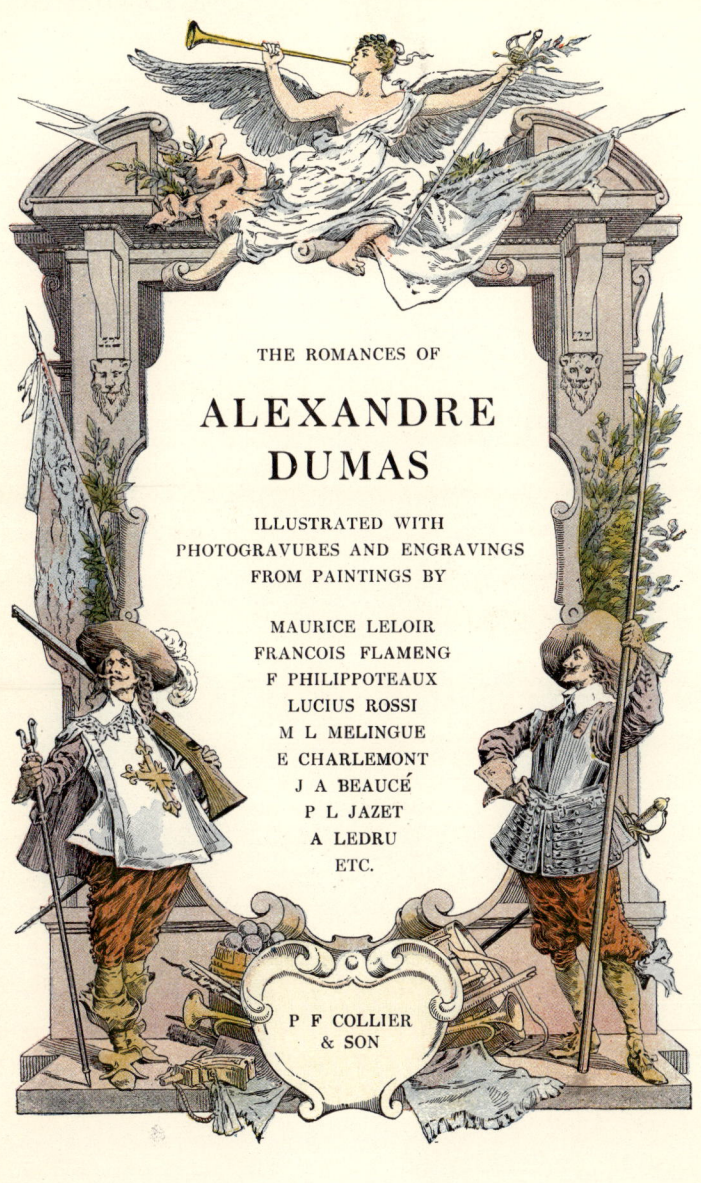

THE CHEVALIER DE MAISON ROUGE

ILLUSTRATED

NEW YORK
P F COLLIER & SON
PUBLISHERS

Copyright, 1910
By P. F. Collier & Son

THE
CHEVALIER DE MAISON ROUGE.

CHAPTER I.

THE ENROLLED VOLUNTEERS.

It was on the evening of the 10th of March, 1793; ten o'clock was striking from Notre Dame, and each stroke, sounding, emitted a sad and monotonous vibration. Night had fallen on Paris, not boisterous and stormy, but cold, damp, and foggy. Paris itself at that time was not the Paris of our day; glittering at night with thousands of reflected lights, the Paris of busy promenades, of lively chat, with its riotous suburbs, the scene of audacious quarrels and daring crime, but a fearful, timid, busy city, whose few and scattered inhabitants, even in crossing from one street to another, ran concealing themselves in the darkness of the alleys, and ensconcing themselves behind their porte-cochères, like wild beasts tracked by the hunters to their lair.

As we have previously said, it was the evening of the 10th of March, 1793. A few remarks upon the extreme situation, which had produced the changed aspect of the capital before we commence stating the events, the recital of which form the subject of this history. France, by the death of Louis XVI., had become at variance with all Europe.

To the three enemies she had first combated, that is to say, Prussia, the Empire, and Piedmont, were now joined England, Holland, and Spain. Sweden and Denmark alone preserved their old neutrality, occupied as they were besides in beholding Catherine II. devastating Poland.

The state of affairs was truly frightful. France, more respected as a physical power but less esteemed as a moral one, since the massacres of September and the execution of the 21st of January, was literally blockaded, like a simple town, by entire Europe. England was on our coasts, Spain upon the Pyrenees, Piedmont and Austria on the Alps, Holland and Prussia to the north of the Pays Bas, and with one accord, from Upper Rhine to Escant, two hundred and fifty thousand combatants marched against the Republic. Our generals were repulsed in every direction. Miacrinski had been obliged to abandon Aix-la-Chapelle, and draw back upon Liege; Steingel and Neuilly were driven back upon Limbourg; while Miranda, who besieged Maestricht, fell back upon Tongres. Valence and Dampierre, reduced to beat a retreat, did so with a loss of half their number. More than ten thousand deserters had already abandoned the army, and cleverly scattered themselves in the interior. At last, the Convention, having no hope except in Dumouriez, despatched courier after courier, commanding him to quit the borders of Bribos (where he was preparing to embark for Holland), and return to take the command of the Army of the Meuse.

Sensible at heart, like an animated body, France felt at Paris—that is to say, at its heart's core—each and every blow leveled at it by invasion, revolt, or treason, even from quarters the most distant. Each victory was a riot of joy; every defeat an insurrection of terror. It is therefore easy to comprehend what tumult was produced by the news of these successive losses, which we are now about to explain.

On the preceding evening, the 9th of March, they had had at the Convention a sitting more stormy than usual; all the officers had received orders to join their regiments at the same time, and Danton, that audacious proposer of improbable things (but which nevertheless were accomplished), Danton, mounting the tribune, cried out:

"The soldiers fail, say you? Offer Paris an opportunity of saving France; demand from her thirty thousand men, send them to Dumouriez, and not only is France saved, but Belgium is reassured, and Holland is conquered."

This proposition had been received with shouts of enthusiasm; registers had been opened in all the sections, inviting them to reunite in the evening. Places of public amusement were closed, to avoid all distraction, and the black flag was hoisted at the Hôtel de Ville, in token of distress. Before midnight five-and-thirty thousand names were inscribed on the registers; only this evening, as it had before occurred in September, in every section, while inscribing their names the enrolled volunteers had demanded that before their departure the traitors might be punished. The traitors were, in fact, the "contre-revolutionists" who secretly menaced the Revolution. But, as may be easily understood, the secret extended to all those who wished to give themselves to the extreme parties who at this period tore France. The traitors were the weaker party, as the Girondins were the weakest. The Montagnards decided that the Girondins must be the traitors. On the next day, which was the 10th of March, all the Montagnard deputies were present at the sitting. The Jacobins, armed, filled the tribunes, after having turned out the women; the mayor presented himself with the Council of the Commune, confirming the report of the Commissioners of the Convention respecting the devotedness of the citizens, but repeating the wish, unanimously expressed the preceding evening, for a Tribunal Extraordinary appointed to judge the traitors. The report of the committee was instantly demanded with loud vociferations. The committee reunited immediately, and in a few minutes afterward they were informed by Robert Lindet that a tribunal would be formed, composed of nine judges (independent of all forms, and acquiring proof by every means), divided into two permanent sections, and prosecuting, directly by order of the Convention, all those who were found guilty in any way of either tempting or misleading the people. This was a sweeping clause, and the Girondins, comprehending it would cause their arrest, rose *en masse*. Death, cried they, rather than submit to the establishment of this threatened imposition.

The Montagnards, in reply to this apostrophe, demanded the vote in a loud tone.

"Yes," replied Ferrand, "let us vote to make known to the world men who are willing to assassinate innocence under the mask of the law."

They voted to this effect; and, against all expectation, the majority decided—first, they would have juries; second, that these juries should be of equal numbers in each department; third, they should be nominated by the Convention. At the moment these three propositions received admission, loud cries were heard; but the Convention, accustomed to receive occasional visits from the populace, inquired their wishes, and were informed, in reply:

"It was merely a deputation of enrolled volunteers, who, having dined at the Halle-au-Blé, demanded to be permitted to display their military tactics before the Convention."

The doors were opened immediately, and six hundred men, armed with swords, pistols, and pikes, apparently half intoxicated, filed off amid shouts of applause, and loudly demanded the death of the traitors.

"Yes," replied Collot d'Herbois, addressing them, "yes, my friends, we will save you—you and liberty, notwithstanding these intrigues."

These words were followed by an angry glance toward the Girondins, which plainly intimated they were not yet beyond reach of danger. In short, the sitting of the Convention terminated, the Montagnards scattered themselves among other clubs, running first to the Cordeliers and then to the Jacobins, proposing to place the traitors beyond the reach of the law, by cutting their throats the same night.

The wife of Louvet resided in the Rue St. Honoré, near

the Jacobins. She, hearing these vociferations, descended, entered the club, and heard this proposition ; then quickly retraced her steps, and warned her husband of the impending danger. Louvet, hastily arming himself, ran from door to door to alarm his friends, but found them all absent ; then fortunately ascertaining from one of the servants they had gone to Petion's house, he followed them there. He found them quietly deliberating over a decree, which ought to be presented on the morrow, and which, by a chance majority, they hoped to pass. He related what had occurred, communicated his fears, informed them of the plot devised against them by the Cordeliers and Jacobins, and concluded by urging them, on their side, to pursue some active and energetic measure.

Then Petion rose, calm and self-possessed as usual, walked to the window, opened it, and then extended his hand, which he drew in covered with moisture.

"It rains," he said ; "there will be nothing to-night."

"Through this half-opened window the last vibration of the clock was heard striking ten.

Such were the occurrences of the 10th of March, and the evening preceding it—occurrences which, in this gloomy obscurity and menacing silence, rendered the abodes destined to shelter the living like sepulchers peopled by the dead. In fact, long patrols of the National Guard, preceded by men marching with fixed bayonets, troops of citizens, armed at hazard, pushing against one another, gendarmes closely examining each doorway, and strictly scrutinizing every narrow alley— those were the sole inhabitants who ventured to expose themselves in the streets. Every one instinctively understood something unusual and terrible was taking place. The cold and drizzling rain, which had tended so much to reassure Petion, had considerably augmented the ill-humor and trouble of these inspectors, whose every meeting resembled preparation for combat, and who, after recognizing one another with looks of defiance, exchanged the word of command slowly and with a very bad grace.

Indeed, it was said, seeing one and the other returning after their separation, that they mutually feared an attack from behind. On the same evening, when Paris was a prey to one of those panics (so often renewed that they ought, in some measure, to have become habitual), this evening the massacre of the lukewarm revolutionists was secretly debated who, after having voted (with restriction for the most part) the death of the king, recoiled to-day before the death of the queen, a prisoner in the temple with her sister-in-law and her children. A woman, enveloped in a mantle of lilac printed cotton, with black spots, her head covered and almost buried in the hood, glided along the houses in La Rue St. Honoré, seeking concealment under a door-porch, or in the angle of a wall, every time a patrol appeared, remaining motionless as a statue, and holding her breath till he had passed, and then again pursuing her anxious course with increasing rapidity, till some danger of a similar nature again compelled her to seek refuge in silence and immobility.

She had already, thanks to the precautions she had taken, traveled over with impunity part of La Rue St. Honoré, when she suddenly encountered, not a body of patrol, but a small troop of our brave enrolled volunteers, who, having dined at La Halle-au-Blé, found their patriotism considerably increased by the numerous toasts they had drunk to their future victories. The poor woman uttered a cry, and made a futile attempt to escape by La Rue du Coq.

"Ah, ah! citoyenne," cried the chief of the volunteers (for already, with the need of command, natural to man, these worthy patriots had elected their chief). "Ah! where are you going?"

The fugitive made no reply, but continued her rapid movement.

"What sport," said the chief; "it is a man disguised, an aristocrat, who thinks to save himself."

The sound of two or three guns escaping from hands rather too unsteady to be depended upon announced to the poor woman the fatal movement she had made.

"No, no," cried she, stopping running, and retracing her steps; "no, citizen; you are mistaken. I am not a man."

"Then advance at command," said the chief, "and reply to my questions. Where are you hastening to, charming belle of the night?"

"But, citizen, I am not going anywhere. I am returning."

"Oh! returning, are you?"

"Yes."

"It is rather a late return for a respectable woman, citoyenne."

"I am returning from visiting a sick relative."

"Poor little kitten!" said the chief, making a motion with his hand, before which the horrified woman quickly recoiled. "Where is your passport?"

"My passport? What is that, citizen? What do you mean?"

"Have you not read the decree of the Commune?"

"No."

"You have heard it proclaimed, then?"

"Alas! no. What, then, said this decree, *mon Dieu?*"

"In the first place, we no longer say God; we only speak of the Supreme Being now."

"Pardon me, I am in error. It is an old custom."

"Bad habit—the habit of the aristocracy."

"I will endeavor to correct myself, citizen; but you said——"

"I said that the decree of the Commune prohibited, after six in the evening, any one to go out without a civic pass. Now, have you this civic pass?"

"Alas! no."

"You have forgotten it at your relation's?"

"I was ignorant of the necessity of going out with one."

"Then come with us to the first post, there you can explain all prettily to the captain; and if he feels perfectly satisfied with your explanation, he will depute two men to conduct you in safety to your abode, else you will be detained for further information."

From the cry of terror which escaped the poor prisoner, the chief of the enrolled volunteers understood how much the unfortunate woman dreaded this interview.

"Oh, oh!" said he, "I am quite certain we hold distinguished game. Forward, forward—to the route, my little *ci-devant*."

And the chief, seizing the arm of the former, placed it within his own, and dragged her, notwithstanding her cries and tears, toward the post Du Palais Egalité.

They were already at the top of the barrier of Sergens, when suddenly a tall young man, closely wrapped in a mantle, turned the corner of La Rue des Petits Champs at the very moment when the prisoner endeavored, by renewing her supplications, to regain her liberty. But, without listening, the chief dragged her brutally forward. The woman uttered a cry of terror, mingled with despair. The young man saw the struggle; he also heard the cry, then bounded from the opposite side of the street, and found himself facing the little troop.

"What is all this? What are you doing to this woman?" demanded he of the person who appeared to be the chief.

"Before you question me you had better attend to your own business."

"Who is this woman, and what do you want with her?" repeated the young man, in a still more imperative tone than at first.

"But who are you, that you interrogate us?"

The young man opened his cloak, when an epaulet was visible, glistening on his military costume.

"I am an officer," said he, "as you can see."

"Officer! in what?"

"In the Civic Guard."

"Well, what of that?" replied one of the troop. "What do we know here of the officers of the Civic Guard?"

"What is that he says?" asked another man, in the drawling and ironical tone peculiar to a man of the people, or, rather, of the Parisian populace, beginning to be angry.

"He says," replied the young man, "that if the epaulet cannot command respect for the officer, the sword shall command respect for the epaulet."

At the same time, making a retrograde movement, the unknown defender of the young woman had disengaged his arms from the folds of his mantle, and drawn from beneath it, sparkling by the glimmer of a lamp, a large infantry saber. Then, with a rapid movement which displayed his familiarity with similar scenes of violence, seized the chief of volunteers by the collar of his blouse, and placing the saber to his throat :

"Now," said he, "let us speak like friends."

"But, citizen," said the chief, endeavoring to free himself.

"I warn you that at the slightest movement made, either by you or any of your men, I pass my saber through your body."

During this time two men belonging to the troop retained their hold of the woman.

"You have asked who I am," continued the young man, "which you had no right to do, since you do not command a regular patrol. However, I will inform you. My name is Maurice Lindey ; I commanded a body of artillerymen on the 10th of August, am now lieutenant in the National Guards, and secretary to the section of Brothers and Friends. Is that sufficient ?"

"Well, Citizen Lieutenant," replied the chief, still menaced with the blade, the point of which he felt pressing more and more, "this is quite another thing. If you are really what you say, that is a good patriot——"

"There, I knew we should soon understand each other," said the officer. "Now, in your turn, answer me ; why did this woman call out, and what are you doing with her ?"

"We are taking her to the guard-house."

"And why are you taking her there ?"

"Because she has no civic pass, and the last decree of the Commune ordered the arrest of any and every individual appearing on the streets of Paris without one after ten o'clock at night. Do you forget the country is in danger, and that the black flag floats over l'Hôtel de Ville?"

"The black flag floats over l'Hôtel de Ville, and the country is in danger, because two hundred thousand slaves march against France," replied the officer, "and not because a woman runs through the streets of Paris after ten o'clock at night. But never mind, citizens. There is a decree of the Commune, it is true, and you only did your duty; and if you had answered me at once, our explanation might have been a much shorter and probably a less stormy one. It is well to be a patriot, but equally so to be polite; and the first officer whom the citizens ought to respect is he, it seems to me, whom they themselves appointed. In the meantime, release that woman, if you please. You are at liberty to depart."

"Oh, citizen," cried she, seizing the arm of Maurice (having listened to the whole of this debate with the most intense anxiety), "oh, citizen, do not abandon me to the mercy of these rude and half-drunken men!"

"Well, then," said Maurice, "take my arm, and I will conduct you with them as far as the Poste."

"To the Poste!" exclaimed the terrified woman, "and why to the Poste, when I have injured no one?"

"You are taken to the Poste," replied Maurice, "not because you have done any one wrong, or because you are considered capable of so doing, but on account of the decree issued by the Commune, forbidding any one to go out without a pass; and you have none."

"But, monsieur, I was ignorant of it."

"Citoyenne, you will find at the Poste brave and honorable men, who will fully appreciate your reasons, and from whom you have nothing to fear."

"Monsieur," said the young woman, pressing Maurice's arm, "it is no longer insult that I fear, it is death; if they conduct me to the Poste, I am lost!"

CHAPTER II.

THE UNKNOWN.

THERE was in this voice an accent of so much terror, mingled with superiority, that Maurice was startled. Like a stroke of electricity, this vibrating voice had touched his heart. He turned toward the enrolled volunteers, who were talking among themselves. Humiliated at having been held in check by a single individual, they were now consulting together with the visible intention of regaining their lost ground. They were eight against one; three were armed with guns, the remainder with pistols and pikes. Maurice wore only his saber. The contest could not be an equal one. Even the woman comprehended this, as she held down her head, and uttered a deep sigh.

As to Maurice, with his brows knitted, his lip disdainfully curled, and his saber drawn from its scabbard, he stood irresolute, fluctuating between the sentiments of a man and a citizen, the one urging him to protect this woman, the other counseling him to give her up. All at once, at the corner of La Rue des Bons Enfans, he saw the reflection of several muskets, and heard also the measured tread of a patrol, who, perceiving a crowd, halted within a few paces of the group, and, through the corporal, demanded:

"Who goes there?"

"A friend," said Maurice. "A friend! Advance, Louis!"

He to whom this order was addressed placed himself at the head of his eight men, and quickly approached.

"Is it you, Maurice?" said the corporal, "Ah, libertine! what are you doing in the streets at this hour!"

"You see, I am going to the section of Brothers and Friends."

"Yes; to visit that of sisters and friends. We know all about that."

> "Ah, listen, ma belle,
> When the dusk midnight hour
> The church-bell shall toll,
> I will haste to thy bower;
> To thy side I will steal,
> Spite of bolts and of bars,
> And my love will reveal,
> 'Neath the light of the stars.

Is it not so?"

"No, *mon ami*; you are mistaken. I was on my way home when I discovered this citoyenne struggling in the hands of these citizen volunteers, and ran to inquire why they wished to detain her."

"It is just like you," said Louis. Then, turning toward the volunteers, "Why did you stop this woman!" inquired the poetical corporal.

"I have already told the lieutenant," replied the chief of the little troop; "because she had no pass."

"Bah! bah!" said Louis, "a great crime, certainly."

"Are you, then, ignorant of the decree of the Commune?" demanded the chief of the volunteers.

"Yes; but there is another clause which has annulled that—which—listen:

> "On Pindus and Parnassus, it is decreed by Love,
> That beauty's witching face,
> That youth and fairy grace,
> Without a pass, by day or night, may through the city rove.

What do you say to this decree, citizen? It is clever, it seems to me."

"Yes; but it does not appear to me peremptory. In the first place, it has not appeared in the 'Moniteur'; then we are neither upon Pindus nor Parnassus; it is not yet day; and, lastly, the citoyenne is perhaps neither graceful, young, nor fair."

"I wager the contrary," said Louis. "Prove that I am in the right, citoyenne; remove your hood, that all may judge if you come under the conditions of the decree."

"Monsieur," said the young woman, pressing closer to Maurice, "having saved me from your enemies, protect me now against your friends, I beseech you!"

"You see," said the chief, "how she hides herself. In my opinion, she is a spy of the aristocrats—some street-walker."

"Oh, monsieur!" said the young woman, stepping before Maurice, and discovering a face radiant with youth and beauty, visible by the light of the lamp, "do I look like what they have termed me?"

Maurice was amazed. He had never even dreamed of beauty equal to that he had caught sight of for a moment, and only for a moment, since the unknown had again enshrouded herself in the hood as quickly as she had previously removed it.

"Louis," said Maurice, in a whisper, "claim the prisoner, that you may conduct her to your post; you have a right to do so, as chief of patrol."

"Very good," said the young corporal; "I understand with half a word."

Then, addressing himself to the unknown:

"Let us go, *ma belle*," continued he; "since you will not afford me the proof that you are within the conditions of the decree, you must follow us."

"Why follow you?" said the chief of the enrolled volunteers, "we shall conduct the citoyenne to the post of l'Hôtel de Ville, where we are on guard, and there she will be examined."

"Not so, not so," said the chief of the first troop; "she belongs to us, and we will keep her."

"Citizens, citizens," said Louis, "you will make me angry"

"Angry or not angry, *morbleu*! it is equally the same to us. We are true soldiers of the Republic, and while you patrol the streets, we go to shed our blood on the frontier."

"Take care you do not shed it by the way, citizens,

which is very likely to occur if you are not rather more polite than you are at present."

"Politeness is a virtue appertaining to the aristocracy, and we belong to the lower orders," replied the chief.

"Do not speak of these things before madame," said Louis; "perhaps she is an English woman. Do not be angry at the supposition, my beautiful bird of the night," added he, gallantly, turning toward the unknown. "Doubtless you are conversant with the poets, and one of them tells us, 'That England is a swan's nest situated in the midst of a large pond.'"

"Ah! you betray yourself," said the chief of the enrolled; "you avow yourself a creature of Pitt's, in the pay of England. A——"

"Silence," said Louis; "you do not understand poetry; therefore I must speak to you in prose. We are National Guards, affable and patient fellows enough, but still children of Paris; that is to say, if we are provoked, we strike rather hard."

"Madame," said Maurice, "from what you have now witnessed you can easily imagine what will soon follow. In five minutes ten or twelve men will be cutting one another's throats for you. Is the cause your defenders have embraced worthy of the blood they are about to shed?"

"Monsieur," replied the unknown, clasping her hands, "I can only assure you that if you permit me to be arrested, the result to myself will be dreadful, but to others fatal; and that rather than you should abandon me, I would beseech you to pierce me through the heart with the weapon you hold in your hand, and cast my corpse into the Seine."

"Madame," replied Maurice, "I will take all the responsibility upon myself;" and letting drop the hand of the lovely *incognita*, which he held in his own:

"Citizens," said he, addressing himself to the National Guard, "as an officer, as a patriot, and a Frenchman, I command you to protect this woman. And, Louis, if any of these *canaille* say a word, put them to the bayonet!"

"Carry arms!" said Louis.

"Oh, *mon Dieu! mon Dieu!*" cried the unknown, enveloping her head still closer in her hood, and supporting herself against a post. "Oh, *mon Dieu*, protect me!"

The volunteers directly placed themselves on the defensive, and one among them fired his pistol, when the ball passed through the hat of Maurice.

"Cross bayonets!" said Louis. "Plan, plan, plan, plan, plan, plan, plan!"

Then, in the darkness of night, a scene of struggling and confusion ensued, during which the sounds of one or two shots were heard, followed by cries, imprecations, and blasphemies; but no one appeared, because, as we have said, there was this evening a secret question of the massacre, and it was believed the massacre had commenced. Two or three windows only were opened for an instant, but were immediately closed. Less in number, and worse armed, the enrolled volunteers were in an instant defeated. Two were badly wounded and four others pinned against the wall, each with a bayonet through his breast.

"There," said Louis, "I hope now you will remain as quiet as lambs. As for you, Citizen Maurice, I order you to conduct this woman to the post of l'Hôtel de Ville. You understand you are answerable for her."

"Yes," said Maurice. Then, in a low tone, "And the password?" added he.

"The devil!" said Louis, rubbing his ear, "the password; it is——"

"Do not fear I shall make a bad use of it."

"*Ma foi!*" said Louis. "make what use you like of it; that is your concern."

"Tell me, then?" said Maurice.

"I will tell you all in good time; but let us first dispose of these tipsy fellows. Then, before we part, I shall not be very sorry to give you a few words of advice."

"Very well. I will wait."

Louis then returned to his National Guards, who still kept the enrolled volunteers at bay.

"Now," said he, "have you had sufficient?"

"Yes, dog of a Girondin!" replied the chief.

"You deceive yourself, my friend," said Louis, coolly; "we are better *sans-culottes* than yourselves, seeing that we belong to the club of Thermopyles, of whose patriotism no one, I hope, entertains a doubt. Let go these citizens," continued Louis; "they resist no longer."

"It is not the less true that this woman is an object of suspicion."

"If she were a suspicious character, she would have made her escape during this skirmish, and not, as you see she has done, waited till it had terminated."

"Hum!" said one of the volunteers. "What the Citizen Thermopyle observes is quite true."

"Besides, we shall know, since my friend goes to conduct her to the post, while we go to drink to the health of the nation."

"Are we going to drink?" said the chief.

"Certainly; I am very thirsty, and I know a pretty little cabaret at the corner of La Rue Thomas du Louvre."

"Why did you not say so at once, citizen? We are sorry to have doubted your patriotism; and, to prove it, let us, in the name of the nation and the law, embrace one another as friends."

"Let us embrace," said Louis.

And the enrolled volunteers and the National Guards embraced with warm enthusiasm. At this moment they were more anxious to embrace than behead one another.

"Let us now go," cried the two united troops, "to the corner of La Rue Thomas du Louvre."

"And we," said one of the wounded, in a plaintive voice, "do you intend to abandon us here?"

"Ah! well, yes," said Louis; "abandon the heroes who have fallen bravely fighting for their country against the patriots—it is true, by mistake, but still true for all that; we will send you some wheelbarrows. Meanwhile, you can sing the 'Marseillaise,' it will divert you."

Then, approaching Maurice, who was waiting for him, with this unknown, at the corner of La Rue du Coq, while the National Guards and enrolled volunteers went back again arm in arm toward La Place du Palais Egalité.

"Maurice," said he, "I promised you some counsel, and this is it. Be persuaded to accompany us, rather than compromise yourself by protecting this young woman, who, it is true, is very charming, and on that account not the less to be suspected; for charming women who run about the streets of Paris at midnight——"

"Monsieur," said the young woman, "judge me not from appearances, I implore you."

"In the first place, you say monsieur, and that is a great fault. Do you understand, citoyenne, what I say?"

"Ah, well! Yes, yes, citizen; allow your friend to accomplish this kind action."

"What is that?"

"By conducting me home, and protecting me on my road."

"Maurice, Maurice," said Louis, "consider well what you are doing; you will compromise yourself terribly."

"I know it well," said the young man; "but what would you have me do? If I leave the poor woman, she will be stopped at every step by the patrols."

"Oh! yes, yes, monsieur, while with you—while with you, citizen, I meant to say—I shall be safe."

"You hear?" said Louis, "safe. She, then, runs great danger?"

"My dear Louis," said Maurice, "let us be just. She must either be a good compatriot or an aristocrat. If an aristocrat, we have erred in protecting her; if a good patriot, it is our duty to preserve her."

"Pardon, pardon, *cher ami;* I am sorry for Aristotle, but your logic is folly. See what he says:

"'Iris my reason steals away,
    And yet she tells me to be wise;
Oh! lady, I can only say,
    Then turn away those glorious eyes.'"

"Louis," said Maurice, "a truce to Dorcit, to Parny,

and to Gentil Bernard, I pray you. Speak seriously; will you, or will you not, give me the password?"

"That is to say, Maurice, you place me in this situation: I must either sacrifice my duty to my friend, or my friend to my duty; but I fear, Maurice, my duty will fall the sacrifice."

"Decide, then, for one or the other, *mon ami;* but, in the name of Heaven, decide quickly!"

"You will not abuse it?"

"I promise you."

"That is not sufficient; swear."

"Upon what?"

"Swear upon the altar of your country."

Louis pulled off his hat, presenting to Maurice the side with the cockade, and Maurice, finding the affair very simple, took, without smiling, the oath required upon this extemporary altar.

"Now," said Louis, "this is the password: France and Lutece; perhaps you would say, France and Lucretia; but let that pass, it is Roman, all the same."

"Citoyenne," said Maurice, "I am at your service. Thanks, Louis."

"*Bon voyage,*" cried he, replacing on his head "the altar of the country," and, faithful to his anacreontic taste, departed, singing:

> "Eleonora, Eleonora!
> Now I've taught you how to love,
> Tell your passionate adorer,
> Does the lesson weary prove?"

CHAPTER III.

LA RUE DES FOSSES ST. VICTOR.

MAURICE, finding himself alone with the young woman, felt for the moment deeply embarrassed. The fear of being duped, attracted by her marvelous beauty, troubled his conscience as a pure and exalted Republican, and caused him to hesitate when about to offer her the support of his arm.

"Where are you going, citoyenne?" said he.

"Alas! monsieur, a long way from here," replied she.

"But how far?"

"By the side of the Jardin des Plantes."

"It is some distance; let us proceed on our way."

"Ah, *mon Dieu!* monsieur," said the unknown, "I plainly perceive I am a constraint upon you; but indeed it is no ordinary danger that I incur. Believe me, I will not abuse your generosity."

"But, madame," said Maurice, who, during his *tête-à-tête*, had totally forgotten the language imposed by the Republican vocabulary, and returned to the language of a gentleman, "how is it, in all conscience, that at this hour you are found in the streets of Paris, where, with the exception of ourselves, you do not see a single individual?"

"Monsieur, I have told you; I had been paying a visit to the Faubourg du Roule. Leaving home at midday, and knowing nothing of what had taken place, I returned, of course, in equal ignorance, all my time having been spent in deep retirement."

"Yes," murmured Maurice, "in some retired house, the resort of the aristocrats. Confess, citoyenne, while publicly demanding my protection, you laugh in your sleeve at my egregious folly."

"Why should I act thus?"

"You are aware that a Republican acts as your guide. Well, this Republican betrays his cause, that is all."

"But, citizen," quickly rejoined the unknown, "I, as well as you, love the Republic; you labor under a mistake concerning me."

"Then, citoyenne, if you are a good patriot, you can have no cause for concealment. Where do you come from?"

"Monsieur, excuse me."

There was in this "monsieur" so much sweetness and modesty of expression, that Maurice believed it to be founded on some sentiment concealed.

"Surely," said he, "this woman is returning from some *rendezvous d'amour.*"

At this moment, without knowing why, he felt deeply oppressed at this thought, and for a short time he remained silent.

When these two noctural promenaders had reached La Rue de la Verrerie, after having encountered three or four patrols, who, thanks to the password, allowed them free passage, an officer at length appeared inclined to raise some difficulties. Maurice here found it necessary to give his name and also his residence.

"That is all that is required from you," said the officer ; "but the citoyenne, who is she ?"

"The sister of my wife."

The officer permitted them to pass.

"You are, then, married, monsieur ?" murmured the unknown.

"No, madame ; why do you think so ?"

"Then," said she, laughing, "you had better have said I was your wife."

"Madame," said Maurice, "the name of wife is rather too sacred to be slightly bestowed. I have not the honor of your acquaintance."

The unknown, in her turn, felt an impression of the heart, and remained silent and confused. At this moment they crossed the bridge Marie. The young woman quickened her pace as they approached the end of their journey. They crossed the bridge De la Tourville.

"We are now, I believe, in your quarter," said Maurice, planting his foot on the quay St. Bernard.

"Yes, citizen," replied the young woman ; "but it is precisely here I most require your assistance."

"Really, madame," said Maurice, "you forbid me to be indiscreet, yet you do all in your power to excite my curiosity. This is not generous. Grant me your confidence. I have merited it, I think. Are you not in honor bound to tell me to whom I speak ?"

"You speak, monsieur," said the unknown, smiling,

"to a woman whom you have saved from the greatest danger she could encounter, to one who owes you a debt of everlasting gratitude."

"I do not require so much, madame ; be less grateful, and pending the second, tell me your name."

"Impossible !"

"You might have told it, nevertheless, to the first sectionary, if you had been taken to the post."

"No, never !" said the unknown.

"But, in that case, you would have gone to prison."

"I had considered all that."

"And prison at this moment——"

"Leads to the scaffold ; I know it all."

"And you would have preferred the scaffold ?"

"To treason—to discover my name was treason ; it is treason to betray others."

"I said truly you compelled me to act a singular part for a Republican."

"You act the part of a truly generous man. You encounter a poor woman subjected to insult ; you do not condemn her because she might be 'one of the people,' but that she may be exempted from fresh annoyances, to save her from shipwreck, you reconduct her to the miserable quarter she inhabits."

"As far as appearances go, you argue correctly, and I might have credited you, had I never either seen or heard you speak ; but your beauty and mode of expression stamp you as a woman of distinction, and it is just this distinction, in opposition with your costume and this miserable quarter, which proves to me that your absence from home at this unseasonable hour conceals some mystery. You are silent—we will speak no more. Are we far from your house, madame ?"

At this moment they entered La Rue des Fosses St. Victor by la Rue de Seine.

"You see that small, dark building," said the unknown to Maurice, extending her hand, and pointing towards a house situated beyond the walls of the Jardin des Plantes. "When we arrive there you must quit me."

"Very well, madame; issue your orders; I am here only to obey."

"You are angry.

"I! angry? Not the least in the world; besides, what does it matter to you?"

"It matters much, since I have yet a favor to ask of you."

"What is that .

"A kind and frank adieu—the farewell of a friend."

"The farewell of a friend! Oh, madame, you do me too great an honor. A singular friend, not to know the name of his friend, who even conceals from him where she resides, no doubt from the fear of being too much troubled with his company."

The young woman hung down her head, but did not reply to this saracasm.

"As to the rest, madame," continued Maurice, "if I have discovered a secret, I did so involuntarily; and without any effort on my part to do so."

"I have now reached my destination, monsieur," said the unknown.

It was facing the old Rue St. Jacques, lined with tall, dark-looking houses, intersected by obscure, narrow alleys, leading to streets occupied by manufactories and tanyards, as within two steps ran the little river Brière.

"Here!" said Maurice, "is it here that you live?"

"Yes."

"Impossible."

"It is so, nevertheless. And now, adieu! my brave chevalier, my generous protector, adieu!"

"Adieu, madame," said Maurice, with slight irony of tone; "but first again assure me you run no risk of any danger."

"None whatever."

"In that case, I will leave you."

Maurice bowed coldly and retired a few paces. The unknown remained for an instant stationary in the same place.

"I do not like to take my leave of you thus," said she. "Come, monsieur, your hand."

Maurice approached, and held out his hand, and then felt the young woman had slipped a ring on his finger.

"Oh! citoyenne, what have you done? Do you not perceive that you have lost one of your rings?"

"Monsieur, you wrong me much."

"The crime of ingratitude is wanting in me; is it not so, madame?"

"Come, I beseech you, monsieur—*mon ami*, do not leave thus. What do you wish to know? What do you ask?"

"Payment—is it not so?" said the young man, bitterly.

"No," said the unknown, with a bewitching expression, "but forgive me the secrecy I am obliged to preserve toward you."

Maurice, seeing in the obscurity those beautiful eyes almost humid with tears, feeling the pressure of that soft hand reposing between his own, hearing the accents of that persuasive voice, which had almost descended to the depths of prayer, felt his anger all at once yield to admiration.

"What do I ask?" said he. "To see you again."

"Impossible! utterly impossible."

"If only for once—one hour, a minute, a second."

"I tell you it is impossible."

"Do you seriously tell me," said Maurice, "that I shall never see you again?"

"Never," said the unknown, in a desponding tone.

"Madame," said Maurice, "you certainly jest with me." Then, raising his noble head, he shook his hanging curls like a man wishing to escape from some power which, in spite of himself, still bound him. The unknown regarded him with an indefinable expression. It was evident she had not altogether escaped the sentiment she had inspired.

"Listen," said she, after a moment's silence, interrupted only by a sigh, which Maurice had in vain endeavored to suppress. "Swear to me, upon your honor, to shut your eyes the moment I desire you to do so, and to keep them closed while you can count sixty seconds. Mind, upon your honor."

"If I swear, what will happen to me?"

"It will happen that I will prove my gratitude to you in a manner that I faithfully promise you I will never again to any other person. Do this for me more than for yourself. As to the rest, it will be difficult."

"But, at least, am I not to know——"

"No; trust to me. You see——"

"In truth, madame, I know not whether you are angel or demon."

"Will you swear it?"

"Yes; I swear to do as you desire me."

"Whatever occurs, you will not open your eyes—whatever happens. You understand? even if you should feel yourself struck with a poniard."

"You bewilder me. My word of honor required with so much urgency."

"Swear, then, monsieur. It appears to me that you run no great risk in so doing."

"Well, I swear," said Maurice, "whatever may happen," closing his eyes.

He hesitated.

"Let me see you only once more—only once more," said he. "I entreat you."

The young woman let fall the hood with a smile not quite free from coquetry, when, by the light of the moon, which at this moment shed its luster between two clouds, he again beheld, for the second time, the raven hair hanging in masses of shining curls, the beautifully arched and penciled eyebrows, o'ershadowing the almond-shaped eyes, so soft and languishing, an exquisitely formed nose, and lips fresh and brilliant as coral.

"Oh, you are beautiful, exquisitely beautiful!" said Maurice.

"Shut your eyes," said the unknown.

Maurice obeyed.

The young woman took both his hands within her own, and placed him in the desired position.

Suddenly he felt a warm perfume pervade his face, and lips slightly touch his mouth, leaving between his lips the disputed ring.

All passed rapid as thought. Maurice experienced a sensation almost amounting to pain. His feelings were inexplicable, even to himself.

He made a brusque movement, and extended his arms before him.

"Your oath," said a voice, already in the distance.

Maurice clasped his hands over his eyes to strenuously resist the strong inclination he felt to perjure himself. He counted no more ; he thought no more ; but remained tottering, his nerves totally unstrung.

In about an instant he heard a noise like that of a door closing a few paces distant from him ; then again everything was silent. Then he removed his hand, and opened his eyes, looking round about him like a man just awakened from a deep sleep, and might, perhaps, have fancied all that had occurred a passing dream, had he not held between his lips the identical ring, proving this unheard-of adventure an incontestable reality.

CHAPTER IV.

MANNERS OF THE TIMES.

When Maurice came to himself, he looked around, but saw only the gloomy, dirty streets extending to his right and left. He essayed to find out exactly where he was, that he might recognize it again; but his mind was disturbed. The night was dark, and the moon which for a moment had appeared to light up the lovely face of the fair unknown, had again retired behind the clouds. The young man, after a moment of cruel incertitude, retraced his steps toward his own house, situated in the Rue de Roule.

Arriving at La Rue St. Avoie, Maurice was much surprised at the number of patrols who circulated in that quarter of the temple.

"What is the matter now, sergeant?" inquired he of the chief of patrol, busily occupied in thoroughly searching La Rue des Fontaines.

"What is it?" said the sergeant. "It is this, *mon officier*. It was intended this night to carry off the woman Capet, and the whole nest beside."

"How was that?"

"A band, forming a patrol, had, I do not know how, procured the password, and introduced themselves into the temple, in the costume of chasseurs of the National Guard. Fortunately, he who represented the corporal, when speaking to the officer on guard, addressed him as 'Monsieur.' He sold himself—the aristocrat!"

"The devil!" said Maurice. "And have they not arrested the conspirators?"

"No. When the patrol reached the street, they were all dispersed."

"And is there any hope of capturing any of these fellows?"

"There is only one among the number of sufficient importance to arrest—that is the chief, a very slight man, who had been introduced among the men on guard by one of the municipals of the service. We had made the villain run, but he had found a door behind, and fled through les Madelonnettes."

Under any other circumstances, Maurice would have remained for the rest of the night with the patriots, who guarded the safety of the public, but since one short hour, love of country was no longer his sole engrossing thought. He continued his way, and the tidings he had just learned were soon obliterated from his memory by the recent events in which he had taken so active a part. Besides, since these pretended attempts had become very frequent, the patriots themselves were aware, under certain circumstances, they made use of them in a political measure; therefore, this news caused our young Republican no great disquietude.

On returning home, Maurice found his "official" (at this epoch they had no longer servants), Maurice, say we, found his official waiting, but who, while waiting, had fallen asleep, and while sleeping, snored uneasily. He awoke him, and with all due regard for his fellow-man, made him pull off his boots, then dismissed him, that he might not interrupt his cogitations, and jumping into bed, it being very late, and he also having youth on his side, slept soundly, notwithstanding the preoccupation of his thoughts.

The next day he discovered a letter on his *table de nuit*. This letter was written in a clear, elegant hand, but unknown to him. He looked at the seal. The seal was engraved with the single word in English, "Nothing." He opened it. It merely contained these words, "Thank you. Everlasting gratitude in exchange for everlasting forgetfulness." Maurice summoned his domestic (the true patriot never rang, the sound denoted servility; indeed, many officials only entered the service of their masters on this express condition).

The official of Maurice had received, nearly thirty years before, at the baptismal font, the name of Jean, but in '92 he was, by private authority, rebaptized (Jean savoring of aristocracy and Deism), and now called himself "Scevola."

"Scevola," demanded Maurice, "do you know where this letter came from?"

"No, citizen."

"Who brought it to you?"

"The concierge."

"And who brought it to him?"

"A commissionaire, no doubt, since it had no postmark."

"Go down, and request the concierge to walk up."

The concierge complied, because it was Maurice who made the request, and he was much beloved by all the officials with whom he was concerned in any way; but at the same time the concierge declared that had it been any other tenant, he should have asked him to walk down.

The concierge was called Aristide.

Maurice interrogated him. It was a stranger who had

brought the letter, about eight in the morning. The young man multiplied his questions and varied them in every possible shape, but could elicit nothing further. Maurice requested his acceptance of six francs, also desiring, if the stranger again presented himself, that he would follow him, without appearing to do so, and inform him where he returned to.

We hasten to say that, much to the satisfaction of Aristide, who felt himself rather insulted by this proposition, the man returned no more.

Maurice remained alone, crushing the letter with vexation; he drew the ring from his finger, and placed it with the crumpled letter upon the *table de nuit,* then turned toward the wall, with the foolish idea of sleeping afresh; but at the end of an hour Maurice returned to this fanfaronade, kissed the ring and reread the letter. The ring was a splendid sapphire; the letter, as we have said, was a charming little billet, displaying its aristocracy in every line.

As Maurice reread and examined it, the door opened. Maurice hastily replaced the ring on his finger, and concealed the note under his pillow. Was this the modesty of newly awakened love, or was it the shame of a patriot, who would not wish it to be known that one in relation with the people was imprudent enough to write a billet, of which the perfume alone was sufficient to compromise both the hand that penned it and the hand that received it?

He who entered was a young man attired as a patriot, but a patriot of surpassing elegance. His blouse was composed of fine cloth, his breeches of cashmere, and his stockings of fine striped silk. As to his bonnet, it might have shamed, from the elegance of its form and splendid purple color, even those of Paris itself. Added to all this, he carried in his belt a pair of pistols of the royal manufacture of Versailles, and a short saber, equal to those of the pupils of the Champ de Mars.

"Ah! thou sleepest, Brutus," said the new-comer, "and the country is in danger. *Fi donc!*"

"No, Louis," said Maurice, laughing, "I do not sleep, I dream."

"Yes, I understand."

"Well, as for me, I cannot understand."

"Bah!"

"Of whom do you speak? Who is this Eucharis?"

"Why, the woman."

"What woman?"

"The woman of La Rue St. Honoré—the woman of the patrol—the unknown—the woman for whom you and I risked our heads last night."

"Oh, yes!" said Maurice, who knew perfectly well what his friend would say, and only feigned ignorance, "the unknown."

"Well, who was she?"

"I know nothing."

"Was she pretty?"

"Pshaw!" said Maurice, pouting his lips disdainfully. "A poor woman forgotten in some love adventure.

> "Yes; sweet creatures that we are,
> 'Tis love that ever tortures man."

"Is this possible?" said Maurice, to whom such an idea was at this moment peculiarly repugnant, and who would have much preferred finding the unknown to be even a conspirator rather than a light woman.

"And where does she live?"

"I know nothing concerning her."

"Come, now; you know nothing; that's impossible."

"Why so?"

"You escorted her back."

"She escaped from me at the Bridge Marie."

"Escaped from you!" said Louis, with a roar of laughter; "a woman escape from you?

> "Say, can the trembling dove elude
> The vulture—tyrant of the air;
> The fawn, on whom the tiger rude
> Springs from his solitary lair?"

"Louis," said Maurice, "I wish you would accustom yourself to speak like other people. You annoy me horribly with your atrocious poetry."

"To speak like other people, indeed! Now, it appears to me I speak better than most people. I speak as the Citizen Demonstur, both in prose and poetry. As for my poetry, *mon cher*, I know a certain Emilie who does not consider is so bad. But to return to yours."

"My poetry?"

"No; your Emilie."

"Have I an Emilie?"

"Ah, ah! your gazelle may turn tigress, and show her teeth in a manner that may not please you, although in love."

"I in love?" said Maurice, shaking his head.

"Yes, you in love."

"Louis," said Maurice, arming himself with a pipe-key which lay upon the table, "I swear that if you will spout verses, I will whistle."

"Then let us talk politics; besides, that brought me here. Have you heard the news?"

"I know that Capet's wife wished to escape."

"Oh! that is nothing."

"What more is there, then?"

"The famous Chevalier de Maison Rouge is in Paris."

"Is it true?" said Maurice, raising himself to a sitting posture. "When did he come?"

"Yesterday evening."

"But how?"

"Disguised as a chasseur of the National Guard. A woman who is thought to be an aristocrat, disguised as a woman of the people, took him these clothes to the barrier gate; an instant afterward they are gone out arm in arm. It was not till after they had passed the sentinel suspicion was excited. He had seen the woman pass with a bundle and repass, accompanied by a soldier, when it suddenly struck him something was wrong, and he ran after them. They had disappeared in a hotel of La Rue St. Honoré, where the door was opened as if by magic.

The hotel had a second point of egress, leading on to the Champs Elysées. *Bon soir* to the Chevalier de Maison Rouge and his companion; they had both vanished. They will demolish the hotel and guillotine the proprietor, but that will not deter the chevalier from renewing the attempt which has just failed; it is four months since the preceding one, and yesterday was the second."

"Is he not arrested?" demanded Maurice.

"Ah; well. Yes, *mon cher*, as well attempt to stop Proteus, arrest Proteus; you know the trouble Aristides had to accomplish it."

"'Pastor Aristæus, fugiens Peneïa Temple.'"

"Take care," said Maurice, carrying the key to his mouth.

"Take care of yourself, for this time you will not whistle at me, but at Virgil."

"That is very true, and as long as you do not translate it I have nothing to say. Now to return to Maison Rouge."

"We agree that he is a brave man."

"The fact is, that to undertake such things he must possess immense courage."

"Or intense adoration."

"Do you believe, then, in the love of the chevalier for the queen?"

"I do not believe it. I only mention what report says. Besides, she has turned the brains of so many others, that this would not be at all surprising. She has seduced Bernais, so they say."

"Never mind; the chevalier must have had confederates in the Temple even."

"Very possible.

"Love breaks through bars,
And laughs at bolts."

"Louis!"

"Ah! it is true."

"Then you think like the rest?"

"Why not?"

"Because, according to your account, the queen has had already two hundred lovers."

"Two, three, four hundred. She is quite handsome enough for that. I do not say she loves them; but, in short, they love her. All the world beholds the sun, but the sun does not see all the world."

"You say, then, that the Chevalier de Maison Rouge——"

"I say they are on the track at this moment, and if he escapes this time the bloodhounds of the Republic, he will be a cunning fox."

"And what does the Commune in all this affair?"

"The Commune is about to issue a decree, by which every house, like an open register, must display on the front the name of every inhabitant, both male and female. This is realizing the dream of the ancients. Why should there not be a window in every breast, that all the world may see what passes there?"

"An excellent idea, that," said Maurice.

"To place windows in men's breasts?"

"No; but to place a list of names on every door."

Maurice felt this might be the means of assisting him to discover the unknown, or, at least, to afford him some clew whereby he might be able to trace her.

"Is it not so?" said Louis. "I have already betted this measure will secure us a batch of five hundred aristocrats. By the bye, we have received this morning, at our club, a deputation of enrolled volunteers; they arrived, conducted by our adversaries of that night, whom I had not abandoned till dead drunk; they are here, I tell you, with garlands of flowers and immortelle crowns."

"Indeed," replied Maurice, laughing; "and how many were there?"

"They were thirty, and were shaved, wearing bouquets in their button-holes."

"Citizens of the Club of Thermopyles," said the orator, "we wish the union of Frenchmen not to be interrupted by any misunderstanding; we, therefore, come to fraternize anew with such excellent patriots as yourselves."

"Well, what then?"

"Then we have fraternized, and in this reiteration, as Diasonis expresses himself, we raised an altar to the country with the table of the secretary and two carafes, in which the nosegays were deposited. As you were the hero of the feat, you were three times summoned to appear, that you might be crowned; but as you did not reply, and it was necessary to crown something, they crowned the bust of Washington. This was the order of the ceremony."

As Louis concluded this statement, which at this epoch had nothing of burlesque, a noise was heard proceeding from the street; the drums, first heard in the distance, now approached nearer and nearer. They easily comprehended the cause of this noise, now too common to be misunderstood.

"What is all that?" said Maurice.

"The proclamation of the decree of the Commune," said Louis.

"I will run to the station," said Maurice, leaping from his bed, and calling his servant to assist him.

"I will return home and go to bed," said Louis. "I had not two hours' sleep last night, thanks to those outrageous volunteers. If they only fight a little, let me sleep; but if they fight much, come and fetch me."

"But why are you so smart to-day?" said Maurice, eying him all over as he rose to withdraw.

"Because on my road hither I am obliged to pass the Rue Bethisy, and in the Rue Bethisy, on the third flat, is a window which always opens when I pass."

"Then you do not fear being taken for a fop?"

"I! a fop? I am, on the contrary, known for a French *sans-culotte*. But one must make some sacrifice to the softer sex. The worship of the country does not exclude that of love; indeed, one commands the other.

"Our Republicans profess
We but follow ancient lore;
Beauty we prize none the less,
That we love our freedom more.

Dare to whistle to that, and I denounce you as an aristocrat. Adieu, *mon ami*."

Louis held out his hand to Maurice, which the young Republican cordially shook, and went out, thinking of a sonnet to Chloris.

CHAPTER V.

WHAT SORT OF MAN THE CITIZEN MAURICE LINDEY WAS.

WHILE Maurice Lindey, having dressed quickly, proceeds to the section of La Rue Lepelletier, of which, as we already know, he was secretary, we will endeavor to lay before the public the antecedents of this young man, introduced upon the scene by one of those impulses so familiar to powerful and generous natures.

The young man had spoken correctly the preceding evening, when in reply he had said his name was Maurice Lindey, resident in La Rue de Roule. He might have added he was a child of that half-aristocracy accorded to the gentlemen of the robe. His ancestors, for two hundred years, had distinguished themselves by that same parliamentary opposition which has rendered so illustrious the names of Moles and Masson. His father, the good Lindey, who had passed his life grumbling against despotism, when on the 14th of July, '89, the Bastile had fallen by the hands of the people, died from sudden fright, and the shock of seeing despotism replaced by a liberty militant, leaving his only son independent by fortune and a republican in principles.

The Revolution which had closely followed this great event found Maurice, in all the vigor and maturity of manhood, becoming a champion prepared to enter the lists; his republican education, improved by his great assiduity to the clubs, and from reading all the pamphlets of that period—God knows how many Maurice had read!—deep and rational contempt for the hierarchy, philosophical consideration of the events which formed the body, absolute denial of all nobility which was not personal, impartial appreciation of the past, ardor for new ideas, sympathy with the people, blended with more aristocratic organizations ; such were the morals, not of those whom we have selected, but which history has given us as the heroes of our tale.

As to his personal appearance, he was in height five feet eight inches, from twenty-five to twenty-six years of age, and muscular as Hercules. His beauty was of the French cast, that is to say, fair complexion, blue eyes, curling chestnut hair, rosy lips, and ivory teeth.

After the portrait of the man comes the position of the citizen. Maurice, not rich, but still independent, bore a name much respected, and, above all, popular. Maurice, known by his education, and principles still more liberal even than his education, Maurice placed himself, so to speak, at the head of a party composed of all the young citizen patriots. It was well that with the *sans-culottes* he passed for rather lukewarm, and with the sectionaries as rather foppish. But the *sans-culottes* no longer remembered his lukewarmness when they saw him snap in twain the knotted cudgels, and the sectionaries pardoned his elegance when he one day scientifically planted a blow between two eyes that had been watching him in an offensive manner for some time past.

And now for the physical, moral, and civic combined. Maurice had assisted at the taking of the Bastile, he had been on the expedition to Versailles, had fought like a lion on the 10th of August, and in this memorable journey, it is only justice to observe, he had killed as many patriots as Swiss, not being more willing to permit an assassin under a blouse than an enemy to the Republic under a red coat. It was he who exhorted the defenders of the château to surrender themselves, and to prevent the shedding of blood ; it was he who placed himself before the mouth of the cannon to which a Parisian artilleryman was putting a light ; he who by a window first entered the Louvre, regardless of the firing of five hundred Swiss and as many gentlemen in ambush ; and when he perceived the signal of surrender, his avenging sword had already cut through more than ten uniforms. Then, seeing his friends leisurely massacring some prisoners, who, having thrown down their arms, and, clasping their hands, supplicated for life, he furiously attacked these fiends, which had gained for him a reputation worthy of the good days of Rome and of Greece. War declared, Maurice enrolled himself, and departed for the frontier in the ranks, as a lieutenant, with the first fifteen hundred volunteers the city sent against the invaders, and who each day had been followed by fifteen hundred others.

At the first battle in which he assisted, that is to say, at Jemappes, he received a ball, which, after having divided the muscles of the shoulder, lodged against the bone. The representative of the people knew Maurice, and he returned to Paris for his recovery.

For a whole month, consumed by fever, he tossed upon his bed of suffering, but in January was able to resume his command, if not by name, at least in fact, of the club of Thermopyles, that is to say, of one hundred young men of the Parisian citizens, armed to oppose any attempt in favor of the tyrant Capet ; and yet more, Maurice, with contracted brows, dilated eyes, and pale face, his heart shrouded with a strange mixture of moral hatred and physical pity, assisted at the execution of the king, and perhaps he alone, of all that throng, remained silent when the head of the son of St. Louis fell on the scaffold, and only raised on high his redoubtable saber, while his friends, loudly shouting, " *Vive la liberté!* " omitted to notice that one voice, at least, did not unite itself with their own.

This was the individual who, on the morning of the 14th of March, bent his steps toward La Rue Lepelletier, and of whose stormy career our history will furnish further detail.

Toward ten o'clock Maurice reached the section of which he was secretary. The commotion was great. The question in agitation was, to vote an address to the Convention, in order to repress the conspiracies of the Girondins. They impatiently awaited the arrival of Maurice.

There was no doubt of the return of the Chevalier de Maison Rouge, of the audacity with which the arch-conspirator had for the second time entered Paris, where he well knew a price was now fixed on his head.

To this circumstance was attributed the attempt made the preceding evening on the temple, and each one expressed his hatred and indignation against the traitors and aristocrats.

Contrary to the general expectation, Maurice appeared preoccupied and silent, wrote down the proclamation, finished his employment in three hours, demanded if the sitting had terminated, and receiving an answer in the affirmative, took his hat, and proceeded toward La Rue St. Honoré.

Arriving there, Paris appeared quite different to him. He revisited the corner of La Rue du Coq, where, during the night, he had first seen the lovely unknown struggling in the hands of the soldiers. Then, from thence he proceeded to the bridge Marie, the same road he had traveled by her side, stopping where the patrols had stopped them, repeating in the same place, as if it had preserved an echo of their words, the sentences exchanged between them; only it was now one o'clock in the afternoon, and the sun, shining brilliantly upon this walk, reminded him at every step of the occurrences of the past night.

Maurice crossed the bridge, and entered directly La Rue Victor, as it was then called.

"Poor woman," murmured Maurice, "she did not reflect yesterday that the duration of the night was only twelve hours, and that her secret would, in all probability, not last longer than the night. By the light of the sun, I will endeavor to find the door through which she vanished, and who knows but I may, perhaps, even see her at a window?"

He then entered the Old Rue St. Jacques, and placed himself in the same spot as the unknown had placed him on the preceding evening. For an instant he closed his eyes, perhaps foolishly expecting the kiss he had then received would again impress his lips. But he felt nothing but the remembrance ; 'tis true that burned yet.

Maurice opened his eyes, and saw two little streets, one to the right, the other to the left. They were muddy, dirty, and badly formed, furnished with barriers, cut by little bridges, thrown over a kennel. There might be seen the beams of arches, nooks, corners, and twenty doors propped up, fast falling into decay. Here, indeed, was misery in all its hideousness. Here and there was a garden inclosed in a fence, others by palisades of poles, some by walls, and skins hanging in the outhouses, diffusing around that disgusting odor always arising from a tan-yard.

Maurice's search lasted for nearly two hours, during which he found nothing, and divined nothing, and ten times he had retraced his steps to consider where he was. But all his efforts were in vain ; his search was a fruitless one, as all trace of the young woman seemed to have been effaced by the fog and rain of the previous night.

"Truly," said Maurice, "I must be in a dream. This filthy place could not for an instant have afforded refuge for my beautiful fairy of last night."

There was, in this wild Republican, more real poetry than in his friend of the anacreontic quatrains, since he clung to this idea, fearful to sully, even in thought, the spotless purity of the unknown. But all hope had now forsaken him.

"Adieu," said he ; "mysterious beauty, you have treated me like a child and a fool. Would she have led me here if she really lived in this wretched locality ? No, she would only pass as a swan over the infected marsh, and, like a bird in the air, leave no trace behind."

CHAPTER VI.

THE TEMPLE.

THE same day, and the same hour, when Maurice, disappointed and unhappy, repassed the bridge De la Tournelle, several municipals, accompanied by Santerre, commandant of the Parisian National Guard, made a visit of inquiry to the temple, transformed into a prison, since the 13th of August, 1793.

The visit was made especially to an apartment in the third story, consisting of an ante-chamber and three rooms. One of these chambers was occupied by two females, a young girl, and a child of nine years old, all dressed in mourning. The elder of the females was about seven or eight and thirty. She was seated at a table reading.

The second, whose age appeared twenty-eight or twenty-nine was engaged on a piece of tapestry.

The young girl of fourteen years was seated near the child, who, ill and in bed, closed his eyes as if asleep, although that was utterly impossible, owing to the noise made by the municipals. While some moved the beds, others examined their clothes and linen; the rest, when their search was concluded, remained rudely staring at the unfortunate prisoners, who never even raised their eyes, the one from her book, the other from her embroidery, and the third from her brother.

The eldest of these women was tall, handsome, and very pale. She appeared to concentrate all her attention on her book, although, in all probability, her eyes read, but not her mind. One of the municipals approached her, brutally snatched away her book, and flung it into the middle of the room. The prisoner stretched her hand across the table, took up the second volume, and continued to read.

The Montagnard made a furious gesture, as if he would take away the second, as he had the first, but at this attempt, which startled the prisoner at her embroidery near the window, the young girl sprang forward, and encircling the reader's head with her arms, weeping, exclaimed: "My poor mother! my poor mother!" and then embraced her. As she did so, the prisoner placed her mouth to her ear, and whispered:

"Marie, there is a letter concealed in the stove; remove it."

"Come, come," said the municipal, brutally dragging the young girl toward him, and separating her from her mother, "shall you soon have finished embracing?"

"Sir," said she, "has the Convention decreed that children shall not embrace their mothers?"

"No; but it has decreed that traitors, aristocrats, and *ci-devants* shall be punished; that is why I am here to interrogate you. Answer, Antoinette."

She who was thus grossly accosted did not even deign to look at her examiner, but turned her head aside, while a flush passed over her face, pale and furrowed with tears.

"It is impossible," said he, "that you are ignorant of the attempt last night. Whence came it?"

The prisoners still maintained silence.

"Answer, Antoinette," said Santerre, approaching her, without remarking the almost frenzied horror which had seized the young woman at sight of this man, who, on the morning of the 21st of January, conducted Louis XVI. from the temple to the scaffold. "Reply. They were conspiring last night against the Republic, and seeking your escape from the captivity in which you are expiating your crimes, by the will of the people. Tell me, do you know who are the conspirators?"

Marie started at contact with that voice, which she endeavored to fly from by removing her chair to the greatest distance possible, but replied no more to this question than to the former one; paid no more deference to Santerre than she had done to the municipal.

"You are, then, determined not to reply?" said Santerre, stamping his foot furiously.

The prisoner took up the third volume from the table. Santerre turned himself away. The brutal power of this man, who commanded eighty thousand men, who had only need of a gesture to cover the voice of the dying Louis XVI., was defeated by the dignity of a poor prisoner, whose head he could cause to fall, but whose will he could not bend.

"And you, Elizabeth," said he, addressing the other female, who at that instant abandoned her tapestry to join her hands in prayer, not to these men, but to God, "will you reply?"

"I do not know what you ask," said she; "therefore, I cannot reply."

"*Morbleu!* Citoyenne Capet," said Santerre, impatiently, "I think what I say is sufficiently clear, too. I again tell you that yesterday an attempt was made for your escape, and you certainly must know the culprits."

"Having no communication with those outside, monsieur, we cannot possibly tell what they do, either for or against us."

"Very well," said the municipal; "we will now hear what your nephew will say."

And he approached the bed of the young dauphin. At this menace, Marie Antoinette suddenly rose.

"Monsieur," said she, "my son is ill, and now asleep—do not wake him."

"Reply, then."

"I know nothing."

The municipal walked straight to the bed of the little prisoner, who, as we have said, feigned sleep.

"Come, wake up, Capet," said he, shaking him roughly.

The child opened his eyes, and smiled.

The municipals then surrounded his bed.

The queen, agitated with fear and grief, made a sign to her daughter, who, profiting by this moment, glided from the apartment into the room adjoining, **opened the mouth of the stove, and drew out a letter.**

"What do you want with me?" asked the child.

"To inquire if you heard nothing during the night."

"No; I was asleep."

"You are very fond of sleep, it seems."

"Yes; for when I sleep I dream."

"And what do you dream?"

"That I again see my father, whom you have killed."

"Then you heard nothing?" said Santerre, quickly.

"Nothing."

"These wolf's cubs are, in truth, well agreed with the she-wolf," said the municipal, furious with rage. "There has been, notwithstanding, a plot."

The queen smiled.

"She bullies us, the Austrian!" cried the municipal. "Well, since it is thus, let us execute in all its rigor the decree of the Commune. Get up, Capet."

"What would you do?" said the queen, forgetting herself. "Do you not see my son is ill, and suffering from fever? Would you wish to kill him?"

"Your son," said the municipal, "is the cause of constant alarm to the council of the temple; he is the point at which all the conspirators aim, and flatter themselves they shall carry you off altogether. Well, let them come. Tison—call Tison!"

Tison was a species of journeyman, charged with all the household work in the prison. He appeared. He was a man of forty years old, much sunburned, of a rude and ferocious aspect, with matted black hair overhanging his eyebrows.

"Tison," said Santerre, "who came yesterday to bring the prisoners' food?"

Tison uttered a name.

"And their linen, who brought it to them?"

"My daughter."

"Then your daughter is a laundress?"

"Certainly."

"And you gave her the washing of the prisoners?"

"Why not? She gains as much by one as another; it

is no longer the tyrant's money, but belongs to the nation, who pays for them."

"You were told to examine the linen with the greatest attention."

"Well, do I ever fail in my duty? In proof of which, they had yesterday a handkerchief tied in two knots. I have taken it to the council, who ordered my wife to wash, iron, and return it to Madame Capet, without saying anything about it."

At this remark of two knots being tied in the pocket-handkerchief, the queen trembled, the pupils of her eyes dilated, and she and Mme. Elizabeth exchanged hasty glances.

"Tison," said Santerre, "your daughter is a person of whose patriotism no one can entertain a doubt; but when she leaves the Temple to-day she returns there no more."

"Ah, *mon Dieu!*" said Tison, terrified. "What are you saying to me? I shall not see my daughter till I go out?"

"You will not go out," said Santerre.

Tison looked wildly around, without allowing his eye to remain fixed on any particular object, and suddenly exclaimed:

"I am not to go out; that is it, is it? Well, then, I will go out altogether. Give me my dismissal. I am neither traitor nor aristocrat, that I should be detainad in prison. I tell you I will go out."

"Citizen," said Santerre, "obey the orders of the Commune, and be silent, or I tell you it may be all the worse for you. Remain here and watch all that passes. There is an eye on you. I warn you of this."

During this time, the queen, who thought herself for a moment forgotten, recovered by degrees, and replaced her son in his bed.

"Desire your wife to come up," said the municipal to Tison.

He obeyed without a word. The threats of Santerre had rendered him meek as a lamb.

Tison's wife came up.

"Come here, citoyenne," said Santerre; "we are going into the ante-chambers; during that time search all the prisoners."

"Listen, wife," said Tison; "they will not permit our daughter to come to the Temple."

"They will not permit our daughter to come here? Then we shall see her no more?"

Tison mournfully shook his head.

"What do you say to this?"

"I say we will make a report to the council of the temple, and the council shall decide it. In the meantime——"

"In the meantime, I will see my daughter again."

"Silence!" said Santerre; "you came here for the purpose of searching the prisoners; search them, then, and afterward we will see——"

"But—now——"

"Oh, oh!" said Santerre, knitting his brows, "you are contaminated, it appears to me."

"Do as the citizen general tells you, wife," he said; "afterward we shall see."

And Tison regarded Santerre with an humble smile.

"Very well," said the woman; "go, then; I am ready to search."

The men went out.

"*Ma chère* Madame Tison," said the queen, "you know——"

"I only know, Citoyenne Capet," said the horrible woman, gnashing her teeth, "that you are the cause of all the misery of the people, and also that I have reason to suspect you, and you know it."

Four men waited at the door to assist Tison's wife, if the queen offered any resistance.

The search commenced on the queen.

There was found on her person a handkerchief tied in three knots, which, unfortunately, appeared a reply to the one spoken of by Tison; a pencil, a scapulary and some sealing-wax.

"Ah! I knew it," said Tison's wife; "I have often

THE CHEVALIER DE MAISON ROUGE. 45

told the municipals she wrote, the Austrian! The other day I found a lump of sealing-wax on the candlestick."

"Ah, madame," said the queen, in a supplicating tone, "only show the scapulary, I entreat you!"

"Yes," said the woman, "I feel pity for you, who have felt so much pity for me, to take my daughter from me."

Mme. Elizabeth and Mme. Royale had nothing found upon them.

The woman Tison recalled the municipals, who entered, Santerre at their head. She showed them the articles found upon the queen, which, as they passed from hand to hand, afforded subjects for an infinite variety of conjectures; but the handkerchief tied in three knots excited, above all, the imagination of these persecutors of the royal race.

"Now," said Santerre, "we are going to read the decree of the Convention to you."

"What decree?" demanded the queen.

"The decree which orders you to be separated from your son."

"Is it, then, true that this decree exists?"

"Yes; the Convention has too much regard for the health of a child confided to its guardianship to leave him in the care of a mother so depraved."

The eyes of the queen flashed like lightning.

"But form some accusation, at least, tigers that you are."

"That is not at all difficult," said a municipal; and he pronounced one of those infamous accusations brought by Suétone against Agrippine.

"Oh! cried the queen, standing, pale with indignation, "I appeal to the heart of every mother!"

"That is all very fine," said a municipal; "but we have already been here two hours, and cannot lose the whole day. Get up, Capet, and follow us."

"Never, never!" cried the queen, rushing between the municipals and the young Louis, preparing to defend the approach to his bed, as a tigress the entrances to her den. "Never will I permit you to carry away my child."

"Oh! messieurs," said Mme. Elizabeth, clasping her hands in an attitude of prayer, "messieurs, in the name of Heaven, have pity on us both."

"Then speak," said Santerre; "state the names, avow the project of your accomplices; explain what they wished to intimate by the knots made in the pocket-handkerchief brought with your linen by Tison's daughter, and the meaning of those tied in the handkerchief found in your pocket, and on these conditions I will leave you your child."

A look from Mme. Elizabeth seemed to implore the queen to submit to this dreadful sacrifice.

Then, quietly brushing from her eye a tear which sparkled like a diamond:

"Adieu, my son," cried she; "never forget your father who is in heaven, or your mother who will soon join him there, and never omit to repeat morning and evening the prayer I have taught you. Adieu, my son."

She gave him a last kiss; then, rising calm and inflexible:

"I know nothing, messieurs," said she; "do as you please."

But the queen must have required more than the usual amount of fortitude contained in the heart of woman, and above all, of a mother. She fell back fainting upon a chair, while they carried away the child, who, with fast-flowing tears, held out his arms, but uttered not a single word or cry.

The door closed behind the municipals who carried away the child, and the three women remained alone. There was for a moment the deep silence of despair, interrupted only by occasional sobs.

"The queen first broke silence.

"My daughter," said she, "that letter?"

"I burned it, as you desired me, *ma mère.*"

"Without reading it?"

"Without reading it."

"Adieu, then, to the last ray of hope—divine hope!" murmured Mme. Elizabeth.

"You are right, my sister, you are right; it is almost beyond endurance." Then, turning toward her daughter: "But you, at least, saw the handwriting, Marie?"

"Yes, *ma mère*, for a moment."

The queen rose, went to the door to make sure she was not observed, then, drawing a pin from her hair, approached the wall, and from a chink drew out a small paper folded like a letter, and showing it to Mme. Royale:

"Collect your thoughts before you reply, my child," said she; "was the writing the same as this?"

"Yes, yes, *ma mère*," cried the princess; "I recognize it."

"God be praised, then!" cried the queen, falling with fervor on her knees. "If he could write since this morning, he is safe. Thanks, *mon Dieu*, thanks! So noble a friend deserves Thy miraclous preservation!"

"Of whom do you speak, *ma mère?*" demanded Mme. Royale. "Who is this friend? Tell me his name, that I may recommend him to God in my prayers."

"You are right, my child; never forget it. This name, for it is the name of a gentleman replete with honor and courage, one not devoted to us through ambition, for he has only revealed himself since our misfortunes. He has never seen the Queen of France, or rather, the Queen of France has never seen him, and he vows his life to her defense. Perhaps he will be recompensed as all virtue is recompensed, by a dreadful death. But—if he dies—Oh! I shall still think of him in heaven—he is called——"

The queen looked uneasily around, then lowering her voice:

"He is called the Chevalier de Maison Rouge. Pray for him."

CHAPTER VII.

THE OATH OF THE GAMESTER.

THE attempted abduction, so contestable was it, because it had had no one to commence the execution of it, had excited the anger of some and the interest of others. That which likewise corroborated this event almost to a certainty, was that the Committee for General Security learned that three weeks or a month before a number of emigrants had entered France from different parts of the frontier. It was evident these people who thus risked their lives did not do so without design, and this design was, in all probability, to cooperate in carrying off the royal family.

Already, upon the proposition of the Conventionalist Asselim, the terrible decree had been promulgated which condemned to death all emigrants convicted of having returned to France, all Frenchmen convicted of having intended to emigrate, particularly all convicted of having assisted in their flight, or in their return, either a female or male emigrant; and, lastly, all citizens convicted of having afforded shelter to an emigrant. With this dreadful law commenced the "Reign of Terror." All that was wanting was the law for suspected persons. The Chevalier de Maison Rouge was an enemy far too active and audacious for his return to Paris, and his apparition in the Temple, not to call forth the gravest measures. More severe inspections than had previously taken place were made in a number of suspected houses, but with the exception of some female emigrants who allowed themselves to be taken, and some old men whose few remaining days they did not trouble themselves to dispute with the executioner, their researches produced no other result.

The sections, as may be imagined, were after this event much occupied for several days, and, consequently, the secretary of the section Lepelletier, one of the most influential in Paris, had little time to think of his unknown fair one. At first, as he had resolved on quitting La Rue Vieille St. Jacques, he had tried to forget her, but, as his friend Louis had observed to him:

> "Alas! endeavoring to forget
> But makes us recollect the more."

Maurice, however, neither said nor confessed anything. He buried in his heart all the details of that adventure which he had been able to conceal from the scrutiny of his friend. But he who knew Maurice to be of a joyous and hilarious nature, and now saw him constantly sad and thoughtful, seeking solitude, doubted not, to use his own expression, that the rogue Cupid had passed that way.

It is remarkable that, during its eighteen centuries of monarchy, France had had few years so mythological as the year of our Lord 1793. In the meantime, the chevalier was not taken, and he was no more spoken of. The widowed queen, cruelly robbed of her child, contented herself by weeping, in company with her sister and daughter. The young dauphin was consigned to the care of "Simon the Shoemaker," this poor little martyr who, in the short space of three years, was reunited to his father. There was a moment's calm. The Montagnard volcano rested before devouring the Girondins.

Maurice felt the weight of this calm, as the heaviness of the atmosphere is felt in stormy weather, and not knowing how to dispose of his leisure, abandoned himself entirely to the ardor of a sentiment, which, if not actually love itself, bordered closely upon it. He reread his letter, again kissed his beautiful sapphire ring, and resolved, notwithstanding his oath, to make one more attempt, promising himself this should indeed be the last. The young man had first thought he would go to the section of the Jardin des Plantes, and there make inquiry from the secretary, his colleague. But the first idea (and, we may add, which he still retained) that the beautiful unknown was mixed up in some political plot, still restrained him, as the thought that any indiscretion on his part might be the means of sending this lovely woman to La Place de la Revolution, and his head to the block, caused his blood to curdle and freeze in his veins. He, therefore, determined on seeking this adventure alone, and without any further information. His plan, besides, was very simple. The catalogue of names inscribed on each door would certainly afford him some clew, and then, by interrogating the porter, he might be able to solve the mystery.

In his capacity of secretary of La Rue Lepelletier, he possessed full and entire right to make all inquiries. Besides, Maurice, ignorant of the name of the unknown, was able to judge of it by analogy. It was impossible so lovely a creature should not possess a name in harmony with her form, some name appertaining to sylph, fairy, or angel, since her arrival on earth must have been hailed as that of a superior and supernatural being. This name would then most infallibly guide him.

Maurice then dressed himself in a blouse of a dark-brown cloth, adorned his head with the "bonnet rouge," worn on great occasions, and set out on his voyage of discovery alone. He had in his hand one of those knotted cudgels called "une Constitution," which, wielded by his vigorous hand, was powerful as the club of Hercules, and in his pocket he placed his commission as secretary of the section of Lepelletier. These were at once his physical security and his moral guarantee.

He prepared himself to review afresh La Rue St. Victor, La Rue Vieille St. Jacques, reading by light of the declining day all those names, inscribed in a hand more or less practised, upon the panels of every door.

Maurice had reached the hundredth house, and consequently, read the hundredth list, and nothing had yet occurred to induce him to imagine that he was in the least degree upon the trail of the unknown, when a good-natured shoemaker, noticing the anxiety and impatience depicted on the young man's countenance, came out with his strap of leather and his punch, and looking at Maurice over his spectacles :

"Do you wish any information respecting the tenants of this house, citizen ?" said he ; "if so, I shall be happy to give it to you."

"Thanks, citizen," stammered Maurice ; "I am looking for the name of a friend."

"Tell me the name, citizen ; I know everybody in this quarter. Where does this friend live ?"

"He lives, I think, in the Old Rue Jacques, but I fear he has removed."

"But how is he named ? I must know that."

Maurice, taken thus unawares, hesitated for a moment, then pronounced the first name that presented itself to his memory.

"René," said he.

"And what trade ?"

Maurice was surrounded by tanneries.

"A working tanner," said he.

"In that case," said a burgess, who stopped and regarded Maurice with a certain good nature not totally exempt from distrust, "it is necessary to address yourself to his master."

"That is true," said the doorkeeper, "it is quite right, the masters know the names of these workmen ; there is the Citizen Dixmer, who is manager of a tannery, has more than fifty workmen in his yard ; he will perhaps tell you."

Maurice turned round and saw a burgess of commanding figure, with a mild countenance, the richness of whose attire denoted opulence.

"Only, as the citizen porter observes, it is necessary I should know the family name."

"I have told you—René."

"René is his baptismal name ; it is the family name I require. All my workmen sign their family name."

"*Ma foi!*" said Maurice, growing impatient under this species of interrogation, "the family name ? I do not know it."

"What," said the burgess, with a smile, in which Maurice thought he discerned more irony than he wished to appear, "what, not know the surname of your friend?"

"No."

"In that case it is not probable you will find him;" and the burgess, gravely bowing to Maurice, walked a short distance and entered a house in the Old Rue St. Jacques.

"The fact is that if you do not know his surname——" said the porter.

"Well, I do not know it," said Maurice, who would not have been sorry to find some occasion to vent his ill-temper, and was at the moment much inclined to seek a quarrel. "What have you to say to that?"

"Nothing, citizen, nothing at all; only, since you do not know the name of your friend, it is, as Citizen Dixmer said, more than probable you will not find him."

And the citizen porter went into his lodge, shrugging his shoulders. Maurice felt a great inclination to thrash this porter, but he was an old man, and his infirmities saved him. Besides, the day was drawing to a close, and he had only a few moments of daylight left. He availed himself of it by returning to the first street, then to the second, examined every door, searched in every nook, looked under every palisade, climbed each wall, threw a glance into the interior of every gateway, looked through the keyholes, knocked at some deserted warehouses without receiving any reply, till at length nearly two hours had elapsed in this useless investigation.

Nine o'clock struck; no more noise was heard, no movement seen in this deserted quarter, whose life seemed to have retired with the light of day. Maurice, in despair, made a retrograde movement, when all at once, at the winding of a narrow alley, he discerned a light burning. He immediately ventured into the dark passage, without remarking that at the moment even where he had thrust himself, a curious head, which for the last quarter of an hour, from the midst of a clump of trees, rising from under the wall, had followed all his movements, and then disappeared suddenly behind this wall. A short time after this head had disappeared, three men came out from a small door in this same wall, went into the alley, where Maurice had preceded them, while a fourth, for greater security, locked the door of entrance into this alley. At the end of this alley, Maurice discovered a court; it was on the opposite side of this court the light was burning. He knocked at the door of a poor solitary house, but at the first sound the light was extinguished. He redoubled his efforts, but no one answered to his call; he saw they were determined to make no reply, so, comprehending that it was only a useless waste of time, he crossed the court and reentered the alley. At this moment the door of the house turned softly on its hinges, three men came out, and then the sound of a whistle was heard.

Maurice turned round, and saw three shadows within a short distance. He saw in the darkness also, his eyes having become accustomed to this obscurity, the reflection of three glittering blades. He knew he was hemmed in. He would have brandished his club, but the alley was so narrow that it touched the wall on either side. At the same moment a violent blow on the head stunned him. This was an unforeseen assault made upon him by the four men who entered through the door in the wall. Seven men at the same time threw themselves upon Maurice, and notwithstanding a desperate resistance, overpowered him, and succeeded in binding his hands and bandaging his eyes.

Maurice had not even uttered a cry, or called for aid. Strength and true courage suffer by themselves, and are tenacious of the help of a stranger. Besides, Maurice had often heard that no one would enter this deserted quarter. Maurice was thus, as we have said, thrown down and bound, but had not uttered a single complaint. He had reflected as to what would follow—that as they had bandaged his eyes they did not intend to kill him directly. At Maurice's age respite becomes hope. He recovered his presence of mind, and listened patiently.

"Who are you?" demanded a voice still breathless from the late struggle.

"I am a man they are murdering," replied Maurice.

"What is more, you are a dead man if you speak so loud, or call for assistance, or even utter the least cry."

"If I had wished to do so, I need not have waited till the present time."

"Are you ready to answer my questions?"

"Let me hear them first, I shall then see whether I ought to reply."

"Who sent you here?"

"No one."

"You came, then, of your own accord?"

"Yes."

"You lie."

Maurice made a desperate effort to disengage his hands, but it was in vain.

"I never lie," said he.

"In either case, whether you came of your own accord or were sent, you are a spy."

"And you are cowards!"

"We cowards?"

"You are seven or eight against one man bound, and you insult that man. Cowards! cowards! cowards!"

This violence on the part of Maurice, instead of enraging his adversaries, appeared to produce a contrary effect. It was even a proof that the young man was not what they deemed him; a true spy would have trembled and begged for mercy.

"There is nothing insulting in that," said a voice, milder yet firmer than any that had previously been heard; "in the times we live in, one may be a spy without being a dishonest man, only it is at the risk of one's life."

"If that is your opinion, you are welcome to question me. I will answer you faithfully."

"What brought you into this quarter?"

"To search here for a woman."

THE CHEVALIER DE MAISON ROUGE. 55

An incredulous murmur followed this assertion. The breeze increased, and became a hurricane.

"You lie!" said the same voice; "it is no woman—there is no woman in this quarter to follow. Avow your intentions, or you die!"

"Well, then," said Maurice, "you surely would not kill me for the mere pleasure of doing so, unless you are true brigands."

And Maurice made a second effort, more strenuous than the first, to disengage his arms from the cord which secured them. It was useless, and at that moment he experienced a sharp pain in his breast, which made him flinch.

"Oh! you feel that?" said one of the men. "There are eight more similar to this with which you will claim acquaintance."

"Kill me, then," said Maurice, with resignation; "it will, at least, be finished at once."

"Who are you?" said the mild but firm voice.

"Do you wish to know my name?"

"Yes, your name."

"I am Maurice Lindey."

"What!" cried a voice, "Maurice Lindey, the revolu—the patriot; Maurice Lindey, the secretary of the section Lepelletier?"

These words were pronounced with so much warmth that Maurice felt they were decisive. This reply was calculated to decide his fate. Maurice was incapable of fear; he drew himself up like a true Spartan, and replied, in a firm voice:

"Yes, Maurice Lindey; yes, Maurice Lindey, secretary to the section Lepelletier; yes, Maurice Lindey, the patriot, the revolutionist, the Jacobin; Maurice Lindey, in short, whose happiest day will be that on which he dies for liberty."

This reply was received with the silence of death.

Maurice presented his breast, expecting every moment the sword, of which he had only felt the point, would be plunged into his heart.

"Is this true?" said a voice full of emotion; "let us see, young man, that you lie not."

"Feel in my pocket," said Maurice, "and you will there find my commission. Look upon my breast, and if not effaced by my blood, you will see my initials, an M and L, embroidered on my shirt."

Maurice felt himself immediately raised by strong arms, and carried to some distance. He first heard one door open, then a second, which he knew was narrower than the first, from the trouble the men found in carrying him through. The murmuring and whispering continued.

"I am lost!" said Maurice to himself; "they will fasten a stone round my neck, and cast me into the Brière."

In an instant he felt the men who bore him were mounting some steps. A warmer air fanned his face, and he was placed upon a seat. He heard a door double-locked and the sound of departing steps. He fancied he was left alone. He listened with as much attention as was possible in a man whose life hung upon a word, and thought he again heard the voice which had already struck upon his ear say, with a mixture of decision and mildness:

"We will deliberate."

CHAPTER VIII.

GENEVIÈVE.

A QUARTER of an hour passed away; it appeared an age to Maurice. And what more natural? Young, handsome and vigorous, highly beloved and esteemed by a hundred devoted friends, with whom he sometimes dreamed of accomplishing great things, he felt himself suddenly, without preparation, liable to lose his life—the victim of a base ambuscade. He knew no one was shut in the chamber; but was he watched? He again exerted all his strength to break his bonds, till his iron muscles swelled, and the cords entered his flesh; but this, like all his former efforts, was useless.

It was the more terrible his hands being tied behind; he was unable to draw up his bandage. If he were only able to see, he might perhaps be able to escape. However, as these various attempts were made without opposition, and hearing no one stirring, he concluded he was quite alone.

His feet pressed upon something soft and heavy, it might be gravel or perhaps soft clay. An acrid, pungent smell announced the presence of vegetable matter. Maurice fancied he was in a greenhouse, or some place very like it. He took a step or two, hit the wall, turned, and, groping with his hands, felt some garden tools. He uttered an exclamation of joy. With unparalleled exertion he began to examine these tools, one after another. His flight now became a question of time. If chance or Providence granted him five minutes, and if among these tools he found a sharp instrument, he was saved. He found a spade. From the way in which Maurice was bound, it required a great struggle to raise the spade a sufficient height for his purpose. He at length succeeded and, upon the iron of the spade, which he supported against the wall with his back, he at last cut, or, rather, wore away, the cord which confined his wrists. The operation was tedious; the iron cut slowly. The perspiration streamed from his face; he heard a noise as of some one approaching; with a tremendous effort, the cord, rather worn, broke. This time it was a cry of joy he gave utterance to; now, at least, he was sure to die in defending himself. Maurice tore the bandage from his eyes. He was not deceived, but found himself in a kind of, not greenhouse, but pavilion, used as a receptacle for the more delicate plants unable to outlive the winter in the open air. In a corner the gardening implements were stowed away, which had been the means of rendering him so important a service. Facing him was a window; he glanced toward it, and saw it was grated, and a man armed with a carbine placed sentinel before it.

On the other side of the garden, about thirty paces distant, perhaps rather less, rose a small turret, fellow to the one where Maurice remained prisoner. The blind was down, but through the blind a light was visible.

He approached the door and listened ; another sentinel was placed before this door. These were the footsteps he had heard. But from the end of the corridor a confusion of voices resounded. The deliberation had evidently degenerated into disputation.

Maurice could not hear distinctly what was said ; some words, however, reached him, and amid these words—as if for them only the distance was short—he distinguished plainly, "Spy ! Poniard ! Death !" Maurice redoubled his attention ; a door opened, and he heard more distinctly.

"Yes," said one voice, "it is assuredly a spy ; he has discovered something, and is certainly sent to take us and our secret unawares. In freeing him we run the risk of his denouncing us."

"But his word," said a voice.

"His word—he will give it only to betray it. Is he a gentleman, that we should trust his word ?"

Maurice ground his teeth at the idea which some folks still retained, that only a gentleman could keep his oath.

"But he does not know us ; how can he denounce us ?"

"No, he does not know us, certainly, nor our occupations ; but he knows the address, and will return ; this time he will be well accompanied."

This argument appeared conclusive.

"Then," said a voice, which several times already had struck Maurice as belonging to the chief, "it is then quite decided."

"Yes, a hundred times, yes ; I do not comprehend you with your magnanimity. *Mon cher,* if the Committee for the Public Safety caught us, you would see if they acted after this fashion."

"You persist, then, in your decision, gentlemen ?"

"Without doubt ; and you are not, we hope, going to oppose it ?"

"I have only one voice, gentlemen ; it has been in

favor of his liberation; you possess six, and they all vote for his death. Let it then be death."

Maurice felt the blood freeze in his veins.

"Of course he will howl and cry!" said the voice; "but have you removed Madame Dixmer?"

"Madame Dixmer!" murmured Maurice; "I begin now to comprehend I am in the house of the master tanner, who spoke to me in the Old Rue St. Jacques, and who went away laughing because I was unable to tell him the name of my friend. But how the devil can it be to his interest to assassinate me?"

Looking round about him, Maurice perceived an iron stake with a handle of ash-tree wood.

"In any case," said he, "before they assassinate me, I will kill more than one of them."

And he sprang to secure this harmless instrument, which, in his hand, was to become a formidable weapon. He then retired behind the door, and so placed himself that he could see without being seen. His heart beat so tumultuously that in the deep silence its palpitations might be heard. Suddenly Maurice shuddered from head to foot. A voice had said:

"If you act according to my advice, you will break a window, and through the bars kill him with a shot from a carbine."

"Oh, no, no! not an explosion," said another voice; that might betray us. Besides, Dixmer, there is your wife."

"I have just looked at her through the blind; she suspects nothing—she is reading."

"Dixmer, you shall decide for us. Do you advocate a shot from the carbine, or a stroke from the poniard?"

"Avoid firearms as far as it is possible—the poniard."

"Then let it be the poniard. *Allons!*"

"*Allons!*" repeated five or six voices together.

Maurice was a child of the Revolution with a heart of flint, and in mind, like many others at that epoch, an atheist. But at the word "*Allons!*" pronounced behind the door, which alone separated him from death, he remembered the sign of the cross, which his mother had taught him when an infant he repeated his prayers at her knee.

Steps approached, stopped; then the key turned in the lock, and the door slowly opened.

During this fleeting moment, Maurice had said to himself:

"If I lose this opportunity to strike the first blow I am a dead man. If I throw myself upon the assassins, I take them unawares—gain first the garden, then the street, and am saved!"

Immediately, with the spring of a lion, and uttering a savage cry, which savored more of menace than terror, he threw down the first two men, who, believing him bound and blindfolded, were quite unprepared for such an assault, scattered the others, took a tremendous leap over over them, thanks to his iron muscles, saw at the end of the corridor a door leading into the garden wide open, rushed toward it, cleared at a bound six steps, and found himself in the garden, debating if it were best to endeavor to run and gain the gate. This gate was secured by a lock and a couple of bolts. Maurice drew back the bolts, tried to open the lock, but it had no key.

In the meantime, his pursuers, who had reached the steps, perceived him.

"There he is!" cried they; "fire upon him, Dixmer, fire! Kill him—kill him!"

Maurice uttered a groan; he was enclosed in the garden; he measured the walls with his eye—they were ten feet in height.

All this passed in a moment. The assassins rushed forward in pursuit of him.

Maurice was about thirty feet in advance, or nearly so; he looked round about him with the air of a condemned man who seeks concealment as the means of saving himself from the reality. He perceived the turret—the blind—and behind the blind the light burning.

He made but one bound—a bound of six feet—seized the blind, tore it down, passed through the window, smashing it, and alighted in a chamber where a female sat reading.

The female rose, terrified, calling for assistance.

"Stand aside, Geneviève—stand aside!" cried the voice of Dixmer; "stand aside, that I may kill him!"

And Maurice saw the carbine leveled at him. But scarcely had the woman looked at him, than she uttered a frightful cry, and instead of standing aside, as desired by her husband, rushed between him and the barrel of the gun.

This movement concentrated all Maurice's attention to the generous woman, whose first impulse was to protect him from danger and death. In his turn he uttered a cry of astonishment.

It was the long sought-for unknown.

"You!" cried he; "you——"

"Silence!" cried she.

Then, turning toward the assassins, who, variously armed, approached the window:

"Ah! you will not kill him!" cried she.

"He is a spy," said Dixmer, whose usually placid countenance had assumed an expression of stern resolution; "he is a spy, and, therefore, must die."

"A spy—he?" said Geneviève; "he a spy! Come here, Dixmer. I need only say one word to prove that you are strangely deceived."

Dixmer and Geneviève approached the window, and in a low voice she uttered a few words. The master tanner raised his head quickly.

"He!" said he.

"He himself," said Geneviève.

"You are certain—quite certain?"

This time the young woman did not reply, but smiling, held out her hand to Maurice.

The features of Dixmer now assumed a singular expression of gentleness and indifference. He placed the butt-end of his musket on the ground.

"This is quite another thing," said he.

Then making a sign to his companions to follow, he

stepped aside with them, and after saying a few words, they disappeared.

"Conceal that ring," murmured Geneviève ; "it is known by every one here."

Maurice quickly drew the ring from his finger, and slipped it into his waistcoat pocket. A moment afterward the door of the pavilion opened, and Dixmer, unarmed, advanced toward Maurice.

"Pardon me, citizen," said he to him, "that I had not known sooner the obligation I am under to you. My wife, while retaining a grateful remembrance of the service you rendered her on the 10th of March, had forgotten your name. We were, therefore, completely in ignorance with whom we were concerned ; independent of this, believe me, we might not for a moment have entertained suspicion either of your honor or intentions. Again, I say, pardon me."

Maurice was bewildered ; with the greatest difficulty he preserved his equilibrium, he felt his head turn round, and was near falling. He supported himself against the mantelpiece. At length :

"Why did you wish to kill me ?" said he.

"That is the secret, citizen," said Dixmer ; "I confide it to your keeping. I am, as you already know, a tanner, and principal in this concern. The greater part of the acids I employ in the preparation of my skins are prohibited goods. Now, the smugglers have received intelligence of an information laid before the counsel-general. I feared you were an informer. My smugglers were more alarmed than myself at your bonnet-rouge and formidable appearance, and I do not conceal from you that your death was resolved upon."

"*Pardieu!* and well I know it," said Maurice ; "you tell me no news. I heard your consultation, and I have seen your carbine."

"I have already apologized," said Dixmer, in a kindly tone. "You must understand that, thanks to the unsettled state of the times, myself and partner, Monsieur Morand, are likely to realize an immense fortune. We have the furnishing of the military bags, and finish from fifteen hundred to two thousand each day. Owing to this blessed state of things in which we live, the municipality are much occupied, and have not time strictly to examine our accounts, so that it must be confessed we fish a little in troubled waters, the more so, as I have told you the preparatory materials we procure by smuggling allow us to gain two hundred per cent."

"*Diable!*" said Maurice, "that appears to me an honest living enough, and I can now understand your dread lest a denunciation on my part should put an end to it; but now you know me, you fear me no longer. Is it not so?"

"Now," said Dixmer, "I only require your promise." Then, placing his hand on his shoulder, and smiling, "As it is only between friends," said he, "may I inquire what brought you here, young man? But remember, if you wish to keep it secret, you are perfectly at liberty to do so."

"I have told you, I believe," murmured Maurice.

"Yes, a woman," said the burgess; "I know there was something about a woman."

"*Mon Dieu!* excuse me, citizen, I am aware some sort of explanation is due to you. Well, then, I sought a female, who the other evening, disguised, told me she resided in this quarter. I neither know her name, position, nor place of abode. I only know I am madly in love with her, that she is short——"

Geneviève was tall.

"That she is fair, and of a lively temperament."

Genevieve was a brunette, with large, pensive eyes.

"A grisette, in short," continued Maurice; "so to please her, I assumed the popular dress."

"This explains it all," said Dixmer, with an affectation of belief, which, at least, did not contradict his sullen look.

Geneviève colored, and feeling herself blush, turned away.

"Poor Citizen Lindey," said Dixmer, "what a miserable evening we have caused you to pass; and you are about the last I would wish to injure, so excellent a patriot, a brother; but, in short, I believed some 'disinfected' usurped your name."

"Let us say nothing more on the subject," said Maurice, who knew it was time for him to withdraw; "put me in the road, and let us forget that this has occurred altogether."

"Put you in your road!" said Dixmer; "you leave us not yet, not yet; I give—or, rather, my partner and myself give—a supper to-night to those brave fellows who wished so much to slaughter you a little while ago. I reckon upon your supping with them, that you may see they are not such devils as they appear to be."

"But," said Maurice, overjoyed at the thought of being for a few hours near Geneviève, "I do not know, really, if I ought to accept——"

"If you ought to accept!" said Dixmer; "I know you ought; these are good and stanch patriots as yourself. Besides, I shall not consider that you have forgiven me unless we break bread together."

Geneviève uttered not a word. Maurice was in torment.

"The fact is," said Maurice, "I fear I may be a constraint upon you, citoyenne; this dress—my ungentlemanly appearance——"

Geneviève looked timidly toward him.

"I accept your invitation, citizen," said he, bowing.

"I will go and secure our companions," said Dixmer; "in the meantime, warm yourself, *mon cher.*"

He went out. Maurice and Geneviève remained alone.

"Ah, monsieur," said the young woman, in an accent to which she in vain tried to convey a tone of reproach, "you have failed in your word, you have been exceedingly indiscreet."

"Madame," cried Maurice, "shall I expose you? Ah! in that case, pardon me, I will retire, and never——"

"*Dieu!*" said she, rising, "you are wounded in the breast; your shirt is stained with blood."

Indeed, upon the fine white shirt of Maurice—a shirt forming a strange contrast to his coarser clothes—a large red spot of blood had spread itself, and had dried there.

"Do not be under any alarm, madame," said the young man, "one of the smugglers pricked me with his poniard."

Geneviève turned pale, and, taking his hand:

"Forgive me," said she, "the wrong that has been done you; you saved my life, and I have nearly caused your death."

"Am I not sufficiently recompensed in finding you? You cannot for a moment imagine it was for another that I sought."

"Come with me," said Geneviève, interrupting him; "I will find you some clean linen. Our guests must not see you thus—it would be too great a reproach to them."

"I am a great trouble to you, madame, I fear," said Maurice, sighing.

"Not at all; I only do my duty; and," she added, "I do it with much pleasure."

Geneviève then conducted Maurice to a large dressing-room, arranged with an air of elegance he had not expected to find in the house of a master tanner. It is true, this master tanner appeared to be a millionaire. She then opened the wardrobes.

"Help yourself," said she; "you are at home."

She withdrew.

When Maurice came out, he found Dixmer, who had returned.

"*Allons, allons!*" said he, "to table; it only waits for you."

CHAPTER IX.

THE SUPPER.

WHEN Maurice entered with Dixmer and Geneviève into the *salle-à-manger*, situated in the body of the basement, where they had first conducted him, the supper was ready, but the room vacant. He saw all the guests enter successively. They were six in number; men of agreeable exterior, for the most part young and fashionably dressed; two or three even wore the blouse and bonnet-rouge.

Dixmer introduced Maurice, naming his titles and qualifications. Then, turning toward Maurice:

"You see," said he, "Citizen Lindey, all those who assist me in my trade. Thanks to the times in which we live, thanks to the revolutionary principles which have effaced all distinction, we all live upon the same footing of sacred equality. Every day we assemble twice at the same table, and I am happy you have been induced to partake of our family repast. *Allons!* to table—citizens, to table!"

"And—Monsieur Morand," said Geneviève, timidly, "do we not wait for him?"

"Ah, true!" said Dixmer. "This citizen, of whom I have already spoken, Citizen Lindey, is my partner. He conducts, if I may so express myself, the moral part of the establishment. He attends to the writing, keeps the cash, superintends the factories, pays and receives money, and, in short, works harder than any of us. The result is, that he is sometimes rather late. I will go and tell him we are waiting."

At this moment the door opened, and the Citizen Morand entered. He was a short man, dark, with bushy eyebrows, and wore green spectacles—like a man whose eyes are fatigued from excess of work—concealing his black eyes, but not so effectually their scintillating gleams. At the first words he uttered, Maurice recognized that mild yet commanding voice engaged in his behalf, when endeavoring to save him from becoming a victim to that terrible discussion. He was habited in a brown coat, with large buttons, a white waistcoat; and his fine cambric shirt-frill was often during dinner smoothed by a hand which Maurice, no doubt from its being that of a tradesman, admired much for its beauty and delicacy of appearance.

They all took their seats. Morand was placed on Geneviève's right hand, Maurice on her left. Dixmer sat opposite his wife. The rest of the guests seated themselves promiscuously round an oblong table. The supper was excellent. Dixmer had a capital appetite, and did the honors of the table with much politeness. The workmen, or those who pretended to be such, under this example, became excellent companions. The Citizen Morand spoke little, and eat still less; drank scarcely anything, and rarely smiled. Maurice, perhaps from the reminiscences his voice awakened, felt for him immediately a lively sympathy, only he was in doubt as to his age, and this rather annoyed him, as sometimes he imagined him to be a man of forty or fifty years, and at others quite young.

Dixmer, on placing himself at table, felt obliged to offer some explanation to his guests for the admission of a stranger into their little circle. He acquitted himself like an artless man, one unaccustomed to deceit; but the guests, as it seemed, were not difficult on this point; for, notwithstanding the awkwardness displayed by this manufacturer of hides in the introduction of e young man, they all appeared perfectly satisfied.

Maurice regarded him with astonishment.

"Upon my honor," said he to himself, "I shall really soon think that I myself am deceived. Is this the same man who, with flaming eyes and furious voice, pursued me gun in hand, and absolutely wished to kill me three quarters of an hour since? At this moment one might take him for a hero rather than an assassin. *Mon Dieu!* how the love of hides transforms a man."

While making these observations, Maurice experienced a strange feeling of joy and grief, and felt unable to analyze his own emotions. He at length found himself near his beautiful unknown, whom he had so ardently sought. As he had dreamed, she bore a charming name; he was intoxicated with the happiness of finding himself at her side; he drank in every word; and at each sound of her voice the most secret chord of his heart vibrated, but he was deeply wounded by all he saw. Geneviève was exactly what he had pictured her; the dream of a stormy night reality had not destroyed. Here was an elegant woman, of refined mind and superior education, affording another instance of what had so frequently occurred during the latter years preceding this present celebrated year, '93. Here was a young woman of distinction compelled, from the utter ruin into which the nobility had fallen, to ally herself to a commoner and a trusty man. Dixmer appeared a brave man. He was incontestably rich, and his manners to Geneviève were those of a man uniting every endeavor to render a woman happy.

But could kindness, riches, or excellent intentions compensate her for what she had sacrificed, or remove the immense distance existing between husband and wife, between a poetical, distinguished, charming girl and a vulgar-looking tradesman ? With what could Geneviève fill up this abyss ? Alas ! Maurice now guessed too well. With love ! And he, therefore, returned to his first opinion of the young woman, influenced by appearances on the evening of their meeting, that she was returning from some *rendezvous d'amour*.

The idea of Geneviève loving any one was torture to Maurice. He sighed, and deeply regretted having exposed himself to the temptation of imbibing a still larger dose of that poison termed love. At other moments, while listening to the ductile voice, so soft and harmonious, examining that pure and open countenance, evincing no fear that he should read every secret of her soul, he arrived at the conclusion that it was utterly impossible that this matchless creature would descend to deceit ; and then he found a bitter pleasure in remembering this lovely woman belonged solely to this good citizen, with his honest smile and vulgar pleasantries, and would never be to him more than a passing acquaintance.

They conversed, of course, on politics. How could it be otherwise at an epoch when politics were mixed up in everything ? Political subjects were even painted on the plates, political designs covered the walls, and politics were daily proclaimed in the streets. All at once, one of the guests who had hitherto preserved silence inquired concerning the prisoners of the Temple.

Maurice started, in spite of himself. He had recognized the voice of that man, a strenuous advocate for extreme measures, who had first struck him with his dagger, and then advocated his death. Nevertheless, this man, an honest tanner, and head of the manufactory, at least so Dixmer represented him, incited the good humor of Maurice by the expression of ideas the most patriotic, and principles the most revolutionary. The young man, under certain circumstances, was not inimical to these extreme measures, so much in fashion at this period, of which Danton was the apostle and hero. In this man's place, whose voice he had heard, and from the effect of whose weapon his wound was still smarting, he would not have attempted to assassinate the man he imagined to be a spy, but would rather have locked him in the garden, and there, equally armed, sword to sword, have fought without mercy, without pity. This is what Maurice would have done; but he comprehended soon that this was too much to expect of a journeyman tanner. This man of extreme measures, who appeared to possess in his political ideas the same violent system as in his private conduct, then spoke of the Temple, and expressed surprise that the prisoners were confided to the guardianship of a permanent council liable to be corrupted, and to municipals whose fidelity had already been more than once tempted.

"Yes," said the Citizen Morand, "but it must be remembered that on every occasion, up to the present time, the municipals have fully justified the confidence reposed in them by the nation, and history will record it is not only Robespierre who merits the title of 'Incorruptible.'"

"Without doubt, without doubt," replied the interlocutor; "but, because a thing has not yet happened, it would be absurd to suppose it never can happen. As for the National Guard," continued the principal of the manufactory, "well, the companies of the different sections are assembled, each in their turn, on duty at the temple, and that indifferently. Will you not admit that there might be, in a company of twenty or five and twenty men, a band of seven or eight determined characters, who, one fine night, might slaughter the sentinels and carry off the prisoners?"

"Bah!" said Maurice, "you see, citizen, this would be a foolish expedient. It would occupy them three weeks or a month, and then they might not succeed."

"Yes," replied Morand; "because one of those aristocrats who composed the patrol had the impudence, in speaking, to let fall the word monsieur, I do not know to whom."

"And then," said Maurice, who wished to prove that the police of the Republic did their duty, "because the entrance of the Chevalier de Maison Rouge into Paris was already known——"

"Bah!" cried Dixmer.

"They knew that Maison Rouge had entered Paris?" wildly demanded Morand; "and did they know by what means he entered?"

"Perfectly."

"Ah! *diable!*" said Morand, leaning forward to look at Maurice, "I should be curious to know that, as up to the present moment, no one can speak positively. But you, citizen, you, secretary to one of the principal sections in Paris, ought to be better informed."

"Doubtless; therefore, what I am about to tell you is the true statement of facts."

All the guests and Geneviève appeared prepared to pay the greatest attention to this recital.

"Well," said Maurice, "the Chevalier de Maison Rouge came from Vendée; as it appears, he had traversed all France with his usual good fortune. Arrived during the day at La Barrière du Roule, he waited till nine o'clock at night. At that hour a woman, disguised as a woman of the people, went out from the barrier, carrying to the chevalier a costume of chasseur of the National Guards. Ten minutes afterward she reentered with him; but the sentinel, who had seen her go out alone, felt rather suspicious when he saw her return with a companion. An alarm was given at the post; the post turned out, when the two culprits, knowing whom they were seeking, flung themselves into a hotel, where a second door opened into Les Champs Elysées.

"It seemed that a patrol devoted to the tyrants waited for the chevalier at the corner of La Rue Burre-du-Bec. You are acquainted with the rest."

"Ah, ah!" said Morand, "this is very strange."

"But positively true," said Maurice.

"Yes, it has an air of truth; but the female, do you know what became of her?"

"No; she has disappeared, and they are quite ignorant who she is or what she is."

The partner of Citizen Dixmer, and Citizen Dixmer himself, appeared to breathe more freely.

Geneviève had listened to the whole of this recital, pale, silent, and immovable.

"But," said Morand, with his usual coolness, "who can say that the Chevalier de Maison Rouge made one of the patrol who caused the alarm at the Temple?"

"A municipal, one of my friends, that day on duty at the Temple. He recognized him."

"He knew him from description."

"He had formerly seen him."

"And what sort of man, personally, is this Chevalier de Maison Rouge?"

"A man of five or six and twenty, short, fair, and of a pleasing countenance, with magnificent eyes and superb teeth."

There was a profound silence.

"Well," said Morand, "if your friend the municipal recognized this pretended Chevalier de Maison Rouge, why did he not arrest him?"

"In the first place, not knowing of his arrival at Paris, he feared being the dupe of a resemblance; and then, my friend, being rather lukewarm, acted as the lukewarm generally act—he let it alone."

"You would not have acted thus, citizen?" said Dixmer, laughing boisterously.

"No," said Maurice; "I confess it; I would rather find myself deceived than allow to escape so dangerous a man as the Chevalier de Maison Rouge."

"And what would you have done, then, monsieur?" timidly inquired Geneviève.

"What would I have done, citoyenne?" said Maurice. "I would have walked direct up to the patrol and placed my hand on the chevalier's collar, saying to him, 'Chevalier de Maison Rouge, I arrest you as a traitor to the nation;' and, my hand once upon his collar, I would not soon release him, I can tell you."

"And what would happen then?" said Geneviève.

"It would happen he had done thus much for himself and friends that the same hour they would be guillotined; that is all."

Geneviève shuddered, and darted on her neighbor a look of affright. But the Citizen Morand did not appear to notice this glance, and phlegmatically emptied his glass.

"The Citizen Lindey is right," said he; "there was nothing else to do; but, unfortunately, it was not done."

"And," demanded Geneviève, "do you know what has become of the Chevalier de Maison Rouge?"

"Bah!" said Dixmer, "in all probability he did not wish to remain longer, and, finding his attempt abortive, quitted Paris immediately."

"And perhaps France even," added Morand.

"Not at all, not at all," said Maurice.

"What! has he had the imprudence to remain in Paris?" asked Geneviève.

"He has not stirred."

A movement of general astonishment followed this assertion, which Maurice had stated with so much confidence.

"This is only a supposition, citizen, on your part," said Morand; "merely a supposition, that is all."

"No; it is a positive fact that I affirm."

"Ah!" said Geneviève, "I acknowledge, for my part,

I cannot believe it is as you say; it would be such an unpardonable imprudence."

"You are a woman, citoyenne, and can comprehend, then, what would outweigh, with a man of such a character as the Chevalier de Maison Rouge, all considerations of personal security?"

"And what can outweigh the dread of losing his life in a moment so dreadful?"

"Eh! *mon Dieu!* citoyenne," said Maurice, "love."

"Love!" repeated Geneviève.

"Doubtless. Do you not know, then, that the chevalier de Maison Rouge is enamored of Marie Antoinette?"

Two or three incredulous laughs were faintly heard. Dixmer looked at Maurice as if he sought to penetrate the very depths of his soul. Geneviève felt the tears suffuse her eyes, and a shuddering she could not conceal from Maurice ran through her frame.

The Citizen Morand poured some wine into his glass, and at this moment carried it to his lips. His paleness would have alarmed Maurice, had not all the young man's attention been at the time centered on Geneviève.

"You are silent, citoyenne," murmured Maurice.

"Have you not said I should understand this because I was a woman? Well, we women, even if opposed to our princes, feel for such devotion."

"And that of the Chevalier de Maison Rouge is the height of devotion, as it is said he has never spoken to the queen."

"Ah! there now, Citizen Lindey," said the man of extreme measures, "it seems to me, permit me to observe, that you are very indulgent to the chevalier——"

"Monsieur," said Maurice, perhaps intentionally making use of a word which had ceased to be in vogue, "I love all brave and courageous natures, which do not refuse to fight when I meet them in the ranks of my enemies. I do not despair of one day encountering the Chevalier de Maison Rouge."

"And——" said Geneviève.

"If I meet him—— Well, I shall fight him."

The supper was finished. Geneviève set the example of retiring by herself rising from table. At this moment the pendulum struck.

"Midnight!" said Morand, coolly.

"Midnight!" said Maurice, "Midnight already?"

"That exclamation affords me much pleasure," said Dixmer; "it proves you are not *ennuyé*, and induces me to hope we may see you again. It is the door of a true patriot which opens to receive you; and, I trust, ere long, you will find it that of a sincere friend."

Maurice bowed, and, turning toward Geneviève:

"Will the citoyenne also permit me to repeat my visit?" demanded he.

"I do more than permit, I request you to do so. Adieu, citizen;" and Geneviève retired.

Maurice took leave of all the guests, particularly saluting Morand, with whom he was much pleased; squeezed Dixmer's hand, and went away bewildered, but, on the whole, more joyful than sad, from the various and unexpected events of the evening.

"Unfortunate encounter, unfortunate encounter!" said the young woman, after Maurice's departure, and then bursting into tears in the presence of her husband, who had conducted her to her room.

"Bah!" said Dixmer, "the Citizen Lindey, a known patriot, secretary to a section, admired, worshiped, and highly popular, is, on the contrary, a great acquisition to a poor tanner who has contraband merchandise on his premises."

"Do you think so, *mon ami?*" asked Geneviève, timidly.

"I think it is a warrant of patriotism, a seal of absolution, placed upon our house; and I thought, when parting this evening, that the Chevalier de Maison Rouge himself would be safe at our house."

And Dixmer kissed his wife with an affection more paternal than conjugal, and left her in the pavilion set apart for her special benefit, passing himself into another part of the building, which he inhabited with the guests we have seen assembled round his table.

CHAPTER X.

SIMON THE SHOEMAKER.

The month of May had commenced. A bright, clear day expanded the lungs tired of inhaling the icy fogs of winter, and the rays of the sun, warm and exhilarating, shone upon the back walls of the Temple. At the wicket of the interior, which separated the tower from the gardens, the soldiers of the post were smoking and laughing. But, notwithstanding the beauty of the day, and the offer made to the prisoners to descend and walk in the garden, the three females refused to do so ; as, since the execution of her husband, the queen had obstinately secluded herself in her chamber, dreading to pass the door of the apartment lately occupied by the king on the second story. When by any chance she took the air, since the fatal occurrence of the 21st of January, she did so on the platform of the tower, where even the battlements were inclosed with shutters.

The National Guards on duty, who knew the three females had received permission to go out, waited in vain all day, wishing much to turn this same authority to some account. Toward five o'clock a man descended and approached the sergeant in command of the post.

"Ah, ah ! is that you, Father Tison ?" said he, who appeared to be a right merry fellow.

"Yes, it is I, citizen ; I bring you, on the part of the municipal, Maurice Lindey, your friend, who is now upstairs, this permission, granted by the Council of the Temple to my daughter, to pay a visit to her mother this evening."

"And you are going out just as your daughter is coming in ? Unnatural father !" said the sergeant.

"I am going much against my inclination, Citizen Sergeant. I also hope to see my poor child, whom I have not seen for two months, and to embrace her this evening. I am going out now. This service, this damned service, compels me to go out. It is necessary I should go to the Commune to make my report. A fiacre is waiting for me at the door, with two gendarmes, and it is exactly the time when my poor Sophie will arrive."

"Unhappy parent!" said the sergeant.

"And, Citizen Sergeant, when my child comes to see her poor mother, who is dying to see her, you will allow her to pass?"

"The order is correct," replied the sergeant, whom the reader has no doubt recognized as our friend Louis; "so I have nothing to say against it. When your daughter comes, she can pass."

"Thanks, brave Thermopyle, thanks," said Tison; and he went out to make his report to the Commune, murmuring, "My poor wife! how happy she will be!"

"Do you know, sergeant," said one of the National Guard, seeing Tison depart, and overhearing the last words, "do you know there is something in this that makes my blood run cold?"

"What is it, Citizen Devaux?" demanded Louis.

"Why," replied the compassionate National Guard, "to see this man, with his surly face and heart of stone, this pitiless guardian of the queen, go out with his eyes full of tears, partly of joy, partly of grief, thinking that his wife will see his daughter, and he shall not. It does not do to reflect upon it too much, sergeant; it really is grievous."

"Doubtless that is why he does not reflect upon it himself, this man who goes out with tears in his eyes, as you term it."

"Upon what should he reflect?"

"That it is three months since this woman he so brutally uses has seen her child. He does not think of her grief, only of his own, that is all. It is true, this woman was queen," continued the sergeant, in an ironical tone, rather difficult of comprehension, "and one is not obliged to feel the same respect for a queen as for the wife of a journeyman."

"Notwithstanding, all this is very sad," said Devaux.

"Sad, but necessary," said Louis. "The best way, then, is, as you say, not to reflect." And he began to sing:

> "Where the branches met
> On a rocky stone,
> There I found Nicette
> Seated all alone."

Louis was in the midst of his pastoral ditty, when suddenly a loud noise was heard from the left side of the post, composed of oaths, menaces, and tears.

"What is that?" demanded Devaux.

"It sounded like the voice of a child," said Louis, listening.

"In fact," said the National Guard, "it is a poor little one they are beating. Truly they ought only to send here those who have no children."

"Will you sing?" said a hoarse and drunken voice.

And the voice sung, in example:

> "Madame Veto promised
> That all our heads should fall——"

"No," said the child, "I will not sing."

"Will you sing?"

And the voice recommenced:

> "Madame Veto promised——"

"No, no!" said the child. "No, no, no!"

"Ah, little beggar!" said the hoarse voice; and the noise of a lash whirring through the air was distinctly heard. The infant screamed with agony.

"Ah, *sacre bleu!*" said Louis, "it is that rascally Simon beating the little Capet."

Several of the National Guards shrugged their shoulders. Two or three tried to smile. Devaux rose and went out.

"I said truly," murmured he, "that parents should never enter here."

All at once a low door opened, and the royal child,

chased by the whip of his guardian, made a flying leap into the court, when something hard struck his leg and fell on the ground behind him.

He stumbled and fell upon his knee.

"Bring me my last, little monster, or else——"

The child rose, and shook his head, in token of refusal.

"Ah! this is it, is it?" said the same voice. "Wait, you shall see."

And the shoemaker, Simon, rushed into his hut as a wild beast to its den.

"Halloo! halloo!" said Louis, frowning. "Where are you going so fast, Master Simon?"

"To chastise this little wolf's cub," said the shoemaker.

"To chastise him, for what?"

"For what?"

"Yes."

"Because the little beggar will neither sing like a good patriot, nor work like a good citizen."

"Well, what have you to do with that?" said Louis. "Did the nation confide Capet to you that you might teach him to sing?"

"And what business have you to interfere, I should like to know, Citizen Sergeant?" said Simon, astonished.

"I interfere, as it becomes every man of feeling to do. It is unworthy of a man to see a child beaten, and to suffer him to be beaten."

"Bah! the son of a tyrant."

"He is a child; and the child has not participated in the crimes of the father. The child is not culpable, and, consequently, ought not to be punished."

"And I tell you he was placed with me to do what I choose with him. I choose him to sing Madame Veto,' and he shall sing it."

"Contemptible wretch!" said Louis. "'Madame Veto' is mother to this child. Would you yourself like your child to be made to sing that you were one of the *canaille?*"

"Me!" cried Simon. "Vile aristocrat of a sergeant!"

THE CHEVALIER DE MAISON ROUGE. 79

"No names," said Louis. "I am not Capet; and they will not make me sing by force."

"I will have you arrested, vile *ci-devant!*"

"You!" said Louis, "you have me arrested? You had better try to arrest a Thermopyle."

"Good, good! He laughs best who laughs last. And now, Capet, pick up my last, and come and finish your shoe, or, *mille tonnerres!*"

"And I," said Louis, turning deathly pale, and advancing a few steps forward, his hands clinched and his teeth set—"I tell you he shall not pick up your last, he shall not make shoes; do you hear, idiot?"

"Ah, yes; you talk very largely, but that will not make me fear you any the more. "Ah, massacre!" roared Simon, turning pale with rage.

At this moment two women entered the court. One held a paper in her hand. She addressed herself to the sentinel.

"Sergeant," cried the sentinel, "it is Tison's daughter, who asks to see her mother."

"Let her pass, since the Council of the Temple permit it," said Louis, who did not wish to leave for a moment, for fear Simon should avail himself of his absence and again beat the child.

The sentinel passed the two women; but hardly had they ascended four steps on the dark staircase, when they encountered Maurice Lindey, who at that moment was descending into the court. It was almost dark, so that he was unable to distinguish their features. Maurice stopped.

"Who are you, citizens?" said he, "and what do you want?"

"I am Sophie Tison," said one of the women; "I obtained permission to visit my mother, and have come to see her."

"Yes," said Maurice; "but this permission was for yourself only, citoyenne."

"I brought my friend, that there might be two of us in the midst of the soldiers, at least."

"Very good ; but your friend cannot go up."

"As you please, citizen," said Sophie Tison, pressing the hand of her friend, who, close against the wall, seemed paralyzed with surprise and terror.

"Citizen Sentinels," said Maurice, raising his voice, and addressing the sentinels who were stationed on every landing, "allow the Citoyenne Tison to pass, but do not permit her friend to pass ; she will remain on the staircase ; see that she is treated with all due respect."

"Yes, citizen," replied the sentinels.

"Go up, then," said Maurice.

The two women then passed on, and Maurice, leaping over the remaining five or six stairs, advanced rapidly into the court.

"What is all this ?" said he, to the National Guard ; "and what is the cause of this noise ? The cries of a child were heard in the prisoner's ante-chamber."

"It is this," said Simon, who, accustomed to the manners of the municipals, believed, on perceiving Maurice, that he came as an ally ; "this traitor, this spy, this *ci-devant*, this aristocrat, prevents me from belaboring Capet ; " and he shook his fists at Louis.

"Yes, *mon Dieu!* I did prevent it," said Louis, drawing his sword ; "and if you again call me *ci-devant*, aristocrat, or traitor, I will run my sword through your body."

"A threat !" cried Simon ; "the guard, the guard ! "

"I am the guard," said Louis ; "so you had better not call, for if I come to you, I will exterminate you."

"Come here, Citizen Municipal, come here," said Simon, now seriously alarmed at Louis' threats.

"The sergeant is quite right," said the municipal to whom he had appealed for assistance ; "you are a disgrace to the nation, coward, to beat a child."

"And why did he beat him ? Do you comprehend ? " said Maurice.

"Because the child would not sing 'Madame Veto,' because the child would not insult his mother."

"Miserable wretch !" said Maurice.

"And you also!" said Simon. "I am surrounded with traitors."

"Rogue!" cried the municipal, seizing Simon by the throat and tearing the last from his hand, "try to prove that Maurice Lindey is a traitor."

And he applied the leather strap pretty heavily to the shoulders of the shoemaker.

"Thanks, monsieur," said the child, who regarded this scene with the air of a stoic; "but he will revenge himself upon me."

"Come, Capet, come, my child," said Louis; "if he beats you again, call for help; I will chastise him, the hangman! And now, Capet, return to your tower."

"Why do you call me Capet? You know very well that Capet is not my name."

"Not your name?" said Louis. "What is your name, then?"

"I am called Louis Charles de Bourbon. Capet is the name of one of my ancestors. I know the history of France; my father taught me."

"And you want to teach a child to make old shoes to whom a king has taught the history of France?" cried Louis. "*Allons donc!*"

"Ah, rest assured," said Maurice, "I will make my report."

"And I mine," said Simon; "and, among other things, I shall say that, instead of one woman being allowed to enter the tower, two were permitted to pass."

At this moment two women went out from the keep. Maurice ran after them.

"Well, citoyenne," said he, addressing the one by his side, "have you seen your mother?"

"Yes, citizen, thank you," said she.

Maurice had wished to see the young girl's friend, or, at least, to hear her voice; but she was enveloped in her mantle, and seemed determined not to utter a single word. He also thought she trembled. This appearance of fear excited his suspicion. He reascended the stairs quickly, and through the glazed partition saw the queen endeavoring to hide something in her pocket which looked like a billet.

"Ah, ah!" said he, "I have been duped."

He called his colleague.

"Citizen Agricola," said he, "enter Marie Antoinette's room, and do not lose sight of her."

"Heyday!" said the municipal, "is it because——"

"Enter, I tell you, and do not lose sight of her for an instant, a moment, a second."

The municipal entered the queen's apartment.

"Call the woman Tison," said he to one of the National Guard.

Five minutes afterward Tison's wife arrived in high spirits.

"I have seen my daughter," said she.

"Where was that?" demanded Maurice.

"Here, of course, in this ante-chamber."

"Well, and did your daughter ask to see the Austrian?"

"No."

"Did she not enter her room?"

"No."

"And during the time you were conversing with your daughter, did no one come out of the prisoners' chamber?"

"How should I know? I was fully occupied with my daughter, whom I had not seen for three months."

"Recollect yourself."

"Ah, yes; I think I remember."

"What?"

"The young girl came out."

"Marie Thérèse?"

"Yes."

"Did she speak to your daughter?"

"No."

"Your daughter restored nothing to her?"

"No."

"Did she pick up nothing from the ground?"

"My daughter?"

"No, the daughter of Marie Antoinette?"
"She picked up her pocket-handkerchief."
"Ah, *malheureuse!*" cried Maurice.

And he rushed toward the string of a bell, which he pulled violently. It was an alarm-bell.

CHAPTER XI.

THE BILLET.

THE other two municipal guards came up hastily. A detachment of the post accompanied them. The doors were shut, and two sentinels intercepted the egress from each chamber.

"What do you want, monsieur?" said the queen to Maurice, when he entered. "I was retiring to bed, when, five minutes since, the citizen municipal suddenly forced his entrance into my chamber, without informing me what may be desired."

"Madame," said Maurice, bowing, "it is not my colleague who desires anything from you, it is myself."

"You, monsieur?" demanded Marie Antoinette, looking at Maurice, whose courteous behavior had inspired her with almost gratitude, "and what do you desire?"

"I request you will be kind enough to show me the letter you were concealing in your pocket when I entered just now."

Mme. Royale and Mme. Elizabeth trembled. The queen turned very pale.

"You are mistaken, monsieur; I concealed nothing."

"You lie, Austrian!" cried Agricola.

Maurice quickly placed his hand on the arm of his colleague.

"One moment, my dear colleague," said he; "leave me to speak to the citoyenne; I am a little bit of a lawyer."

"Go on, then; but you will not contrive it, *morbleu!*"

"You have concealed a letter, citoyenne," said Maurice,

austerely. "Now, it is necessary we should see this letter."

"But what letter?"

"The letter that Tison's daughter brought you, and which the citoyenne, your daughter" (Maurice alluded to the young princess), "picked up with her pocket-handkerchief."

The three females looked at one another with terror.

"But, monsieur, this is worse than tyranny," said the queen; "these women! these women!"

"Do not mistake," said Maurice, with firmness; "we are neither judges nor executioners, we are overseers; that is to say, your fellow-citizens, commissioned to guard you. We have our order; to violate it is treason. Citoyenne, I pray you to give me the letter you have concealed."

"Messieurs," said the queen, with much hauteur, "since you are overseers, search, and deprive us of our rest to-night, as usual."

"God forbid we should lay our hands upon these women. I am now going to inform the Commune and await its orders; but you cannot retire to bed; you must sleep upon these fauteuils, if you please, and we must guard you. If necessary, they will search you."

"What is the matter?" said Tison's wife, appearing at the door, quite bewildered.

"It is this, citoyenne," said Maurice, "that by lending yourself to treasonable practises, you will debar yourself from seeing your daughter any more."

"From seeing my daughter? What do you tell me, then, citizen?" demanded Tison's wife, who could not yet comprehend why she was not to see her daughter.

"I tell you that your daughter did not come here to see you, but to bring a letter to the Citoyenne Capet; and, therefore, she will return here no more."

"But if she does not come here, I shall not be able to see her, as we are forbidden to go out."

"This time you have no one to blame but yourself—it was your fault," said Maurice.

"Oh!" screamed the poor woman, "why do you say it is my fault? Nothing has happened, I tell you. If I thought anything would happen, woe to you, Marie Antoinette; you should pay dearly for it."

And the exasperated woman shook her fist at the queen.

"Threaten no one," said Maurice; "but rather gain by kindness what we demand; for you are a woman, and the Citoyenne Marie Antoinette, who is herself a mother, will take pity on you. To-morrow your daughter will be arrested—to-morrow imprisoned; then, if they discover anything, and you know that when they choose they always can do so, she is lost, and also her companion."

The woman Tison, who had listened to Maurice with terrified credulity, turned wildly toward the queen.

"You hear, Antoinette? My daughter! It is you who will ruin my child!"

The queen, in her turn, appeared bewildered, not by the fury which sparkled in the eyes of her female jailer, but by the despair legible there:

"Come, Madame Tison," said she, "I have something to say to you."

"Halloo! No cajolery; there are not too many of us," said Maurice's colleague. "Before the municipality—always before the municipality."

"Never mind, Citizen Agricola," said Maurice; "provided the permission comes from us, it does not matter in what fashion."

"You are right, Citizen Maurice; but——"

"Let us pass behind the glazed partition, Citizen Agricola; and if you think with me, we will turn our backs, and I am certain the individual for whom we evince this consideration will not make us repent it."

The queen heard these words, intended for her to hear, and cast upon the young man a look of grateful acknowledgment. Maurice carelessly turned his head, and walked to the other side of the glazed partition. Agricola followed him.

"You see this queen," said he to Agricola; "as a

queen she is very culpable, as a woman she is high-minded and dignified. They destroyed the crown—woe to the model!"

"*Sacre bleu!* you speak well, Citizen Maurice; I love to listen to you and your friend Tison. Is this also poetry you are reciting?"

Maurice smiled.

During this conversation, the scene which Maurice had anticipated was passing on the other side.

The woman Tison approached the queen.

"Madame," said the queen, "your despair grieves me. I do not wish to deprive you of your daughter—that would be too cruel; but do you consider that by doing what these men require your child will be equally lost?"

"Do as they tell you," cried the woman, "do as they say."

"But first, at least, hear what the question is."

"What the question is?" demanded the woman, with an almost savage curiosity.

"Your daughter brought a friend with her."

"Yes, an artificial, like herself. She did not like to come alone, because of the soldiers. This friend committed a letter to your daughter—your daughter let it fall. Marie, who was passing, picked it up. It is, doubtless, a paper of no consequence, but still one upon which evil-minded people might put a bad construction. Has not the municipal just told you, if they wish to do so, they can do so?"

"What next? What next?"

"Well, this is all; you wish me to send back this paper—do you wish me to sacrifice a friend, without, perhaps, benefiting your daughter?"

"Do as they say," cried the woman, "do as they say."

"But if this paper implicates your daughter," said the queen; "do you understand?"

"My daughter is, like myself, a good patriot," cried the housekeeper. "*Dieu merci!* The Tisons are well known. Do what they tell you."

"*Mon Dieu!*" said the queen, "what can I say to convince you?"

"My child! I want them to return me my child!" cried Tison's wife, stamping her feet. "Give me the paper, Antoinette, give me the paper!"

"There it is, madame."

And the queen tendered a paper to the wretched creature, which she seized, and held joyfully above her head, crying:

"Come here, come here, Citizen Municipals. I have the paper; take it, and give me back my child!"

"You would sacrifice our friends, my sister," said Mme. Elizabeth.

"No, my sister," replied the queen, mournfully, "I only sacrifice ourselves. This paper implicates no one."

At the cries of the woman Tison, Maurice and his colleague came toward her, when she immediately held out the paper to them. They opened and read:

"A l'Orient! again an old friend."

Maurice had no sooner cast his eyes on this paper, than he started.

The writing was not quite unknown to him.

"*Mon Dieu!*" cried he, "can it be that of Geneviève? But no; it is impossible, and I am mad. It resembles hers, certainly; but what communication can she have with the queen?"

He turned round, and observed that Marie Antoinette was watching him attentively. As for the woman Tison, as she awaited her fate, she devoured Maurice with her eyes.

"You have done a good action," said he to Tison's wife; "and you, citoyenne, a great one," addressing the queen.

"Then, monsieur," replied Marie Antoinette, "follow my example. Burn this paper, and you will perform a charitable one."

"You are joking, Austrian," said Agricola. "Burn a paper that may, perhaps, enable us to discover a whole covey of aristocrats? *Ma foi!* no; that would be too much like blockheads."

"Do what? Burn it! That might compromise my daughter," said the woman Tison.

"I believe you; your daughter and some others," said Agricola, taking the paper from the hands of Maurice, which, had he been alone, would most assuredly have been destroyed.

Ten minutes afterward, the letter was deposited on the bureau of the members of the Commune, and commented upon in various ways.

"'A l'Orient—an old friend.' What the devil can this mean?" said a voice.

"*Pardieu!*" replied a geographer; "to Lorient, that is clear enough. Lorient is a little town of Brittany, situated between Vannes and Quimper."

"*Morbleu!* they ought to burn the town, if it be true that it shelters aristocrats, who keep watch still upon the Austrian."

"It is the more dangerous," said another, "that Lorient being a seaport, they might establish communication with England."

"I propose," said a third, "that a mandate be forwarded to Lorient, that an inquiry may be made."

This proposition made the minority smile, but excited the majority; they decreed a mandate should be sent to Lorient to watch the aristocrats.

Maurice had been informed of the consultation.

"I think it may, perhaps, mean the East," said he; "but I am quite sure it is not in Brittany."

The next day the queen, who, as we have previously said, would no more enter the garden to avoid passing the door of the apartment where her husband had been imprisoned, requested permission to ascend the tower to take the air, with her daughter and Mme. Elizabeth. Her wish was instantly acceded to; but Maurice followed her, and, mounting the stairs, ensconced himself behind a little turret. There, concealed, he awaited the result of the letter of the preceding evening. The queen at first walked indifferently with Mme. Elizabeth and her daughter, then stopped, while the two princesses continued their promenade ; then turned toward the "East," and observed very attentively a house, at the windows of which were visible several persons. One of the number held a white pocket-handkerchief.

Maurice, on his part, drew a telescope from his pocket, and while he adjusted it, the queen made a quick movement, as if to request those at the window to retire ; but Maurice had already remarked the head of a man, with fair hair and pale complexion, whose salutation was so respectful as almost to border on humility. Behind this young man, for he appeared to be five or six and twenty years of age, a woman remained partially concealed from view. Maurice directed his glass toward her, and thought he recognized Geneviève. Immediately the female, who also held a telescope in her hand, drew back, dragging the young man away with her. Was this really Geneviève? Had she also recognized Maurice ? Had this couple only retired at the signal given him by the queen ? Maurice waited a moment to see if this young man and woman would reappear ; but seeing the window remain unoccupied, he recommended the strictest vigilance to his colleague, Agricola, quickly descended the staircase, and went to lie in ambush at the angle of La Rue Porte Foin, to see if they came out of the house. It was in vain ; no one appeared. He could not resist the suspicion which had entered his mind at the moment the companion of Tison's daughter had persisted in maintaining so obstinate a silence. Maurice directed his course toward the Old Rue St. Jacques, where he arrived, bewildered by the strangest suspicions, doubts, and fears. When he entered, Geneviève, attired in a white morning-dress, was seated under an arbor of jasmine, where they were accusstomed to take their breakfast. She, as usual, accorded Maurice a friendly greeting, and invited him to take a cup of chocolate with her. Dixmer, on his part, who had in the meantime arrived, expressed the greatest joy at meeting Maurice at this unexpected hour of the day ; but before he permitted Maurice to take the cup of chocolate he had accepted (always enthusiastically attached to his trade), he insisted that his friend, the secretary to the "Section Lepelletier," should make a tour through the manufactory with him. Maurice consented.

"My dear Maurice," said he, "I have important news for you."

"Political?" asked Maurice, always occupied with one idea.

"Ah! dear citizen," said Dixmer, smiling, and taking the young man's arm, "do you think we trouble ourselves about politics? No, no; relating to business, *Dieu merci!* My honored friend, Morand, who, as you know, is a celebrated chemist, has discovered the secret of staining leather red in an unequaled manner; that is to say, unalterable—a process never discovered until now. It is this color I want to show you. Besides, you will see Morand at work; he is quite an 'artiste.'"

Maurice did not exactly comprehend how making a red dye constituted an "artiste;" but, nevertheless, accepted his offer, and followed Dixmer across the tan-yards, and in a separate sort of office saw the Citizen Morand at work. He wore blue spectacles, was in his working-dress, and seemed fully occupied in changing a skin from dirty white to purple. His hands and arms, visible under his sleeves, which were turned up, were red to the elbow.

He merely moved his head to Maurice, so entirely was he preoccupied.

"Well, Citizen Morand," said Dixmer, "what say we?"

"We shall gain one hundred thousand livres by this process alone; but I have not slept for eight days, and these acids have affected my sight."

Maurice left Dixmer with Morand, and joined Geneviève, murmuring softly:

"It must be confessed the trade of municipal stupefies the hero. About eight days in the Temple, one might fancy one's self an aristocrat, and denounce one's self. Good Dixmer! Brave Morand! Sweet Geneviève! And for an instant they suspected me."

Geneviève awaited Maurice with a sweet smile calculated to make him forget all his latent cause for suspicion. She was, as usual, sweet, amiable, and charming. The hours passed in Geneviève's society were those only in which Maurice could be said really to exist.

At all other times he was infected with that fever which might be termed the fever of '93, by which Paris was separated into two camps, and existence rendered a perpetual combat. Toward noon he quitted Geneviève, and returned to the tower of the Temple.

At the extremity of La Rue St. Avoie, he encountered Louis, now relieved from guard. He left the ranks and came to meet Maurice, who still wore upon his countenance the impress of the happiness he had enjoyed in the society of the lovely Geneviève.

"Ah!" said Louis, cordially shaking his friend by the hand:

> "In vain you seek your anguish
> Within your heart to hide,
> I know for whom you languish,
> For whom so long you've sighed;
> Within your heart, within your eyes,
> Love reigns, and triumphs in his prize."

Maurice put his hand in his pocket to search for the key. This was the method he adopted to put a stop to his friend's poetical vein. But he saw the movement and ran away, laughing.

"Apropos," said Louis, retracing his steps, "you have three days more at the Temple; I recommend the little Capet to your care."

CHAPTER XII.

LOVE.

In fact, Maurice for some time had experienced a strange mixture of happiness and misery. It is always thus at the commencement of *des grandes passions*. His daily occupation at the Section Lepelletier, his evening visits to the Old Rue St. Jacques, and some occasional visits to the club of the Thermopyles, filled up his days.

He did not dissimulate. He well knew that to see Geneviève daily was to imbibe large draughts of love, unaccompanied by hope. Geneviève was a woman of retired manners and pleasing appearance, who would frankly tender her hand to a friend, and would innocently approach his face with her lips, with the confidence of a sister and the ignorance of a vestal, before whom the words of love appear as blasphemy.

Thus, in the purest dreams that the first style of Raphael has traced upon the canvas, is a Madonna with smiling lips, chaste eyes, and heavenly expression. It is necessary to borrow from the divine pupil of Perugino to portray the likeness of Geneviève.

In the midst of flowers, she imbibed their freshness and perfume; isolated by the occupation of her husband, and by her husband himself, she appeared to Maurice each time he saw her like a living enigma, of which he could not divine the meaning, and dare not ask it. One evening, when, as usual, he remained alone with her, they were both seated at the same window by which he had entered, a few nights since, with so little ceremony; the perfume of the lilacs in full bloom floated upon the soft breeze that had succeeded the radiant sunset.

After a long silence, Maurice, having, during this silence, followed the intelligent and holy eye of Geneviève, as she watched the appearance of the stars in the azure vault of heaven, ventured to inquire concerning the great disparity between herself and husband. She so young, and he already past the middle age; she so *distingué*, while everything around announced him a man of inferior birth and education; she so refined in her tastes, while her husband had not an idea beyond his manufactory.

"Here, at the abode of a master tanner, are harp, piano, and drawings, which you acknowledge to be your own. How is it that this aristocracy which I detest in others I adore in you?"

Geneviève fixed upon Maurice a look full of candor.

"Thanks," said she, "for this inquiry; it proves to me

you have not sought information concerning me from any one else."

"Never! madame," said Maurice, "I have a devoted friend who would die for me; I have a hundred comrades ready to follow wherever I may lead them; but among all these hearts, when a woman is concerned, and, above all, such a woman as Geneviève, I know but of one I would trust, and that one is myself."

"Thanks, Maurice," said the young woman; "I will myself tell you all you desire to know."

"Your maiden name first," said Maurice. "I only know your married one at present."

Geneviève detected the selfishness of love in this question, and smiled.

"Geneviève du Treilly," said she.

Maurice repeated, "Geneviève du Treilly."

"My family," continued Geneviève, "was ruined after the American war, in which both my father and elder brother had taken part."

"Both gentlemen?" said Maurice.

"No, no," said Geneviève, blushing.

"And yet you said your maiden name was Geneviève du Treilly."

"My family, Monsieur Maurice, was rich, but not noble."

"You challenge me," said the young man, smiling.

"Oh, no, no," replied Geneviève. "In America my father was connected with the father of Monsieur Morand. Monsieur Dixmer was managing man to Monsieur Morand. We were ruined, and Monsieur Morand, knowing that Monsieur Dixmer was a man of independent fortune, presented him to my father, who, in his turn, presented him to me."

"I saw he had beforehand formed a resolution of marriage. I understood it was the wish of my family. I did not love, neither had I ever loved any one, and I accepted him.

"I have now been Dixmer's wife for three years, and I am bound to say he has proved to me so good and excellent a husband, that notwithstanding the difference of taste and the disparity of age, I have never even for a moment experienced the slightest feeling of regret."

"But," said Maurice, "when you married Monsieur Dixmer he was not at the head of this manufactory?"

"No; we lived at Blois. After the 10th of August, Monsieur Dixmer purchased this house and the adjoining work-shops, and that I might not be annoyed by the workmen, and to spare me the sight of many things repulsive to a person of my habits, which are, as you observed, Maurice, a little aristocratic, he gave me this pavilion, where I live alone, retired, gratifying my various fancies and desires, and happy when a friend like yourself, Maurice, comes either to distract or partake in my reveries."

And Geneviève tendered her hand to Maurice, which he ardently kissed. Geneviève blushed slightly.

"Now, my friend," said the young woman, drawing away her hand, "you know how I became the wife of Monsieur Dixmer."

"Yes," said Maurice, regarding Geneviève with great attention; "but you have not told me how Monsieur Morand came to be associated with your husband."

"Oh, that is very simple," said Geneviève. "Monsieur Dixmer had, as I have told you, some fortune, but still not sufficient to engage alone in a large concern like this. The son of Monsieur Morand, his protector, as I have before said, this friend of my father, you will remember, provided half the funds, and as he possesses a good knowledge of chemistry, he devotes himself to various improvements with the energy you have remarked, and, thanks to which, the business of Monsieur Dixmer has extended considerably."

"Monsieur Morand is also a great friend of yours, is he not, madame?" said Maurice.

"Monsieur Morand is a noble-hearted being, one of the worthiest men in existence," gravely replied Geneviève.

"If he has given you no other proofs," said Maurice, a little piqued at the importance accorded by Geneviève to the young man, the partner of her husband, than, dividing the expenses of this establishment with Monsieur Dixmer, and inventing a new color for the morocco, allow me to say you rather overrate his merits."

"He has given me many other proofs, monsieur," said Geneviève.

"He is young, is he not?" said Maurice. "His wearing green spectacles renders it difficult to tell his age."

"He is thirty-five."

"You have known him, then, a long time?"

"From infancy."

Maurice bit his lips; he had always suspected Morand loved Geneviève.

"Oh!" said Maurice, "that explains his familiarity with you."

"It seems to me, monsieur," said Geneviève, smiling, "that this familiarity, which at least is only that of a friend, does not need any explanation."

"Oh, pardon me, madame; you know all affectionate natures are jealous, and my friendship was jealous of that you appear to feel for Monsieur Morand."

He was silent. Geneviève also remained silent. There were no more questions to-day respecting Morand, and Maurice quitted Geneviève more than ever in love, for he was jealous.

So blinded was the young man by his passion, that he had not remarked, during the recital of Geneviève, many gaps, much hesitation, and many concealments, which, although at the moment had escaped his notice, now returned to his memory, and strangely tortured him; and then he might not be able to secure to himself the liberty allowed him by Dixmer, of conversing with Geneviève as often and as long as he pleased, and in solitude, as they now found themselves every evening; and more, not only had he become a constant and expected guest at the house—not only remained in perfect security with Geneviève, who seemed guarded by her angelic purity from any advances on the part of the young man, but he now escorted her in all the excursions made from time to time in that quarter. In the midst of this established **intimacy** one thing surprised him. The more he sought (perhaps the better to watch his sentiments for Geneviève) the friendship of Morand, by whose genius, notwithstanding his prejudice, he felt himself captivated, and whose pleasing manners won him more and more every day, the greater the inclination evinced by this whimsical man to avoid him.

Of this he complained bitterly to Geneviève; for he did not doubt but that Morand had discerned in him a rival, and therefore his conduct was actuated by jealousy.

"The Citizen Morand hates me," said he, one day, to Geneviève.

"You?" said Geneviève, with a look of astonishment. "You—Monsieur Morand hate you?"

"Yes; I am sure of it."

"And why should he hate you?"

"Do you wish me to tell you?" cried Maurice.

"Without doubt," replied Geneviève.

"Well, then, because I——"

Maurice stopped; he was going to say, "Because I love you."

"I cannot tell you why," replied Maurice, coloring.

The fierce Republican near Geneviève was timid and confused as a young girl.

Geneviève smiled.

"Say," replied she, "there is no sympathy between you, and I may, perhaps, believe you. You possess an ardent mind, an ambitious spirit, are a man of birth and education; while Morand is a merchant grafted on a chemist. He is timid and retiring. It is this timidity that deters him from taking the first step toward your acquaintance."

"And who asks him to make the first advance toward me? I have made fifty to him, and he has never responded."

"What is it, then?" said Geneviève.

Maurice chose to remain silent.

The day after this conversation with Geneviève, he

The exasperated woman shook her fist at the Queen.

The Chevalier de Maison-Rouge
—p. 85

arrived there at two o'clock in the afternoon, and found her ready dressed to go out.

"Welcome," said she; "you will act as my chevalier?"

"Where are we going?" demanded Maurice.

"I am going to Auteuil. It will be a delightful excursion. I mean to walk part of the way. Our carriage will convey us to the barrier, where it will wait for us. We will then walk to Auteuil, and when I have finished my business there, we will return to take——"

"Oh!" said Maurice, "what a delightful day you offer me!"

The two young people went out. Beyond Passy the carriage put them down. They sauntered along slowly, and continued their journey on foot.

On arriving at Auteuil, Geneviève stopped.

"Wait for me," said she, "at the entrance to the park. When I have finished, I will rejoin you."

"Where are you going, then?" demanded Maurice.

"To a friend's house."

"Where I cannot accompany you?"

Geneviève smilingly shook her head.

"Impossible!" said she.

Maurice bit his lips.

"Very well," said he; "I will wait."

"Ah! what?" said Geneviève.

"Nothing," replied Maurice. "Shall you be long?"

"If I had thought it would inconvenience you, Maurice, if I had known you were engaged," said Geneviève, "I would not have requested you to do me the slight favor to accompany me to-day. I might have asked——"

"Monsieur Morand," interrupted Maurice, sharply.

"No; you are aware Monsieur Morand is at the manufactory, at Rambouillet, and does not return till this evening."

"Then, to what do I owe the preference?"

"Maurice," said Geneviève, softly, "I cannot keep the person I came to see waiting; but if I am the least constraint upon your return to Paris, only send back the carriage."

"No, no, madame," replied Maurice, quickly; "I am at your service."

He bowed to Geneviève, who, sighing softly, proceeded on her way, and entered Auteuil.

Maurice went to the appointed place, and continued walking backward and forward with long, impatient strides, cutting off with his cane, like Tarquin, all the heads of the weeds, and flowers of the thistles, which he found upon the road; and this road being narrow and retired, left him at full liberty to trace and retrace his footsteps as often as he pleased. And what occupied his thoughts? The desire to know whether Geneviève loved him or not. Her manner to him was that of a friend or sister; but he felt this was not sufficient. He loved her with an entire love. She had become his sole thought by day, his renewed dream by night. At one time he only asked to see her again; he now required her to love him. Geneviève was absent for an hour, which to him had appeared an age; when he saw her returning with a smile upon her lips, Maurice, on the contrary, went to meet her with a frowning brow.

Geneviève, smiling, took his arm.

"Here I am," said she; "pardon me, *mon ami*, for having made you wait."

Maurice only replied by a bow; and they then entered a shady lane, which, by a winding path, conducted them into the high-road.

It was one of those delicious evenings in spring, when every plant sends its fragrance on high, when every bird, either seated on the branches, or skipping from spray to spray, warbles its song of praise to God; one of those evenings that seem destined to live forever in our memory. Maurice was silent, Geneviève pensive. She plucked with one hand flowers for a bouquet, the other rested on the arm of Maurice.

"What is the matter with you?" said he, all at once, to Geneviève; "and what makes you so sad to-day?"

Geneviève might have answered—my happiness. She regarded him tenderly.

"But you," said she, "are you not more than usually sad to-day?"

"I," said Maurice, "have reason to be sad; I am unhappy; but you——"

"You unhappy?"

"Doubtless; do you not perceive sometimes from my tremulous tones how much I suffer? Does it not often happen, when I am talking with you, or your husband, I am compelled suddenly to seek the air, because I feel as if my heart would burst?"

"But," demanded Geneviève, embarrassed, "to what do you attribute this suffering?"

"If I were an affected lady," said Maurice, attempting a laugh, "I should say it was a nervous attack."

"And at this moment do you suffer?"

"Much," said Maurice.

"Let us return, then."

"What, already, madame?"

"Without doubt."

"True," said the young man; "I forgot Monsieur Morand would return from Rambouillet this evening; and it is fast approaching."

Geneviève looked at him reproachfully.

"Oh, again!" said she.

"Why, then, did you the other day, favor me with so high an eulogium on Monsieur Morand? It is your own fault."

"How long is it since, to people we esteem," demanded Geneviève, "we may not express our real opinion of an estimable man?"

"It must be a very lively esteem to cause you to accelerate your pace, as you at this moment are doing, for fear of being too late by a few minutes."

"You are to-day absolutely unjust, Maurice. Have I not passed part of the day with you?"

"You are right; and I am indeed too exacting," replied Maurice, subduing his impetuosity. "Let us return to meet Monsieur Morand."

Geneviève felt her anger pass from her mind to her heart.

"Yes," said she. "Let u return to Monsieur Morand. He, at least, is a friend who never causes me pain."

"They are, indeed, valuable friends," said Maurice, "and I, for my part, should like a few such."

They were now upon the high-road; the horizon, crimsoned as the departing rays of the setting sun, glistened upon the gilt moldings of the Dome des Invalides. A star, which on the previous evening had attracted the attention of Geneviève, sparkled in the azure of heaven. Geneviève quitted Maurice's arm with melancholy submission.

"Why have you made me suffer?" said she.

"Ah!" said Maurice, "I am not so clever as some people, and do not know how to make love."

"Maurice!" said Geneviève.

"Oh, madame, if he is certainly so worthy and so just, he ought not to suffer."

Geneviève again placed her white hand within the powerful arm of Maurice.

"I pray you," said she, in an altered tone, "to speak no more—to speak no more!"

"And why is that?"

"Because your voice makes me ill."

"You are displeased with everything, even my voice?"

"Be silent, I conjure you."

"I will obey you, madame."

And the impetuous young man passed his hand over his face, damp with perspiration.

Geneviève saw that he really suffered.

"You are my friend, Maurice," said Geneviève, looking at him kindly; "do not deprive me of your valuable friendship."

"Oh! you would not long regret it," said Maurice.

"You are mistaken," said Geneviève; "I should regret it very long, and forever."

"Geneviève, Geneviève!" cried Maurice, "have pity on me."

Geneviève shuddered. It was the first time Maurice had uttered her name in these passionate accents.

"And now," continued Maurice, "since you have di

vined me, let me tell you all, Geneviève, for might you kill me with a look, I have been silent too long; I will speak, Geneviève."

"Monsieur," said the young woman, "I have supplicated you, in the name of our friendship, to remain silent; I still pray you to do so, if not for my sake, for your own. Not another word; in the name of Heaven, not another word."

"Friendship, friendship! if it be a friendship like this you profess for me, that you feel for Monsieur Morand, I wish for no more of your friendship—I, Geneviève, require more than others."

"Enough," said Mme. Dixmer, with the gesture of a queen, "enough, Monsieur Lindey; here is our carriage, please to conduct me to my husband's house."

Maurice trembled with fever and emotion when Geneviève, to rejoin the carriage, which indeed was only a few paces distant, placed her hand on his arm.

They both entered the carriage; Geneviève took the front seat, and Maurice the one opposite. They traversed Paris without either one or the other having uttered a word. Only, all the way, Geneviève had held her handkerchief before her eyes. When they entered the building, Dixmer was occupied in his counting house, Morand had just returned from Rambouillet, and was changing his dress. Geneviève held out her hand to Maurice, as she entered her chamber.

"Adieu, Maurice; you have wished it."

Maurice said nothing, but walked directly to the mantelpiece, where hung a portrait of Geneviève. He ardently kissed it, pressed it to his heart, replaced it, and went out. Maurice reached home without knowing how he arrived there; he had passed through Paris without seeing anything, without hearing anything; all that surrounded him appeared like a dream; he was unable to account for his actions, his words, or the sentiments which induced them. There are moments when the most serene spirits succumb under the violence of their own emotions.

It was, as we have said, rather a race than a return on the part of Maurice. He undressed himself without the assistance of his *valet de chambre*, neither replied to his cook, who displayed his supper duly prepared for him, but taking the day's letters from the table, he read them all, one after the other, without comprehending a single word. The burning jealousy, that intoxication of reason, was not yet dissipated. At ten o'clock, Maurice mechanically sought his bed, as, indeed, he had done everything else since his parting with Geneviève.

If Maurice, in his cooler moments, had been told of this extraordinary behavior in another, he would not have been able to comprehend it, but would have considered him mad to have pursued this desperate conduct, totally unauthorized either by too much reserve or too much *abandon* on the part of Geneviève. He now only felt this was a terrible blow to all his hopes, of which he had never, even to himself, rendered an account, and upon which, vague as they were, reposed all his visions of happiness, dreams which, like an unseizable vapor, floated shapelessly towards the horizon, and there disappeared. Thus it happened, as in similar cases, that Maurice, stunned by this blow, dropped asleep directly he found himself in bed, where he remained free from all sentiment till the morrow. He was awakened by the noise of the official opening the door, who came as usual to unclose the windows, which opened upon a large garden, and to bring some flowers.

At that time, in the year '93, much attention was paid to the culture of forced flowers, and Maurice dearly loved all flowers; but now, without even bestowing a glance upon them, he half raised his heavy head, and supporting it on his hand, endeavored to recall the events of the preceding evening. Maurice asked himself, without being able to account for it, the cause of this mad folly; the sole cause was jealousy of Morand; but the moment was certainly badly chosen to amuse himself by being jealous of a man, when this man was at Rambouillet, and while enjoying a *tête-à-tête* with the woman one loves, surrounded by the most enchanting scenery, on one of the lovely days of spring. It was not suspicion of the inmates at the house at Auteuil, where Geneviève had remained an hour; no, the incessant torment of his life was the idea that Morand loved Geneviève, and yet, singular fantasy of the brain, strange combination of caprice, not a gesture, a look, not even a word from Dixmer's partner had afforded the slightest grounds for this belief. The voice of the *valet de chambre* aroused him from this reverie.

"Citizen," said he, showing him the open letters on the table, "have you selected those you wish to keep, or shall they all be burned?"

"Burn what?" said Maurice.

"The letters the citizen read last night before he retired to bed."

Maurice could not remember having read one.

"Burn all," said he.

"Here are two days' letters, citizen," said the official.

He presented a packet of letters to Maurice, and threw the others under the grate. Maurice took the letters, felt the impression of a seal, and fancied that he recognized the perfume of a friend, and looking over his correspondence, he found an envelope and handwriting that made him tremble. This man, who bravely faced danger, trembled before the odor of a letter. The official approached Maurice, to inquire what he would take, but he signified a wish to be alone. Maurice turned and re-turned this letter; he felt a presentiment it contained misery for him, and started and trembled before unknown misfortune. Having collected all his courage, he at length opened it, and read as follows:

"CITIZEN MAURICE,—It has become necessary that we should burst these bonds—bonds which, on your side, affect to exceed the bounds of friendship. You are a man of honor, citizen, and now a night has passed since the occurrences of yesterday evening, you ought to comprehend that your presence at our house is no longer desirable. I leave it to you to excuse yourself in any way you think best to my husband. On the arrival this day of your letter to Monsieur Dixmer, I am convinced I shall regret the loss of an unfortunate friend, whom all social propriety will deter me from meeting for the future. Adieu forever. GENEVIÈVE.

"P.S.—The bearer awaits your reply."

Maurice called ; the *valet de chambre* reappeared.

"Who brought this letter?"

"A citizen commissionaire."

"Is he waiting?"

"Yes."

Maurice did not for a moment hesitate, but, partly dressing, seated himself before his writing-desk, and taking the first sheet of paper that came to hand (he found it had on it the impression of a heart with the name of the section), he wrote:

"CITIZEN DIXMER,—I respected you, and I still do so, but I cannot visit you any longer."

Maurice considered what reason he could assign for not visiting Dixmer, and one idea alone presented itself to his mind, that which at this epoch occurred to every one. He thus continued :

"Certain rumors are afloat relative to your lukewarmness in public affairs. I have no wish to accuse you, and no mission to defend you. Receive my respects, and feel assureed your secrets will remain forever buried in my heart."

Maurice did not even read this letter, written, as we have said, under the impression of the first idea that presented itelf. He did not doubt the effect it would produce. Dixmer, an excellent patriot, as Maurice imagined from his conversation, at least, would be much grieved at receiving it, his wife and M. Morand would no doubt influence him not to reply, and forgetfulness would gradually spread itself like a dark veil over the past, laughing at the melancholy transformation. Maurice signed and sealed his letter, gave it the official, and the commissionaire departed. Then a slight sigh escaped the Republican; he took his hat and gloves and proceeded to the section. He hoped, poor Brutus, to recover his stoicism by occupying himself with public affairs. These were indeed terrible; the 31st of May was preparing. The *terreur*, which like a torrent, precipitated itself from the height of La Montagne, endeavored to carry away this dike, opposed to it by the Girondins, those audacious Modérés who had dared to demand vengeance for the massacres of September, and to wrestle for an instant to save the life of the king.

While Maurice pursued his way with a rapidity that drove the fever from his heart to his head, the messenger had reentered the Old Rue St. Jacques, filling the dwelling there with terror and astonishment. The letter, after passing through Geneviève's hands, was given by her to Dixmer. Dixmer opened and read it, without at first understanding it; he then communicated the contents to the Citizen Morand, who supported his head upon his hand. His face was pale as death. In the situation in which Dixmer, Morand, and their companions found themselves (a situation totally unknown to Maurice, but which our readers have penetrated) this letter was like a thunder-bolt.

"Is this an upright, honest man?" asked Dixmer, much grieved.

"Yes," replied Morand, without the least hesitation.

"Never mind," said the advocate for extreme measures, "you see we were very wrong not to kill him."

"My friend," said Louis, "we struggle against violence, we brand it with the name of crime. We have acted rightly, whatever may be the result, in not assassinating this man. I again repeat, I believe Maurice to possess a noble, generous spirit."

"Yes; but if so noble and generous a spirit belongs to this warm Republican, perhaps he may regard it in the light of crime, if he has made any discovery, not to immolate his own honor, as they say, 'on the altar of the country.'"

"But," said Morand, "do you think he knows anything?"

"Do you not hear? he speaks of secrets buried in his own heart."

"These secrets are evidently those confided to him by me, relative to our contraband transactions. He knows no others."

"But this interview at Auteuil? does he suspect anything? you know he accompanied your wife?"

"It was I who told Geneviève to take Maurice with her as a protection."

"Listen," said Morand; "we shall soon see if these surmises be true. The turn of our battalion to guard the temple arrives on the 2d of June, that is to say, in eight days. You are captain, Dixmer, and I lieutenant; if our battalion, or even our company, receives a counter-order, like that received the other day by the battalion of La Butte-des-Moulins, which Santerre has replaced by that of Gravilliers, all is discovered, and we have only to flee from Paris, or die fighting. But if all follows in the usual course of things——"

"We are lost, all the same," replied Dixmer.

"How so?"

"*Pardieu!* does not all revolve upon the cooperation of this young municipal? Was it not he who, without knowing it, must open the road for us to the queen?"

"That is true," said Morand, confounded.

"You see, then," said Dixmer, knitting his brows, "that, at any price, we must renew our intimacy with this young man."

"But if he refuse, if he fears to compromise himself?"

"Listen," said Dixmer; "I will question Geneviève; she saw him last; perhaps she may know something more."

"Dixmer," said Morand, "it is with pain I see you mixing Geneviève with all our plots, not that I fear any indiscretion on her part. Oh, great God! the drama we are acting is a dreadful one, and I blush and tremble at the same time to place the head of a woman at stake, as well as our own."

"The head of a woman," said Dixmer, "ponders as gravely as that of a man, when stratagem is required, and often achieves more by candor and beauty than by force, strength, power, or courage. Geneviève shares in our convictions and our sympathies. Geneviève shall also share our fate."

"Well, my friend," said Morand, "I have said all I ought to say. Geneviève is in every way worthy of the mission you have given her, or, rather that she has taken upon herself. It is martyrs who become saints."

And he held out his delicate and effeminate hand to Dixmer, who roughly pressed it between his own. Then Dixmer, recommending Morand and his companions to watch with increased vigilance, quitted them, and entered Geneviève's apartments. She was seated before a table, bending over a piece of embroidery. She turned round at the noise of the opening door, and recognized Dixmer.

"Ah! is it you, *mon ami?*" said she.

"Yes," said Dixmer, with a placid, smiling countenance. "I have received a letter from your friend Maurice, which I cannot understand in the least. Read it, and then tell me what you think of it."

Geneviève took the letter with a hand, of which (with all her self-command) she could not disguise the tremor, and read. Dixmer followed her eyes as they ran over every line.

"Well?" said he, when she had finished.

"Well, I think that Monsieur Maurice Lindey is an honest man, and from him we have nothing to fear," replied Geneviève, with the greatest calmness.

"You think he is ignorant who the persons are you visited at Auteuil?"

"I am certain."

"Why, then, this sudden determination? Did he appear yesterday less friendly and more silent than usual?"

"No," said Geneviève; "I believe he was just the same."

"Consider well before you answer me, Geneviève, for you must understand your reply will greatly influence our future projects."

"Listen, then," said she, with an emotion that overthrew all her attempts at calmness. "Wait——"

"Well," said Dixmer, all the muscles of his face slightly contracting, "collect your thoughts, Geneviève."

"Yes," said the young woman, "yes, I remember, yesterday he was not particularly civil. Monsieur Maurice," continued she, "is a little tyrannical in his friendship, and," hesitatingly added, "sometimes we have quarrelled for a whole week."

"This is, then, merely a simple quarrel?" demanded Dixmer.

"Most probably."

"Geneviève, understand this, in our position it is not probability that will suffice; it is certitude we require."

"Ah, well, *mon ami*, I am certain."

"This letter, then, would be only a pretext for not visiting us again?"

"*Mon ami*, as you wish it, I will tell you."

"Speak, Geneviève, speak; of any other woman I would not ask it."

"It is a pretext," said Geneviève, looking down.

"Ah!" said Dixmer.

Then, after a moment's silence, he replaced it in his waistcoat, and placed his hand upon his wife's chair to compress the beatings of his heart.

"Will you do me a service?" said he.

"What service?" said Geneviève, turning round, surprised.

"To prevent even the shadow of danger. Maurice is, perhaps, deeper in our secrets than we imagine. That which you believe a pretext may, perhaps, be a reality. Write him one word."

"I?" said Geneviève, starting.

"Yes, you. Tell him that you have opened the letter and desire an explanation. He will then call, you can interrogate him, and will easily discover what is the matter."

"Oh, no!" cried Geneviève; "I cannot do as you wish me; I will not do it."

"Dear Geneviève, when interests so powerful as those that rest upon us are at stake, will you recoil before the paltry consideration of self-love?"

"I have told you my opinion of Maurice, monsieur," said Geneviève; "he is honest and brave, but capricious, and I do not choose to submit to any other authority but that of my husband."

This answer, returned with so much calmness, and, at the same time, firmness, convinced Dixmer that to insist further at this moment would be worse than useless. He did not add another word, but looked at Geneviève, without seeming to do so, and went out. Morand was awaiting his return with great anxiety. Dixmer repeated word for word all that had occurred.

"Well," said Morand, "we will wait and think no more about it. Rather than I would cast a shadow of suspicion on your wife, rather than wound her self-love, I would renounce——"

Dixmer placed his hand upon his shoulder.

"You are mad, monsieur," said he to him, "or else you do not know what you are saying."

"Do you think so, Dixmer?"

"I think, chevalier, that you have no more self-command than I have, to give utterance to sentiments on the impulse of the moment. Neither you, I, nor Geneviève belong to ourselves, Morand. We are the chosen defenders of a certain cause, and this cause depends upon its supporters."

Morand trembled, and preserved a gloomy and thoughtful silence. They took several turns round the garden without exchanging a word. Then Dixmer left Morand.

"I have some orders to give," said he, in a calm voice. "I must leave you, Monsieur Morand."

Morand held out his hand to Dixmer, and looked after him as he turned away.

"Poor Dixmer!" said he. "I fear much that in all this you risk the most."

Dixmer returned to the manufactory, and having issued several orders, looked over the day-book, and distributed bread and fuel to the poor of the section, went home, and changed his working-dress for his walking costume immediately on his arrival there.

An hour afterward, Maurice Lindey, while deeply engaged in his readings and allocutions, was interrupted by the voice of his official, whispering in his ear:

"Citizen Lindey, some one who, so he pretends, at least, has something of importance to say to you, is waiting at your house."

Maurice, on entering, was much surprised at meeting the master tanner, who had there comfortably installed himself, and was turning over the newspapers. All the way along he had questioned the domestic, who, of course, not knowing Dixmer, could afford him no clue to his recognition. On perceiving Dixmer, Maurice stopped at the threshold of the door, and blushed in spite of himself. Dixmer smilingly arose, and held out his hand.

"What ails you? and what have you written to me?" he inquired of the young man. "Indeed, my dear Maurice, I feel it sensibly. You designate me as 'lukewarm and a false patriot.' Now, as you dare not repeat these accusations to my face, acknowledge you wish to seek a quarrel with me."

"I will avow anything you please, my dear Dixmer, for your conduct to me has always been that of a worthy man; but I have, nevertheless, made a resolution, and that resolution is irrevocable."

"But how is that," said Dixmer, "when, according to your own account, you have nothing to reproach me with, and yet, notwithstanding, you leave us?"

"My dear Dixmer, believe me, acting as I now am, and depriving myself of such a friend, I must be actuated by powerful motives."

"Yes; but under any circumstances," said Dixmer, affecting to smile, "these reasons are not those you have written. What you have written to me is merely a subterfuge."

Maurice reflected an instant.

"Listen, Dixmer," said he; "we live in an epoch when

a doubt conveyed in a letter could and would annoy you, I can well understand. It would then be acting like a dishonorable man to allow you to remain in this state of inquietude. Yes, Dixmer, the reasons I gave you were not the true ones."

This avowal, which should have cleared the face of the merchant, only seemed the more to cloud it.

"But at least tell me the true motive," said Dixmer.

"I cannot tell you," said Maurice, "and yet I am certain, if you knew it, you would afford me your approval."

Dixmer still continued to press him.

"Then you really wish to know it," said Maurice.

"Yes," replied Dixmer.

"Well, then," replied Maurice, who felt a sensation of relief as he approached the truth, "this is the truth. You have a young and beauteous wife, virtuous as she is beautiful; yet it is well known that I cannot visit at your house without my visits being misinterpreted."

Dixmer turned rather pale.

"Truly, then, my dear Maurice," said he, "you ought to thank the wife for the wrong you do the friend."

"Understand," said Maurice, "I have not the folly to suppose my presence can be dangerous to your repose, or that of your wife; but it might, perhaps, afford subject for calumny, and you are aware that the more absurd the scandal, the easier it gains belief."

"Absurd!" said Dixmer, shrugging his shoulders.

"Absurd, as much as you please," said Maurice; "but separate, we shall not the less be good friends, for we shall have nothing to reproach ourselves with, while, on the contrary, if near——"

"Well, what then?"

"There would be food for scandal."

"Do you think, Maurice, that I should believe——"

"Eh, *mon Dieu!*" said the young man.

"But why did you not write this instead of telling it to me, Maurice?"

"Just to avoid the scene of this moment."

"And are you vexed, Maurice, that I respected you sufficiently to demand an explanation?"

"No; on the contrary, I swear I am glad to have seen you once again before our final separation."

"Our final separation, citizen; you whom we esteem so much!" taking Maurice's hand and pressing it between his own.

Maurice started.

"Morand," continued Dixmer, who failed not to notice this start, "Morand said to me only this morning, 'Do all in your power to bring back Maurice.'"

"Monsieur," said the young man, frowning, and drawing away his hand, "I do not believe I stand very high in the estimation of Monsieur Morand."

"You doubt it?" said Dixmer.

"Me!" replied Maurice. "I neither believe nor doubt it, and have no motive to inquire on the subject. When I went to your house, it was to visit yourself and your wife, and not on account of Monsieur Morand."

"You do not know him, Maurice," said Dixmer; "Morand possesses a noble soul."

"I grant it," said Maurice, smiling bitterly.

"Let us, however, return to the object of my visit," continued Dixmer.

Maurice bowed, like a man who hears all, but has nothing more to say.

"You say, then, that these reports have already circulated?"

"Yes, citizen."

"Well, then, let us speak frankly. Why should you pay any attention to the silly prattling of idle neighbors? Have you not your own clear conscience, Maurice; and Geneviève, has she not a sense of honor?"

"I am younger than you," said Maurice, who began to be astonished at this pertinacity, "and perhaps view things with more susceptibility. This is why I declare that on the reputation of such a woman as Geneviève a shadow even should not be permitted to be cast. Permit me, therefore, my dear Dixmer, to adhere to my former resolution."

"And now," said Dixmer, "since we are in order for confession, tell me one thing more."

"What?" said Maurice, coloring. "What more do you wish me to avow?"

"That it is neither politics nor the report of your assiduities at my house that induces you to leave us."

"What is it, then?"

"The secret you have discovered."

"What secret?" demanded Maurice, with so naïve an expression of curiosity as completely to reassure the tanner.

"The secret of the smuggling affair, which you discovered the same evening when our singular acquaintance commenced. You have never forgiven me this fraud, and accuse me of being a bad Republican, because I employ English produce in my manufacturing."

"My dear Dixmer, I solemnly declare to you that when I visited at your house, I had totally forgotten I was in the house of a contrabandist."

"Truly?"

"Truly."

"You really, then, had no other reason for abandoning the house, than that you have stated?"

"Upon my honor."

"Well," said Dixmer, rising and offering his hand to the young man, "I hope you will consider this resolution, which has been productive of pain to us all, and will again return to us as usual."

Maurice bowed, but made no reply, which was, of course, equivalent to a refusal. Dixmer left, annoyed at not having been able to reestablish an intimacy with this man, whom certain circumstances had rendered not only useful to him, but absolutely indispensable. Maurice was agitated by a variety of emotions of a contrary nature. Dixmer entreated him to return. Geneviève would pardon him. Why, then, should he despond? Louis, in his place, would have selected a crowd of aphorisms from his favorite authors. But then he had Geneviève's letter, that formal adieu, which he had carried with him to the section and placed near his heart ; also the little word received from her the day after he had rescued her from the cowards who insulted her ; and, lastly, the obstinate jealousy still retained by this young man against the detestable Morand, the first cause of his rupture with Geneviève.

Maurice remained inflexible in his resolution. But it must be acknowledged, the privation of his daily visits to the Old Rue St. Jacques formed a sad blank in his existence ; and when the hour arrived at which he had been accustomed to pay his daily visit to the quarter St. Victor, he fell into a profound fit of melancholy, and began, from that moment, to survey every aspect of hope or regret. Each morning, on awakening, he expected to receive a letter from Dixmer, and acknowledged to himself that he who had so firmly resisted all persuasion would now at last yield to a letter ; each day he sallied out in hopes of meeting Geneviève, and, beforehand, had arranged a thousand ways of speaking to her ; each evening he returned in hopes of there finding a letter or message left since the morning, though, doubtless, it would bring an addition to the grief, now become his constant companion. Often, in his hours of despair, his strong nature rebelled at the idea of enduring so much torture, without retaliating upon the primary cause of all his suffering and all his misery, Morand. Then he formed a project to go and seek some quarrel with Morand, but Dixmer's partner was so inoffensive and gentlemanly, that to insult or provoke him would be a cowardly proceeding on the part of a Colossus like Maurice.

It was fortunate Louis came to distract the attention of his friend from troubles which he obstinately concealed in his own heart, without having the power to destroy them. He had used every argument of theory and practise to secure to its country that heart totally engrossed by another love. But although this was to be regretted, and although, in another state of mind, it might have dragged Maurice into the center of the political whirlpool, it had not restored to the young Republican that first activity which had distinguished him as a hero on the 14th of July and the 10th of August. These two systems, for the last ten months in view of each other, and which, thus far, had only carried on light attacks, and commenced a few skirmishes, prepared to meet body to body, when it was evident that the struggle, once begun, would end fatally for one or the other. These two systems born from the breast of the revolution itself, were those of moderation, represented by the Girondins, that is to say, by Bressot, Petion, Vergniaud, Valais, Lanjuinais, Barbaroux, etc., etc., and La Terreur, or La Montagne, represented by Danton, Robespierre, Chenier, Fabre, Marat, Collot d'Herbois, Hébert, etc., etc.

After the 10th of August, as after every action, the power appeared to pass into the hands of the Modérés. A ministry had been formed from the wreck of the former ministry, and of a new adjunction. Roland, Servien, Clavières, former ministers, had been recalled. Danton, Monge, and Le Brun had been nominated afresh. With one exception only, all these ministers belonged to the moderate party. Of course, when we say "moderate," we speak relatively. But the 10th of August had had its echo from afar, and the coalition hastened to march, not to the assistance of Louis XVI. personally, but to the royalist principles tottering at its basis. Then were heard the menacing words of Brunswick, and, as a terrible realization, Longwy and Verdun had fallen into the power of the enemy. Then a dreadful reaction had taken place—then Danton had dreams of the days of September, and realized the bloody dream, which displayed before the enemies of France an entire scene of immense assassination, ready to struggle for an existence, compromised with all the energy of despair.

September had saved France; but all, in saving her, had exceeded the limits of the law. France saved, energy became useless; the Modérés had regained some strength, and then wished to recriminate those dreadful days. The words murderer and assassin had been uttered, a new name had even been added to the national vocabulary—it was that of Septembriseurs—Danton had bravely accepted. Clovis had for a moment inclined his head under the baptism of blood to raise it only still more lofty and menacing. Another opportunity to renew La Terreur presented itself; it was the procès of the king. Violence and moderation entered, not altogether to wrestle against persons, but principles. The hope of relative strength was founded on the royal prisoner. Moderation was overcome, and the head of Louis XVI. fell upon the scaffold. On the 10th of August, the 24th of January had rendered to the coalition all its energy. It was still the same man they opposed, but not the same fortune. Dumouriez, arrested in his progress by the disorder of all the administrations which prevented the succor of men or money reaching him, declared against the Jacobins, whom he accused of causing this disorganization, adopted the party of the Girondins, and ruined them in declaring himself their friend. Then La Vendée rose, threatening the districts, misfortune producing treason, and treason misfortune. The Jacobins accused the Modérés, and wished to strike the blow on the 10th of March that is to say, during the evening when our story commences. But too much precipitation on the part of their adversaries saved them, and perhaps also the rain, which had caused Petion (that profound anatomist of the Parisian mind) to remark:

"It rains; there will be nothing to-night."

But since the 10th of March everything threatened ruin to the Girondins. Marat was accused and acquitted. Robespierre and Danton were reconciled as a lion and tiger would reconcile themselves before fighting the bull they both intended to devour; Henriot, the Septembriseur, nominated commandant-general to the National Guard; everything presaged that awful day, which would carry away by storm the last dike the Revolution opposed to La Terreur. Such were the great events in which, under any other circumstances, Maurice would have taken an active part, for which his powerful nature and exalted patriotism so fully qualified him. But happily or unhappily for Maurice, neither the exhortations of Louis, nor the terrible preoccupations abroad, had been able to divert his mind from the one idea that possessed it; and when the 31st of May arrived, the fierce assailants of the Bastile and the Tuileries was laid upon his bed, devoured by that fever which destroys the strongest, and yet only requires a word to dissipate, a look to heal.

CHAPTER XIII.

THE THIRTY-FIRST OF MAY.

DURING the morning of the 31st of May, when the tocsin and beat of drum had been sounding since the break of day, the battalion of the Faubourg St. Victor entered the temple. When all the usual formalities had been gone through, and the posts distributed, the municipals on service arrived, bringing with them four pieces of cannon, in addition to those already forming the battery at the gate of the temple. At the same time, Santerre arrived, with his epaulets of yellow wool and a coat on which his patriotism was displayed by large spots of grease. He reviewed the battalion, which was in a proper state, but on counting the municipals, found only three.

"Why are there only three municipals?" inquired he; "and who is the bad citizen who fails us?"

"The absent citizen, general, is not, however, *un tiede*," replied our old acquaintance, Agricola; "for it is the secretary of the Section Lepelletier, the chief of the brave Thermopyles, the Citizen Maurice Lindey."

"Well, well," said Santerre, "I know as well as yourself the patriotism of the Citizen Maurice Lindey; but that will not deter me, if he is not here in five minutes, from inscribing his name in the list of the absent."

And Santerre passed on to other details. A few paces

from the general, at the moment he pronounced these words, a captain of chasseurs and a soldier had stationed themselves, one leaning against his gun, the other seated on a cannon.

"Did you hear?" said the captain to the soldier, in a low tone. "Maurice has not yet arrived."

"Yes; but rest assured he will arrive; he will not remain quiet at least."

"In case he should not come," said the captain, "I will place you sentinel on the staircase; and as she ascends to the tower, you will be able probably to speak a word to her."

At this moment a man, evidently a municipal, from his tricolored scarf, entered; but this man being a stranger to the captain and the chasseur, they both regarded him attentively.

"Citizen General," said the newcomer, addressing Santerre, "I request you to accept me in place of Citizen Maurice Lindey, who is ill. Here is the medical certificate; my turn of guard arrives in eight days. I now exchange with him; in eight days he will do duty for me, as to-day I will for him."

"Provided Capet and the Capets live eight days longer," said one of the municipals.

Santerre replied by a slight smile to this pleasantry, and turning toward Maurice's proxy:

"Very good," said he; "sign the register, in lieu of Maurice Lindey, and consign to the column of observations the reason for this exchange."

The captain and chasseur exchanged looks of delight mingled with astonishment.

"In eight days," said they.

"Captain Dixmer," said Santerre, "take your position in the garden with your company."

"Come, Morand," said the captain to the chasseur, his companion. The drum sounded, and the company, led by the master tanner, filed off in the direction prescribed. They placed their arms altogether, and the company divided itself into groups, which dispersed themselves

THE CHEVALIER DE MAISON ROUGE. 119

according to their inclination, far and wide. Their place of promenade was the same garden where, in the time of Louis XVI., the royal family came sometimes to take the air. This garden was naked, barren, and desolate, completely despoiled of trees, flowers, or verdure of any kind. At about five and twenty paces, or perhaps rather nearer, that portion of the wall built on the Rue Porte Foin, rose a species of cottage, which the foresight of the municipality had established for the convenience of the National Guard stationed at the temple, who, during the days of riot, when they were not permitted to go out, found it an accommodation to take their meals in this little cottage. The direction of this little ale-house had been a matter of contention, till at length concession was made in favor of an excellent patriot, wife of a Fabourien, killed on the 10th of August, and who bore the name of Plumeau. This little cabin, built of planks and mud, rose in the middle of a border, of which the bounds may still be recognized by a hedge of dwarf box-trees. It was composed of a simple chamber, twelve feet square, under which extended a cave, entered by steps rudely cut in the earth itself. Here the widow Plumeau stowed away her wine and provisions. This department was ultimately managed by herself and daughter, a girl of twelve or fifteen years of age. Hardly established at their bivouac, the National Guards separated, as we have said, some to saunter in the garden, while others chatted with the hostess. Some amused themselves by criticising the designs traced upon the walls, which were all of a patriotic tendency, such as the king pendant, with this expression: "Monsieur Veto taking an air-bath;" or the king guillotined, with this: "Monsieur Veto spitting in the sack;" while some offered hints to Mme. Plumeau concerning her gastronomical designs, that might more or less excite their appetites. Among the latter were the captain and the chasseur whom we have previously remarked.

"Ah, Captain Dixmer," said the cantinière, "I have some famous vin de Saumer."

"But, Citoyenne Plumeau, in my opinion, at least, the

vin de Saumer is nothing without the cheese of Brie," replied the captain, who, before he stated this opinion, had carefully looked round, and detected the absence of his favorite commodity.

"Ah, captain, it is true; but the last morsel has been consumed."

"Well," said the captain, "if there is no cheese of Brie, no vin de Saumer for me; and remark, Citoyenne Plumeau, the consumption is worth the trouble; listen to what I intend to propose to the company."

"But, captain, I ask you to wait only five minutes, and I will run and procure some at the house of the citoyenne concièrge, who competes with me, and who always has it. I shall pay very dear, and you, I am sure, are too good a patriot to injure me."

"Yes, yes," replied Dixmer, "and in the meantime we will go into the vault, and select our own wines."

"Make yourself at home, captain, pray do."

And the widow Plumeau began to run with all her might toward the lodge of the concièrge, while the captain and chasseur, provided with a light, raised the trap-door, and then descended into the cave.

"Good," said Morand, after an instant's examination, "the cave advances in the direction of the Rue Porte Foin. It is nine or ten feet in depth, and there is no brick-work."

"What is the nature of the soil?" inquired Dixmer.

"Sand-stone; it is all made earth; these gardens have been thrown into confusion, and then restored many times. There is no rock in any part."

"Be quick!" cried Dixmer; "I hear the sabots of our vivandière; take two bottles of wine, and let us go up."

They both appeared at the entrance of the trap-door as Mme. Plumeau entered, carrying the cheese so strenuously insisted on by Dixmer, while several chasseurs followed her, attracted by the presence of the said cheese. Dixmer did the honors; he offered twenty bottles of wine to his company, while the Citizen Morand recounted the devotion of Curtius. the disinterestedness of Fabricius, and the patriotism of Brutus and Cassius, histories almost as much appreciated as the cheese of Brie and the vin d'Anjou offered by Dixmer, which is not saying a little. Eleven o'clock struck. At half-past the sentinels were relieved.

"Does not the Austrian take her walk in half an hour?" asked Dixmer of Tison, who passed the cabin.

"Half an hour after noon, exactly," and he began to sing.

He was received with a shout of laughter from the National Guard. Dixmer immediately summoned those men in his company whose duty it was to mount guard at half-past eleven o'clock for an hour and a half, and recommended them to hasten their breakfast, and made them take the arms to Morand, to place them, as it was agreed, on the highest story of the tower, in the same turret behind which Maurice was hidden the day he intercepted the signs intended for the queen from the window of the Rue Porte Foin. If any one had noticed Morand at the moment he received this message, simple as it was, he would have seen him blush beneath the masses of his long black hair. Suddenly a dull noise shook the court of the temple, and sounds were heard like the roaring of a hurricane in the distance.

"What is that?" said Dixmer to Tison.

"Oh!" replied the jailer, "it is nothing; some little uproar they are making as these rascally Brissontins go to the guillotine."

The noise increased, the roar of artillery was heard, and a crowd of people rushed past, near the temple, shouting:

"Long live the Sections!" "Long live Henriot!" "Down with the Brissontins!" "Down with the Rolandists!" "Down with Madame Veto!"

"Ah!" said Tison, clapping his hands, "I will go and open the door for Madame Veto, that, without any disturbance, she may enjoy the love the people evince for her."

He approached the wicket of the donjon.

"Halloo, Tison!" cried a loud voice.

"Yes, general," replied he, stopping short.

"Not to go out to-day," said Santerre; "the prisoners are not to quit their chambers to-day."

This order was peremptory.

"Good!" said Tison; "so much the less trouble."

Dixmer and Morand exchanged looks of disappointment; then, waiting till the hour for duty had struck (though now uselessly), they both left to walk between the cabin and the wall built on the Rue Porte Foin. Morand began walking fast a distance of easy and geometrical steps, that is to say, of three feet.

"What distance?" inquired Dixmer.

"Sixty to sixty-one feet," replied Morand.

"How many days will be required?"

Morand considered, then traced upon the ground some geometrical signs, which he effaced directly.

"Seven days, at least, are necessary," said he.

"Maurice is guard in eight days," murmured Dixmer. "It is then absolutely imperative that within eight days we should be reconciled to Maurice."

The half-hour struck, Morand, sighing, resumed his gun, and, conducted by the corporal, went to relieve the sentinel who paraded the platform before the tower.

CHAPTER XIV.

DEVOTION.

The day following these events, that is to say, the 1st of June, at ten o'clock in the morning, Geneviève was seated in her accustomed place near the window. She asked herself why, for the last three weeks, the days for her rose so sad, while they passed so slowly, and, lastly, why, instead of anticipating each evening with delight, she now dreaded its return. Her nights, above all, were wretched, those nights that used to be so happy, those nights passed in dreaming of the past and of the future.

At this moment her eyes fell upon a case of magnificent striped and crimsoned carnations, which since the winter she had removed from the little greenhouse where Maurice had been imprisoned, to bloom in her own apartment. Maurice had taught her to cultivate them in this case where they were inclosed; they were watered and daily trimmed, as if Maurice had been there; for when he came in the evening, she delighted to show him, thanks to their united care, the progress they had made during the night. But since the cessation of Maurice's visits, the poor carnations had been quite neglected, and for want of requisite care and attention, the opening buds had withered, turned yellow, and fallen down outside the balustrade. Geneviève now comprehended from this sight alone the reason of her own melancholy. She said to herself: "It is with flowers as with certain friendships, which we nourish and cultivate with ardor, till they bloom in the heart, and then, in a moment of suspicion, a caprice, an unkindness, strikes at the root of this friendship, and the heart that this friendship has bound up and brought to life languishes and dies." The young woman experienced a sensation of anguish. She examined her inmost thoughts; the sentiments she had endeavored to combat, and which she had hoped to conquer, she feared now more than ever, would only die with her; then she felt a moment's despair, for she knew the struggle would become more and more impossible. She slowly bowed her head, imprinted a kiss upon the withered flowers, and wept. Her husband entered at this moment. He, on his side, was too much preoccupied with his own thoughts to pay any attention to the emotion exhibited by his wife. It is true, Geneviève rose quickly to meet him, and in so doing turned her face from the window.

"Well?" said she.

"Well, nothing new; impossible to approach her, impossible to pass her, impossible even to see her."

"What?" cried Geneviève, "with all the noise there has been in Paris?"

"It is the very noise which has made the guard redouble their vigilance, from the fear that any one might avail themselves of the general excitement to make an attempt on the temple, and the very moment when her majesty was about to walk upon the platform, an order was issued by Santerre that neither the queen, Madame Royale, nor Madame Elizabeth should go out to-day."

"The poor chevalier! he must be much annoyed?"

"He was in despair when he saw this chance had thus escaped us, and turned so pale that I trembled lest he should betray himself."

"But," asked Geneviève, timidly, "is there not, then, at the Temple, any municipal of your acquaintance?"

"There ought to have been one, but he did not come."

"Who?"

"The Citizen Maurice Lindey," said Dixmer, in a tone he endeavored to render indifferent.

"And why did he not come?" said Geneviève, in her turn making a similar effort at self-command.

"He was ill."

"He—ill?"

"Yes, and seriously so. Patriot as you know him to be, he was obliged to cede his turn to another."

"This is most unfortunate!"

"*Mon Dieu!* Geneviève," replied Dixmer, "if he had been there, as matters now stand, it might have been just the same. Unfriendly as we are at present, he might perhaps have avoided even speaking to me."

"I think, *mon ami*," replied Geneviève, "you exaggerate the unpleasantness of our situation. Monsieur Maurice may have taken a whim not to come here, but is not on that account our enemy. Coolness does not exclude politeness, and I am convinced, on seeing you, he would meet you half way."

"Geneviève," replied Dixmer, "what we require from Maurice needs something more than politeness—a firm and attached friendship. This feeling is destroyed; we have nothing further to hope from him."

And Dixmer heaved a deep sigh, while his usually placid face bore a troubled expression.

"But," said Geneviève, hesitatingly, "if you think that Monsieur Maurice is necessary to your projects——"

"That is to say," replied Dixmer, "that I despair of being able to succeed without him."

"Well, then, why do you not try some new method with the Citizen Lindey?"

It seemed to her that in speaking of the young man by his surname, her voice sounded less tender than when she called him by his Christian name.

"No," replied Dixmer, shaking his head, "any new proceeding would appear singular and necessarily awaken suspicion; and then, Geneviève, I see further than you into this affair; Maurice feels deeply wounded."

"Wounded, *mon ami!* What would you say? Speak."

"You know as well as I do, Geneviève, that in our rupture with the Citizen Lindey there is more than caprice."

"To what, then, do you attribute this rupture?"

"To pride, perhaps," said Dixmer, quickly.

"To pride?"

"Yes; he did us honor, in his opinion, at least, this good bourgeois of Paris—this *demi-aristocrat de robe*—concealing his susceptibilites under his patriotism; he conferred honor upon us, this Republican so powerful in the section, in his club, in the municipality, by according his friendship to a manufacturer of hides. Perhaps we have made too few advances; perhaps we have forgotten ourselves."

"If we had even been guilty of this, I think your last step would have redeemed all that," replied Geneviève.

"Yes, supposing the offense came from me; but if, on the contrary, it proceeded from you."

"From me! Do you imagine I have any ill-feeling toward Monsieur Maurice?" said Geneviève, astonished.

"Who knows? In a similar manner did you not at first even accuse him of caprice? I, therefore, still return to my first opinion, Geneviève; you did very wrong not to write to him."

"Me!" cried Geneviève; "do you think so?"

"Not only now do I think so, but have done so ever since this rupture of the last three weeks."

"And——" said Geneviève, timidly.

"I look upon this step as indispensable."

"No, no! Dixmer, do not require this of me."

"You know, Geneviève, I require nothing of you; I only entreat you. Well, listen: I request you to write to the Citizen Maurice."

"But——" said Geneviève.

"Hearken!" said Dixmer, interrupting her; "there is between you and Maurice either some serious cause of quarrel—for, as far as I am concerned, there is no complaint against my proceedings—or it emanates from childish folly."

Geneviève did not reply.

"If this is merely a silly disagreement, it is folly to render it lasting; and if you have serious motives for quarreling, situated as we are, you ought not even to value your dignity or self-respect. We must not place in the balance the quarrels of young people against objects of high interest. Make one effort; subdue your own feelings, and write one word only to Maurice Lindey, and he will return."

Geneviève reflected for a moment.

"But," said she, "could we not find some means less compromising to renew the friendly intercourse between Monsieur Maurice and yourself?"

"Compromising, do you call it? It appears to me to be the most natural way possible."

"No, not for me, *mon ami*."

"You are very opinionated, Geneviève."

"Allow me to tell you, it is the first time, at least, that you have discovered it."

Dixmer, who for some time had been crushing his handkerchief between his hands, now wiped the perspiration from his brow.

"Yes," said he, "and it is this increases my astonishment."

"*Mon Dieu!*" said Geneviève, "and is it possible, Dixmer, that you do not divine the cause of my resistance, and that you wish to force me to speak?"

And, overcome with contending emotions, her head sank upon her breast, and her arms fell listlessly by her sides. Dixmer appeared to make a strenuous effort to command himself, took Geneviève's hand, compelled her to raise her head, looked into her eyes, and began to laugh; but in a manner so forced and unnatural that, had Geneviéve been less agitated at the moment, it must have been perceptible even to her.

"I see how it is," said he; "you are in the right, and I was blind. With your wit and distinction, you have been fearful that Maurice ought not to admire you so much."

Geneviève felt as if an icy chill had penetrated to her heart. This irony on the part of her husband relative to Maurice's affection for her—that love of which, from the knowledge she possessed of the character of the young man, she could estimate the violence, and in which, though only acknowledged with deep remorse, she participated in the depths of her heart—this irony petrified her. She felt it was utterly impossible to reply.

"I have guessed rightly, have I not?" said Dixmer. "Well, reassure yourself, Geneviève; I know Maurice to be a fierce Republican, whose heart contains no other love than love of country."

"Monsieur," exclaimed Geneviève, "are you certain of what you say?"

"Eh! without doubt," replied Dixmer. "If Maurice loved you, instead of quarreling with me he would redouble his attentions and civilities to one whom it was his interest to deceive. If Maurice loved you, he would not so easily renounce his title of 'friend of the family,' generally used to cover these treasons."

"Do not, I beseech you," cried Geneviève, "make a jest of these things."

"I do not jest, madame; I only tell you Maurice does not love you, that is all."

"And I—I," said Geneviève, "tell you that you deceive yourself."

"In that case," replied Dixmer, "Maurice, who has had sufficient strength to tear himself away, is an honest man, and as they are rare, Geneviève, one cannot do too much to reclaim them when once lost. Geneviève, you will write to Maurice, will you not?"

"Oh, *mon Dieu!*" cried the young woman, resting her head between her hands, for he to whom she looked for support in a moment of danger had precipitated instead of restraining her fall.

Dixmer regarded her for a moment, then, forcing a smile:

"*Allons, chère amie,*" said he; "no woman's *amour propre*. If Maurice wishes to recommence a declaration, laugh at the second as you did at the first. I know you, Geneviève; you have a noble and excellent heart. I can depend on you."

"Oh, *mon Dieu!*" said the young woman, sinking on her knees, "who can feel confidence in those who have no confidence in themselves?"

Dixmer turned pale, as if all his blood had retreated back to his heart.

"Geneviève," said he, "I have acted very wrong to cause you so much anguish of mind. I ought to have explained myself at once. Geneviève, we live at an epoch of self-sacrifice. I have devoted myself to the queen, our benefactress, and not only my arm, not only my head, but my happiness. Others will give their lives; I do more than give her my life, I risk my honor, and if that perishes, only one more tear will fall into the ocean of miseries which are preparing to swallow up France. But my honor runs no risk under the guardianship of such a woman as Geneviève."

For the first time Dixmer had revealed the whole truth. Geneviève raised her head, and fixed her beautiful eyes, full of admiration, upon him; then slowly rose, and presented her face to him to kiss.

"You wish it?" said she.

Dixmer made a sign in the affirmative.

"Dictate, then;" and she took up a pen.

"No; it is sufficient to use, not to abuse, this worthy young man," said Dixmer; "and when he will reconcile himself to us on receipt of a letter from Geneviève, this letter should be from Geneviève, and not from Monsieur Dixmer."

And Dixmer a second time kissed his wife's forehead, thanked her, and went out.

Then Geneviève tremblingly wrote:

"CITIZEN MAURICE,—You know how much my husband respects you. Three weeks of separation, which to us have appeared an age, have made you forget. Come, we await you; your return will be a real fête.

"GENEVIÈVE."

CHAPTER XV.

THE GODDESS REASON.

As Maurice had informed General Santerre the preceding evening, he was seriously ill while he kept his chamber. Louis, in his daily visits, had made use of every argument to induce him to enter into some amusements; but Maurice continued obstinate. There are some maladies we do not desire to heal. On the 1st of June, he arrived toward one o'clock.

"Is there anything particular going on to-day," asked Maurice, "that you are so superb?"

Indeed, Louis was most splendidly attired. The "bonnet-rouge," the "carmagnole," and the tricolored girdle, ornamented with two instruments then called the "cruets of the Abbé Maury," but which before and since have been honestly termed pistols.

"In the first place," said Louis, "it is generally the breaking of the ice of the Bironde which is in train for execution; but the drum beats. At this moment, for example, the 'bonnets-rouges' chafe upon La Place du Carrousel ; then, in particular, there is a grand solemnity to which I invite you, after to-morrow."

"But what is there to-day ? You came to seek me, do you say ?"

"Yes ; to-day we have the rehearsal."

"What rehearsal ?"

"Why, the rehearsal of this great solemnity."

"*Mon cher*," said Maurice, "you know that it is now eight days since I last went out, consequently I am ignorant of everything ; and, therefore, the more require to be fully informed."

"What ! Have I not told you ?"

"You have told me nothing."

"First, you already know we had suppressed 'God' for some time past, and have replaced it by the 'Supreme Being.'"

"Yes ; I know all that."

"*Eh bien !* it seems they have found out one thing : that the 'Supreme Being' was a Modéré, a Rolandist, and, in short, a Girondin."

"Do not make a jest of anything holy, Louis ; you know I do not like it."

"What would you have, *mon cher?* it is necessary to accord with the age. I like the ancient God well enough ; first, because I am accustomed to it. As for the 'Supreme Being,' it appears He has been really wrong, and since He has been above, everything has been playing at cross-purposes, consequently, our legislators have decreed His downfall."

Maurice shrugged his shoulders.

"Shrug your shoulders as much as you please," said Louis ; "but now we are going to worship the 'Goddess Reason.'"

"And are you engaged in all these masquerades ?" said Maurice.

"Ah, *mon ami*, if you knew the Goddess Reason as I know her, you would be one of her warmest partisans. Listen : I wish you to know her, and will present you to her."

"A truce with all this folly. I am out of spirits, you well know."

"The very thing, *morbleu!* she will enlighten you ; she is a nice girl. Ah! but you know the austere goddess whom the Parisians wish to crown with laurels, and promenade about in a gilded paper chair! It is— Guess."

"How can I guess?"

"It is Arthemise."

"Arthemise!" said Maurice, taxing his memory in vain to recollect the name.

"Yes ; a handsome brunette, with whom I formed an acquaintance last year at the ball at the Opera ; by the same token, you came to sup with us, and made her tipsy."

"Ah, yes," said Maurice. "I remember now. It is she, is it?"

"She has the best chance. I presented her to the concourse. All the Thermopyles have promised me their votes. In three days the general election will take place. To-day we enjoy the preparatory dinner, to-day we spill the wine of Champagne, perhaps after to-morrow we may spill blood. Let them spill what they like, Arthemise shall be goddess, or may the devil carry me away! *Allons,* come ; we will help to put on her tunic."

"Thanks ; but I have always entertained a repugnance for things of this sort."

"To robe goddesses? *Peste! mon cher,* you are difficult to please. Let me see if that does not suit you, I will put it on, and you shall take it off."

"Louis, I am ill, and not only out of spirits, but the gaiety of others makes me miserable."

"Ah, that is it! You frighten me, Maurice ; you neither laugh nor fight. Are you by any chance engaged in some plot?"

"Me? Would to God!"

"You ought to say, 'Would to the Goddess Reason!'"

"Leave me, Louis ; I cannot, and will not, go out. I am in bed, and there let me rest in peace."

Louis scratched his ear.

"Well," said he, "I see how it is."

"What do you see?"

"That you wait for the Goddess Reason."

"*Corbleu!*" cried Maurice, "spiritual friends are very troublesome. Go, or I shall utter a few imprecations on you and your goddess."

"Charge! Charge!"

Maurice raised his hand to curse him, when he was interrupted by his official, who at this moment entered, bearing in his hand a letter for the citizen, his brother.

"Citizen Agricola," said Louis, "you enter at an unfortunate moment. Your master was about to become superb."

Maurice let fall his hand, which he listlessly extended for the letter; but the instant he had touched it he started; and having eagerly examined both the seal and handwriting, grew very pale in the anticipation of bad tidings, and broke the seal hastily.

"Oh! our interest is awakened at last," said Louis, "it seems to me."

Maurice heard him not; his whole soul was merged in the four lines of Geneviève. He read and reread them three or four times over; and then raising his head, gazed at Louis like a man quite stupefied.

"*Diable!*" said Louis, "the sight of a letter, it appears, makes all fierce feeling subside."

Maurice read the letter for the fifth time, and a hue of vermilion suffused his face, the moisture disappeared from his eyes, and a deep sigh relieved his breast; then, forgetting at once his illness and attendant weakness, he leaped from his bed.

"My clothes!" cried he, to the astonished official; "my clothes, my dear Angesilas. Oh, my dear Louis—my poor Louis, I will attend you every day. Indeed, I did not expect or hope for this. Here; my white trousers or frilled shirt, that they may dress my hair and shave me."

The official hastened to execute the orders of Maurice.

"Ah, Louis!" cried the young man, "I never till this moment knew what happiness meant."

"My poor Maurice," said Louis, "I think you require the visit I recommended to you."

"Oh! my dear friend, pardon me; for truly, reason has forsaken me."

"Then I offer you mine," said Louis, laughing at his own execrable pun.

The most surpassing thing was, Maurice laughed also. His present happiness rendered this easy.

This was not all.

"Wait," said he, cutting some orange-blossoms from a tree in full bloom; "present this from me to the worthy widow of Mansole."

"*A la bonne heure!*" said Louis. "In consideration of your gallantry, I pardon you. Then it appears to me you are absolutely in love, and I always feel profound respect for its unfortunate victims."

"Yes, I am in love," said Maurice; and his heart dilated with joy. "I am in love; and now, since she loves me, I may declare it; for since she has recalled me, must she not love me, Louis?"

"Doubtless," complacently replied the adorer of the Goddess Reason; "but take care, Maurice, for the fashion in which you take this makes me fear for you."

"Bravo! bravo!" cried Maurice, clapping his hands; then, taking to his heels, he descended the stairs, four at once, and directed his steps toward the well-known Old Rue St. Jacques.

"He is worse than I thought him," said Louis, in his turn descending the staircase in a rather calmer mood. Arthemise was not Geneviève.

Hardly had Louis and his orange-blossom arrived at the Rue St. Honoré, when a crowd of young citizens, to whom he had been accustomed to administer either kicks or half-pence, according to the humor he happened to be in, respectfully followed him—mistaking him, no doubt, for one of those virtuous individuals to whom St. Just had proposed they should offer the white robe and a bunch of orange-blossoms. As the cortége every moment increased in numbers—for even at this epoch a virtuous man was a rare sight to behold—there were several thousand young citizens present when the bouquet was offered to Arthemise, a homage which made several other "Reasons" who had joined the ranks very ill with sick headache next day. It was on the same evening that the famous song was circulated through Paris :

> "Long life to Goddess Reason—
> The pure, clear dawn of day."

And as it has arrived thus far without any knowledge of the author—a fact which has exceedingly exercised the sagacity of the revolutionary historian—we have almost the audacity to affirm it was composed for *la belle* Arthemise by our poetical friend, Hyacinthe Louis.

CHAPTER XVI.

THE PRODIGAL CHILD.

MAURICE could not have been quicker, had he even possessed wings. The streets were crowded, but Maurice only remarked the crowd as it retarded his course. It was said everywhere that the Convention was sitting; that the majesty of the people was offended through the representatives, whom they prevented from coming out; and of this there seemed some probability, as the tinkling of the tocsin was heard, and the thunder of the cannon sounding an alarm. But what, at this moment, to Maurice, mattered either the tocsin or the cannon? What cared he whether the deputies were or were not able to come out, when the prohibition did not extend to him ? So he quickened his pace—that was all. While running, he pictured to himself Geneviève waiting at the little window overlooking the garden, in order to see him, and that she would perceive him far off ; and then her smile, more than ever charming, would welcome him back again. Dixmer also was no doubt informed of this happy return, and would tender him his coarse, large hand, so frank and loyal in its greetings. He loved Dixmer; now, even his love almost extended to Morand, with his black locks and his green spectacles, behind which he fancied he could see the glitter of his brilliant but saturnine eyes. He loved the whole world, for he was happy, and would willingly have showered flowers on the heads of all mankind, that they might be as happy as himself. But for once he was deceived. Poor Maurice! he deceived himself, as a man generally does when he reckons according to his wishes.

Instead of the sweet smile awaiting Maurice, which was to receive him when he would be seen from afar, Geneviève had determined on meeting Maurice with the most distant politeness—a feeble rampart with which to oppose the torrent that threatened to invade her heart. She had retired to her chamber on the first floor, and did not intend coming down till sent for. Alas! she also deceived herself. Dixmer alone was not deceived; he watched for Maurice through a wired lattice, and smiled ironically. Morand was gravely occupied in dyeing black some tails which are placed on white catskin to imitate ermine.

Maurice pushed open the little door of the alley, to enter unceremoniously through the garden, as of old; the door opening produced a peculiar sound, which indicated the arrival of Maurice.

Geneviève, who had stationed herself behind the closed window, started, and let fall the curtain she had drawn on one side.

The first sensation experienced by Maurice on entering his friend's house was disappointment. Not only was Geneviève absent from the window on the ground floor, but on entering the little salon where he had uttered his last adieu, he found no one, and was compelled to announce himself, as if an absence of three weeks' duration had transformed him into a stranger. His heart was oppressed.

It was Dixmer whom Maurice first saw. He came forward and embraced him with exclamations of joy.

Geneviève then came down. She tried in vain to restore some color to her pallid cheek; but before she had proceeded twenty steps the blood receded to her heart. Maurice saw Geneviève appear in the shadow of the door; he advanced toward her, smiling, intending to kiss her hand, and then only perceived how sadly she was changed. She, on her part, noticed with anxiety the attenuated frame of Maurice, and his fevered look of wild excitement.

"You are here, then, monsieur," said she, in a voice of which she could not subdue the emotion.

She had determined to address him with perfect indifference.

"*Bonjour*, Citizen Maurice; why have your visits been so rare of late?"

This fickleness appeared more strange still to Maurice; and now what a shadow was cast upon all.

Dixmer cut short this examination, and put an end to all reciprocal reproaches by ordering dinner to be served; it was nearly two o'clock. They passed into the *salle-à-manger*, where Maurice saw a cover was placed for him. Then the Citizen Morand arrived, dressed in the same chestnut-colored coat and waistcoat—he always wore his green spectacles—and white frilled shirt.

Maurice was so affectionately disposed to all present, that while assembled before him he dismissed the suspicions and fears which intruded themselves upon his mind when absent from them. In short, what probability was there that Geneviève loved this little chemist? He was in love, and in consequence a fool to allow such folly to enter into his head.

Besides, the moment was badly chosen for jealousy. Maurice carried within his waistcoat pocket Geneviève's last letter, and his heart, bounding with joy, beat beneath it. Geneviève had recovered her serenity.

There is this peculiarity in the organization of women, that the present is able to efface all hues of the past, and distances all fears for the future. Geneviève felt happy, having resumed her self-command; that is to say, she became calm and dignified, though still kind—another shade which Maurice had not the requisite skill to comprehend. Louis would have found the explanation in "Parny," in "Berlin," or the "Gentil Bernard." The conversation turned upon the Goddess Reason. The fall of the Girondins, and the new mode of worship, were the prevailing topics of the day. Dixmer pretended he should not have been sorry to see this unparalleled honor offered to Geneviève. Maurice felt inclined to laugh, but Geneviève concurred in the opinion of her husband, while he regarded them both with astonishment, wondering that patriotism could so far mislead a sensible man like Dixmer, and a woman of so poetical and refined a nature as Geneviève. Morand developed the theory of female politicians. He cited "Theroigne de Mirecourt," the heroine of the 10th of August, and Mme. Roland, the "Soul" of the Girondins. Then, *en passant*, he launched out against the "Tricoteuses." These words made Maurice smile. It was, however, a cruel joke against these female patriots that they were latterly termed "the female leeches of the guillotine."

"Ah, Citizen Maurice," said Dixmer, "we respect patriotism, even when it is mistaken."

"As for me," said Maurice, "as far as I know of patriotism, I always find the women sufficiently good patriots, if not too high aristocrats."

"You are quite right," said Morand; "and as for myself, I frankly confess I consider a woman very contemptible when she affects the demeanor of a man, and a man a coward, unworthy of the name, when he insults a woman, even were she his bitterest enemy."

Morand was gradually drawing Maurice on to delicate ground. Maurice, on his side, replied by an affirmative sign. The lists being opened, Dixmer, like the sounding herald, added:

"One moment, one moment, Citizen Morand; you except, I hope, those women who are known enemies of the the nation?"

A silence of some moments succeeded this "parry and thrust" to the response of Morand and the sign of Maurice. Maurice first interrupted the silence.

"Let us except no one," said he, sadly; "those females who have been enemies to the nation are now, it appears to me, sufficiently punished."

"You allude to the prisoners of the Temple; to the Austrian, the sister and daughter of Capet?" cried Dixmer, with a rapidity which deprived his words of all expression.

Morand changed color while awaiting the reply of the young Republican. It has been said that, could we have seen it during this suspense, the marks of his nails were visible indented in his breast.

"Just so," said Maurice, "it is of them I am speaking."

"Who?" said Morand. "Is what they say of them true?"

"What do they say?" demanded the young man.

"That the prisoners are cruelly maltreated, sometimes even by those whose duty it is to protect them."

"There are individuals," said Maurice, "who do not deserve the name of men. There are some cowards who, totally deficient in real courage, retain a desire to torture the vanquished, in order to persuade themselves that they are the conquerors."

"You are not one of those men, Maurice, I am quite certain," said Geneviève.

"Madame," replied Maurice, "I who now speak to you, I have mounted guard near the scaffold on which perished the late king. With drawn saber in my hand, I was prepared to slay any one who attempted to rescue him. Notwithstanding, on his approach, I removed my hat, and turning toward my men, said: 'Citizens, I here warn you that the man who first insults the king receives my saber through his body.' And I defy any one to assert that a single shout was heard to proceed from my company. From my hand first enunciated those ten thousand placards affixed to the walls of Paris after the king's return from Vincennes: 'Whoever acknowledges the king shall be flogged. Whoever insults the king shall be hung.'

"Well," continued Maurice, without noticing the fearful effect his words had produced upon his listeners, "well, I have proved to you that I am a frank, good patriot, that I hate all kings and their partisans. Yet I declare, notwithstanding my opinion, which is nothing short of a deep conviction, that, notwithstanding the certainty I feel that the Austrian is, in a great measure, the cause of the miseries that desolate France, never, never shall any man, let him be who he may, even Santerre himself, insult the ex-queen in my presence."

"Citizen," said Dixmer, shaking his head as if he disapproved of so much hardihood, "are you aware you ought to be very sure of us before you speak of these things in our presence?"

"Before you, and before every one, Dixmer; and I will add, she may perhaps perish on the same scaffold as her husband, but I am not one to inspire a woman with fear, and I respect all those who are weaker than myself."

"And the queen, Monsieur Maurice?" demanded Geneviève, timidly, "has she sometimes evinced her sense of this delicacy, to which she is so little accustomed?"

"The prisoner has thanked me several times for my consideration for her, madame."

"Then she must witness your turn to guard with pleasure?"

"I believe she does, madame," replied Maurice.

"Then," said Morand, tremulous as a woman, "since you have confessed to what no one can now doubt—that is to say, a generous heart—you will not persecute the child any more?"

"Me!" said Maurice. "Ask the infamous Simon the weight of the arm of the municipal before whom he had the audacity to beat the little Capet."

This answer produced a spontaneous movement at Dixmer's table. All the guests rose respectfully; Maurice alone remained seated, and did not imagine he had elicited this mark of admiration.

"What is the matter?" said he, astonished.

"I thought some one called from the manufactory," said Dixmer.

"No," said Geneviève; "at first I thought so, too, but we are mistaken."

And every one resumed their seats.

"Ah! it is you, then, Citizen Maurice," said Morand, in a tremulous voice, "who are the municipal so much talked about, and who so nobly defended a child?"

"Talked about?" said Maurice, with a naïveté almost sublime.

"Yours is a noble heart," said Morand, rising from the table. That he might give way to his feelings, he retired to the manufactory, as if some pressing business there awaited him.

"Yes, citizen," replied Dixmer, "they do speak about it, and it should be said that all those possessed with generous hearts applaud without knowing you."

"And let him remain unknown," said Geneviève. "The glory he would acquire would be replete with danger."

Thus, in this singular conversation, without knowing it, each had contributed his word of heroism, devotion, and sensibility.

There had nearly been the word—Love.

CHAPTER XVII.

THE MINERS.

At the moment they left the table, Dixmer was told that his notary awaited him in his study. He excused himself to Maurice, besides, he was accustomed to leave him thus, and proceeded to attend his man of business. He was negotiating for the purchase of a house in the Rue de la Corderie, facing the garden of the Temple. It was rather, as to the rest, a ruin than a house that Dixmer was purchasing, for the actual basement was in a state of dilapidation; but it was his intention to rebuild it. The bargain had not been delayed with the proprietor; that same morning the notary had seen him and agreed to pay nineteen thousand five hundred livres. He, therefore, brought the agreement for signature, and came to receive the requisite money for the purchase, as the proprietor would that day clear out the building, that the workmen might commence operations on the morrow.

The contract signed, Dixmer and Morand accompanied the notary to the Rue de la Corderie, to view this new acquisition, for they had purchased without seeing it. It was a house situated near where No. 20 now stands—three stories in height, and surmounted by a curved roof. The lower part at one time had been let to a wine-merchant, and contained some most excellent cellarage.

The proprietor, above all things, vaunted his cellars; they were the best part of the house. Dixmer and Morand appeared to attach very little interest to these cellars, yet both, as if from mere politeness, descended with the proprietor into what he called his vaults.

An exception to the general rule, he had not exaggerated. The cellars were magnificent; one of them extended under the Rue de la Corderie, and from this cellar they they could hear the voitures roll over their heads. Dixmer and Morand did not appear to appreciate this advantage. They even spoke of filling them up, observing that, however convenient they might be to a wine-merchant, they became perfectly useless to honest bourgeoises, who intended to occupy the whole of the house. After the cellars they visited the first, second, and third stories; from the third they completely overlooked the garden of the Temple. It was as usual, invaded by the National Guard, who enjoyed this privilege, since the queen never walked there now. Dixmer and Morand recognized their friend, the widow Plumeau, with her usual activity, doing the honors of her cantine, but doubtless their anxiety to be in their turn remembered by her was not very great, as they kept themselves concealed behind the proprietor, while he expatiated on the advantages of this view, at once so varied and agreeable.

The purchaser then wished to see the roof. The proprietor, doubtless, was unprepared for this emergency, since he had not got the key, but, influenced by the bundle of papers of assignment shown him, he descended to search for it.

"I was not deceived," said Morand, "and this house will answer our purpose exactly."

"And what do you say to the vaults?"

"That is an interposition of Providence which will spare us two days' labor, at least."

"Do you think it may be in the direction of the cantine?"

"It inclines a little to the left, but that is of no consequence."

"But," said Dixmer, "how will you be able to follow your subterranean line with the certainty of its terminating where you wish?"

"Rest assured," said Morand; "that is my affair."

"If we were every day to give a signal from here that we are watching?"

"But from the platform the queen could not see it, for the curved roofs alone are less in height than the platform, and yet I doubt it."

"Never mind," said Dixmer; "either Maury or Toulun may see an opening somewhere, and they will inform the queen."

And Dixmer tied several knots in a white calico curtain, passing it backward and forward before the window, as if shaken by the wind.

Then both, equally impatient to visit the roof, awaited the proprietor's return on the staircase, having first closed the door, not wishing to afford the worthy man a sight of his waving curtain.

The roofs, as Morand had foreseen, did not reach the height of the summit of the tower.

This was at once an advantage and disadvantage. A difficulty, because they could not communicate by signs with the queen, and an advantage, because the very impracticability alone disarmed all suspicion.

The highest houses were naturally the objects of the strictest surveillance.

"It is necessary, either by means of Toulun, Maury, or Tison's daughter, to find some way to tell her to keep upon the watch," murmured Dixmer.

"I have thought of that," said Morand.

They descended; the notary waited in the salon with the contract signed.

"It is all right," said Dixmer; "the house suits me, so hand over to the proprietor the sum of nineteen thousand five hundred lives in payment, and let him give a receipt."

The proprietor did so, first scrupulously counting the money.

"You understand, citizen," said Dixmer, "the principal clause, that the house must be vacated this evening; that, in short, I must put the workmen in to-morrow."

"Well, citizen, I agree to do so; you can take the keys this evening at eight o'clock; all will be free."

"Pardon me," said Dixmer, "but did you tell me, Citizen Notary, there was a way out leading into the Rue Porte Foin?"

"Yes, citizen," said the proprietor; "but I had it closed; for, having only one official, the poor devil had too much fatigue, being obliged to watch both doors. But it is so fastened up that at any time it can be reopened in two hours at least. Would you wish to convince yourselves, citizens?"

"Thanks, it is not necessary," said Dixmer. "I attach no importance to this way out; it is useless to me."

They then both left, having for the third time reminded the landlord of his promise that the apartments should be empty at eight o'clock that evening. At nine o'clock they both returned, followed by five or six men at a distance, of whom, in the confusion then reigning in Paris, no one took any notice. They both entered first. The landlord kept his word; the house was totally empty. They closed the shutters with the greatest care, sounded the brick-work, struck the steel, and lighted some wax-candles which Morand carried in his pocket.

Then one after another the six men entered. These were the ordinary guests of the master tanner, the same contrabandists who one evening wished to kill Maurice, but had now been converted into his friends. They closed the doors, and descended into the vault. This vault, so contemptuously treated during the day, had become this evening the most important part of the house. Having first stopped up every crevice through which a curious eye might penetrate to the interior, Morand placed a cask upright, and began to trace geometrical lines upon a piece of paper laid upon it, with a stick of chalk. While he was thus engaged, his companions, conducted by Dixmer, left the house, following Rue de la Corderie, and at the corner of the Rue de Bennie stopped before a covered carriage. In this carriage was a man, who silently distributed to each one the instrument of a pioneer, to one a spade, to another a mattock, to this one a lever, to that a pick-ax; each man concealed his under his riding-coat or mantle. The miners retraced the road to the small house, and the carriage disappeared. Morand had finished his calculation. He went straight to an angle of the cave.

"There," he said, "dig."

And the work of deliverance immediately commenced.

The situation of the unhappy prisoners in the Temple became daily more serious and hourly more wretched. For an instant Mme. Elizabeth and Mme. Royale had indulged some hope. The municipals, Toulun and Lepetre, touched with compassion for the august prisoner, had evinced some interest in them. At first, little habituated to the marks of sympathy, the poor women were suspicious; but suspicion ceases to exist with hope. Besides, what now could happen to the queen, separated from her son by a prison, from her husband by death? To follow him to the scaffold, this idea had possessed her for some time, and she finished by becoming accustomed to it. The first time Toulun and Lepetre returned on guard, the queen particularly requested, if they really felt any interest in her misfortunes, they would describe to her the last moments of the king. This was putting their sympathy to a sad test. Lepetre had assisted at the execution; he obeyed the order of the queen. The queen demanded the journals containing the report of the execution. Lepetre promised to bring them when next on guard; it would be his turn again in three weeks. In the king's time they had at the Temple four municipals; the king dead, they had only three, one to watch during the day, two during the night. Then Toulun and Lepetre invented a stratagem that they might always keep watch together at night. The hours of guard were arranged thus: they wrote one ballot "day," on two others "night." Each drew his ballot from a hat, and chance decided the night watch. Every time that Toulun and Lepetre were on guard they wrote "day" on three ballots, and presented the hat to the municipal they wished to dispossess, and he, thrusting his hand into the improvisatory, necessarily drew forth a ballot on which was inscribed "day." They then destroyed the other two, murmuring against the hazard which always decreed them the most wearisome watch of the two—that is to say, the night. When the queen was sure of her guards, she corresponded with the Chevalier de Maison Rouge. Then an escape was attempted, but the attempt was arrested. The queen and Mme. Elizabeth were to flee disguised as municipal officers, with cards that would be provided for them.

As to the two children—that is to say, Mme. Royale and the young dauphin, they had remarked that the man who came to light the lamps of the Temple was always accompanied by two children, the same age apparently as the princess royal and the dauphin. It was, therefore, arranged that Turgy, of whom we have previously spoken, should dress himself as a lamp-lighter, and carry away the prince and princess. We will mention, in a few words, who Turgy was. Turgy was an old waiter of the king's, introduced at the Temple with part of the family from the Tuileries, for the king had at first been permitted a well-appointed table. The first month this consideration cost the nation thirty or forty thousand francs. It may easily be understood this prodigality could not last. The Commune decreed otherwise. They dismissed the chiefs, cooks, and scullions; one single man-servant only was retained—that man was Turgy. He was naturally the medium of communication between the prisoners and their partisans, for Turgy was permitted to go out, and consequently was enabled to forward their letters and introduce the replies. These billets were generally twisted round the stoppers of the *carafes*, containing the milk of almonds, brought to the queen and Mme. Elizabeth. They were written in lemon juice, and perfectly illegible, till held near the fire. All was prepared for their escape, when one day Tison lighted his pipe with the paperstopper of the *carafe*. As the paper burned, the writing became visible. He instantly extinguished the half-burned paper, and carried the remaining fragment to the Council of the Temple, when, being held near the fire, they could only read a few disjointed words, the other part being burned to ashes. They could merely recognize the handwriting of the queen. Tison, being questioned, mentioned some slight marks of attention and sympathy he fancied he had observed on the part of Lepetre and Toulun. They were immediately denounced to the municipality, and allowed no more to enter the Temple. Turgy remained. But suspicion was now excited to the highest degree. The princesses were never left a moment alone. All communication with the exterior was now utterly impossible. Mme. Elizabeth had one day given Turgy a gold-handled knife to clean, which she used for cutting her fruit. Turgy, suspecting something, opened the blade, and in the handle found a letter. This letter contained an alphabet of signs. He returned the knife to Mme. Elizabeth; but a municipal then present prevented him, and in his turn, securing the knife, opened the blade; but, fortunately, the letter was no longer there. The municipal, nevertheless, confiscated the knife. It was at that time the indefatigable Chevalier de Maison Rouge dreamed of this second attempt, which they intended to carry into execution by means of the house which Dixmer had purchased. The prisoners, however, by degrees had now lost all hope. That day the queen, terrified by the noise in the streets, which reached her ears, and learning from these cries they were debating the accusation of the Girondins, the last supporters of moderation, felt dreadfully depressed. The Girondins dead, the royal family lost their only defense against the Convention.

At seven o'clock the supper was served. The municipals examined every plate, as usual, unfolded each napkin successively, searched the bread, the one with a fork, the other with his fingers, and concluded by breaking into pieces the macaroons and walnuts, for fear any letter should reach the prisoners. These precautions being concluded, the royal family were invited to their meal in these simple words :

"Widow of Capet, you may eat."

The queen shook her head, signifying she was not hungry. But at this moment Mme. Royale advanced, as if to embrace her mother, and whispered :

"Seat yourself at table, madame. I fancy Turgy made a sign."

The queen tremblingly raised her head. Turgy was opposite to her. The napkin laid over his left arm, and with his right hand he touched his eye. She immediately rose, without any further objection, and resumed her usual place at table. The two municipals assisted at their meals, being strictly prohibited from leaving the princesses alone for an instant with Turgy. The feet of the queen and Mme. Elizabeth met, and pressed each other under the table. As the queen was seated opposite Turgy, not one of his gestures escaped her notice besides, they were all so natural, that they neither could nor did inspire the municipals with any suspicion whatever. At the removal of the supper the same precautions were used as before ; the smallest pieces of bread were broken and examined. After which, Turgy went out first, the two municipals following ; the woman Tison remained.

This woman had become ferocious since her separation from her daughter, of whose fate she was totally ignorant. Every time the queen lavished a caress on Mme. Royale, it threw her into an excess of rage almost bordering on frenzy; so much so, that the queen, who so well understood the griefs of a mother, often denied herself this consolation, now, alas! the only one left her, of pressing her daughter to her heart.

Tison came now to seek for his wife, who at first declared she would not leave till Capet's wife was in bed.

Mme. Elizabeth then wished the queen good night, and entered her chamber. The queen and princess having also retired, Tison's wife took the candle and went out. The municipals had already thrown themselves upon their beds in the corridor. The moon, pale visitant of the unhappy princesses, glided by the opening of the first house, casting a diagonal ray across the window at the foot of the queen's bed. For an instant everything remained calm and silent in the chamber, then a door turned softly on its hinges, a shadow passed over the rays of the moon, and approached the queen—it was Mme. Elizabeth.

"Did you see it?" said she, in a whisper.

"Yes," replied the queen.

"And you understood it?"

"So well that I dare not believe it."

"Let us see, repeat the signs."

"First, then, he touched his eyes to indicate he had some news for us; then he passed his napkin from his left to his right; by that he meant to say they were occupied in our deliverance. Then he put his hand to his face, to signify that the expected aid would reach us from the interior, and not from a stranger; then when you asked him not to forget the milk of almonds to-morrow, he made two knots in his pocket-handkerchief. Thus it is again the Chevalier de Maison Rouge—noble-hearted man that he is."

"It is he," said Mme. Elizabeth.

"Are you asleep, my child?" demanded the queen.

"No, *ma mère*," replied Mme. Royale.

"Then pray for you know whom."

Mme. Elizabeth quietly regained her chamber, and for some minutes during the silence of the night the soft, sweet voice of the youthful princess might be heard addressing her prayer to God. It was at that moment, at a signal from Morand, the first stroke of the pick-ax sounded in the small house at the Rue de la Corderie.

CHAPTER XVIII.

CLOUDS.

OPPOSED to the intoxication of first appearances, Maurice was certainly much disappointed at the reception of Geneviève, and reckoned upon solitude to regain the road he had lost, or seemed to have lost, the route to her affections. But Geneviève had wisely arranged her plan, and did not intend to allow him an opportunity for a *tête-à-tête*, being conscious of their danger even from the happiness they afforded her. Maurice anticipated the morrow. A kinswoman of Geneviève, no doubt previously invited, came to call upon her, and Geneviève had retained her. This time there was nothing to be said; it could not be the fault of Geneviève. When leaving, Maurice was requested to escort this relation to the Rue des Fosses St. Victor, where she resided. Maurice went away pouting, but Geneviève smiled, and he construed this smile into a promise.

Alas! Maurice deceived himself. The next day, the 2d of June, that terrible day that witnessed the downfall of the Girondins, Maurice dismissed his friend Louis, who absolutely wished to carry him off to the Convention, and that he should put everything aside, and accompany him to visit his fair friend. The Goddess of Liberty had a frightful rival in Geneviève. Maurice found Geneviève in her little salon, all grace and amiability, but near her was a young *femme de chambre* with the tricolored cockade, engaged in marking pocket-handkerchiefs in the angle of the window; she never left her place.

Maurice knit his brows, and Geneviève, perceiving he was not in the best temper possible, redoubled her assiduities; but since her amiability was not carried so far as to dismiss the young official, he impatiently left an hour earlier than usual. This might have happened by chance, perhaps. Maurice grew patient. The evening, besides, from other causes, was so fearful, that long as it was since he had interested himself in politics, the report reached even him. It required nothing less than the downfall of a party who had reigned in France for ten months to withdraw his attention from his all-engrossing passion for Geneviève. The next day witnessed the same management on the part of Geneviève, and Maurice, having foreseen this, had arranged his plan. So, ten minutes after his arrival, seeing that the young woman, having finished marking a dozen pocket-handkerchiefs, commenced six dozen of table-napkins, Maurice, we say, drew out his watch, rose, bowed to Geneviève, and went out without saying one word. Still more, as he left, he did not even once look back. Geneviève, who had risen to watch him across the garden, remained an instant speechless, pale, and trembling, then dropped into her chair, thunderstruck at the effect of her diplomacy. At this moment Dixmer entered.

"Maurice gone?" said he, with astonishment.

"Yes," stammered Geneviève.

"But he had only just arrived."

"He was here a quarter of an hour, or nearly so."

"Then he will return?"

"I much doubt it."

"Leave us, Magnet," said Dixmer.

The *femme de chambre* had assumed the name from hatred to that of Maria, from its unfortunately being the same as that of the Austrian. She rose at the command of her master, and quitted the room.

"Well, dear Geneviève," said Dixmer, "is peace restored between you and Maurice?"

THE CHEVALIER DE MAISON ROUGE. 151

"On the contrary, *mon ami*, I think we are cooler than ever."

"And this time who is to blame?" said Dixmer.

"Maurice, without the slightest doubt."

"Permit me to judge."

"You cannot guess," said Geneviève, blushing.

"Why he is angry? No."

"It seems to me, it is some whim about Magnet."

"Bah! truly; then you must send the girl away. I will not deprive myself of a friend like Maurice for the sake of a *femme de chambre*."

"Oh!" said Geneviève, "he is not, I think, so angry as to require her to be sent away; it will suffice to——"

"What?"

"To exile her from my chamber."

"And Maurice is right," said Dixmer; "it is you he comes to visit, and not Magnet; it is therefore quite unnecessary that she should be present."

"But, my dear Dixmer," replied she, regarding her husband with astonishment.

"Geneviève," replied Dixmer, "I hoped to have found in you an ally who would render more easy the task imposed upon me, and find, on the contrary, that your fears redouble our dangers and difficulties. Four days since, I thought all was arranged between us, and now all must commence over again. Have I not told you that I confide in you, in your honor? have I not told you that it is positively necessary that Maurice should become our friend, more intimately than before, but less suspicious than ever? Oh, *mon Dieu!* these women are an everlasting obstacle to our projects."

"But, *mon Dieu!* is there no other way? I have told you before, that for all our sakes it would be better if Monsieur Maurice returned here no more."

"Yes, for our sakes, perhaps, but for the sake of those far above us, those for whom we have promised to sacrifice our lives, fortune, and happiness, it is necessary that this young man should return. Are you aware they begin to suspect Turgy, and talk of placing another servant near the queen.'"

"Well, I will send away Magnet."

"*Mon Dieu!* Geneviève," said Dixmer, with a movement of impatience very unusual with him, "why do you speak to me thus? why stifle the ardor of my ideas by your own? why strive to create difficulties where too many already exist? Geneviève, act like an honorable, devoted woman, act as you feel you ought to act. I tell you, to-morrow I go out—to-morrow I take Morand's place as engineer. I shall not dine with you, but he will; ne has something to ask Maurice, and I will explain to you what it is. What he has to request you may imagine, Geneviève, is a thing of vital import; it is not only the goal to which we march, but the way leading to it. It is the last hope of that devoted, noble-minded man, our protector, to whom we are bound to dedicate our lives."

"And for whom I will freely give mine," cried Geneviève, with enthusiasm.

"Well, this man, Geneviève, I cannot tell why, as you must have seen, is not loved by Maurice, by whom, above all things, it is necessary he should be respected. In short, from the bad temper in which you have put Maurice to-day, he may perhaps refuse Morand that which it is so imperative we should obtain at any price. Will you now that I have told you, Geneviève, assist Morand with all your tact and delicacy of sentiment?"

"Oh, monsieur!" cried Geneviève, clasping her hands and turning pale, "let us speak no more on this subject."

"Then," said Dixmer, pressing his lips on his wife's forehead, "reflect upon it, and form your resolution." And he went out.

"Oh! *mon Dieu! mon Dieu!*" murmured Geneviève, with anguish, "they compel me to accept this love by violence, toward which my whole soul inclines!"

The next day, as we have already said, was Sunday. It was customary in the family of Dixmer, as in all the bourgeoise families at that period, that the dinner should be longer and more ceremonious on that day than on any other. Since their intimacy, Maurice having received a general invitation, never omitted to dine with them on that day. Although they did not dine till two o'clock, Maurice had not arrived at noon. From the manner of their parting, Geneviève had almost despaired of seeing him. In short, twelve o'clock struck, then half-past, then one. It would be impossible to describe during this period what passed in the heart of Geneviève. She was at first dressed with the greatest simplicity; then, seeing that he delayed his coming, she, with a feeling of coquetry natural to the heart of woman, had placed a flower at her side, a flower in her hair, and still listened, her heart each moment more and more compressed. The dinner-hour had almost arrived, and Maurice had not appeared. About ten minutes to two, Geneviève heard the sound of horse's steps—that sound she knew so well.

"Oh!" cried she, "his pride could not wrestle against his love. He loves me; he loves me!"

Maurice dismounted, and gave his horse to the gardener, desiring him to remain where he was. Geneviève saw with anxiety that the gardener did not lead the horse to the stables. Maurice on this day looked superlatively handsome. A splendid black coat, a white waistcoat, breeches of chamois leather, designed for limbs after the model of Apollo, a white cambric stock, and his waving hair, displayed a fresh, a beaming face, formed altogether a type of manly beauty. He entered. As we have already said, his presence dilated the heart of Geneviève, who received him joyfully.

"Ah!" said she, holding out her hand, "you are come to dine with us, are you not?"

"On the contrary, citoyenne," said Maurice, coldly, "I came to ask your permission to absent myself."

"To absent yourself?"

"Yes; the sectional affairs claim my attention. I feared you might wait, and would accuse me of being wanting in politeness, therefore came to make my excuses in person."

Geneviève again felt her heart sinking within her.

"Ah, *mon Dieu!*" cried she, "and Dixmer, who does not dine at home, counted upon finding you here on his return, and desired me to detain you."

"Ah, then, madame, I comprehend your insistence, it is a command of your husband; and I not to guess all this. I shall never cure myself of conceit."

"Maurice!"

"It is for me, madame, to draw my inference from your actions rather than your words; it is for me, therefore, to comprehend, that if Dixmer is absent, the greater the reason I should not remain. His absence would surely add to your constraint."

"Why so?" timidly inquired Geneviève.

"Because you appear, since my return, sedulously to avoid me, because I returned for your sake, and yours only; you well know, *mon Dieu*, that ever since my return I have invariably found some one with you."

"Then," said Geneviève, "you are still angry, *mon ami*, although I endeavor to act for the best."

"No, Geneviève, you would do much better to receive me as before, or drive me away altogether."

"Maurice," said Geneviève, tenderly, "understand my situation, consider my anguish, and do not enact the tyrant over me any longer."

And the young woman regarded him mournfully.

Maurice remained silent.

"What do you require, then?" continued she.

"I require your love, Geneviève, since I now feel I cannot live without that love."

"Maurice, have pity on me."

"Then, madame, you leave me to die."

"To die?"

"Yes, to die; or to forget."

"You could, then, forget?" said Geneviève, the tears rushing from her heart to her eyes.

"Ah, no, no," said Maurice, falling on his knees before her; "no, Geneviève, I may die, perhaps, but forget you, never, never!"

"And yet," replied Geneviève, with firmness, "that would be the best, Maurice, for this love is criminal."

"Have you said this to Monsieur Morand?" said Maurice, suddenly resuming his frigidity of manner.

"Monsieur Morand is not a madman like yourself, and has never yet compelled me to indicate to him how he should conduct himself in the house of a friend."

"I wager," said Maurice, smiling ironically, "that if Dixmer dines out Morand is not absent. Ah, I see, this is necessary to deter me, for while Morand is there, Geneviève, forever at your side, not quitting you even for a single moment," continued he, contemptuously, "I should not love you, or, rather, I should not declare that I loved you."

"And I," cried Geneviève, driven to extremity by this eternal suspicion, and seizing the young man's arm with a species of frenzy, "I swear solemnly, Maurice, and let it be once for all, that whether you ever return here again or not, Morand has never breathed a word of love, that he neither loves me nor ever will love me. I swear this on my honor—I swear this by the soul of my mother!"

"Alas! alas!" said Maurice, "I wish I could believe you."

"Oh, believe me, poor fool!" said she, with a smile (which, although anything but jealous, might have been a charming confession), "believe me. Besides, if you wish to know more, Morand loves a woman in whose presence all others sink into insignificance, as the flowers of the field fade before the stars of heaven."

"And who is this woman able to eclipse all other women?" demanded Maurice, "when among the number we find Geneviève."

"Do we not always," said Geneviève, smiling, "consider the one we love as the *chef d'œuvre* of the creation?"

"Then," said Maurice, "if you do not love me, Geneviève——" The young woman waited with anxiety the end of the sentence. "If you do not love me," continued Maurice, "will you swear never to love another?"

"Ah! that, Maurice, I will swear with all my heart," cried the young woman, delighted that he had thus compromised with her conscience.

Maurice seized her raised hands, and covered them with ardent kisses.

"And now," said he, "I will be kind, indulgent, and confiding. I will even be generous. I wish to see you smile, and myself to be happy."

"And you will ask me nothing more?"

"I will endeavor."

"And now," said Geneviève, "I think it will be useless to hold the horse any longer. The section will wait."

"Oh, Geneviève! the whole world might wait, if I could only stay with you!"

Steps were heard in the courtyard.

"They come to tell us that dinner is ready," said Geneviève. They silently pressed each other's hands.

It was Morand who came to tell them they only awaited their presence at table. He also was in full dress for the Sunday's dinner.

CHAPTER XIX.

THE REQUEST.

In the meantime, Morand did not a little excite the curiosity of Maurice. The most refined of fops could not discover a fault in the tie of his cravat, the folds of his boots, or the texture of his linen; but it must be allowed his hair and spectacles were always the same. It then appeared to Maurice, so much was he reassured by the oath of Geneviève, that he now, for the first time, viewed these locks and spectacles in a proper light.

"The devil!" said Maurice to himself—"the devil take me if I am now ever again jealous of this worthy Citizen Morand. Put on every day, if you choose, your full-dress coat, or even make yourself one of cloth of gold, since from this time I promise to see nothing but your wig and spectacles, and, above all, never again to accuse you of loving Geneviève."

We can easily understand the shake of the hand bestowed upon the Citizen Morand at the conclusion of this soliloquy was more frank and cordial than usual. Contrary to custom, the party was small, covers being placed for only three on a narrow table. Geneviève was seated nearly opposite Maurice, between himself and the light, which reflected on her luxuriant black curls, tinged them with the blue hue of the raven's wing, enhancing the brilliancy of her eyes and complexion. Beyond his pigeon-colored suit, Morand appeared to have dismissed all recollection of the day from his mind—that brilliant mind, which Maurice had sometimes heard burst fresh from the lips of this singular man, which would no doubt have been accompanied by the flashes from his eyes, had they not been totally obscured by the green spectacles. He uttered a thousand witticisms, but never himself smiled ; indeed, what added piquancy to his witticisms, and a strange charm to his sallies, was his own impenetrable gravity. This merchant, who had made numerous voyages, and visited various countries, trading in every sort of skin, from the skin of the panther to that of the rabbit ; this chemist with arms dyed with his own chemical preparations, was as conversant with Egypt as Herodotus, Africa as Lavaillant, and the opera and the boudoir as any fop.

"But the devil take me, Monsieur Morand," said Maurice, "you are not only a clever man, but a scholar also."

"Ah! I have both seen and read much," said Morand ; "and then it is necessary I should prepare myself in some degree for the life of pleasure I intend to lead, when I retire on my fortune. It is time, Citizen Maurice, it is time."

"Bah!" said Maurice ; "you talk like an old man. What age, then, are you?"

Morand turned round, startled by this question, natural as it certainly was.

"I am thirty-eight," said he. "Ah! see what it is to be a scholar, as you term it. It makes one old."

Geneviève began to laugh, and Maurice joined in; but Morand merely smiled.

"You have then, made several voyages?" demanded Maurice, pressing Geneviève's foot between his own.

"Part of my youth," replied Morand, "was passed among foreigners."

"And you have seen much? Pardon me, I ought to say, have observed much; for a man like yourself can not see without observing," replied Maurice.

"*Ma foi!* yes; seen much?" replied Morand; "I have almost seen everything."

"Everything, citizen?" replied Maurice, laughing gaily, "that is saying a great deal. If you were to search——"

"Ah! yes, you are right; there are two things I have never seen. It is true, in our days, these two things have become rare."

"What are they, then?" demanded Maurice.

"The first," said Morand, "is a god."

"Ah!" said Maurice, "but in lieu of a god, I shall be able to show you a goddess, Citizen Morand."

"How so?" interrupted Geneviève.

"Yes, a goddess of modern creation—the Goddess Reason. I have a friend, of whom you have sometimes heard me speak—my dear and brave Louis, with a heart of gold, whose only fault is that of making verses and vile puns."

"Well?"

"Well, he selected for Paris a Goddess Reason, of good repute, and in whom they can discover nothing at all objectionable. It is the Citoyenne Arthemise, ex-dancer of the Opera, and at present *parfumeuse*, Rue Martin. As soon as she is definitely received as goddess, I will show her to you."

Morand bowed his head in token of thanks, and continued:

"The other," said he, gravely, "is a king."

"Ah! that is more difficult," said Geneviève; "there are no more of them," she added, forcing a smile.

"You should have seen the last," said Maurice; "it would have been prudent to have done so."

"The result is," said Morand, "I have not the least idea of a crowned head; it must be very sad."

"Very sad, indeed," said Maurice; "I respond to you. I who see one nearly every month."

"A crowned head?" demanded Geneviève.

"At least," said Maurice, "one that has borne the weight and miserable burden of a crown."

"Ah, yes, the queen," said Morand; "truly, Monsieur Maurice, it must be a melancholy sight——"

"Is she as proud and beautiful as they say?" demanded Geneviève.

"Have you never seen her, then, madame?" demanded Maurice, surprised in his turn.

"I? never!" replied the young woman.

"Indeed," said Maurice; "that is strange."

"And why strange?" said Geneviève. "We lived in the province till '91; since '91 we have resided in the Old Rue St. Jacques, which much resembles the province, only there they have neither light nor air, and, still less, flowers. You are acquainted with my life, Monsieur Maurice? It has always been the same. How do you suppose I could have seen the queen when I have had no opportunity whatever of so doing?"

"And I do not think you will avail yourself of that which, unfortunately, perhaps, may present itself," said Maurice.

"What do you mean to say?" demanded Geneviève.

"The Citizen Maurice," replied Morand, "alludes to one thing no longer a secret."

"To what?" demanded Geneviève.

"To the probable condemnation of Marie Antoinette, and to her death upon the same scaffold where her husband died. The citizen said, in short, that you would not avail yourself of the opportunity offered you of seeing her the day when she will quit the Temple for La Place de la Revolution."

"Oh, certainly not!" cried Geneviève, as Morand pronounced these words with the greatest *sang froid*.

"Then you can only lament," said the impassible chemist; "for the Austrian is well guarded, and the Republic a fairy that renders invisible what seems best to her."

"I acknowledge, however," said Geneviève, "I have been very much wishing to see this poor woman."

"Let us see," said Maurice, anxious to gratify all the wishes of Geneviève; "have you really such an inclination? Then only say the word. I agree with the Citizen Morand, the Republic is a fairy; but I, in the quality of municipal, am somewhat of a wizard."

"Could you allow me a sight of the queen—you, monsieur?" cried Geneviève.

"Certainly I can."

"And how?" exclaimed Morand, exchanging a rapid glance with Geneviève, which escaped the notice of the young man.

"Nothing more simple," said Maurice. "There are certainly some municipals of whom they are mistrustful; but as for me, I have given sufficient evidence of my devotion to the cause of liberty to render me above all suspicion. Besides, admittance to the Temple depends conjointly on the municipals and the chiefs of the post. Now, the chief of the post is, just at this moment, my friend Louis, who appears to me to be called indubitably to replace General Santerre, seeing that, in three months, he has risen from the rank of corporal to that of adjutant-major. Well, come to me the day I shall be on guard; that is to say, next Thursday, at the Temple."

"Well," said Morand, "I hope now your wishes may be gratified. Take care that you find him."

"Oh! no, no," said Geneviève, "indeed, I cannot."

"And wherefore not?" said Maurice, who only anticipated in this visit to the Temple an opportunity of seeing

Geneviève on a day when he could enjoy this happiness alone, without the presence of others.

"Because it might, perhaps, dear Maurice, expose you to some unpleasant dispute; and if anything were to happen to you through gratifying a whim of mine, I should never, while I lived, forgive myself."

"You have spoken wisely, Geneviève," said Morand. "Suspicion is very great, the best patriots are now even suspected. Renounce this project, which, as you say, is, after all, a mere caprice of curiosity."

"They will say that you are envious, Morand, and that, not having yourself seen either king or queen, you do not wish others to do so. Come, to end all discussion, join the party."

"Me? *Ma foi!* no."

"It is, then, no longer the Citoyenne Dixmer who wishes to visit the Temple; it is I who entreat you to come there, to divert a poor prisoner. For the great door, once closed upon me, I remain for twenty-four hours as much a prisoner as the king would be, or a prince of the blood." And pressing between his own the foot of Geneviève, "Come, then," said he, "I entreat you."

"*Voyons*, Morand," said Geneviève, "come with me."

"It will be losing a day," said Morand, "and will prevent my going where I ought on business."

"Then I shall not go," said Geneviève.

"But why?" demanded Morand.

"Because I cannot depend upon my husband to escort me; and if you will not accompany me—you, a respectable man, thirty-eight years of age—I have not the hardihood to encounter alone all the chasseurs, cannoniers, and grenadiers, requesting to speak to one of the municipals only three or four years older than myself."

"Then," said Morand, "since you deem my presence indispensable, citoyenne——"

"*Allons, allons!* learned citizen, be as gallant as if you were a kind-hearted, ordinary man, and sacrifice half a day to the wife of your friend," said Maurice.

"Well, let it be so," said Morand.

"Now," said Maurice, "I only require one thing from you, that is discretion. Any one visiting the Temple is considered a suspicious proceeding, and, consequently, should any accident occur afterward, we should all be guillotined. The Jacobins do not jest. *Peste!* you see how they have treated the Girondins."

"*Diable!*" said Morand, "this observation of the Citizen Maurice requires consideration. It would be a sort of retiring from business if I could not go out at all."

"Have you not heard," said Geneviève, smiling, "that the Citizen Maurice said all ?"

"*Eh, bien,* all ?"

"All."

"Yes, without doubt," said Morand, "your company is very agreeable, but I much prefer, *belle sentimentale,* to live in your society than to die in it."

"What the devil was I thinking of ?" said Maurice to himself, "when I imagined this man loved Geneviève ?"

"Then it is all settled," said Geneviève. "I address myself to you, Morand, thoughtful, absent man that you are; remember it is on Thursday next ; so do not on the Wednesday evening commence some chemical experiment that will occupy your time and attention for the next twenty-four hours, as it very frequently happens."

"You may be perfectly easy on that point," said Morand. "Besides, you can remind me."

Geneviève then rose from the table, and Maurice followed her example. Morand was about to leave also, and perhaps to follow them, when one of the workmen brought the chemist a small vial containing some liquid, which instantly engrossed all his attention.

"Let us make haste," said Maurice, drawing away Geneviève.

"Oh ! be assured," said she, " he will remain there for an hour at the very least."

And the young woman allowed him to take her hand, which he tenderly pressed between his own. She felt remorse for her treachery, and compensated for it by her kindness.

"Do you see," said she to Maurice, crossing the garden, and showing him the carnations, which had been removed into the air, with the hope of reviving them, "do you see my flowers are all dead?"

"What killed them?" said Maurice; "your neglect? Poor carnations!"

"It was not my neglect, but your desertion, *mon ami*."

"They required, my little Geneviève, some water; that was all; besides, my absence should have left you plenty of time."

"Ah!" said Geneviève, "but if the flowers were watered with tears, the poor carnations, as you call them, would they not, then, die?"

Maurice threw his arms round Geneviève, and, drawing her to him, before she had time to prevent him, pressed his lips upon the half-smiling, half-languishing eye now fixed upon the drooping, dying flowers. Geneviève felt so much self-reproach, it made her lenient to others.

Dixmer returned home late, and on his return found Morand, Maurice, and Geneviève botanizing in the garden.

CHAPTER XX.

THE FLOWER-GIRL.

At length the anticipated Thursday, the day of Maurice's guard, arrived. It was now the month of June. The sky was of a deep and cloudless blue, and against this sheet of blue rose the heavy white mass of nine houses. The coming of that dreadful day was already foreseen, represented by the ancients as thirsting with an unquenchable thirst, and which, to borrow the phraseology of the plebeian Parisians, licked the pavement very dry. Paris was clean as a carpet, and perfumes filled the air, mounting to the trees, emanating from the flowers circulating and intoxicating with joy, as if to render the inhabitants of the capital forgetful for a few moments of that vapor of blood which rose without intermission from the pavement of these places.

It was Maurice's duty to enter the temple at nine o'clock; his two colleagues were Meruvault and Agricola. At eight o'clock he was in the Rue Vieille St. Jacques, in a grand costume as citizen municipal; that is to say, in tricolored scarf tightly fastened round his tall and elegant frame. He, as usual, rode there on horseback, and on his route had an opportunity of receiving the sincere approbation, admiration, and eulogiums of the worthy patriots who saw him pass. Geneviève was already prepared; she wore a simple muslin dress, a species of light taffeta mantle, and a small bonnet, ornamented with a tricolored cockade. Thus attired, she appeared of dazzling beauty. Morand, who, as we have seen, had been earnestly solicited to accompany them, had, no doubt for fear of being mistaken for an aristocrat, attired himself in his usual costume—half bourgeois, half artisan. He entered alone, and his countenance betrayed great fatigue; he pretended to have been at work all night, in order to complete some urgent business.

Dixmer had gone out immediately after the return of his friend Morand.

"Well," demanded Geneviève, "what have you decided on, Maurice, and how are we to see the queen?"

"Listen," said Maurice, "I have arranged everything. I shall arrive at the Temple with you, and then introduce you to my friend Louis, who commands the guard; I then take my post, and at a favorable moment I will come to seek you."

"But," demanded Morand, "when are we to see the prisoners, and how are we to see them?"

"At either their breakfast or their dinner, if that will suit you, through the glazed partition of the municipal."

"Perfectly," said Morand.

Maurice then saw Morand approach a sideboard at the further end of the *salle-a-manger*, and drink hastily a glass of pure wine, which rather surprised him, Morand being usually very abstemious, and indulging only in wine and water.

Geneviève saw that he regarded him with astonishment.

"Can you not fancy," said she, "he must be half dead with fatigue; he has taken nothing since yesterday morning."

"Did he not dine here?" asked Maurice.

"No; he was trying some experiments in the city."

Geneviève took a useless precaution, with respect to Maurice, since, lover-like, he was an egotist, and had merely bestowed upon the action of Morand that superficial attention which an amorous man might accord to any one, except the woman he loves. To his glass of wine Morand added a crust of bread, which he hastily swallowed.

"And now," said he, "dear Citizen Maurice, I am quite ready; when you choose we will depart."

Maurice, who was stripping the decayed petals from one of the dead carnations he had plucked in passing, now offered his arm to Geneviève, saying:

"Let us set out."

They went, in short, Maurice so happy he could scarcely contain himself; he would have uttered cries of joy had he not restrained his emotion. What could he desire more? Not only had he acquired the certainty that she did not love Morand, but also the hope that he possessed her affection. The glorious sun shone upon the world, the arm of Geneviève was reposing within his own, while the public criers, shouting at the top of their voices the triumph of the Jacobins and the defeat of Brissot and his companions, announced that the country was saved.

There are truly moments of life when the heart of man seems too small to contain the joy or grief concentered there.

"Oh! what a lovely day!" exclaimed Morand.

Maurice turned round in surprise. This was the first burst of feeling he had ever heard issue from the lips of this singularly reserved and absent man.

"Oh, yes, it is indeed lovely," said Geneviève, pressing

closer the arm of Maurice, "if it would only continue till evening, pure and cloudless as it is now!"

Maurice applied this word, and his happiness redoubled each moment. Morand at the same time regarded Geneviève through his green spectacles with a peculiar expression. Perhaps he also applied her expressions. They thus crossed Le Petit Pont, La Rue de la Janerie, and the bridge of Notre Dame; they then proceeded to La Place de l'Hôtel de Ville, La Rue Bur du Bec, and La Rue St. Avoye. As they progressed, Maurice's step became more and more elastic, while, on the contrary, those of his male and female companions waxed slower and slower. They had reached the corner of La Rue des Vieilles Audriettes, when all at once a flower-girl impeded their passage by offering them her basket filled with flowers.

"Oh! what magnificent carnations!" cried Maurice.

"Oh, yes, very beautiful!" said Geneviève; "it seems the cultivator of these had no other preoccupation, for they are not withered and dead."

This speech sunk deep into the heart of the young man.

"Ah! my brave municipal," said the flower-girl, "purchase a bouquet for the pretty citoyenne. She is dressed in white; look at these superb crimson carnations; white and purple look well together; she will place the bouquet upon her heart, and as her heart is near to your blue coat, there you have the national colors."

The flower-girl was young and pretty; her compliment was well turned and well chosen, for had it been made expressly for that occasion, it could not better have applied to the circumstances. Besides, the flowers were almost symbolical; they were similiar to those now dead.

"I will purchase one," said Maurice, "since they are carnations; all other flowers I detest."

"Ah, Maurice," said Geneviève, "it is useless; we have so many of them in the garden."

But although her lips uttered the refusal, her eyes expressed a longing desire to possess them.

Maurice selected the most beautiful of the bouquets. It was the one the pretty flower-girl had presented to him. It consisted of twenty deep-red carnations, emitting an odor at once sweet and pungent; in the center, towering above the rest, rose a magnificent carnation.

"Here," said Maurice, to the *marchande*, throwing on her basket an assignat of five livres, "that is for you."

"Thanks, my brave municipal," said the flower-girl, "a thousand thanks."

And she went toward another couple, trusting the day commenced thus auspiciously would continue to its close. During this apparently simple scene, which had only occupied a few seconds at most, Morand seemed scarcely able to support himself, and wiped the perspiration from his pallid brow, while Geneviève also turned pale and trembled.

She received the nosegay which Maurice presented to her, and clasping it in her lovely hand, held it to her face, less to inhale the odor than to conceal her emotion. The remainder of the journey was pleasant, at least as far as concerned Maurice. As for Geneviève, his gaiety was a constraint upon her, and Morand passed his day in a fashion peculiar to himself, that is to say, in smothered sighs or startling bursts of laughter, and occasionally uttering some formidable witticism, which fell upon the passers-by like sparks of fire.

At nine o'clock they reached the Temple.

Santerre called over the municipals.

"I am here," said Maurice, leaving Geneviève under the care of Morand.

"Welcome," said Santerre, holding out his hand to the young man.

Maurice took care not to refuse the hand thus offered to him. The friendship of Santerre was certainly most valuable at this epoch. At sight of this man who had commanded the famous rolling of drums, Geneviève shuddered, and Morand turned pale.

"Who is this handsome citoyenne?" demanded Santerre of Maurice, "and what does she do here?"

"She is the wife of the brave Citizen Dixmer; you have heard this excellent patriot spoken of, Citizen General?"

"Yes, yes," replied Santerre, "the chief of a tannery, captain of chasseurs of the Legion Victor."

"The same."

"*Bon, bon! Ma foi!* she is pretty. And this ugly fellow, who has given her his arm?"

"That is the Citizen Morand, her husband's partner, and chasseur in Dixmer's company."

Santerre approached Geneviève.

"*Bon jour*, citoyenne," said he.

Geneviève made an effort.

"*Bon jour*, Citizen General," replied she, smiling.

Santerre felt flattered by both title and smile.

"And what brings you here, *belle patriote?*" continued Santerre.

"The citoyenne," replied Maurice, "has never seen the Widow Capet, and she wishes to see her."

"Yes," said Santerre, "before——" and he made an atrocious gesture.

"Precisely," replied Maurice, coldly.

"Very well," said Santerre, "only mind they are not seen entering the keep; it would be a bad example; besides, I confide all to you."

Santerre again shook hands with Maurice, made an inclination of his head to Geneviève in a friendly and protecting manner, and quitted them to attend to his other various engagements.

After a great many evolutions of gendarmes and chasseurs, after some maneuvering with cannon, the dull resounding of which it was considered carried to the environs a salutary lesson or admonition, Maurice took Geneviève's arm, and followed closely by Morand, advanced toward the post, at the door of which Louis was vociferating loudly, commanding the maneuvers of his battalion.

"*Bon!*" cried he, "why, there is Maurice. *Peste!* with a female, too, who appears to me rather agreeable.

Does the stupid fellow wish to compare her with my Goddess Reason ? If it were so, poor Arthemise!"

"Well, Citizen Adjutant," said the captain.

"Ah! that's right; attention," said Louis. "Files to the left—left! *Bon jour*, Maurice ; not so quickly——"

The guns rolled, the company dispersed to their respective places, and when each was at his post, Louis hastened away to exchange compliments with his friend. Maurice presented Louis to Geneviève and Morand. Then an explanation commenced as to the purport of their visit.

"Yes, I understand," said Louis, "you wish your friends to enter the keep; that is easily managed. I will go directly and station the sentinels, then I will order them to admit you and your friends."

In ten minutes afterward Geneviève and Morand entered the suite of the three municipals, and placed themselves behind the glazed partition.

CHAPTER XXI.

THE CRIMSON CARNATIONS.

THE queen rose alone. Having been indisposed for two or three days, she had remained in bed longer than usual, but having heard from her sister that the sun was rising magnificently, she made an effort to quit her couch, and that she might be enabled to breathe the pure air with her daughter, had requested permission to walk on the platform, which had been granted her without the slightest difficulty. She had also been induced to act thus from another cause. Once, and it is true, once only, from the height of the tower she had seen the dauphin playing in the garden. But at the first signal of recognition between the mother and child, Simon interfered, and compelled the boy to retire immediately. Never mind, she had seen him, that was a great source of happiness to her. True, the poor little prisoner was very pale and much changed. Then he was dressed as a child of the people, in a blouse and large trousers. But his beautiful, fair, waving curls were still left him, forming around him a glory which God, no doubt, intended to guard the infant martyr to heaven. If she could only see him once again, oh! what a cordial to the heart of the unhappy mother! There was yet another motive.

"My sister," Mme. Elizabeth had said to her, "you know we found in the corridor a straw standing upright in an angle of the wall. In the language of our signs this desires us to pay attention to everything around us, and to warn us of the approach of a friend."

"That is true," replied the queen, who, regarding her sister and child with pity, had even herself encouraged them not to despair of their ultimate safety. The duties of the service accomplished, Maurice was then higher in authority in the keep of the Temple, since chance had elected him as a guard during the day, and the other municipals, Agricola and Meruvault, as guards during the night. These municipals had left, after laying the procès-verbal before the Council of the Temple.

"*Eh, bien*, Citizen Municipal," said the woman Tison, coming forward to salute Maurice, "you bring company, then, to see our caged pigeons? It is only I who am condemned no more to see my poor Héloise."

"They are friends of mine," said Maurice, "who have never yet seen the female Capet."

"Ah, well, they will see admirably behind the partition."

"Assuredly," said Morand.

"Only," said Geneviève, "we shall present the appearance of the cruel impertinents who come from the other side of the iron grate to mock the misery of the unfortunate prisoners."

"*Eh, bien!*" why should not your friends see them on their way to the tower, since the woman will walk there to-day, with her sister and her daughter, for they have left her a daughter, while I, who am not guilty, they have deprived of mine. Oh, these aristocrats! it will always be the case; let them do what they will, favor is always shown to them, Citizen Maurice."

"But they have removed her son," replied he.

"Ah! if I had a son," murmured the jaileress, "I should lament my daughter less."

Geneviève, during this time, had exchanged looks with Morand several times.

"*Mon ami,*" said the young woman to Maurice, "the citoyenne is in the right. If you could by any means place me in the way of Marie Antoinette, it would be less repugnant to my feelings than gazing at her here. It seems to me this manner of viewing people is at once humiliating both to them and us."

"Kind Geneviève," said Maurice, "you possess true delicacy of mind."

"*Pardieu!* citoyenne," said one of Maurice's colleagues, who was at that moment breakfasting in the ante-chamber on bread and sausages, "if you were the prisoner, and Capet's wife felt curiosity to see you, she would not be so very particular about the indulgence of her fancy—the jade."

Geneviève, with a movement quicker than lightning, threw a rapid glance toward Morand to note the effect of these words upon him. In effect, Morand started, a strange, phosporescent light gleamed from under his eyelids, and his hands were clinched for an instant, but all this was so momentary that it passed unperceived.

"What is the name of this municipal?" asked she of Maurice.

"It is the Citizen Meruvault," replied the young man; and then added, as if to apologize for his coarseness, "a stone-cutter."

Meruvault heard it, and in his turn stared at Maurice.

"*Allons, allons!*" said the woman Tison; "finish your sausage and your half bottle, that I may take it away."

"It is not the fault of the Austrian if I finish them now," grumbled the municipal; "for if she could have murdered me on the 10th of August, she would have done so; thus the day when she 'sneezes in the sack,' I shall be in the first rank, firm at my post."

Morand turned pale as death.

"*Allons*, Citizen Maurice," said Geneviève, "let us go where you promised to take us; here it seems as if I were a prisoner; I feel suffocated."

Maurice conducted Geneviève and Morand out, when the sentinels, previously instructed by Louis, allowed them to pass without any difficulty. They installed themselves in a little passage on the upper story, so that the moment when the queen, Mme. Royale, or Mme. Elizabeth ascended to the gallery, these august personages could not do otherwise than pass before them.

As the promenade was fixed for ten o'clock, and they had only a few minutes to wait, Maurice not only did not quit his friends, but further, in order that the slightest suspicion might not be excited by this rather illegal proceeding, having met Agricola, he took him with him. It struck ten.

"Open!" cried a voice from the base of the tower, which Maurice knew to be that of General Santerre. Immediately the guard assumed arms, and closed the iron gratings; the sentinels also prepared arms. There was then heard in all the court a confused noise of iron, stones, and footsteps, which vividly impressed both Morand and Geneviève, for Maurice observed them both turn pale.

"And all these precautions to guard three poor women," murmured Geneviève.

"Yes," said Morand, endeavoring to smile; "if those who tempt them to escape were now here, and in our place saw what we see it would disgust them with the trade."

"In fact," continued Geneviève, "I begin to think they will not save themselves."

"And I to hope," said Maurice, inclining toward the staircase as he spoke.

"Attention!" cried he; "here are the prisoners."

"Name them to me," said Geneviève, "for I do not know either of them."

"The two first who are ascending are the sister and

daughter of Capet. The last one, preceded by a little dog, is Marie Antoinette."

Geneviève made a step in advance. Morand, on the contrary, instead of looking at them, pressed himself close against the wall, his lips more livid and earthy than the stones of the keep.

Geneviève, with her white robe and bright, pure eyes, appeared like an angel awaiting the prisoners, to cheer them on their dark and dreary road, and to administer in passing a ray of comfort to their desolate and blighted hearts. Mme. Elizabeth and Mme. Royale pursued their way, having only thrown a glance of astonishment at the strangers. No doubt the former imagined they were those whom the signals announced, for, turning round quickly to Mme. Royale, she pressed her hand, and, while so doing, dropped her pocket-handkerchief, as if to inform the queen.

"Pay attention, my sister," said she ; " I have dropped my pocket-handkerchief."

And she passed on with the young princess.

The queen, with panting breath, accompanied with a short, dry cough, indicating ill health, stooped to pick up the handkerchief which had fallen at her feet, when her little dog, more agile than its mistress, seized it, and ran forward to convey it to Mme. Elizabeth. The queen continued her ascent slowly, and after some steps found herself in her turn before Geneviève, Morand, and the young municipal.

"Flowers !" cried she, "Oh ! how long is it since I have seen any flowers ! How deliciously they smell ! You are happy to possess these flowers, madame."

Quick as the idea formed in her mind, prompted by these melancholy words, Geneviève extended her hand to offer her bouquet to the queen.

Then Marie Antoinette raised her head, looked at her, and an almost imperceptible blush passed over her colorless face.

But by a natural movement, from a habitual passive obedience to regulation, Maurice put out his hand to arrest the arm of Geneviève. The queen then remained hesitating, when, looking at Maurice, she recognized him as the young municipal who had always spoken to her with so much firmness, but at the same time tempered with equal respect.

"Is this forbidden, monsieur?" said she.

"No, no, madame. Geneviève, you can offer your bouquet," said Maurice.

"Oh! thanks, thanks, monsieur," said the queen, with grateful acknowledgments; and bowing with gracious affability to Geneviève, the queen extended her emaciated hand, and selected at hazard a single carnation from the mass of flowers.

"Take all, madame, take all," timidly said Geneviève.

"No," said the queen, with a fascinating smile; "this bouquet may come perhaps from one you love. I will not deprive you of it."

Geneviève blushed, and at this blush the queen smiled.

"*Allons, allons!* Citoyenne Capet," said Agricola, "you must continue your route."

The queen bowed, and ascended the steps, but before she disappeared, turned round and murmured:

"The carnations smell very sweet, and she is very lovely."

"She has not seen me," murmured Morand, who, almost kneeling in the shade, had effectively escaped the notice of the queen.

"But you had a good view of her, had you not, Morand? had not you, Geneviève?" said Maurice, doubly happy, first from the sight he had procured his friends, and also that he had afforded ever so slight a gratification to the unhappy prisoner.

"Oh, yes, yes!" said Geneviève; "and were I to live for a thousand years, I should never forget her."

"And what do you think of her?"

"She is charming."

"And you, Morand?"

Morand clasped his hands, but made no reply.

"Tell me," said Maurice, in a whisper, to Geneviève; "is it the queen whom Morand worships?"

Geneviève started, but recovering herself instantly, replied, smilingly:

"It really looks like it."

"You have not yet told me what you think of her, Morand," persisted Maurice.

"I thought her very pale," replied he.

Maurice retook the arm of Geneviève to descend toward the court. In the dark staircase it seemed to him that Geneviéve kissed his hand.

"What does that mean, Geneviève?"

"It means, Maurice, that I shall never forget that to gratify a whim of mine you have risked your life."

"Oh!" said Maurice, "what exaggeration of danger, Geneviève. Between you and me, you well know that gratitude is not the sentiment I wish to inspire you with."

Geneviève pressed his arm softly.

Morand followed with faltering steps.

On quitting the court, Louis came to identify the two visitors, who then left the Temple; but before quitting it, Geneviève made Maurice promise to dine the next day in the Old Rue St. Jacques.

CHAPTER XXII.

SIMON THE CENSOR.

WHEN Maurice returned to his post, in a state of transcendent happiness, he found Tison's wife weeping.

"What have they done to you now, mother?" asked Maurice.

"All this makes me furious!" replied the jaileress.

"What?"

"Because there is nothing but injustice for poor people in this world."

"But how?"

"You are rich, you are a bourgeois, you come here only

for a day, and they permit pretty women to visit you here, who present bouquets to the prisoners, while I who nestle everlastingly in this dove-cot am not allowed to see my poor Sophie."

Maurice took her hand and slipped into it an assignat of ten livres.

"There, good woman, take that, and do not despair. *Mon Dieu!* the Austrian will not last forever."

"Ten livres!" said the jaileress; "that is kind of you, but I would rather have even a papilotte that had curled my poor girl's hair."

As she finished these words, Simon, who was then coming up, heard them, and saw the jaileress place in her pocket the money Maurice had given her. We will mention what sort of a temper Simon was in. As he entered the court he encountered Louis. Now, a decided antipathy existed between these two men. This hatred was less induced by the violent scenes with which our readers are already familiar, than by the difference of race, an everlasting source of detestation, which however mysterious it may at first appear, is easily explained. Simon was hideous, Louis handsome; Simon was low, Louis the very opposite; Simon was a Republican bully, Louis one of those ardent patriots who had sacrificed everything to the Revolution; and then, if they must come to blows, Simon instinctively felt that the fist of the fop lost none of its elegance when Maurice had decreed him to a plebeian punishment.

Simon, on perceiving Louis, stopped short, and turned pale.

"It is still this battalion that mounts guard," growled he.

"Well," said a grenadier, who overheard this apostrophe, "one is as good as another, it seems to me."

Simon drew a pencil from his pocket, and pretended to note down something on a piece of paper almost as black as his own hands.

"Ah!" said Louis, "you know how to write, then, Simon, since you are tutor to young Capet? Look, citizens, upon my honor, he takes notes; it is Simon the Censor."

A universal shout of laughter proceeded from the ranks of the young National Guards, almost all men of education, at the ridiculous title bestowed upon the wretched cobbler.

"Very well, very well," said he, grinding his teeth, and coloring with rage; "they say you have permitted strangers to enter the keep, and that without the consent of the Commune. Very well, I am going to draw out the procès-verbal for the municipal."

"At least, he knows how to write that," said Louis; "it is Maurice, you know, brave Simon—Maurice with the Iron Hand, you remember that."

At this moment Morand and Geneviève went out. At this sight, Simon rushed into the keep, at the very moment, as we have said, when Maurice, by way of consoling her, presented the woman Tison with the assignat for ten livres. Maurice paid no attention to the presence of this miserable wretch, whom by a natural instinct he always avoided if he by any chance encountered him, regarding him in the light of a disgusting and venomous reptile.

"Ah, well!" said Simon to Tison's wife, "so you wish to bring yourself to be guillotined, citoyenne?"

"I!" said the woman, who had just dried her eyes with her apron; "and why is that?"

"Why? because you receive money from the municipal for allowing aristocrats entrance to the Austrian."

"I!" said the woman Tison. "Be silent; you are mad!"

"This shall be consigned to the procès-verbal," said Simon, emphatically.

"Well, then, they are friends of the Municipal Maurice, one of the best patriots that ever existed."

"Conspirators, I tell you; besides, the Commune shall be informed; it will judge for itself."

"*Allons*, you mean to denounce me, then, spy of the police?"

"Exactly so, if you do not denounce yourself."

"Denounce what? What do you wish me to denounce?"

"All that has happened."

"But nothing has happened."

"Where were these aristocrats?"

"There, upon the staircase."

"Has Capet's wife ascended the stairs?"

"Yes."

"And they spoke to her?"

"They exchanged two words."

"Two words! and what perfume of this aristocrat's do I smell here?"

"It is the scent of the carnations."

"Carnations! what carnations?"

"Why, the citoyenne had a bunch of them, which perfumed the whole place."

"What citoyenne?"

"The one who saw the queen pass."

"You see plainly—and tell the queen so—that conversing with these aristocrats will be your ruin. But what is this I am treading upon?" continued Simon, stooping down.

"Ah!" said the woman Tison, "it is a flower, a carnation; it must have fallen from the hand of the Citoyenne Dixmer, when Marie Antoinette took one from her bouquet."

"The woman Capet took a flower from the Citoyenne Dixmer's bouquet?" said Simon.

"Yes, and it was given her by me," said Maurice, in a loud and menacing tone, who had been for some moments listening to this colloquy till his patience was nearly exhausted.

"It is all very well, it is all very well; one sees what one does see, and one knows what one says," growled Simon, who still held in his hand the carnation crushed by his huge foot.

"And I also know one thing," replied Maurice, "which I am now going to tell you; it is that you have nothing whatever to do in this keep, and that your honorable post of tormentor is down there with the little Capet, whom I would, for your own sake, recommend you not to chastise to-day, as I am here to defend him."

"Do you threaten me? do you call me tormentor?" cried Simon, crushing the flower in his hand. "Ah! we shall see if it is permitted in these aristocrats— Why, what can this be?"

"What?" asked Maurice.

"That I feel in this carnation! Ah, ah!"

The eyes of Maurice were transfixed with astonishment, as Simon drew from the calyx of the flower a small paper, rolled with the most exquisite care, which had been artistically introduced into the center of the clustering leaves.

"Oh, *mon Dieu!*" said Maurice, "what can this mean?"

"We will know, we will know!" said Simon, approaching the window. "Ah! you and your friend Louis told me I did not know how to read. "Well, you shall see."

Louis had calumniated Simon; he had learned both to read and write. But the billet was so minute that Simon was obliged to have recourse to his spectacles. He consequently placed it on the window, while he proceeded to take an inventory of the contents of his pockets; but while thus engaged, the Citizen Agricola opened the door of the ante-chamber exactly facing the little window, thereby causing a current of air, which blew away the little paper, light as a feather from a bird's wing, so that when Simon, after a momentary exploration, had discovered his spectacles, placed them on his nose, and turned himself round, his search was useless—the paper had disappeared.

"There was a paper here!" screamed Simon, crimson with rage; "there was a paper here. Look to yourself, Citizen Municipal, for it must and shall be found."

And he descended precipitately, leaving Maurice in a state of stupefaction. Ten minutes afterward three members of the Commune entered the keep. The queen was still upon the platform, and strict orders had been issued that she should remain in total ignorance of all that had just occurred. The members of the Commune desired to be conducted to her presence. The first object which met their view was the crimson carnation, which she still retained in her hand. They regarded her with surprise, and approaching her:

"Give us this flower," said the president of the deputation.

The queen, who had not previously noticed this interruption, started and hesitated.

"Surrender your flower, madame," said Maurice, in terror, "I entreat you."

The queen tendered them the carnation. The president took it and retired, followed by his colleagues, into a neighboring apartment, to make an examination, and draw up the procès-verbal. They opened the flower—it was empty. Maurice breathed afresh.

"Wait a moment," said one of the members, " the heart of the carnation has been removed. The socket is empty, it is true, but in this, socket most unquestionably, a letter has been introduced."

"I am quite ready and willing," said Maurice, "to furnish all necessary explanation; "but, first of all, I request that I may be arrested."

"It would not be right to avail ourselves of your proposition," said the president. " You are known as a stanch patriot, Citizen Lindey."

"And I will answer with my life for the friends I had the imprudence to bring with me."

"Answer for no one," replied the procurator.

A great conversation was now heard in the court. It was Simon, who, having long and vainly sought for the little billet wafted away by the wind, now went to inform Santerre that an attempt had been made to carry off the queen, with all the accessories which the charms of his excited imagination could lend to such an event. Santerre was in great haste—he investigated the Temple and changed the guard, to the great disgust of Louis, who strongly protested against this offense to his battalion.

"Ah! vile cobbler," said he to Simon, menacing him with his saber, "I have you to thank for this; but only wait a little, I will have my revenge, and pay you in your own coin."

"I think rather that the nation will pay you," said the shoemaker, rubbing his hands.

"Citizen Maurice," said Santerre, "hold yourself in readiness for the command of the Commune, who will examine you."

"I await your orders, commandant; but I have already told you I desire to be arrested, and I again repeat my former request."

"Wait, wait," murmured Simon, sullenly; "since you feel so sure, we will soon settle that business for you." And he went to find the woman Tison.

CHAPTER XXIII.

THE GODDESS REASON.

THEY searched during the whole day in the court, in the garden and its environs, for the little billet which had caused all this tumult, and which they no longer doubted contained the whole plot. They interrogated the queen, after having first separated her from her daughter and sister, but elicited nothing more from her, than having, on the staircase, encountered a young woman carrying a bouquet, she had drawn a single flower from the center.

"Had she not plucked this flower with the consent of the Municipal Maurice?"

She had nothing more to tell. This was the truth in all its force and simplicity. This was all reported to Maurice, and he in his turn declared the deposition of the queen to be quite correct.

"But," said the president, "there was still a plot."

"Impossible," said Maurice; "I was dining at Madame Dixmer's and proposed that she should see the prisoners, hearing her remark she had never done so; but neither the day nor the manner of so doing was arranged."

"But the flowers were purchased," said the president; "the bouquet had been made beforehand."

"Not at all; I myself purchased these flowers from a flower-girl, who offered them to us at the corner of La Rue des Vieilles Audriettes."

"But at least, this flower-girl presented the bouquet to you?"

"No, citizen; I selected it myself from ten or twelve others. Certainly, I purchased the most beautiful."

"But was there a possibility of secreting this billet on your road to the tower?"

"Impossible, citizen. I never quitted Madame Dixmer's side for a moment, and to perform the operation named on each flower—for remark that every flower, according to Simon's account, contained a like billet—would, at least, occupy half a day or more."

"But, in short, could not two prepared billets have been placed in the flowers?"

"It was in my presence the prisoner took one at hazard, after having declined the rest."

"Then, in your opinion, Citizen Lindey, there was not a plot at all."

"If it were a plot," replied Maurice, "and I am the first not only to believe but to affirm it, my friends were not concerned in it. However, as the nation must necessarily experience alarm, I offer security by constituting myself prisoner."

"Not at all," said Santerre; "this act alone is sufficient proof. If you constitute yourself prisoner to answer for your friends, I constitute myself prisoner to answer for you. The thing is simple enough. There is no positive denunciation. Is it not so? No one will know what has passed. Inspect every occurrence more strictly, redouble your own vigilance especially, and we shall arrive at the bottom of this thing by avoiding publicity."

"Thanks, commandant," said Maurice; "but I reply to you as you would answer were you in my place. We ought not to stop here; it is necessary that the flower-girl should be discovered."

"The flower-girl is far away, but be perfectly easy on that point; she will be sought after. As for you, watch your friends, while I guard the prison correspondence."

No one had thought of Simon, but he had formed his own project. He arrived toward the conclusion of the sitting, and learned the decision of the Commune.

"Ah! then it only requires a regular denunciation," said he, " to settle this affair. Wait five minutes, and I will bring it to you."

"Who is it?" said the president.

"It is," said Simon, "the courageous Citoyenne Tison who denounces the secret practises of that partisan of aristocracy, Maurice, and the intrigues of another equally false patriot, one of his friends, named Louis."

"Take care, take care, Simon; your zeal for the nation perhaps misleads you. Maurice and Louis are tried and proved patriots."

"That will be seen at the tribunal," replied Simon.

"Consider well, Simon; this will be a disgraceful proceeding for all true patriots."

"Disgraceful or not, what difference will that make to me? Do I dread disgrace? They shall, at least, learn all the truth concerning those who wish to betray them."

"Then you persist in a denunciation in the name of the woman Tison?"

"I will denounce myself, even this very night, to the Cordeliers, and you among the rest, Citizen President, if you are still unwilling to command the arrest of the traitor Maurice."

"Well, let it be so," said the president, who, according to custom in these miserable times, trembled before those who clamored the loudest, "they shall be arrested."

While this decision was forming against him, Maurice had returned to the Temple, where the following billet awaited him:

"Our guard being violently broken up, I shall not be able, in all probability, to see you before to-morrow morning. Come, then, and breakfast with me; during that meal you shall give me a true and particular account of the plots and conspiracies discovered by Simon.

"Yours, faithfully, LOUIS."

Maurice replied:

"There is nothing new, so sleep in peace to-night and breakfast without me to-morrow, as on reviewing the incidents of the day, I find I shall not, in all probability, be able to leave till noon.

"Yours, faithfully, MAURICE.

"P.S.—As to the rest, I believe the conspiracy was only a false alarm, after all."

Louis had, indeed, left at one o'clock, with the whole of his battalion, thanks to the brutal conduct of the shoemaker; he, however, consoled himself with a quatrain, and went to visit Arthemise. Arthemise was delighted to see Louis. The weather, as we have said, was magnificent; she therefore proposed a walk along the quay, to which Louis, of course, assented. They had walked some distance, discoursing on politics, Louis recounting his expulsion from the Temple, and vainly endeavoring to divine the cause, when, on reaching the height of La Rue des Barres, they perceived a flower-girl, who, like themselves, remounted the bank to the right of the Seine.

"Ah! Citizen Louis," said Arthemise, "I hope you are going to present me with a bouquet?"

"Two, if you wish it," said Louis; and they both redoubled their speed to overtake the flower-girl, who walked at a rapid pace. On arriving at the bridge Marie, the young girl, stopped, and stooping under the parapet, emptied the contents of her basket into the river. The flowers separated, whirled round for an instant in the air, while the bouquets, dragged down by their own weight, fell more quickly, till at last both flowers and bouquets floated upon the surface, following the course of the water.

"Stop!" said Arthemise, regarding the flower-girl thus strangely occupied; "it is said—but yes—but no—but if —ah! this is strange!"

The flower-girl placed her finger on her lips, as if to entreat her silence, and disappeared.

"Who is this, then?" said Louis. "Do you know this mortal goddess?"

"No; I fancied at first—but certainly I am deceived."

"She, however, made a sign to you," persisted Louis.

"But why is she a flower-girl this morning?" said Arthemise to herself.

"You acknowledge, then, that you know her, Arthemise?" said Louis.

"Yes," replied Arthemise; "she is a flower-girl I sometimes deal with."

"At all events," said Louis, "she has a strange method of disposing of her merchandise."

And both, after having looked for the last time at the flowers which, already arrived at the wooden bridge, had received a fresh impetus from the arm of the river which passed under its arches, continued their route toward the Rapée, where they anticipated dining *tête-à-tête*. This incident was forgotten for the moment, but as it was at least singular, and of rather a mysterious character, it vividly impressed Louis' poetical imagination. In the meantime, the denuciation brought by Tison's wife against Maurice and Louis caused a great tumult at the club of the Jacobins; and Maurice was informed at the Temple by the Commune that his safety was endangered by the public indignation. This was a recommendation to the young municipal to conceal himself if he were guilty; but with conscious rectitude Maurice remained at the Temple, where he was found at his post when they came to arrest him. At the same time, Maurice was interrogated. Remaining firm in his resolution not to endanger the safety of his friends, in whom he felt the most implicit confidence, Maurice yet was not the man to sacrifice himself by a ridiculous silence worthy of a hero of romance, and therefore demanded the flower-girl should be tried. It was five o'clock in the afternoon when Louis returned home and heard, at the same moment, of the arrest of Maurice, and also the demand made by him. The flower-girl of the bridge Marie instantly recurred to his mind like a sudden revelation. This singular individual casting her flowers into the Seine; the coincidence of quarters; the half admission of Arthemise; all these facts combined instinctively convinced him this was the solution of the mystery demanded by Maurice. He bounded from his chamber, flew rather than ran down four flights of stairs, and precipitated himself into the presence of the Goddess Reason, who was engaged in embroidering golden stars on a robe of azure blue, It was her robe of divinity.

"A truce to the stars, *chère amie*," said Louis; "they have arrested Maurice, and in all human probability before evening I shall share the same fate."

"Maurice arrested!"

"*Mon Dieu!* yes. In these times nothing is more common than the recurrence of these events; but they excite little attention, because they come in troops, that is all. Almost all great events originate in trifles. Never neglect trifles. Who was that flower-girl we met this morning, *chère amie?*"

Arthemise started.

"What flower-girl?"

"The one who so recklessly cast her flowers into the Seine."

"Ah! *mon Dieu!*" said Arthemise, "is this circumstance, then, so serious that you return to urge me on that point?"

"So serious, *chère amie*, that I entreat you to answer my question without loss of time."

"*Mon ami*, I cannot do so."

"Goddess, with you nothing is impossible."

"I am in honor bound to keep silence."

"And I am bound in honor to make you speak."

"But why do you insist upon it thus?"

THE CHEVALIER DE MAISON ROUGE. 187

"Why? *Corbleu!* that Maurice may not have his throat cut."

"*Mon Dieu!* Maurice guillotined?" cried the young woman, much alarmed.

"Unless you speak; indeed, unless you dare to reply while my head still remains upon my shoulders."

"Ah! No, no," said Arthemise; "it would be utter ruin."

At this moment Louis' official rushed into the apartment.

"Ah, citizen!" cried he, "save yourself! save yourself!"

"And why?" demanded Louis.

"Because the gendarmes have arrived, and while they were forcing an entrance, I gained the next house by the roof, and hastened to prevent your return."

Arthemise uttered a heartrending cry, for she truly loved Louis.

"Arthemise," said Louis, "do you really place the life of a flower-girl in comparison with that of Maurice and of your lover? If it is so, I declare to you that I no longer regard you as the Goddess Reason, but shall proclaim you the Goddess Folly."

"Poor Héloise!" exclaimed the ex-danseuse of the Opera; "if I betray you, it is not my fault."

"Well, well, *chère amie*," said Louis, presenting a paper to Arthemise, "you have already favored me with her Christian name; oblige me now with her surname and address."

"Oh! write it, never, never!" cried Arthemise; "I would rather tell you."

"Tell me, then, and rest assured I will not forget."

And Arthemise, in an agitated voice, gave the name and address of the false flower-girl to Louis. "She is called Héloise Tison, and lives in the Rue des Nonandières, No. 24."

At this name, Louis uttered an exclamation, and fled. He had not reached the corner of the street, when a letter was delivered to Arthemise. It only contained three lines.

"Not a word concerning me, dear friend; the revelation of my name would infallibly ruin me. Wait till to-morrow. I quit Paris this night. Thine,

"HÈLOISE."

"Oh, *mon Dieu!*" cried the future goddess, "if I could only have divined this, I would have waited till to-morrow;" and she glanced from the window to recall Louis, if there was yet time, but he had disappeared.

CHAPTER XXIV.

THE MOTHER AND DAUGHTER.

WE have already said that in a few hours the news of this event had circulated through Paris. In short, there were at this epoch various indiscretions easy to comprehend on the part of a government of which the political schemes were concocted and unraveled in the street. This rumor gradually gained ground, till it at length reached the Old Rue St. Jacques, and two hours after the arrest of Maurice they heard of his detention. Thanks to the activity of Simon, the details of the plot were quickly reported beyond the Temple; but, as of course every one added to the original, the news arrived in an unintelligible form at the master tanner's. One said a poisoned flower had been conveyed to the queen, by means of which the Austrian would stupefy her guards, and thus be enabled to escape from the Temple; others said the report originated from certain suspicions entertained of the fidelity of the battalion dismissed by Santerre on the preceding evening. Already more victims were designated for the hatred of the people.

But the inhabitants of the Old Rue St. Jacques were not, of course, deceived as to the real nature of this event, and Morand on one side, Dixmer on the other, went out immediately, leaving Geneviève a victim to the most violent despair. If this misfortune had befallen

Maurice, it was she who had been the sole cause of it. It was her hand that conducted this young man blindfold to the entrance of the dungeon which now inclosed him, and which, in all human probability, he would quit only for the scaffold. But, under any circumstances, Maurice should not lose his head on account of his devotion to her wishes. If Maurice were condemned, she would accuse herself before the tribunal, and would then confess all. She would take all the responsibility upon herself, to feel assured that, at the expense of her life, she might save Maurice. And Geneviève, instead of feeling any fear of death, experienced, on the contrary, almost a degree of happiness at the idea of dying for Maurice.

On quitting the house, Dixmer and Morand separated, the former took the road to La Rue de la Corderie, the latter hastened to La Rue des Nonandières. Arriving at the end of the bridge Marie, Morand perceived a crowd of idlers and common people, at that time stationed at Paris, had congregated at the scene of the late event, as crows assemble on the field of battle. At this sight Morand stopped short, a universal tremor shook his frame, and he leaned for support against the parapet. At length, after a few seconds, he regained the almost miraculous power which, under trying circumstances, he exercised over his feelings, and mingling with the various groups, commenced his inquiries, and learned that a short time before they had taken from La Rue des Nonandières, 24, a young woman, most certainly guilty of the crime of which she stood then accused, as they surprised her while occupied in forming these packets. Morand inquired before what club the poor girl would be interrogated, and found they had conducted her to the Section Mère, where he immediately followed her.

The club was thronged, but by making free use of his elbows and fists, he succeeded in forcing an entrance. The first sight he encountered was the tall and noble figure of Maurice, standing haughtily before the bench of the accused, and annihilating Simon by his looks.

"Yes, citizens," cried Simon, "the Citoyenne Tison

accuses the Citizen Lindey and the Citizen Louis. The Citizen Lindey mentions a flower-girl, upon whom he endeavors to cast all the blame ; but, as I told you before, the flower-girl will not return, or be found again, and that is a vile plot formed by a body of aristocrats, who toss back the ball from one to the other, like cowards, as they are. You have seen, besides, that the Citizen Louis had decamped when his presence was required, and he will return no more than the flower-girl."

"Then you have lied, Simon," cried a furious voice; " and he will return, for he is here."

And Louis strode into the hall.

"Room for me," said he, pushing aside the spectators. "Room for me."

And he placed himself near Maurice.

The entrance of Louis, so natural, and without affectation, yet combining all the freedom and strength inherent in the character of the young man, produced an immense effect upon the tribunes, who instantly greeted him with cries of applause. Maurice contented himself by smiling and holding out his hand to his friend—the friend concerning whom he had said to himself, " I shall not long stand alone at the bench of the accused."

The spectators gazed with visible interest on these two handsome young men, accused (like a demon envious of their youth and beauty) by the foul shoemaker of the Temple. He soon perceived the unfavorable impression he had made, and determined to strike the last blow.

" Citizens ! " roared he, " I demand that the generous Citoyenne Tison should be heard, that she may speak, and bring forward her accusation."

" Citizens," said Louis, " I demand that the flower-girl, who is about to be arrested, and who no doubt will be brought before you, may be first heard."

"No, no," said Simon ; " it is just some false evidence —some partisan of the aristocrats. Besides, the woman Tison is most impatient to forward the means of justice."

During this time Louis took the opportunity to whisper to Maurice.

"Yes," cried the tribunes; "the deposition of the woman Tison; let her depose."

"Is the woman Tison in the hall?" demanded the president.

"Without doubt she is here," cried Simon. "Citoyenne Tison, answer for yourself."

"I am here, president; but if I depose will they give me back my daughter?" said the jaileress.

"Your daughter has nothing at all to do with the affair with which we are at present engaged," said the president. "Make your deposition first, and then appeal to the Commune to redeem your child."

"Do you hear?" said Simon; "the citizen president commands you to make your deposition. Do it quickly."

"A moment," said the president, turning toward Maurice, astonished at the calmness of a man generally so impetuous. "One moment. Citizen Municipal, have you nothing to say first?"

"No, Citizen President—except that before Simon attached the words 'traitor and coward' to a man like myself it would have been better to have waited till he was more correctly informed on that subject, that is all."

"You say that? you say that?" replied Simon, with the blustering accent peculiar to the plebeian Parisian.

"I say, Simon," replied Maurice, with more sorrow than anger, "that you will experience your punishment when you see who it is will presently be brought here."

"Who will arrive here, then?" demanded Simon.

"Citizen President," said Maurice, without deigning to notice the question of his hideous accuser, "I unite with my friend Louis in demanding that the young girl about to be arrested may be heard before this poor woman is compelled to speak, who, no doubt, has been prompted to this deposition."

"Listen, citoyenne," said Simon; "listen. They say down there that you are a false witness!"

"I a false witness!" cried the woman Tison. "You shall see—you shall see. Wait."

"Citizen," said Maurice, "in pity, desire this woman to remain silent."

"Ah! you are afraid," said Simon; "you are afraid."

"Citizen President, I require the deposition of the woman Tison."

"Yes, yes; the deposition!" cried the tribunes.

"Silence!" cred the president; "the Commune returns."

At this moment the sound of a voiture was heard rolling outside, amid the noise and shouts of arms.

Simon turned uneasily toward the door.

"Quit the box," said the president to him; "you have nothing more to tell."

Simon descended.

At this moment some gendarmes entered, with the tide of curious idlers, which soon. ebbed, and a woman was pushed toward the judgment hall.

"Is it she?" whispered Louis to Maurice.

"Yes, it is," replied Maurice. "Miserable woman, she is utterly ruined and lost."

"The flower-girl! the flower-girl!" murmured the tribunes, whose curiosity was raised to the highest pitch. "Is this the flower-girl?"

"I demand, before everything else," roared Simon, "the deposition of the woman Tison. You commanded her to depose, president, and she has not yet done so."

The woman was recalled, and entered upon a dreadful and circumstantial deposition. The flower-girl, it was true, was alone criminal, but Maurice and Louis were her accomplices. This denunciation produced an incredible effect upon the public mind, and now, indeed, Simon was in the ascendant.

"Gendarmes," said the president, "bring forward the flower-girl."

"Oh! this is frightful," said Maurice, concealing his face in his hands.

The flower-girl was called and placed before the tribune, exactly opposite to Tison's wife, whose testimony had convicted her of a capital crime the moment before. She raised her veil.

"Héloise!" cried the woman Tison; "my child. You here?"

"Yes, *ma mère*," replied the young woman, in a low tone.

"And why do you enter between two gendarmes?"

"Because I am accused, *ma mère*."

"You! accused, and by whom?" cried the startled woman.

"By you, *ma mère*."

A frightful silence, like the precursor of death fell suddenly upon this noisy assemblage, while the miserable feeling excited by this affecting scene weighed down every heart. "Her daughter," was whispered, as if by voices in the distance, "her daughter!" Unhappy woman! Maurice and Louis regarded both the accuser and the accused with sentiments of deep commiseration mingled with respectful pity for their unhappy fate. Simon, anxious to witness the conclusion of this tragedy, in which he hoped both Maurice and Louis would remain actors, endeavored to concentrate the attention of the woman, who gazed wildly around.

"What is your name, citoyenne?" said the president to the young girl, himself affected at the scene.

"Héloise Tison, citizen."

"What is your age?"

"Nineteen years."

"Where do you reside?"

"Rue des Nonandières, 24."

"Did you sell the Citizen Lindey, whom you now see on the bench, a bouquet of carnations this morning?"

The young girl turned round and looked at Maurice.

"Yes, citizen, I did," she said.

The mother herself gazed at her daughter, her eyes dilated with terror.

"Are you aware that every carnation contained a billet addressed to the widow of Capet?"

"I know it," replied the accused.

A movement of horror and admiration spread itself through the hall.

"Why did you offer these carnations to the Citizen Maurice?"

"Because I perceived that he wore the scarf of a municipal, and I imagined he was going to the Temple."

"Who are your accomplices?"

"I have none."

"What! have you, then, concocted this plot alone?"

"If it is a plot, I alone am concerned in it."

"But the Citizen Maurice——"

"Did he know that the flowers contained these billets?"

"Yes."

"The Citizen Maurice is a municipal, the Citizen Maurice could converse with the queen at any hour of the day or the night. The Citizen Maurice, if he wished to say anything to the queen, had no occasion to write, he could speak."

"And you do not know the Citizen Maurice Lindey?"

"I have sometimes seen him come to the Temple, while I was there, with my poor mother, but I only know him by sight."

"Do you see, miserable wretch," said Louis, shaking his finger at Simon, who, dismayed at the turn of affairs, with his head lowered, was attempting to sneak away unperceived, "do you see what you have done?"

Every one regarded Simon with looks of deep indignation.

The president continued:

"Since you made up these bouquets, you, of course, are aware that each one contained a paper, and therefore you must know also what was written upon that paper?"

"Of course I know it."

"Well, then, tell us what it was?"

"Citizen," said the young girl, with firmness, "I have told all I either can or will tell."

"Then you refuse to answer this question?"

"Yes."

"Do you know to what you expose yourself?"

"Yes."

"You trust, perhaps, to your youth and beauty?"

"I trust in God."

"Citizen Maurice Lindey, Citizen Hyacinth Louis," said the president, "you are free. The Commune recognizes your innocence, and admires your loyal spirit. Gendarmes, conduct the Citoyenne Héloise to the prison of the section."

At these words the woman Tison seemed to awake, and uttering a piercing cry, attempted to rush forward once more to embrace her daughter, but was withheld by the guards.

"I forgive you, mother," said the young girl, as they led her away.

The woman Tison rushed forward, uttered a savage roar, and fell down as if dead.

"Noble girl," murmured Morand, filled with emotions too miserable to describe.

CHAPTER XXV.

THE BILLET.

IMMEDIATELY following the events we are about to relate, the last scene of the drama enrolled itself, as a sad finale to this sudden change in the wheel of fortune. The woman Tison, struck as by a thunderbolt at what had occurred, and totally abandoned by those who had escorted her (for there is something even revolting in an involuntary crime, and it certainly amounts to a great crime when a mother condemns her own daughter to an ignominious death, were it even from excess of zealous patriotism), the woman, after remaining for some time in a state of insensibility, at length raised her head, looked wildly around, and finding herself deserted and alone, uttered a loud cry, and rushed toward the door.

At this door a few idlers more curious than the rest still remained congregated together, who dispersed when they beheld her, and pointing with their fingers, said one to another, "Do you see that woman? It is she who denounced her daughter."

The wretched woman uttered a cry of despair and rushed toward the Temple. But on reaching the third house of La Rue Michel de Comte, a man placed himself in front of her, impeding her progress, and concealing his face and figure in his mantle:

"Are you content," said he, "now you have killed your child?"

"Killed my child!" cried the poor woman, "killed my child! No, no, it is not possible!"

"It is so, notwithstanding, for your daughter has been arrested."

"And where have they taken her?"

"To the conciergerie; from there she will be sent to the Revolutionary Tribunal, and you know what becomes of those who are sent there."

"Stand aside," said the woman Tison, "and let me pass."

"Where are you going?"

"To the conciergerie."

"What are you going there for?"

"To see her again."

"They will not allow you to enter."

"They will permit me to lie at the door, to live there, to sleep there. I will remain there till she goes out, and then, at least, I shall see her once more."

"Suppose some one promised to restore you your child?"

"What is that you say?"

"I ask you, supposing a man were to promise to give you back your child, would you do what this man required of you in return?"

"Everything for my child; all for my Héloise!" cried the woman, wringing her hands. "All, all, all!"

"Listen," said the unknown. "It is God who now punishes you."

"And for what?"

"For the tortures you have inflicted so mercilessly on a poor mother as unhappy as yourself."

"Of whom do you speak? What do you mean?"

"You have often driven the unhappy prisoner to the very verge of despair, where you are yourself at this moment, by your revelations and brutalities. God now punishes you for all this by conducting this daughter, whom you loved so much, to the scaffold."

"You said there was some man who could save her; where is this man? what does he want? what will he demand?"

"This man requires that you cease to persecute the queen, that you demand pardon for the outrages already committed against her, and if at any time you perceive that this woman, who is also a weeping, despairing mother, by any unforeseen circumstance, or by some miracle from Heaven, is upon the point of saving herself, instead of opposing her flight, you do all in your power to aid and abet it."

"Listen, citizen," said the woman Tison. "You are the man—is it not so?"

"Well?"

"It is you who promise to save my child?"

The unknown remained silent.

"Will you engage to do it? Will you promise? Will you swear it? Answer me."

"All that a man can do to save a woman I will do to save your daughter."

"He cannot save her," cried the woman, uttering piercing cries, "he cannot save her. When he promised me he lied."

"Do what you can for the queen, and I will do all in my power for your daughter."

"What care I for the queen? She is not my daughter. If they must decapitate some one, it shall not be my daughter, it shall be her. They may cut my throat so that they spare my child's. They may lead me to the guillotine, so that they do not harm a hair of her head, and I will go there singing:

"Ah! ça ira, ça ira, ça ira."

And she commenced singing in a frightful voice, then suddenly stopped short, and burst into a fit of frenzied laughter. The man in the mantle himself appeared alarmed at this burst of folly, and retreated a step or two from her.

"Ah! you shall not escape me thus," said the woman Tison, in despair, and retaining her hold of his mantle; "you shall not at one moment say, 'Do this and I will rescue your child,' and afterward say, 'perhaps.' Will you save her?"

"Yes."

"How?"

"The day she is conducted from the conciergerie to the scaffold."

"But why wait—why not to-night? this evening—this moment, even?"

"Because I cannot do so."

"Ah! you know you cannot; you well I know you cannot!" cried the woman Tison. "But as for me, I can."

"What can you do?"

"I can persecute the prisoner, I can watch the queen, as you term her, aristocrat as you are, and I can enter the prison any hour of the day or night. All this will I do. We will see how much she will escape; we will see. Yes, we shall see, since they will not save my daughter, who ought to do so if they could. Head for head. Do you like that? Marie Antoinette has been queen. Héloise Tison is only a poor girl. I know all this very well; but on the guillotine they are equals—all distinction ceases there."

"Well, it may be so," said the man in the mantle. "But you perform your part, and I will fulfil mine."

"Swear."

"I swear it."

"But what do you swear?"

"Anything you choose."

"Have you a child?"

"No."

"Well, then," said the woman, in a disappointed tone, "by what can you swear?"

"Listen. I swear by God!"

"Bah!" exclaimed the woman Tison, "you know very well they have demolished the ancient and have not yet decided on the new."

"I swear by the tomb of my father!"

"Swear not by a tomb, for that is prophetic of evil. Oh, my God! my God! When I think that perhaps in three days I may swear by the tomb of my child also. My daughter! My poor Héloise!" cried the woman Tison, frantically; till at the sound of her voice, raised to a shrill scream, several windows were opened. At sight of the opened windows, another man, who seemed to detach himself from the wall, advanced toward the first.

"There is nothing can be done with this woman," said he; "she is mad."

"No; she is a mother," replied the former, and dragged his companion away. When she saw them leaving her, the woman Tison again returned to the subject.

"Where are you going?" cried she. "Are you going to rescue Héloise? Wait for me, then—I will go with you. Wait for me; do wait for me."

And the poor wretch followed them, screaming, till at the corner of the nearest street she lost sight of them altogether; and not knowing which way to turn, she remained for an instant undecided, looking on every side, when seeing only in the silence and darkness of the night a double symbol of death, she uttered a cry of horror and fell on the pavement without sense or motion. The clock struck ten. During this time, and while the same hour was resounding from the Temple clock, the queen, as usual, sat in her chamber, between her daughter and her sister. Near her was a lighted lamp, concealed from the sight of the municipal, by Mme. Royale, who pretended to embrace her mother, who was reading over again a small billet written on the smallest piece of paper imaginable, and in characters so minute that her eyes, already nearly blinded by her scalding tears, scarcely retained strength to decipher it. The billet contained the following lines:

"To-morrow, Tuesday, demand permission to walk in the garden; this will be accorded without any difficulty, as an order has been issued to grant you this favor whenever you think proper to solicit it. After two or three turns, feign to feel fatigued, approach the cabin, and ask the widow Plumeau to allow you to sit down. Then, in moment, pretend to feel worse, and faint away. They will then close all the doors, that they may be able to render you assistance, and you will remain with Madame Elizabeth and Madame Royale. Immediately the trap-door of the cellar will open. Precipitate yourself, your sister, and daughter through this aperture, and you are all three saved."

"*Mon Dieu!*" said Mme. Royale, "our evil destiny tires in the pursuit."

"If this billet should prove only a trap," said Mme. Elizabeth.

"No, no," said the queen; "these characters have always indicated to me the presence of a mysterious but equally brave and faithful friend."

"Is it the chevalier?" demanded Mme. Royale.

"He himself," replied the queen.

Mme. Elizabeth clasped her hands.

"Let us each read the billet again very softly," replied the queen, "so that if one of us forget any particulars, the others can supply them."

They all three reread the letter, and had just finished so doing, when they heard the door of their chamber turn slowly on its hinges. The two princesses turned round; the queen alone remained stationary, except by an imperceptible movement, she raised her hand to her hair and hid the billet in her head-dress. It was a municipal who opened the door.

"What is your business, monsieur?" demanded Mme. Elizabeth and Mme. Royale at the same moment.

"Hum!" said the municipal, "it appears to me that you retire very late to-night."

"Is there, then," said the queen, with her usual dignity, "a new decree from the Commune, stating the hour at which I am to go to bed?"

"No, citoyenne," said the municipal; "but, if necessary, they will make one."

"In the meantime, monsieur," said Marie Antoinette, "respect—I do not say the chamber of the queen—but that of a woman."

"Truly," growled the municipal, "these aristocrats always speak as if they were something."

But, in the meantime, subdued by the haughty dignity of her prosperity, but which three years of suffering had calmed down, he withdrew. An instant afterward the lamp was extinguished, and the three females retired in darkness, as usual.

The next morning, at nine o'clock, the queen having reread the letter before she arose, in order that she might not misconstrue any of the instructions contained there, tore it into almost invisible fragments. She then hastily finished her toilet, awoke her sister, and entered the chamber of the princess. A minute afterward she came out and called the municipals on guard.

"What do you want, citoyenne?" said one of them, appearing at the door, while the other did not even discontinue his breakfast to answer the royal appeal.

"Monsieur," said Marie Antoinette, "I have just left my daughter's chamber, and found her very ill. Her limbs are swollen for want of exercise; and you know, monsieur, it is I who have doomed her to this life of inaction. I received permission to walk in the garden; but, in descending, I must necessarily pass before the door of the room occupied by my husband in his lifetime. When I made the attempt, my heart failed me, and I had not courage to do so, and have since limited my walks to the platform. Now, however, I find this exercise insufficient for my poor child. I therefore, entreat you, Citizen Municipal, in my name, to claim to General Santerre the renewal of this privilege."

The queen had pronounced these words in a manner at once so mild, yet dignified, had so strenuously avoided all allusions to anything that could wound the feelings of the Republican, that he who had entered her presence with his head covered, as for the most part was the custom of these men, gradually raised the bonnet-rouge, and said, when she had finished, bowing respectfully to her:

"Rest assured, madame, your petition shall be laid before the citizen general." Then, on retiring, as if to convince himself he had yielded to justice rather than weakness: "It is just," said he; "after all, it is only right."

"What is just?" demanded the other municipal.

"That this woman should be permitted to walk in the garden with her child, who is an invalid."

"Bah!" said the other; "when she asks to be allowed to walk from the Temple to La Place de la Revolution, that will be permitted her fast enough."

The queen heard these words, and turned very pale, but still drew from them fresh courage for the great attempt she meditated. The municipal finished his breakfast, and descended. The queen requested she might take hers in her daughter's room, which was granted. Mme. Royale, to confirm the statement concerning her ill health, did not quit her bed; the queen and Mme. Elizabeth remained near her.

At one o'clock, as usual, Santerre arrived. His coming was announced by the drums beating the march, and by the entrance of a fresh battalion, and other municipals, who came in their turn to relieve those on guard. When Santerre had fully reviewed the battalion leaving, and the one about to take its place, and had paraded his large, heavy-limbed horse round the court of the Temple, he stood still for a moment. This was for the purpose of receiving any claims, denunciations, or requests. The municipal, availing himself of this halt, approached him.

"Well, what do you want?" said Santerre, brusquely.

"Citizen," said the municipal, "I come to entreat on the part of the queen——"

"Who is the queen?" interrupted Santerre.

"True!" said the municipal, astonished at his own mistake. "What have I said? I must be mad. I came to speak on the part of Madame Veto."

"All in good time," said Santerre. "Now I understand you; what have you to say to me?"

"The young Veto is ill, it appears, from want of proper air and exercise."

"Well, is it necessary again to bring this before the public? The nation granted her permission to walk in the garden, and she refused it. *Bon soir.*"

"That is exactly it. She regrets this now, and requests you will permit her to do so."

"There is no difficulty about that. You all hear," said Santerre, "that Capet's wife will come down to walk in the garden. Now," addressing the whole battalion, "take care she does not abuse this favor granted her by the nation, by making her escape over the walls; for if that happens I will cut off every one of your heads." A roar of laughter followed this pleasantry of the citizen general. "Now that is settled," said Santerre, "adieu. I am going to the Convention. It appears they are about to reunite Roland and Barbaroux, and the question is to deliver their passport to another world." It was this intelligence that had put the citizen general in such good humor. He then galloped away. The battalion just quitted guard followed him, then the municipals also gave place to those who had received Santerre's instructions respecting the queen. One of the municipals who went up to Marie Antoinette perceived, while thanking him, that her daughter turned from red to pale, while the sister seemed engaged in thanks to God.

"Ah!" thought she, looking through the window toward heaven, "your soul reposes there, seigneur; but will your terrible doom be allowed to fall heavily on us?"

"Thanks, monsieur," said she, with that fascinating

smile which had proved the ruin of Bernane, and turned the heads of so many of his fellow-men, "thanks!"

Then, turning round to her little dog, who leaped after her, walking on his hind-legs, for he well understood, from the looks of his mistress, that something unusual was about to take place:

"Come, Jet," said she, "we are going for a walk."

The little animal began to frisk and jump, and after looking at the municipal attentively, comprehending, no doubt, that from this man originated the intelligence which had made his mistress so happy, ran toward him, and wagging his long and silky tail, ventured even to caress him. This man, who perhaps might be insensible to the prayers of a queen, could not resist the caresses of a little dog.

"If only on account of this little beast, you should go out more frequently, Citoyenne Capet. Humanity commands us to take care of every creature."

"At what hour shall we go out, monsieur?" demanded the queen. "Do you not think the sun would do us good?"

"You can go out when you please," said the municipal; "there has been no restriction on the subject. If you like to go out at midday, as that is the time they change the sentinels, there will be less bustle in the court."

"Then let it be at midday," said the queen, pressing her hand to her side to still the beating of her heart. And she regarded this man, who appeared to her less stern than his associates, and who, perhaps, for kindly yielding to the wishes of a prisoner, might fall a sacrifice to the conspiracy which they meditated. But at the moment when compassion was stealing over the heart of the woman, the mind of the queen was aroused. She thought of the corpses of her faithful friends strewed upon the floor of the palace on the 10th of August; she recalled to memory the 2d of September, and the head of the Princess Lamballe, carried on a pike before her windows; she remembered the 21st of January, when her husband died upon the scaffold, the noise of the drums extinguishing his feeble voice; then again she thought of her son, whose cries of distress had more than once reached her ears, and her heart became hardened. "Alas!" cried she, "misfortne is like the blood of the ancient Hydras—it is is teemful of crops of future evils!"

CHAPTER XXVI.

THE LITTLE DOG JET.

THE municipal left to call his colleagues, and to read the procès-verbal left by the former municipals. The queen remained alone with her sister and child. They all three regarded one another. Then Mme. Royale threw her arms round the queen, and warmly embraced her. Mme. Elizabeth approached her sister, and held out her hand.

"Let us offer up our prayers to God," said the queen, "but in a manner that no one hears us."

It was one of those fatal epochs when prayer, that natural hymn of praise which God has implanted in every human heart, became suspicious in the eyes of these men, since prayer is an act of praise and acknowledgment for mercies received. But in the ideas of these guardians hope and gratitude afforded subject for inquietude, since the queen could only hope for flight, and could thank God only for affording her the means of effecting it. This mental prayer concluded, all three remained without uttering a word.

Twelve o'clock struck, then three quarters, then one. But the moment when the last stroke resounded from the bronze timbrel, the noise of arms was heard on the spiral staircase ascending to the queen.

"They are relieving sentinels," said she; "they come to seek us."

She saw her sister and daughter turn very pale.

"Courage!" said she, trembling herself with emotion.

"It is one o'clock," said a firm voice below. "Let the prisoners descend."

"We are here, gentlemen," replied the queen, who, with a sentiment almost of regret, embraced at a glance the black walls and the rude appurtenances which had been more or less the companions of her captivity.

The first wicket opened, they gained the corridor, which, being dark, enabled the three captives to conceal their emotions. Before them frolicked little Jet; but when they arrived at the second—that is to say, the door from which Marie Antoinette endeavored to turn her eyes—the faithful little animal first placed his nose to the ground, then laid his head upon his paws, and gave utterance to a succession of plaintive cries, which terminated in a prolonged howl. The queen passed on quickly, not having strength sufficient to recall her dog, and supported herself against the wall; then, essaying to advance again a few steps, her limbs refused their office, and she felt herself compelled to stop. Her sister and daughter approached her, and for a few moments the three females remained motionless, forming a melancholy group, the mother resting her face upon the head of her daughter, when little Jet rejoined them.

"Well!" cried the voice, "do you or do you not mean to come down?"

"We are coming," said the municipal, who had remained standing, respecting this grief in all its simplicity.

"Let us go now," said the queen, as she prepared to descend.

When the prisoners had reached the bottom of the staircase, opposite the door, under which the sun shed his rays of bright gold, the rolling of the drum was heard summoning the guard; then a profound silence, the effect of curiosity, ensued, and the massive door opened, revolving slowly upon its creaking hinges. A woman was seated on the ground, or, rather, on the corner of the stone contiguous to this door. It was the woman Tison, whom the queen had not seen for four-and-twenty hours, and whose absence at supper the preceding evening, and at their morning's meal, had excited her surprise. The queen already saw the light, the trees, the garden, and beyond the barrier which enclosed the garden her eyes eagerly sought the little hut of the canteen, where her friends so impatiently awaited her coming; when, at the sound of footsteps, the woman removed her hands, and the queen beheld a pale and care-worn face beneath the mass of gray, disheveled locks. The change wrought in these few hours was so great that the queen stood overwhelmed with astonishment. Then, with the deliberation peculiar to those deficient in reason, she knelt down before the door, impeding the passage of Marie Antoinette.

"What do you want, my good woman?" demanded the queen.

"He said it was necessary that you should pardon me."

"Who said so?" demanded the queen.

"The man in the mantle," replied the woman Tison.

The queen looked at Mme. Elizabeth and her daughter, surprised at this appeal.

"Go along, go," said the municipal; "let the Widow Capet pass; she has permission to walk in the garden."

"I know it," said the old woman; "that is why I came to wait for her here, since they will not allow me to go up; and I ought to ask her forgiveness. I was obliged to wait for her coming out to see her."

"But why, then, are you not permitted to go up?" demanded the queen.

The woman began to laugh.

"Because they pretend that I am mad," said she.

The queen looked at her, and saw indeed that the wild eyes of the unhappy being reflected a strange light—that vague expression denoting all absence of intellect.

"Oh, *mon Dieu!*" said she. "Poor woman, what has happened?"

"Happened? Do you not know?" said the woman; "but if——You know very well, since it was on your account she was condemned."

"Who?"

"Héloise."

"Your daughter?"

"Yes, she—my poor child."

"Condemned by whom? How? Why?"

"Because she sold a bouquet."

"What bouquet?"

"A bouquet of carnations. She is not a flower-girl," continued the old woman, as if endeavoring to collect her thoughts, "then how could she sell this bouquet?"

The queen shuddered; she felt an invisible link connected this scene with her present situation, and convinced her the time must not be lost in useless conversation.

"My good woman," said she, "allow me to pass, I entreat you; you can tell me all this by and by."

"No, now; you must pardon me, and I must assist you to escape, that he may save my daughter."

The queen turned pale as death.

"*Mon Dieu!*" murmured she, raising her eyes to heaven, then, turning toward the municipal. "Monsieur," said she, "have the kindness to remove this woman; you see that she is mad."

"Go, go, mother," said the municipal; "decamp."

But the woman clung to the wall, still reiterating, "She must pardon me, that he may save my daughter."

"But who is he?"

"The man in the mantle."

"Sister," said Mme. Elizabeth, "try to console her."

"Oh, willingly," said the queen; "I believe, indeed, that will be the shortest way;" then, turning toward the mad woman, "What do you desire, good woman?" said she.

"I wish you to pardon me all the suffering I have caused you by my unjust behavior—all the denunciations I have made; and trust that when you see the man in the mantle you will command him to save my daughter; for he will do all that you desire."

"I do not know whom you mean by the man in the mantle," said the queen; "but that is not the question. If it is necessary to your peace of mind to obtain my pardon for all the offenses you imagine you have committed against me, I freely forgive you, my poor woman, from the depths of my heart, and trust only that any one I may have offended will as sincerely pardon me."

"Oh!" cried the woman Tison, with an indescribable accent of joy, "he will save my child, since you have forgiven me. Your hand, madame, your hand——"

The queen, astonished, and at a loss to comprehend the meaning, presented her hand to the woman, who seized it, and ardently pressed her lips upon it. At this moment the hoarse voice of a hawker was heard in the Temple resounding from the street.

"This," cried he, "is the judgment and decree condemning Héloise Tison to the penalty of death for the crime of conspiracy."

Scarcely had these words reached the ears of the woman Tison, than rising from her knees, with an air of dogged resolution, she extended her arms to impede the passage of the queen.

"Oh, *mon Dieu!*" cried the queen, who had not lost one word of this sentence, so dreadful to her ears.

"Condemned to death!" cried the mother. "My child condemned! my Héloise lost! He has not, then, saved her—and now he cannot save her. Too late—too late!"

"Poor woman!" said the queen, "believe me, I feel for you."

"You!" said she, looking at her fiercely with her bloodshot eyes. "You pity me? Never—never!"

"You are mistaken. I pity you from my heart; but do pray allow me to pass."

The woman burst into a hoarse laugh.

"Let you pass? No, no. I would have assisted you to escape, because he promised, if I did so, he would rescue my daughter; but since she is condemned to death, you shall not alone be saved."

"Messieurs," cried the queen, "come to my aid. Do you not see that this woman is quite mad?"

"No, I am not mad; I know well what I am saying!" cried the woman. "It is the truth—there was a conspiracy, and Simon discovered all. It was my poor daughter who sold the bouquet. She confessed it before the Revolutionary Tribunal. A bouquet of carnations; they had some papers concealed in them."

"Madame," said the queen, "in the name of Heaven!"

The voice of the crier was again heard repeating:

"This is the judgment and decree condemning the girl Héloise Tison to the punishment of death for the crime of conspiracy."

"Do you hear it?" screamed the lunatic, to the groups of National Guards scattered around, "do you hear? Condemned to death; it is you who have killed my daughter—you, Austrian, you!"

"Messieurs," said the queen, "if you will not release me from this mad woman, allow me, at least, to return to my apartments. I can not support the reproaches of this woman, unjust as they are; it crushes my heart;" and she turned away, sighing deeply.

"Yes, yes—weep, hypocrite!" cried the maddened wretch; "your bouquet will cost you dear. She must have suspected you. Thus it is you doom all those to death who serve you. You carry misery, Austrian, everywhere! Your friends are dead—your husband and your defenders have all perished—and now they will sacrifice my unhappy child! When will your turn come, that no more may die for you?" And the miserable creature accompanied these last words with threatening gestures. The queen hid her face between her hands.

"Unhappy woman!" observed Mme. Elizabeth, venturing to speak, "are you aware that she whom you address is the queen?"

"The queen!" repeated the maniac, whose madness every moment increased, "if she is the queen, let her defend my poor girl against the hangman who seeks her life. Who will show mercy to my poor Héloise? Kings can show mercy. Render me back my child, and I will acknowledge her as queen. Till then, she is only a woman, and a woman who brings misery upon all, and kills all——"

"Oh! have pity, madame," cried Marie Antoinette; "you see my tears and distress;" and she again made an attempt to pass, not from any hope of escape, but to free herself from this cruel attack.

"You shall not pass!" roared the old woman. "You want to escape, Madame Veto—I know it all; the man in the mantle told me you want to go and rejoin the Prussians. But you shall not escape," continued she, clasping the robe of the queen. "I will prevent you. *A la lanterne,* Madame Veto! To arms, citizens! let us march——"

And with her arms wrestling, her grizzled locks disheveled, and hanging over her haggard countenance—her bloodshot eyes—the unfortunate creature fell to the ground, in her fall tearing the robe she still held in her hand. The queen, terrified, but disembarrassed at least of the maniac, was flying to the side of the garden, when all at once a terrible cry resounded, mingled with loud barking, and accompanied with a strange uproar, arousing the National Guards from their stupor, who, attracted by the scene, immediately surrounded Marie Antoinette.

"To arms! to arms! Treason!" shouted a man, whom, from his voice, the queen recognized as the shoemaker Simon. Near this man, who, sword in hand, guarded the threshold of the cabin, little Jet was barking furiously.

"To arms! every one to his post!" cried Simon; "we are betrayed! Compel the Austrian to turn back. To arms! to arms!"

An officer ran forward, when Simon spoke to him, pointing with enraged gestures to the interior of the hut. The officer in his turn then cried:

"To arms!"

"Jet! Jet!" called the queen, advancing some steps.

But the dog only continued to bark more furiously.

The National Guard ran to arms, and rushed toward the hut, while the municipals took possession of the queen, her daughter, and sister, and compelled them to reenter the wicket, which they closed behind them.

"Prepare your arms!" cried the municipals to the sentinels. And the sound of firearms was heard.

"It is there! it is there!" cried Simon, "under the trap. I saw it shut again. I am certain of it. Besides, the Austrian's dog, a good little animal, who was not in the plot, barked at the conspirators, who are no doubt still in the cave. Hold! he barks again."

Indeed, Jet, instigated by Simon's cries and shouts, began to bark again more strenuously than before. The officer seized the ring of the trap, but seeing he was unable to raise it, two of the grenadiers went to his assistance, but without the slightest success.

"You perceive they hold the trap-door from below. Fire through the trap-door, my friends, fire!" said Simon.

"Oh!" cried Mme. Plumeau, "you will break my bottles."

"Fire!" repeated Simon, "fire!"

"Be silent, brawler!" said the officer, "and bring some hatchets, and begin to open the planks. Now, let a few men hold themselves in readiness, and fire into the trap-door the instant an opening is made."

The groaning of planks and a sudden jerk informed the National Guards that some movement was taking place in the interior. Directly afterward they heard a motion underground, like an iron portcullis being closed.

"Courage!" said the officer to the sappers, who worked indefatigably. The hatchets entered the planks. Twenty guns were lowered in the direction of the opening, which enlarged every moment. But through the aperture no one could be seen. The officer lighted a torch and threw it into the cave. It was empty. They then raised the trap-door, which now offered no resistance. "Follow me!" said the officer, bravely descending the ladder.

"*En avant, en avant!*" cried the National Guards, following the example of their officer.

"Ah! Madame Plumeau," said Simon, "you lent your cellar to the aristocrats!"

The wall was broken down, the humid soil was trampled by numerous feet, and a conduit of three feet wide and five feet high, like the branch of a trench, plunged in the direction of La Rue de la Corderie. The officer ventured into this opening, resolved to follow these aristocrats into the bowels of the earth; but when he had advanced three or four steps, he found all further progress impeded by an iron grating.

"Stop!" said he to those who were closely pressing behind him; "we can proceed no longer; here is a physical impediment."

"Well," said the municipal, who, having placed the prisoners in security, anxiously awaited the news; "well, well, what have you discovered?"

"*Parbleu!*" said the officer, reappearing, "it was doubtless a conspiracy; the aristocrats wanted to carry off the queen, and, of course, she connived with them."

"*Peste!*" cried the municipal, "send some one after Citizen Santerre, that he may inform the Commune."

"Soldiers," said the officer, "remain in this cellar, and if any one presents himself, kill him."

And the officer, having issued his orders, remounted to make his report.

"Ah, ah!" said Simon, rubbing his hands—"ah, ah! will they still say I am a fool? Brave Jet! Jet is a famous patriot; Jet has saved the Republic. Come here, Jet, come." And the brute who had coaxed the poor little dog, the moment he approached him, raised his foot and kicked him to a distance of several feet. "I like you, Jet," said he. "Ah! you will cut your mistress's throat. Come here, Jet, come."

But instead this time of obeying him, Jet ran away, howling, on the road toward the keep.

CHAPTER XXVII.

THE MUSCADIN.

It was near two o'clock. Louis was promenading up and down in Maurice's room, while Agesilas polished his master's boots in the ante-chamber, only for the greater convenience of conversation the door remained open, and during his walk Louis stopped, and often addressed a few questions to the official.

"And you say, Citizen Agesilas, that your master left home this morning?"

"Oh, *mon Dieu!* yes."

"At the usual hour?"

"It might be ten minutes earlier, or ten minutes later, I cannot say exactly."

"And you have not seen him since?"

"No, citizen."

Louis continued his walk, and after three or four turns again stopped, and renewed his questions.

"Had he his sword with him?" demanded he.

"When he goes to the section, he invariably carries it."

"Are you sure he has gone to the section?"

"At least, he told me so."

"In that case, I shall join him," said Louis, "and if we miss each other, tell him I have been here, and left to rejoin him."

"Wait," said Agesilas.

"Why?"

"I hear his footstep on the staircase."

Almost at the same moment the door opened, and Maurice entered. Louis bestowed a hasty glance upon him, and perceived nothing extraordinary in his appearance.

"So you are come at last," said he. "I have been waiting here these two hours."

"So much the better," said Maurice, smiling, "that

has afforded you plenty of time to compose distichs and quatrains."

"Alas! *mon ami*, I have made none."

"Why, is the world coming to an end?"

"My dear Maurice, I am very unhappy."

"You unhappy?"

"Yes, I am miserable. I am suffering from remorse."

"Remorse?"

"Eh, *mon Dieu!* yes," said Louis. "Between you and her there was no alternative—between you and her I would not hesitate; but, you see, Arthemise is in despair, for she was her friend."

"Poor girl!"

"And it was she who gave me her address."

"You had much better have allowed things to take their natural course."

"Yes; and at this very moment you would have been condemned in her stead."

"Powerfully argued, dear friend. But I, who come to ask your advice, think you are too wise for that."

"Never mind; ask away."

"This poor girl—do you understand? I wish to attempt some means of saving her. Even if I could only give or receive a blow in her defense, I feel as if it would do me good."

"You are mad, Louis," said Maurice, shrugging his shoulders.

"If I made an appeal to the Revolutinary Tribunal?"

"It is too late, she is condemned."

"Truly," said Louis, "it is dreadful to see this poor girl sacrificed thus."

"The more so since it was my safety that has entailed her death. But, after all, Louis, we have one consolation. She was a conspirator."

"*Mon Dieu!*" said Louis, "does not every one conspire nowadays? She has done no more, poor girl, than every one else does."

"Neither complain too much nor too loudly, my friend," said Maurice, "for we have to bear our share in this trouble. Believe me, we are not so fully cleared from the accusation of being her accomplices that no stain remains behind. To-day, at the section, I was termed 'Girondin' by the captain of the Chasseurs of St. Leu ; and I, at the same time, found it necessary to convince him, by a blow from my sword, that he was mistaken."

"Then that was the reason you returned so late ?"

"Just so."

"But why did you not inform me ?"

"Because in affairs of this nature one cannot restrain one's self, and it is necessary to conclude them immediately, that they may make no noise."

"And this *canaille* called you 'Girondin,' Maurice ?"

"Eh, *mon Dieu!* yes; and this will convince you that another adventure of this nature, and we become unpopular; and you well know, Louis, in these times unpopular is a symbolical term for suspect."

"I well know it," said Louis; "and that word appalls the bravest heart; but never mind. It is repugnant to my feelings to allow this poor girl to die without soliciting her pardon, this poor Héloise to be led to the guillotine without asking her forgiveness."

"What do you wish to do ?"

"I wish you to remain here; you have nothing to reproach yourself with. With me, you see, the case is very different. Since I can do nothing for her, I will meet her on her way. I wish to go there, Maurice ; do you comprehend me ? She might even only give me her hand."

"I will accompany you, then," said Maurice.

"Impossible, my friend ; you are a municipal secretary to a section, and you have been tried, while I have only been your defender; they will think you guilty, therefore remain here. As for me, it is quite another thing. I risk nothing, and therefore may go."

"Go, then," said he; "but be prudent."

Louis smiled, shook Maurice's hand, and went out. Maurice opened his window, and looked a sad adieu; but before Louis had turned the corner of the street, he looked back more than once, and each time, as if drawn by magnetic influence and sympathy, Louis turned round, looked at him, and smiled. At last, when he disappeared at the corner of the quay, Maurice closed the window, threw himself into a fauteuil, and fell into one of those dreamy moods which in people of strong mind and vigorous constitution often are the presentiments of misfortune, as they resemble the calm generally precursor of the storm. He was softly awakened from his reverie, or, rather, state of stupor, by his official, who, on returning from the execution of some commission, entered with the sprightly air of a servant anxious to communicate his budget of news. Seeing his master preoccupied, he dared not interrupt him, and therefore contented himself by constantly passing and repassing before him, without any reasonable cause for so doing.

"What is it?" at length said Maurice; "speak, if you have anything to tell me."

"Ah, citizen, another desperate conspiracy!"

Maurice merely shrugged his shoulders.

"A conspiracy enough to make the hair of one's head stand upright," continued Agesilas.

"Indeed!" replied Maurice, like a man accustomed to hear daily of thirty conspiracies at this epoch.

"Yes, citizen," replied Agesilas; "it drives me to frenzy, you see. Nothing else is thought of; it makes one's flesh creep."

"Let us hear this conspiracy," said Maurice.

"The Austrian has failed in her attempt to escape."

"Nonsense," said Maurice, beginning to listen with the greatest avidity.

"It seems," continued Agesilas, "that the Widow Capet was in communication with the girl Tison, who is to be guillotined to-day. She has not escaped, unfortunate creature!"

"How had the queen communication with this girl?" demanded Maurice, who felt the perspiration exuding at every pore.

"Through a carnation. Can you imagine, citizen, how they could have conveyed the plan to her in a carnation?"

"In a carnation ! Who did this ?"

"Monsieur le Chevalier de—wait, then. He bears a fine title ; but as for me, I forget all these names. A Chevalier de Château—what a fool I am ! it is not a Château—a Chevalier de Maison."

"De Maison Rouge ?"

"That is it."

"Impossible !"

"How impossible ? When I told you they have found the trapdoor, the subterranean passage, and coaches."

"On the contrary, you have told me nothing about all this."

"Well, I am going to tell you, then."

"Go on, then. If it is a story, it is, at least, a good one."

"No, citizen ; it is not a story, and, in proof of that, I had it from a citizen porter. The aristocrats had dug a mine, and this mine commenced at La Rue de la Corderie, and terminated in the cellar of the little cabin belonging to Madame Plumeau, who has narrowly escaped being arrested as an accomplice. This widow Plumeau—you see it all now, I hope ?"

"Yes," replied Maurice ; "but afterward ?"

"Capet's wife was to escape, by the subterranean passage. She already had her foot on the first step, when Simon caught her by her robe. They beat to arms in the city, and the recall in the sections. Do you not hear the drum ? There ! It is said that the Prussians are at Dumartin, and have reconnoitered as far as the frontiers."

In the midst of this flow of words, a mixture of truth and falsehood, probability and impossibility, Maurice seized the winding thread. All sprung from the carnation presented before his eyes to the queen, and purchased by himself from the poor, miserable flower-girl. This carnation contained the plan of the plot, the whole of which now burst upon him, connected as it was with the events, more or less true, detailed by Agesilas. At this moment the noise of the drum was heard still, and Maurice listened to the crier in the street.

"Tremendous conspiracy discovered at the Temple by the Citizen Simon. Grand conspiracy in favor of the Widow Capet, discovered at the Temple."

"Yes, yes," said Maurice; "it is just as I thought. There is some truth in all this. And Louis, in the midst of this popular excitation, goes to offer himself to this girl, and makes himself a suspect."

Maurice took up his hat, clasped his sword-belt, and with two bounds was in the street.

"Where can he be?" said Maurice to himself. "Probably on the road to the conciergerie."

And he rushed toward the quay.

At the extreme end of the Quai de la Megisserie, some pikes and bayonets, standing in the midst of the crowd, attracted his attention, and he fancied in the center he could distinguish the costume of a National Guard, and in the group signs of hostile movements. He ran, his heart oppressed with the dread of impending misfortune, toward the assemblage on the banks of the river. The National Guard pressed by the company of Marseillais was Louis. He was very pale, his lips compressed, his eyes menacing, his hand upon the handle of his sword, measuring the place best calculated to strike the blows he fully intended to inflict on his cowardly assailants. Within two feet from Louis stood Simon. He was laughing ferociously, and pointing him out to the Marseillais and the populace, saying:

"Look at him! look well at him! He is one of those that I drove from the Temple yesterday for an aristocrat. He is one of those who favored the correspondence with the carnations. This is an accomplice of the girl Tison, who will pass here presently. Well, do you see? he walks quietly on the quay while his coadjutor goes to the guillotine; and, perhaps, she was even more to him than an assistant. She might be his mistress, and he is here to bid her farewell, or to try and save her!"

Louis was not the man to endure much more. He drew his sword from its scabbard. At the same time, the crowd opened to admit a man, who rushed headlong into the group, whose broad shoulders had already knocked down two or three spectators who were preparing to become actors in this scene.

"Be happy, Simon," said Maurice. "You regretted, no doubt, that I was not with my friend to enable you to turn your new title of denunciator to full account. Denounce, Simon, denounce! I am here."

"*Ma foi!* yes," said Simon, with his hideous laugh; "and your arrival is very apropos. This," continued he, "is the elegant Maurice Lindey, who was accused at the same time as the girl Tison, but was acquitted because he was rich."

"*À la lanterne! À la lanterne!*" cried the Marseillais.

"Yes, forsooth, you had better make the attempt," said Maurice; and, advancing a step, he pricked one of the foremost cut-throats in the forehead, so that the blood from his wound nearly blinded him.

"Have at the murderer!" cried the latter.

The Marseillais lowered their pikes, raised their hatchets, and loaded their guns, while the frightened crowd dispersed, leaving the two friends to contend alone against this storm of blows. They regarded each other with a last sad yet sublime smile, while calmly awaiting their destruction from the whirlwind of iron and flame which threatened them, when, all at once, the door of the house against which they were leaning suddenly opened, and a swarm of young people, attired in the habits of those termed "Muscadins," or fops, each wearing a sword and brace of pistols in his girdle, rushed upon the Marseillais, and were instantly engaged in a terrific contest.

"Hurrah! hurrah!" cried Maurice and Louis, simultaneously, animated by this unexpected relief, without reflecting that to fight in the ranks of the new-comers was to confirm Simon's accusation, "Hurrah!" But if they were forgetful of their own safety, another thought for them. A short young man, about five-and-twenty years of age, with blue eyes, who fought without any intermission, with infinite science and valor, with a heavy sword, which any one would have thought his delicate and feminine hand incapable of wielding, perceiving that Maurice and Louis, instead of escaping by the door, which seemed to have been left open with that intention, remained fighting by his side, turned round, saying in a low voice :

"Fly directly through this door; pay no attention to what we may do here, or you will uselessly compromise yourselves."

Then, seeing the two friends hesitate, he suddenly cried out, addressing himself to Maurice :

"Away!" said he; "no patriots among us, Citizen Lindey; we are aristocrats here."

At these words, united to the audacity which would induce a man publicly to accuse himself of what at this period must lead to certain death, the crowd uttered a loud shout. But the fair young man, without evincing any symptoms of alarm, pushed Maurice and Louis into the alley, where he closed the door behind them. He then, with the three or four friends who had been assisting him, threw himself into the *mêlée*, which was now considerably augmented hy the approach of the fatal cart. Maurice and Louis, thus miraculously saved, regarded each other in amazement; but comprehending they had no time to lose, sought for some outlet. This seemed to have been managed expressly for them. They entered a court, and at the end discovered a small door concealed, which opened into La Rue St. Germaine l'Auxerrois. At this moment a detachment of gendarmes opened from Pont au Change, who had soon swept over the quay, although, from the traverse street where our two friends had concealed themselves, they heard for an instant the noise of an obstinate struggle. They preceded the cart which conducted the hapless Héloise to the scaffold.

"Gallop!" cried a voice, "gallop!"

The cart proceeded at a quick pace, and Louis saw the unfortunate girl standing, a smile upon her lips, and calm reliance in her eye, but was unable to exchange even a gesture with her, as she passed without seeing him, in the midst of a whirlwind of people, shouting, "To the guillotine with the aristocrat! to the guillotine!" The noise decreased in the distance till they reached the Tuileries. Then the little door through which Maurice and Louis had escaped again opened, and three or four Muscadins, with their clothes torn and stained with blood, passed through. It was probably all that remained of the little troop. The fair young man went through the last.

"Alas!" said he, "this cause is, then, accursed!"

And, casting from him his sword, notched and bloody, he rushed toward La Rue des Lavandières.

CHAPTER XXVIII.

THE CHEVALIER DE MAISON ROUGE.

MAURICE hastened to return to the section to enter a complaint against Simon. It is true that before quitting Maurice Louis had found a more expeditious way; this was to collect some Thermopyles to lie in wait for him and kill him in a pitched battle. But Maurice was strenuously opposed to this plan.

"You are ruined," said he, "if you make use of these means. Crush Simon, but do it legally. That ought to be an easy thing enough to the lawyers."

Consequently, the next morning, Maurice laid a formal complaint before the section, but was both astonished and annoyed when the president turned a deaf ear, excusing himself by saying he could not interfere between two good citizens, each incited by the love of country.

"Good!" said Maurice. "I know now how to act to merit the reputation of a good citizen. To assemble the people and to assassinate a man who displeases you; this you call being 'incited by love of country.' Well, I return to Louis' opinion, which I was wrong to dispute. After to-day, as you hear, I shall adopt patriotism and shall first experimentalize upon Simon."

"Citizen Maurice," said the president, "you are, after all, perhaps more to blame in this affair than Simon.

He has discovered a conspiracy, which it was not his province to do so. You have seen nothing, although the discovery formed part of your duty ; and more, you have held communication, accidentally or intentionally, we know not which, with the enemies of the nation.''

"I ?" said Maurice. "Well, this is something new. And with whom, pray, Citizen President ?"

"With the Citizen Maison Rouge."

"I ?" said Maurice, stupefied. "I had communication with the Chevalier de Maison Rouge ? I do not even know him—I never——"

"You have been speaking to him."

"I ?"

"To shake his hand."

"I ?"

"Yes."

"Where ? when, Citizen President ?" said Maurice, carried away by the firm conviction of his own innocence. "You have lied."

"Your zeal for your country carries you too far, Citizen Maurice," said the president, "and you will regret what you have said, when I tell you I can prove what I say to you be true. I have advanced nothing but the truth. Here are three different reports accusing you."

"Now," said Maurice, "do you really think me simple enough to believe in your 'Chevalier de Maison Rouge' ?"

"And why should you not believe it ?"

"Because it is only the ghost of a conspirator, with whom you always have a conspiracy ready to amuse your enemies."

"Read the denunciations."

"I will read nothing," said Maurice. "I protest I have never seen the chevalier—never spoken to him. Let any one who doubts my word of honor come and tell me so. I shall know how to answer him."

The president shrugged his shoulders. Maurice, who did not wish to be in arrears with any one, did the same.

An air of gloomy silence pervaded the remainder of the sitting. After the meeting was concluded, the president, a stanch patriot, raised to the highest rank in the district by the votes of his fellow-citizens, approached Maurice, and said :

"Come, Maurice, I want to speak to you."

Maurice followed the president, who conducted him into a little cabinet contiguous to that where the sittings were held. On arriving there he regarded Maurice for a moment in silence, then, placing his hand on his shoulder :

"Maurice," said he, " I knew and esteemed your father; this makes me esteem and love you. Believe me, you incur great danger from want of faith—the first falling off of a truly revolutionary spirit. Maurice, my friend, they who lose their faith also lose their fidelity. You do not believe in the enemies of the nation, therefore you pass near without seeing them, and become the instrument in their plots without being aware of it."

"What the devil!" said Maurice. "I know, citizen, I am a man of feeling, and possess some share of patriotic zeal, but my zeal does not render me a fanatic. There are twenty pretended conspiracies, to which the public assign the same name. I demand to face my accuser."

"You will not believe in the conspirator, Maurice," said the president; "then, tell me, do you believe in the red carnations for which Héloise Tison was yesterday guillotined ?"

Maurice started.

"Do you believe in the subterranean passage under the Temple garden, communicating from the cellar of the Citoyenne Plumeau to a certain house in La Rue de la Corderie ?"

"No," said Maurice.

"Then do as Thomas the Apostle did—'Go and see.'"

"I am not on guard at the Temple, and they would not allow me to enter there."

"Any one may enter the Temple now."

"How is that ?"

"Read the report, since you are so incredulous. I shall only proceed by official information."

"Well," said Maurice, reading the report, "this is to the point."

"Continue."

"They have transported the queen to the conciergerie!" cried Maurice.

"Do you think that, from a dream, or what you call an imaginary idea, or an idle story, the Committee of Public Safety would have adopted so grave a measure?"

"This measure has been adopted, but will never be executed, like many more I have seen, and all——"

"Read to the end," said the president; and he presented him with the last paper.

"The receipt of Richard, the jailer of the conciergerie," cried Maurice; "she has been there these two hours."

This time Maurice remained deep in thought.

"The Commune, as you know," continued the president, "acts with profound judgment. It is digging a furrow long and straight in its course; its measures are not puerile, and it has put in execution the principle of Cromwell: 'It is not necessary to strike the king except upon the head.' Read this secret note from the minister of the police."

Maurice read:

"Seeing that we possess the certainty that the *ci-devant* Chevalier de Maison Rouge is in Paris—that he has been in several places—that he has left traces of his appearance in various plots, happily frustrated, I request all chiefs of the different sections to redouble their vigilance——"

"Well?" said the president.

"I must believe this," said Maurice; and he continued:

"Description of the Chevalier de Maison Rouge. In height, five feet three inches, fair hair, blue eyes, straight nose, chestnut-colored beard, dimpled chin, soft voice, and hands like a female's."

At this description a strange light burst upon Maurice; he thought of the young man who commanded the troop of Muscadins, and who, on the preceding evening, saved the lives of himself and Louis, and so valiantly drew his sword upon the Marseillais in their defense.

"*Mordieu!*" exclaimed Maurice, "it must be he; in that case, the denomination would not be false. I spoke to him, but I cannot remember taking his hand."

"Maurice," said the president, "what do you say to all this now, *mon ami?*"

"That I believe it," said Maurice, musing sadly, who, for some time past, without understanding what evil influence saddened his life, had noticed everything darkening around him.

"Do not jest thus with popularity," said the president. "In these days, Maurice, popularity is life. As for unpopularity, it is to be suspected of treason, and the Citizen Maurice Lindey ought not even to be suspected of being a traitor."

Maurice had nothing to reply to sentiments so much in accordance with his own. He thanked his old friend and quitted the section.

"Ah!" murmured he, "there is too much suspicion and skirmishing. Now," drawing a deep breath, "now for peace, innocence, and joy—now to Geneviève."

And Maurice took the road to the Old Rue St. Jacques.

When he reached the abode of the master tanner, Dixmer and Morand were supporting Geneviève, who was suffering from a violent attack of hysterics. Thus, instead of entering unceremoniously, as he was accustomed to do, a servant met him in the passage.

"Announce me," said he, "and if Dixmer cannot conveniently receive me, I will retire."

The domestic entered the little pavilion, while Maurice remained in the garden. It seemed to him that something strange was going on in the house, and the workmen, instead of being occupied in their usual employment, were walking listlessly about the garden. At length, Dixmer himself appeared.

Come in, dear Maurice," said he; "come in, you are not one of those against whom the door is closed."

"What is the matter?" inquired the young man.

"Geneviève is ill," said Dixmer; "indeed, more than ill—she is delirious."

"Ah, *mon Dieu!*" cried the young man, overcome at again encountering trial and suffering. "What, then, is the matter with her?"

"You are aware, *mon cher*," said Dixmer, " one never knows anything concerning the illness of women, especially their husbands."

Geneviève was lying down on a chaise-lounge; near her stood Morand, offering her some salts, which she smelled occasionally.

"Well?" said Dixmer.

"Always the same thing," replied Morand.

"Héloise! Héloise!" murmured the young woman, from between her closed teeth and white lips.

"Héloise!" repeated Maurice, in much surprise.

"*Mon Dieu!* yes," replied Dixmer, quickly; "Geneviève most unfortunately saw the cart pass conveying the unhappy girl to the scaffold. Since then she has had five or six attacks of hysterics, and keeps on continually calling upon Héloise. But the most astonishing thing of all is that in her she recognized the girl who sold the carnations, which you already know about," said Morand.

"Certainly I do know," said Maurice, "when they barely failed of cutting my throat."

"Ah! we have heard all that, dear Maurice, and believe me, we have not been slightly alarmed; but Morand was at the sitting, and saw you fully acquitted and liberated."

"Silence!" said Maurice; "she again speaks."

"Oh, those empty, unintelligible words!" said Dixmer.

"Maurice," murmured Geneviève; "they are going to kill Maurice. To him, chevalier—to him!" A profound silence followed these words. "Maison Rouge," again murmured Geneviève, "Maison Rouge!"

Maurice felt a slight suspicion, but he could make out nothing clearly, and was too much affected by the suffering of Geneviève to comment much upon her words.

"Have you called in a physician ?" demanded Maurice.

"Oh! it will prove nothing," said Dixmer; "a slight delusion, that is all."

And he shook his wife so violently by the arm that she revived, and uttering a shrill cry, opened her eyes, which till now had remained closed.

"Ah, you are both here, and Maurice with you. Oh, I am so glad to see you, *mon ami;* if you knew what I have"—she corrected herself—"what we have suffered for the last two days."

"Yes, we are all here," said Maurice ; "have no more terror on that account. But there is one name, above all others, you must not accustom yourself to pronounce, seeing that at this moment it does not bear a very high repute."

"What name ?" quickly demanded Geneviève.

"The Chevalier de Maison Rouge."

"Have I named the Chevalier de Maison Rouge ?" inquired Geneviève, bewildered.

"Without doubt you have," said Dixmer ; "but understand, Maurice, there is nothing surprising in that, since it is said he was an accomplice of the girl Tison, and that it was he who concocted the whole plan of escape so happily frustrated yesterday."

"I do not say there is anything surprising," said Maurice ; "I only say it is better to keep it concealed."

"Who ?" demanded Dixmer.

"The Chevalier de Maison Rouge, *parbleu!* The Commune seeks for him, and the bloodhounds have a fine scent."

"Provided that, before they arrest him," said Morand, "he has not accomplished some new enterprise that may succeed better than the last."

"At all events," said Maurice, "it will not be in favor of the queen."

"Why not ?" demanded Morand.

"Because she is henceforth shielded from his bold attempts."

"Where is she, then?" inquired Dixmer.

"At the conciergerie," replied Maurice; "she was taken there this evening." Dixmer, Geneviève, and Morand uttered a cry which Maurice mistook for one of surprise. "Thus, you see," continued he, "adieu to the chevalier's plans for the queen. The conciergerie is more secure than the Temple."

Morand and Dixmer exchanged looks, unperceived by Maurice.

"Ah, *mon Dieu!*" said Maurice, "Madame Dixmer has turned faint again."

"Geneviève!" said Dixmer, "you must go to bed, my child; you suffer."

Maurice took the hint. He respectfully kissed Geneviève's hand and quitted the house. Morand left with him, and accompanied him as far as the Old Rue St. Jacques, where he parted with him to exchange some words with a man, a superior sort of domestic, who held a horse ready saddled and bridled. Maurice was so much occupied with his own thoughts, that he did not even inquire the man's name; indeed, he and Morand had not exchanged a word since they quitted the house together. He took the road to the Rue de Fosses St. Victor, and gained the quay.

"It is strange," said he, walking on. "Is my mind weakened, or are these events assuming importance? But everything appears to me as if viewed through a magnifying-glass."

And, to recover his equanimity, Maurice presented his face to the breeze, and, leaning against the parapet of the bridge, was soon lost in thought.

CHAPTER XXIX.

THE PATROL.

As he lost himself in these reflections, and, leaning against the parapet of the bridge, enjoyed a melancholy pleasure in gazing on the dark, still water, he heard the measured tread of a little troop, like that of a patrol. Maurice turned round; it was a company of the National Guard, arrived by the other extremity; and in the obscurity he fancied he recognized Louis. It was he, indeed. The instant he saw his friend Maurice, he ran toward him with open arms.

"Found at last!" cried Louis. "*Morbleu!* it is not without some trouble that we have rejoined you.

"'But since I find a friend so fond,
My fate assumes an aspect new.'

This time you will not complain, I hope, for I have given you Racine instead of Louis."

"But what do you do here as patrol?" inquired Maurice, anxiously.

"I am chief of the expedition, *mon ami;* the business is to establish our blemished reputation upon its original footing." Then, turning toward his company: "Carry arms! Present arms! Shoulder arms! There, *mes enfants*, it is not yet sufficiently dark, so you can talk over your little affairs, while we follow your example." Then, returning to Maurice: "I have heard great news at the section to-day," continued Louis.

"What?"

"First, that you and I are beginning to be suspected."

"I know it. What next?"

"Secondly, that the whole conspiracy of the carnations was conducted by the Chevalier de Maison Rouge."

"I know that also."

"But this you do not know: that the conspiracy of the carnations and that of the subterranean passage are one and the same."

"Again, I know it."

"Then, let us pass on to the third piece of news. This, I am certain, you cannot know. We go this night to capture the Chevalier de Maison Rouge."

"To take the Chevalier de Maison Rouge?"

"Yes."

"Have you, then, turned gendarme?"

"No; but I am a patriot. A patriot owes something to his country. Now, my country is horribly ravaged by this chevalier, who forms plot upon plot. Well, my country commands me, being a patriot, to free her from this Chevalier de Maison Rouge, who distresses her horribly, and I obey my country."

"It is all the same," said Maurice, "but it is singular that you should be charged with this commission."

"I am not charged; I charge myself, or, rather, I should say, I solicited the commission. It required a brilliant stroke to reinstate us in our former position, while our reestablishment will not only prove security for our lives, but still more the right of putting, at the very first opportunity offered, six ounces of lead into the belly of that hideous Simon."

"But how are they sure it was the chevalier who was the instigator of this subterranean plot?"

"They are not yet certain, but they presume so."

"You proceed, then, upon inference?"

"No, we proceed by certainty."

"How have you arranged all this?"

"Listen."

"I am listening."

"I had scarcely heard the cry, 'Grand conspiracy discovered by the Citizen Simon,' that beast Simon (the miserable is everywhere) than I wished to judge of the truth for myself. Then they named the subterranean passage."

"Does it really exist?"

"It does; I have seen it—seen it with both my eyes. That I call seeing."

"There, why do you not whistle?"

"Because that is Molière; and besides, these events, I must confess, appear to me rather too serious for pleasantry."

"What could we jest about, if we did not jest about serious things?"

"You say, then, that you have seen it?"

"I repeat that I have seen the subterranean passage. It extends from the cellar of the widow Plumeau, to a house in the Rue de la Corderie, No. 12 or 14, I cannot remember which."

"Have you passed through it, Louis?"

"I have, the whole length, and, *ma foi!* it is a trench prettily cut, I can assure you ; and, moreover, it was divided by three iron gratings, which they have been obliged to drive out one after the other, but which, in case these conspirators had succeeded, would have given them time, by sacrificing two or three of them, to have placed Madame Widow Capet in a place of safety. Happily, it is not so, and this hideous Simon has discovered all."

"But it appears to me," said Maurice, "those who ought to have been first arrested were the inhabitants of the houses in the Rue de la Corderie."

"This would have been done, had they not found the house perfectly uninhabited."

"But, at least, this house must belong to some one?"

"Yes, to a new proprietor, but no one knows who; they know the house changed masters three weeks since, and that is all. The neighbors have often heard a noise, but the house, being very old, they had imagined it was undergoing thorough repair. As to the late proprietor, he has left Paris. In the meantime I arrived.

"'*Pour Dieu!*' said I to Santerre, drawing him aside, 'you are in an awkward situation.'

"'Indeed we are,' replied he.

"'This house has been sold, has it not?'"

"'Yes; it was about three weeks ago.'

"'Was it sold in the presence of a notary?'

"'Yes.'

"'Then we must find out all the notaries in Paris, discover which of them sold this house, and then make him produce the agreement, and underneath will be found the name of the purchaser.'

"'Well and good!' said Santerre, 'that is capital advice, and coming, too, from a man they accused of not being a good patriot. Louis! Louis! I will reestablish you, or may the foul fiend seize me!'

"To be brief," continued Louis, "this was what was said and done. The notary was sought for, the act was found, and upon the agreement the name of the culprit was signed. Then Santerre took me aside, and I have engaged to arrest him."

"Was this man the Chevalier de Maison Rouge?"

"No; only his accomplice; that is to say, in all probablity, he was so."

"Then, how is it you say you are going to arrest the Chevalier de Maison Rouge?"

"We are going to arrest them altogether."

"Do you, then, know this Chevalier de Maison Rouge?"

"Perfectly."

"Have you seen the description of him?"

"*Parbleu!* Santerre gave it to me. Five feet two or three inches, fair hair, blue eyes, straight nose, etc.; besides, I have seen him."

"When?"

"This very day."

"You have seen him?"

"And so have you, also."

Maurice started.

"The short, fair young man who rescued us this morning—he who commanded the troop of Muscadins, who fought so valiantly and struck so hard."

"Was that the chevalier?" demanded Maurice.

"Himself. They followed and lost him in the environs of the domicile of our proprietor of the Rue de la Corderie, so that we surmise they live together."

"It seems probable."

"It is certain."

"But it seems to me, Louis," added Maurice, "that if this evening you arrest those who rescued you this very morning, you are much wanting in gratitude."

"Go along, then," said Louis. "Why, you don't suppose he saved us for our own sakes, do you?"

"For what else, then?"

"Not at all; they were in ambush to carry off the poor girl, Héloise Tison, as she passed to the scaffold. Our cut-throats embarrassed them, so they fell upon the cut-throats; that was the whole of it. We have been saved by a *contre-coup*. Now, as the intention is everything, and there was no intention, I have nothing to accuse myself with on the score of ingratitude. Besides, do you see, Maurice, the capital point is necessity, and the necessity is that we should reinstate ourselves by a brilliant achievement. And then I have promised him for you."

"To whom?"

"To Santerre; he knows that you command this expedition."

"How can that be?"

"'Are you sure of arresting these criminals?' said he to me.

"'Yes,' I replied; 'if Maurice is with me.'

"'But are you sure of Maurice? Some time since he was looked upon as rather lukewarm.'

"'Those who say that are totally deceived. Maurice is no more lukewarm in the cause than I am myself.'

"'And you will answer for his fidelity?'

"'As for my own.'

"I then went to your house, but could not find you at home. I took this road first, because it lay in my way, and then I remembered it was the one you usually frequented; so at last we have met."

"My dear Louis, I am in despair. I do not feel the slightest taste for this expedition. Say that you were not able to find me."

"Impossible! All our men have seen you."

"Well, then, say you met me, and I was not willing to join you."

"Again impossible."

"But why so?"

"Because this time you will not only be considered lukewarm, but *un suspect,* and you well know the fate of these suspects; they are conducted to La Place de la Revolution, and there invited to salute the statue of liberty, only, instead of doing so with the hat, they substitute the head."

"Well, Louis, I hardly care how soon; but without doubt it seems strange to you to hear me say so."

Louis opened his eyes wide, and looked at Maurice.

"Well," said Maurice, "I am weary of life."

Louis burst into a roar of laughter.

"Ah, ah!" said Louis, "we have a quarrel with our beloved, and that fills us with melancholy ideas. *Allons, bel* Amadis! let us return to the man, and from that we shall pass to the citizen. As for me, I am never a better patriot than when I am embroiled with Arthemise. Apropos, her divinity, the Goddess Reason, charged me with a thousand gracious messages for you."

"Pray thank her for me. Adieu, Louis."

"Adieu! How adieu?"

"Yes, I am going."

"Where are you going?"

"I am going home."

"Maurice, you will ruin yourself."

"I laugh at the idea."

"Maurice, reflect; my friend, reflect."

"I have done so."

"I have not repeated all——"

"What?"

"That Santerre said to me."

"What did he say?"

"When I asked for you to be chief of this expedition, he said to me:

"'Take care.'"

"Of whom?"

"Of Maurice."

"Of me?"

"Yes, Maurice; and he also added:

"'He often goes into that quarter.'"

"Into what quarter?"

"Into that of Maison Rouge."

"How?" cried Maurice, "it is not here he hides himself."

"They fancy so, since it is here his supposed accomplice resides, the purchaser of the house in the Rue de la Corderie."

"Faubourg Victor?" demanded Maurice.

"Yes, Faubourg Victor."

"And in what street?"

"In the Old Rue St. Jacques."

"Ah! *mon Dieu!*" murmured Maurice, as if struck by a thunderbolt.

And he pressed his hand before his eyes. But after a moment's interval, during which he had collected all his courage:

"What trade?" said he.

"A master tanner."

"His name?"

"Dixmer."

"You are right, Louis," said Maurice, by a violent effort controlling his emotion; "I will go with you."

"And you do well; are you armed?"

"I always carry my sword."

"Then also take a pair of pistols."

"And you?"

"I have my gun. Carry arms! lower arms! *en avant!* march!"

The patrol commenced its march, accompanied by Maurice, who walked near Louis. They were preceded by a man dressed in gray, who directed their movements. This was an agent of police. From time to time a shadow might be seen emerging from the angles of the streets or the doors of the houses, exchanging some words with the man in gray. This was the inspector. On arriving at the little street, the man in gray did not hesitate for an instant. He was well instructed, and entered the street at once. Before the door of the garden where Maurice had been so nearly garroted, he stopped.

"It is here," said he.

"What is here?" demanded Louis.

"It is here we shall find the two principals."

Maurice supported himself against the wall; he felt as if he were sinking to the ground.

"Now," said the man in gray, "there are three entrances: the principal entrance, this one, and another which leads into a pavilion. I shall enter with six or eight men through the principal entrance, in the meantime keep guard here with four or five men, and place three sure men at the entrance to the pavilion."

"I will get over the wall," said Maurice, "and watch in the garden."

"The very thing," said Louis, "as from the interior you can open the door to us."

"Willingly," said Maurice; "but do not ungarrison the passage, or come till I call you. All that passes in the interior I shall see from the garden."

"You are acquainted with the house then?" demanded Louis.

"Some time back I wished to buy it."

Louis proceeded to conceal his men in the corners of the hedges and angles of the doors, while the agent of police retired with six or eight National Guards to force his way by the principal entrance. In an instant the noise of their receding steps was deadened in the distance, without having awakened the least suspicion. Maurice's men were at their post. They declared everything had remained perfectly quiet, and that nothing extraordinary was passing in the Old Rue St. Jacques. Maurice then began to climb the wall.

"Listen," said Louis.

"To what?"

"The word."

"Right."

"Carnation and Vault. Stop all those who cannot repeat these two words. Permit all to pass who can. This is the password."

"Thanks," said Maurice, dropping from the top of the wall into the garden.

CHAPTER XXX.

THE PASSWORD.

The first blow was terrible. It indeed required all Maurice's self-command to enable him to conceal from Louis how powerfully he was affected by these startling events, but once in the garden, once alone, in the silence of night, his mind became more calm, and his ideas, instead of running disordered through his brain, became once more under the control of reason.

What! this house that Maurice had so often visited with the purest pleasure, this house which had formed for him a paradise on earth, was in reality only a den of sanguinary intrigues; the kind and flattering receptions bestowed on his ardent friendship resulted, then, from sheer hypocrisy, the love of Geneviève from fear. The plan of the garden is well known, our readers having more than once followed our young folks there. Maurice glided from bush to bush till he was shaded from the moon's rays by the little outhouse where he had been imprisoned previous to his first introduction to the house. This outhouse was opposite the pavilion inhabited by Geneviève. But this evening, instead of a stationary light gleaming from her chamber, it moved frequently from one window to another. Maurice saw Geneviève through the curtain, evidently raised by accident, hastily packing some things in a portmanteau, and with astonishment beheld some weapons in her hands. He raised himself upon a post to enable him to penetrate further into the room. A large fire was blazing on the hearth, where Geneviève was destroying papers. In a moment the door opened, and a young man entered the room. At first Maurice imagined this man was Dixmer. The young woman ran toward him, seized his hands, and held them for an instant, while they stood facing each other, evidently the subjects of some deep emotion. What this emotion meant he could not divine, as their words did not reach his hiding-place. But all at once Maurice measured his height with his eye.

"This is not Dixmer," murmured he.

Indeed, the man who had entered was small and delicate, while Dixmer was tall and masculine. Jealousy is an active stimulant, and in a second he had analyzed the height of this man in contrast to her husband.

"This is not Dixmer!" murmured he, compelled, as it were, to repeat it, to convince himself in reality of the perfidy of Geneviève.

He approached still nearer to the window, but the nearer he came the less he saw. His brain was on fire. Near him stood a ladder; the window was seven or eight feet high. He seized it, and planting it firmly against the wall, ascended and placed his eye at an aperture in the curtain.

Geneviève's unknown visitor was a fair young man, about twenty-six or twenty-seven years of age, with blue eyes and an elegant demeanor; he retained both the young woman's hands within his own, and was speaking soothingly, endeavoring fruitlessly to assuage the grief of Geneviève, which was plainly evinced by the tears which suffused her charming countenance. A slight noise accidentally made by Maurice caused the young man to turn his face toward the window. Maurice suppressed a cry of astonishment, he recognized his mysterious deliverer of the Place du Châtelet. At this moment Geneviève withdrew her hands from those of the unknown, and went toward the fireplace to ascertain that the papers were utterly consumed.

Maurice could no longer command his indignation.

All those fierce passions which torture the heart of man—love, vengeance, and jealousy—lacerated him with their fangs of fire. He knew his time, pressed with violence against the badly closed window, and vaulted into the chamber. At the same moment two pistols were pointed at his breast.

Geneviève, who had turned round at the noise, remained dumb on perceiving Maurice.

"Monsieur," said the young Republican, coldly, to him who, for the second time held his life at his disposal, "monsieur, you are the Chevalier de Maison Rouge."

"And what if I am?" replied the chevalier.

"It is this: you are a brave man, and consequently, a cool man; and I am about to say a few words to you."

"Speak," said the chevalier, without lowering his pistols.

"You can kill me if you choose, but you cannot do so before I have uttered a cry, or, rather, I will not die without giving an alarm. Should I do so, the thousand men who surround this house will have reduced it to ashes ere the lapse of ten minutes; so lower your pistols and listen to what I have to say to madame."

"To Geneviève!" said the chevalier.

"To me!" murmured the young woman.

"Yes, to you."

Geneviève, pale as a statue, seized his arm, but he repulsed her coolly.

"You know what you have affirmed, madame," said Maurice, with profound contempt. "I now see that you have told the truth. You, indeed, do not love Monsieur Morand."

"Maurice, listen to me!" said Geneviève.

"I have nothing to hear, madame; you have severed with a single stroke every cord that united my heart with your own. You told me you did not love Morand, but you did not tell me you loved another."

"Monsieur," said the chevalier, "you spoke of Morand; of what Morand do you speak?"

"Of Morand, the chemist."

"Morand, the chemist, stands before you. Morand, the chemist, is the Chevalier de Maison Rouge."

And extending his hand toward the table, he in an instant replaced his black wig, which for so long a period had concealed him from the young Republican.

"Ah, yes," said he, with redoubled disdain; "yes, I understand it is not Morand that you love, since Morand does not exist, but his subterfuge; but, to speak more plainly, this is not the less contemptible."

The chevalier made a threatening movement.

"Monsieur," said Maurice, "will you permit me to speak for a moment to madame? Join in the conversation, if you like; she will not be long, and then I will answer you."

Geneviève made a sign to Maison Rouge to entreat his patience.

"Thus, Geneviève, thus," continued Maurice, "you have made me a laughing-stock for my friends and a curse to myself. You have rendered me, blind fool that I was, an instrument in all your plots, and an easy tool in your hands. Listen to me. It was an infamous deed, but you will be punished, madame, and monsieur, who was going to kill me before your eyes. Before five minutes have elapsed he will be there, lying at your feet; and if his life be spared, it will only be to lose his head upon the scaffold."

"He die!" cried Geneviève, "he lose his head upon the scaffold! But you do not know, then, Maurice, that he is my protector, and that of my family; that I will give my life for his, that if he dies I will die, and that if you are my love he is my religion."

"Ah!" said Maurice, "perhaps you still mean to pretend that you love me. Really, women are sadly weak and contemptible." Then turning to the young Royalist, "Now, monsieur," said he, "you must either kill me or die yourself."

"Why so?"

"Because, if you do not kill me, I shall arrest you."

Maurice extended his hand to seize him by the collar.

"I shall not dispute my life with you," said the Chevalier de Maison Rouge. And he flung his pistols on a chair.

"And why do you not dispute your life?"

"Because my life is not equivalent in value to the remorse I should experience in feeling that I had killed a brave man, and more than all since Geneviève loves you."

"Ah!" cried the young woman, clasping her hands, "you are always kind, brave, loyal, and generous, Armand."

Maurice regarded them both, almost stupefied with astonishment.

"Allow me," said the chevalier, "to return to my chamber. I give you my word of honor it is not to escape; I wish to conceal a portrait."

Maurice turned his eyes quickly toward that of Geneviève; it hung as usual in its place. Perhaps the chevalier divined Maurice's thoughts; perhaps he wished to try his generosity to the utmost.

"I know," said he, "you are a Republican, but I know also that you possess a pure and loyal heart. I will trust you to the end."

And he drew a miniature from his breast, and displayed it to Maurice. He beheld before him the portrait of the queen. Maurice bowed his head, and rested his forehead on his hand.

"I await your orders, monsieur," said Maison Rouge; "if you still desire my arrest, will you knock at this door when it is time to give myself up to you? I value my life only while it is sustained by the hope of serving the queen."

The chevalier quitted the room without a gesture from Maurice offering to detain him.

As he left the chamber, Geneviève cast herself at the young man's feet.

"Pardon, Maurice," sobbed she, "pardon for all the evil I have done; forgive my deception, forgive me, if only on account of my tears and suffering, for believe me, I have wept much and suffered much. My husband left me this morning; I do not know where he is gone, and perhaps I may see him no more. And now I have only one friend left, a more than friend, a brother, and you will destroy him. Pardon, Maurice, pardon!"

Maurice raised the young woman.

"What do you wish?" said he. "There is fatality in all this. Every one stakes his life in these days; the Chevalier de Maison Rouge has played like all the rest, but he has lost the game, and he must, therefore, pay."

"That means that he must die, if I understand you rightly?"

"Yes."

"He must die, and it is you who tell me this?"

"It is not I, Geneviève, it is fatality."

"Fatality has not uttered the last word, since you can save him."

"At the expense of my word, and, consequently, of my honor. I comprehend, Geneviéve."

"Shut your eyes, Maurice; it is all that I ask; and as far as a woman may evince her gratitude, I will promise you mine."

"I should close my eyes to little purpose, madame, I assure you; there is a password given, and without this password no one could go out. Besides, the house, as I have told you, is already surrounded."

"And you know it?"

"Doubtless, I know it."

"Maurice!"

"Well?"

"*Mon ami*, my dear Maurice, tell me this password; I must know it."

"Geneviève," cried Maurice, "do you mean to say to me, 'Maurice, for the love I bear you, sacrifice your word and your honor, betray your cause, abjure your opinions? What do you offer, Geneviève, in exchange for all this, you, who tempt me thus?"

"Oh, Maurice, save him, save him first, and then ask of me my life."

"Geneviève," replied Maurice, in a desponding tone,

"listen to me. I have one foot on the road to infamy; before I make a final descent, I wish, at least, to find a sufficient cause for so doing. Geneviève, swear to me you do not love the Chevalier de Maison Rouge."

"I love him as a sister and a friend, not otherwise, I swear."

"Geneviève, do you love me?"

"Maurice, I do love you; it is true, as God now hears me."

"If I do what you ask me, will you henceforth abandon relatives, friends, country, and fly with the traitor?"

"Maurice! Maurice!"

"She hesitates! she hesitates!" And he turned from her with all the violence of disdain. Geneviève, who was leaning upon him, feeling suddenly her support give way, fell upon her knees.

"Maurice," said she, rising and wringing her hands, "I will swear to do all that you require of me. Order, and I will obey."

"You will be mine, Geneviève?"

"I will."

"Swear it, by Christ!"

Geneviève extended her arms.

"*Mon Dieu!*" cried she, "Thou didst pardon one poor sinful creature; I trust in Thy mercy Thou wilt also pardon me."

And the large tears rained down her cheeks, falling upon her long curls hanging disheveled on her bosom.

"Not thus!" said Maurice; "swear not thus, or I cannot accept that oath."

"*Mon Dieu!*" replied she, "I swear to devote my life to Maurice, to die with him, and, if requisite, for him, if he will save my friend, my brother, my protector, the Chevalier de Maison Rouge."

"He shall be saved," said Maurice.

And he went toward his chamber.

"Monsieur," said he, "resume your costume of the tanner Morand; I return your parole; you are free. And **you, madame,**" said he, turning to Geneviève these are the two passwords 'Carnation and Vault.'" And as if he entertained a horror of visiting the chamber where he had just pronounced the words which constituted him a traitor, he opened the window, and sprang from the room into the garden below.

CHAPTER XXXI.

THE SEARCH.

MAURICE had returned to his post in the garden, opposite the window of Geneviève, only it was now quite dark, she having left her apartment to enter that of the chevalier.

It was time Maurice returned, for scarcely had he reached the angle of the outhouse when the garden door opened, and the man in gray appeared, followed by Louis and five or six grenadiers.

"Well?" asked Louis.

"You see I am at my post," said Maurice.

"And no one has attempted to force the watchword from you?" said Louis.

"No one," replied Maurice, happy to escape by an evasion, from the way in which the question was put to him. "No one. And what have you done?"

"Why, we have acquired the certainty that the chevalier entered the house an hour ago, and has not left it since," replied the agent of police.

"Do you know his chamber?" said Louis.

"His room is only separated from the Citoyenne Dixmer's by a corridor."

"Ah, ah!" said Louis. "It appears this Chevalier de Maison Rouge is a gallant."

Maurice felt the hot blood rush to his forehead; he closed his eyes, yet saw a thousand lights.

"Let us see," said he, in a choking voice; "upon what do we decide?"

"We have decided," said the police agent, "to arrest him in his chamber, perhaps in his bed."

"He does not, then, suspect anything?"

"Absolutely nothing."

"What is the ground plan?" inquired Louis.

"We have had an exact plan," said the man in gray. "A pavilion situated at an angle of the garden; there it is; you ascend four steps, do you see them here? and find yourself on a landing; to the right is the apartment of the Citoyenne Dixmer; no doubt it is that of which we see the window. Facing this window, at the back part, is a door opening on the corridor, and in this corridor the entrance to the chamber of the traitor."

"Well, with so careful a specimen of topography," said Louis, "we might, I think, as easily find our way blindfolded as with our eyes open. Let us march."

"Are the streets well guarded?" said Maurice, with an interest which the assistants very naturally attributed to his fear lest the chevalier should escape.

"The streets, the passages, even the crossings," said the man in gray. "I defy any one to pass who has not the watchword."

Maurice shuddered; all these precautions being taken made him fear that he had uselessly parted with his honor to add to his happiness.

"Now," said the man in gray, "how many men do you require to secure the chevalier?"

"How many men?" said Louis. "I hope Maurice and I are sufficient for that. Is it not so, Maurice?"

"Yes," murmured he; "we are certainly sufficient."

"Attend!" said the police agent; "now, no pretending. Do you mean to take him?"

"*Morbleu!* Do we mean?" said Louis; "I should think so! Is it not, Maurice, necessary that we should take him?"

Louis laid a stress upon these words, for, as he had truly said, suspicion began to settle upon them, and it was not wise to allow time for suspicion (which marched with such rapid strides at this epoch) to assume a firmer consistence, for Louis comprehended that no one would presume to doubt the stanch patriotism of two men who captured the Chevalier de Maison Rouge.

"Well, then," said the police agent, "if you are in earnest, better take three men than two, and four than three, with you. The chevalier invariably sleeps with pistols under his pillow, and his sword on a table by his side."

"Eh, *mordieu!*" said one of the grenadiers of Louis' company. "Let us go in without preference for any one; if he resists, we will cut him to pieces; if he surrenders, we will reserve him for the guillotine."

"Well done!" said Louis. "Do we go in by the door or by the window?"

"By the door," said the police agent; "perhaps by chance the key may remain in it, and if we enter by the window, we must break some panes, and that would make a noise."

"Let us go by the door, then," said Louis; "as long as we enter, it little matters how. *Allons*, sword in hand, Maurice!"

Maurice mechanically drew his sword from the scabbard, and the little troop advanced toward the pavilion. The information of the man in gray proved perfectly correct; they first found the steps, then the landing, and at last entered the vestibule.

"Ah!" cried Louis, joyfully, "the key is in the door."

In short, extending his hand in the dark, his fingers had encountered the cold key.

"Then open it, Citizen Lieutenant," said the man in gray.

Louis cautiously turned the key in the lock. The door opened. Maurice wiped the perspiration from his brow.

"We shall find him here," said Louis.

"Not yet," said the man in gray, "if our chart is correct this is the apartment of the Citoyenne Dixmer."

"We can soon ascertain that," said Louis; "light the wax candle, some fire still remains."

"Light the torches," said the man in gray; "they are not so soon extinguished as candles."

At the same time, taking two torches from the hand of a grenadier, which he lighted by the dying embers. He placed one in the hand of Maurice, the other of Louis.

"You see," said he, "I was not deceived; here is the door opening into Citoyenne Dixmer's sleeping apartment, and here the one opening into the corridor."

"Now, for the corridor," said Louis.

They opened the door at the further end, which was not more firmly secured than the first, and found themselves fronting the door of the chevalier's chamber. Maurice had seen this door twenty times before, and never thought of inquiring where it led to. All his world was centered in the room where he was received by Geneviève.

"Oh, oh!" said Louis, in a low voice, "we must change our tactics—no more keys, and the door locked."

"Are you," asked Maurice, at length able to articulate, "sure that he is here?"

"If our plan is correct, it ought to be here," replied the police agent; "besides, we are about to ascertain that. Grenadiers, force open the door, and you, citizens, hold yourselves in readiness, and the instant the door is opened precipitate yourselves into the chamber."

Four men, selected by the emissary of police, raised the butt-ends of their muskets, and on a signal from the man who conducted this enterprise gave one blow altogether, when the door flew into a thousand fragments.

"Surrender, or you are a dead man!" cried Louis, rushing into the chamber.

No one replied, and the curtains of the bed were closely drawn.

"Make way," said the emissary of police, "and at the first movement of the curtains, fire!"

"Wait," said Maurice, "I will open them."

And no doubt in the hope that the Chevalier de Maison Rouge might be concealed behind it, Maurice, hastily pulled back the curtain, which, rolling along the iron rods, left the tenantless bed exposed to view.

"*Mordieu!*" said Louis, "there is no one here."

"He must have escaped," murmured Maurice.

"Impossible, citizen, impossible!" said the man in gray. "I tell you he was seen to enter here an hour ago, and no one has been seen to go out, and all the outlets from the garden are well guarded."

Louis opened the cabinets, the wardrobes, and looked everywhere, even where it was morally impossible a man could be concealed.

"You see, however, that no one is here?"

"No one!" repeated Maurice, with emotion easily understood. "You see no one is here."

"To the chamber of the Citoyenne Dixmer," said the police agent; "perhaps he may be there?"

"Eh!" said Maurice, "respect the chamber of a woman.

"Certainly we will respect it, and the Citoyenne Dixmer also; but for all that, we must visit it."

"What, the Citoyenne Dixmer?" said one of the grenadiers, delighted at the idea of making a wretched joke

"No," said Louis; "the chamber only."

"Then," said Maurice, "permit me to pass first."

"Pass on, then," said Louis. "You are captain in all honor;" and leaving two men to guard the apartment, they returned to that where they had lighted their torches. Maurice approached the door opening into the chamber of Geneviève. It was the first time he had ever entered there. His heart beat violently. The key was in the door. Maurice laid his hand upon the key, but still hesitated. "Well," said Louis, "open!"

"But," said Maurice, "if the Citoyenne Dixmer should be in bed?"

"We will look in her bed, under her bed, in the chimney, in the wardrobes, and then, if we find no one there but herself, we will wish her good-night," said Louis.

"No, not so," said the police agent; "we shall arrest her. The Citoyenne Dixmer is an aristocrat who has been recognized as an accomplice of the girl Tison and the Chevalier de Maison Rouge."

"Open it yourself, then," said Maurice. "I do not arrest women."

The agent of police looked at Maurice sideways, and the men murmured among themselves.

"Oh, you grumble, do you?" said Louis; "then you shall have two to grumble about. I am of Maurice's opinion," and he made a step forward.

The man in gray seized the key, opened the door, and the soldiers rushed into the chamber. Two wax lights burned upon a little table, but the chamber of Geneviève, like that of the Chevalier de Maison Rouge was uninhabited.

"Empty!" cried the police agent.

"Empty!" cried Maurice, turning pale; "where is she, then?"

Louis regarded Maurice with astonishment.

"Let us search," said the agent of police; and, closely followed by the militia, he began to rummage the house from the cellars to the work-shops. At length, when their backs were turned, Maurice, who had followed them impatiently with his eyes, in his turn darted into the chamber, opening the presses, which had already been opened, and, calling, in a voice replete with anxiety, "Geneviève! Geneviève!" But Geneviève made no reply; the chamber was indeed vacated. Then he began to search the house in a species of frenzy, the greenhouse, even the outhouses, nothing was omitted, but all without success. Suddenly a noise was heard, a troop of armed men presented themselves at the door, exchanged the password with the sentinel, entered the garden, and dispersed themselves over the house. At the head of this reinforcement waved the red plume of Henriot.*

"Well," said Louis, "where is the conspirator?"

"How! where is the conspirator?"

"Yes; I ask what have you done with him?"

"I shall ask you that question. If your detachment had guarded the outlets properly, ere this he must have

* The name of Santerre has been incorrectly introduced, as since the 3d of May, Henriot commanded the National Guard.

been arrested, since he was not in the house when we entered it."

"What! do you mean to say," cried the furious general, "that you have really allowed him to escape?"

"We could not allow him to escape, since we have never taken him."

"Then I can comprehend nothing," said Henriot.

"Why?" said Louis.

"Of the message you sent me by your envoy."

"We have sent none."

"Yes; a man in a brown coat, with black hair, and green spectacles, who came from you to inform me you were on the eve of capturing Maison Rouge, but that he defended himself like a lion, upon hearing which I hastened to your assistance."

"A man in a brown coat, black hair, and green spectacles?" repeated Louis.

"Yes; with a female on his arm."

"Young and pretty?" cried Maurice, glancing toward the general.

"Yes, young and pretty."

"It was she—the Citoyenne Dixmer."

"And he? Maison Rouge. Oh, miserable that I am, not to have killed them both!"

"Let us go, Citizen Lindey," said Henriot; "we may perhaps overtake them."

"But how the devil," said Louis, "came you to let them pass?"

"*Pardieu!*" said Henriot, "I allowed them to pass because they knew the password."

"They had the password?" said Louis; "then there is surely a traitor among us."

"No, no, Citizen Louis; you know, and we all know, we have no traitors among us."

Louis looked around him as if to detect the miscreant, and publicly proclaim his shame. He encountered the gloomy face and wandering eye of Maurice.

"Ah!" murmured he, "who could have foretold this?"

"This man cannot be very far off," said Henriot; "let us search the environs; perhaps he has fallen in with some patrol who, more clever than ourselves, will not fail to secure him.

"Yes, yes, let us search," said Louis; and, under the pretense of so doing, he seized Maurice by the arm, and drew him into the garden.

"Yes, let us search," said the soldiers; "but before we search——" and one of them flung his still burning torch into an adjacent outhouse filled with bundles of dried cow-hair and rotten planks.

"Come," said Louis, "come."

Maurice offered no resistance. He followed Louis like a child; they both ran as far as the bridge without speaking again. When there, they stopped, and Maurice turned round. The sky was red from the horizon to the faubourg, and from above the houses ascended innumerable crimson stars.

CHAPTER XXXII.

THE FIRE.

MAURICE shuddered as he extended his hand toward La Rue St. Jacques.

"The fire!" said he, "the fire!"

"Yes," said Louis, "the fire! What then?"

"Oh, *Mon Dieu! mon Dieu!* if she has returned."

"Who?"

"Geneviève."

"Geneviève means Madame Dixmer, does it not?"

"Yes."

"There is no danger of her return; she did not go away for that purpose."

"Louis, I must find her. I will have my revenge."

"Oh, oh!" said Louis.

"You will assist me in my search, will you not, Louis?"

"*Pardieu!* there will be no difficulty in that."

"Why so ?"

"Without doubt, if you are so much interested, as far as I am able to form an opinion on the Citoyenne Dixmer's fate, you being intimate with her, ought, knowing her, also to know her friends. She has not quitted Paris; it is all the rage to remain there ; she has taken refuge in the house of some confidential acquaintance, and to-morrow morning you will receive a billet from some 'Rose,' or some ' Menton,' requesting you to present yourself at the house of the concierge, such a number, such a street, and inquire for Madame ——; that is all."

Maurice shrugged his shoulders ; he well knew there was no one with whom Geneviève could take refuge.

"We shall not find her," said he.

"Will you permit me to say one thing, Maurice ?"

"What ?"

"That it will be no great misfortune if we should not find her."

"If we do not, Louis, I shall die."

"*Diable!*" said the young man, "it is only this love, then, that has hitherto kept you alive ?"

"Yes," replied Maurice.

Louis reflected an instant.

"Maurice," said he, "it is now nearly eleven o'clock ; this quarter is deserted , here is a stone seat, particularly adapted for the reception of two friends. Accord me the favor of a private interview, as they described it under the ancient régime."

They both seated themselves upon the bench.

"Speak," said Maurice, resting his aching head upon his hand.

"I give you my word of honor I will speak only in prose, *mon ami*, without exordium, periphrase, or commentary ; I tell you one thing, it is that we are ruining ourselves, or, rather, you are ruining us."

"Why so ?" demanded Maurice.

"There is, my friend, a decree issued by the Committee of Public Safety, which declares every man a traitor to his country who enters into any relationship with the acknowledged enemies of the said country. Alas! do you know this decree?"

"Doubtless I do," said Maurice.

"Well, it seems to me you are not a vile traitor to your country. What say you? as Manlius says."

"Louis! At least, you do not regard with idolatry in this country those who give house-room, table, and bed to Monsieur le Chevalier de Maison Rouge, who is not a high Republican, as I suppose, and has not been accused at any time of having taken part in the days of September. Ah! Louis," said Maurice, sighing heavily.

"Still, it appears to me," continued the moralist, "that you have been, and still are, too intimate with the enemies of your country. *Allons, allons! cher ami*, do not rebel, and, like the fire, Enceladus, you will remove the mountain as you turn back."

Louis pronounced these words in the kindest manner possible, and glossed them over with an artifice truly Ciceronian. Maurice merely made a gesture of assent, but the gesture was considered an admission, and Louis continued:

"If we exist in a greenhouse temperature, a healthy atmosphere, where the barometer invariably points to sixteen degrees (this, my dear Maurice, is elegant, *comme il faut*, we are occasionally rather aristocratic), we flourish and do well, but if scorched in a heat of thirty or forty degrees, the sap burns, so that it rises slowly, and from the excess of heat seems cold; when cold, then comes the blight of suspicion; you know this, Maurice, and, once suspected, you possess too much good sense not to know that we shall ere long be no more."

"Well, then," said Maurice, "they can kill me, and there will be an end of me, for I am weary of my life."

"A quarter of an hour ago, indeed, scarcely so long," said Louis, "I left you to act according to your own pleasure on this subject; and then to die now it is necessary to die a Republican, while you would die an aristocrat."

"Ah!" said Maurice, whose blood began to boil from

impassioned grief, resulting from the consciousness of his own criminality, "you go too far, *mon ami*."

"I shall go further still, and inform you, that if you turn aristocrat——"

"You will denounce me?"

"For shame! No. I will confine you in a vault, and have you sought after to the sound of the drum, like a wild object; then I will proclaim that the aristocrats, knowing what was in reserve, had seized, victimized, and starved you, so that like the Prevot Elie de Beaumont, Monsieur, Latude, and others, when found, you will be publicly crowned with flowers by the ladies of La Halle and the rag-pickers of the section. Make haste, then, to appear an Aristides, else your business is quite concluded."

"Louis! Louis I feel that you are right, but I am dragged along. I am sliding down the precipice. Leave me to my fate, for I am drawn to it."

"I shall not leave you, but I shall quarrel with you. Call to mind a few of the scenes enacted daily between Pylades and Orestes—scenes which prove beyond all doubt that friendship is a paradox, since these model friends quarreled without ceasing."

"Leave me to my fate, Louis; you had much better do so."

"I will never abandon you."

"Then allow me to love, to be mad, at my ease; to be criminal, perhaps, for if I again see her I fear I shall kill her."

"Or fall upon your knees. Ah, ah, Maurice, Maurice, to have loved an aristocrat, I never could have credited it. It is like poor Asselin with the Marquis de Charry."

"No more, Louis, I beseech you."

"Maurice, I will cure you, or may the devil take me. I do not wish you to be drawn in the lottery of St. Guillotine, as the grocer of La Rue des Lombards observes. Maurice, you will exasperate me! Maurice, you will render me bloodthirsty! I feel as if I wanted to set fire to the Isle of St. Louis! A torch! a fire-brand!"

Maurice smiled in spite of himself.

"You exasperate me with your folly," continued Louis. "Drink, Maurice, become a drunkard, do anything; study political economy; but, for the love of Jupiter, let us fall in love with nothing but Liberty."

"Or Reason!"

"Ah! the goddess talks much about you. She thinks you a charming mortal."

"Are you not jealous?"

"Maurice, to save a friend I feel capable of any sacrifice.

"Thanks, my poor Louis, and I truly appreciate your devotion; but the best way to console me is to saturate me with grief. Adieu, Louis, go to Arthemise."

"And you, where are you going?"

"I shall return home."

And Maurice turned toward the bridge.

"You live, then, on the side of the Old Rue St. Jacques now?"

"No; but it pleases me to go that way. To look once again upon the place inhabited by your fair inconstant?"

"To see if she has not returned where she knows I am awaiting her. Ah! Geneviève, I could not have believed you capable of so much deceit."

Maurice, a tyrant who well knew the fair sex, since he died from having loved them too well, said:

> "Woe to the man who trusts his heart
> To woman, changeful as the breeze."

Maurice sighed, and the two friends took the road to the Old Rue St. Jacques. As they approached they heard a great noise and saw the light increase; they listened to patriotic chants, which, on a brilliant day, in the glorious sunshine, or in the atmosphere of combat, sounded like hymns of heroism; but which, by the red light of an incendiary fire, savored more of the degrading accents of a drunken rabble.

"Oh, *mon Dieu, mon Dieu!*" cried Maurice, forgetting that God was abolished, as he wiped the perspiration from his face.

Louis watched him attentively, and muttered:

> "Alas! when caught in Cupid's snare,
> To Prudence we must bid adieu."

All the inhabitants of Paris appeared moving toward the theater of these events we are about to narrate. Maurice was obliged to cross a hedge formed by the grenadiers, the range of the sections, then the impetuous crowd of this always furious populace, at this epoch easily aroused, and who ran howling from spectacle to spectacle, without intermission. As they approached, Maurice impatiently hastened his steps; Louis, with some trouble, kept close behind him, for he did not like to leave him to himself for a moment. It was nearly all over. The fire had communicated from the outhouses, where the soldier had flung his torch, to the work-shops, constructed of planks, so put together as to allow the free circulation of air, the merchandise was consumed, and the house itself was now in flames.

"Oh, *mon Dieu!*" said Maurice; "if she has returned, should she find herself in a chamber encircled by the devouring element, waiting for me, calling on me——" and Maurice, nearly insensible from grief, liked better to think of the folly of those who loved than of his treason.

Maurice stooped and entered the door he caught sight of through the mass of burning flame. Louis still followed him. He would have pursued him to the confines of hell. The whole was in flames; the fire had now indeed commenced its work of destruction on the staircase. Maurice hastened to visit the first floor, the salon, the chamber of Geneviève, of the Chevalier de Maison Rouge, and the corridors, calling, in a choking voice:

"Geneviève! Genevèive!"

No one replied. On returning from the search our two friends saw volumes of flame now entering the door; but, not heeding the shouts of Louis, who had clambered to the window, Maurice passed through the midst of them, then ran to the house, crossed, notwithstanding all impediments, a courtyard strewed with broken marbles, discovered the *salle-à-manger*, the salon of Dixmer, Morand's cabinet of chemistry, all filled with smoke, with fragments and broken glass. The fire had reached this part of the house, and the work of destruction would soon be complete. Maurice, as in the pavilion, did not omit visiting a single chamber, or leave unexamined even a corridor. He then descended to the cellars; perhaps Geneviève had taken refuge from the fire there. He found no one.

"*Morbleu!*" said Louis, "no one but a salamander could take refuge here, and it is not that fabulous animal that you are in search of. Let us go; we can make inquiry in this assemblage; some one has perhaps seen her."

It needed all Louis' force to drag away Maurice—hope still detained him there. Then they commenced their investigation; they visited the environs, stopped all the females who passed, searched all the alleys, without any result. It was now one o'clock in the morning, and Maurice, notwithstanding his athletic vigor, was overpowered and broken down with fatigue, and at length desisted from his worse than useless efforts. A carriage passed; Louis hailed it.

"*Mon cher*," said he to Maurice, "we have done all in the range of human possibility that we can do to recover Geneviève. We have broken our backs, been roasted, and have been cruelly cuffed for her. Cupid, however exacting he may be, could require no more from a man in love, and, above all, from one who is not. So jump into the carriage, and let us return home."

Maurice submitted without making any reply. They arrived at Maurice's door without either of the friends having uttered a single word. As he descended from the carriage, they heard the window of his apartment close.

"All right!" said Louis; "he is waiting. I shall rest easy now. Knock, however."

Maurice knocked; the door opened.

"*Bon soir*," said Louis; "wait for me to-morrow morning to go out."

"*Bon soir*," said Maurice, mechanically, as the door closed behind him.

Upon the first steps of the staircase he met his official.

"Ah, Citizen Lindey," said he, "how much uneasiness you have caused us."

The word "us" struck Maurice.

"You?" said he.

"Yes, I, and the little lady, who is waiting for you."

"The little lady!" repeated Maurice, feeling the moment ill-chosen to remind him of his former loves. "You were right to tell me. I shall sleep at Louis'."

"That is impossible; she was at the window, and saw you alight, and cried out, 'There he is!'"

"What can it matter anything she knows to me? I have no heart for love. Go up-stairs, and tell this woman she is deceived."

The official made a movement as if to obey him, then stopped.

"Ah, citizen," said he, "you are wrong. The little lady is already very sad; your message will drive her to despair."

"But," said Maurice, "who is this woman?"

"Citizen, I have not seen her face; it is concealed by her mantle, and weeps, that is all I know."

"She weeps?" said Maurice.

"Yes, but very softly, stifling her sobs."

"She weeps?" again repeated Maurice; "there is, then, some one in the world who loves me sufficiently to feel anxious in my absence!" and he ascended slowly behind the official.

"Here he is, citoyenne, here he is!" cried he, rushing into the chamber.

Maurice entered behind him.

He beheld, then, in the corner of the room, the trembling form (its face hid in the cushions) of a woman, whom he would have thought dead but for the convulsive groaning, which made him start. He signed to his official to leave the room, who went out, closing the door behind him. Then Maurice ran to the young woman, who raised her head :

"Geneviève!" cried the young man, "Geneviève here! *Mon Dieu!* am I, then, mad?"

"No; you are in possession of your senses, *mon ami*," replied the young woman. "I had promised to be with you if you would save the Chevalier de Maison Rouge. You have saved him, and I am here; I await you."

Maurice mistook the meaning of these words; he recoiled a step, and looked sadly at the young woman.

"Geneviève," said he, "you do not love me."

Geneviève regarded him with tearful eyes; then, turning from him, leaned her head on the pillow of the sofa and gave free utterance to her sobs and tears.

"Alas!" said Maurice, "it is evident that you no longer love me, and not only that you love me no more, Geneviève, but that you must entertain a feeling of hatred toward me to experience this despair."

Maurice had spoken so nobly, yet with so much feeling, that Geneviève, anxious to correct him, took his hand, and attempted some explanation.

"*Mon Dieu!*" she said, "those we think the best will always be egotists."

"Egotists, Geneviève! What do you mean to say?"

"Can you not, then, imagine what I suffer? My husband a fugitive, my brother proscribed, our house in flames, and all this in one night; and then that dreadful scene between you and the chevalier was added to the rest."

Maurice listened with delight, for it was impossible even for the most foolish passion not to admit that this accumulation of trouble was more than sufficient excuse for Geneviève's deep and violent grief.

"And now you are come, I shall keep you; you will not leave me more?"

Geneviève started.

"Where should I go?" replied she, with bitterness. "Have I an asylum, a shelter, a protector, save he who has put a price upon his protection ? Oh ! rash and foolish that I am. I stepped over the Pont Neuf, Maurice, and in passing I stopped to gaze at the dark water dashing angrily against the angles of the arches ; it attracted and fascinated me. Then, said I to myself, 'There, poor woman, is a shelter for you—there a grave, rest, and obliviousness.'"

"Geneviève ! Geneviève !" said Maurice, "you said that ? Then you do not love me ?"

"I promised," replied Geneviève, "I promised to come, and I am here."

Maurice drew a deep breath, and cast his eyes upon the floor.

"Geneviève," murmured he, "weep no more. Geneviève, console yourself for all your grief, since you love me. Tell me, Geneviève, for the sake of Heaven, that it was not the violence of my menaces that brought you hither. Assure me that even had you not seen me this evening, on finding yourself alone, isolated and without an asylum, you would have come and received my oath, to return to you that which I had compelled you to take."

Geneviève regarded the young man with a look of intense gratitude.

"Generous !" said she. "Oh, *mon Dieu !* I thank Thee ; he is generous."

"Listen, Geneviève," said Maurice. "God, whom they have here driven from their temples, they cannot expel from our hearts, where He has implanted love. This evening, apparently so dark and gloomy, conceals behind its somber curtain a silvery cloud. God has conducted you to me, Geneviève, and speaks to you through me. God is at length willing to compensate us for all the sufferings we have endured, for the virtues we have displayed in combating this love, as if this sentiment so long entertained, and so profound, could be a crime. Weep no more, Geneviève, weep no more ; give me your hand. Do you wish to live in the house of your brother ? do you wish he should kiss the hem of your robe, and pass over the threshold of his door without turning his head ? Well, say but one word, make but one sign, and I am gone, and you are free. But, on the other side, my adored Geneviève, will you call to mind how ardently I have loved you, and have only existed in this love, which it remains with you to render so fatal or so fortunate to me ? I have been a traitor to my friends, and am become vile and contemptible in my own eyes; will you now remember that in all this I regarded your happiness for the present and the future ? Ah ! Geneviève, what will you reply? Ah ! Geneviève, you who are an angel of mercy, will you render a man so happy that he no longer regrets life, and ceases to desire eternal felicity ? Then, instead of repelling me, smile, my Geneviève; let me place your hand upon my heart, and incline toward one who worships you from the inmost recesses of his soul. Geneviève, my love, my life, do not take back your vow !"

The heart of the young woman swelled at these words. The fatigue of her late suffering had worn out her strength, and though her tears no longer flowed, occasional sobs relieved her overcharged bosom.

"You still weep, my Geneviève," continued Maurice, with profound melancholy; "you still weep. Oh! reassure yourself. I will never impose my love on scornful grief, and never soil my lips with a kiss impoisoned by a single tear of regret."

He averted his face, and coldly turned away.

"Ah! Maurice," murmured Geneviève, "do not abandon me, Maurice; I have no one left me in the world but you."

CHAPTER XXXIII.

THE MORROW.

A BEAUTIFUL sun beamed across the green window-blinds, gilding the leaves of three large roses placed in a flower-stand before the window of Maurice. These flowers, more precious as the season was on the decline, perfumed with a delicious fragrance the little *salle-à-manger* of spotless neatness, where at a table served with every elegancy, but without profusion, sat Maurice and Geneviève. The door was closed, for as the table contained all that was requisite, it was understood they waited on themselves. They heard the official stirring in the adjoining room. The warmth and life of the last few lovely days entered through the half-open jalousie, making glitter like emeralds and rubies the rose leaves caressed by the rays of the sun. Geneviève let fall upon her plate the golden fruit she held in her hand. She appeared to be in deep thought, and smiling only with her lips, while her eyes languished with a melancholy expression. She remained thus silent, abstracted, and happy in the sun of her love, as the beautiful flowers in the sun of heaven. Soon her eyes sought those of Maurice, and encountered his gazing upon her. She placed her soft white arm upon the young man's shoulder, and leaned against his breast with that faith and confidence far exceeding love. Geneviève looked at him without speaking, and blushed as she regarded him. Maurice slightly inclined his head to imprint a kiss upon the half-open lips of Geneviève. He bent his head, while she turned pale, and closed her eyes, as the delicate flower conceals its calyx from the rays of light. They remained dreaming thus, when a sharp ring at the door-bell suddenly startled them.

The official entered mysteriously, and closed the door.

"Here is the Citizen Louis," said he.

"Ah, dear Louis!" said Maurice, "I will go and dismiss him. Pardon, Geneviève."

Geneviève stopped him.

"Dismiss your friend, Maurice?" said she, "and such a friend; one who has consoled, assisted, and sustained you? No; I would no more drive such a friend from your house than from your heart. Let him come in, Maurice, let him come in."

"With your permission," said Maurice.

"I wish it," said Geneviève.

"Ah! you will find that to love you is not enough,"

cried Maurice, delighted with her delicacy; "it is necessary to adore you."

Geneviève held her blushing face to the young man. He opened the door, and Louis entered, smart as usual in his costume of demi-Muscadin. On perceiving Geneviève he manifested great surprise, which was succeeded by a respectful salute.

"Come here, Louis, come here, and look at madame; you are dethroned, Louis. I have now some one I prefer. I would have given my life for you; for her—I tell you nothing new, Louis—for her I have sacrificed my honor."

"Madame," replied Louis, in accents of deep emotion, "I shall endeavor to love Maurice the more that he has not altogether ceased to love me."

"Sit down, monsieur," said Geneviève, smiling.

"Yes, sit down," said Maurice, who, having pressed in his right hand that of his friend, and in his left that of his mistress, presented the appearance of a man arrived at the height of human felicity.

"Then you do not wish to die now? do not wish any longer to kill yourself?"

"What was that?" said Geneviève.

"Ah! *mon Dieu!*" said Louis, "man is a most versatile animal, and philosophers have good cause to despise his levity. Here is one, would you believe it, madame, who no later than yesterday evening wished to fling himself into the fire, throw himself into the water; who declared there was no more happiness for him in this world, and behold him this morning, gay, joyous, with a smile upon his lips, his countenance resplendent with happiness, life in his heart, seated at a well-furnished table; it is true, he has not eaten much, but that does not prove he is unhappy."

"Did he wish to do all this?" said Geneviève.

"All this, and much more still. I will tell you all some day, but at this moment I am very hungry; it is all Maurice's fault, for making me, yesterday evening, run all over the quarter St. Jacques. Permit me, then, to make an attack upon the breakfast, which I perceive you have neither of you yet touched."

"That is right," said Maurice, with childish joy; "I have not breakfasted, neither have you, Geneviève."

He watched Louis' eyes as he uttered her name, but he evinced no surprise.

"Ah!" said Maurice, "you have already surmised who it was, Louis."

"*Parbleu!*" said Louis, cutting himself a large slice of white and rosy ham.

"I also am hungry," said Geneviève, holding her plate.

"Louis," said Maurice, "I was ill yesterday."

"You were worse than ill; you were mad."

"Well, I think it is you who are suffering at this moment."

"Why?"

"You have not yet given us any verses."

"I will sing you one this moment," said Louis.

> "Phœbus, in the midst of the Graces,
> The lyre in his hand still retained,
> Till following of Venus the traces,
> 'Twas lost, and could not be regained."

"Always ready with a quatrain," said Maurice, laughing.

"I am glad that you are contented, as it is now necessary to turn our attention to more serious affairs."

"Has anything new occurred, then?" said Maurice, anxiously.

"I am ordered on guard at the conciergerie."

"At the conciergerie?" said Geneviève, "near the queen?"

"Near the queen. I believe so, madame."

Geneviève turned pale. Maurice frowned, and made a sign to Louis, who cut himself another slice of ham double the size of the first. The queen had indeed been removed to the conciergerie, where we will follow.

CHAPTER XXXIV.

THE CONCIERGERIE.

At an angle of the Pont au Change, and of the Quai aux Fleurs, rose the remains of the old palace of St. Louis, called *par excellence* the palace, as Rome is called the city, and which still continues to retain the royal cognomen, when the only kings who inhabit it are the registrars, the judges, and the pleaders. The house of justice was a large and somber building, exciting more fear than love for the goddess. There might be seen united in this narrow space all the instruments and attributes of human vengeance. In the first ward were those who had been arraigned for crime; further on where they were tried; and lower down the dungeons of the condemned. By the door was a small space where the red-hot iron stamped its mark of infamy; and about one hundred and fifty paces from the first, another space, far more extensive, where the last act of the fearful tragedy took place—that is to say, La Greve, where they finished the work previously sketched out for them at the palace. Justice, as we see, reigned paramount over all. All these portions of the edifice joined one with another, sullen-looking, dark, and gray, pierced by iron-grated windows, where the gaping arches resemble the grated dens extending along the side of the Quai des Lunettes. This is the conciergerie. This prison contains dens washed by the black mud from the waters of the Seine; it also possesses mysterious issues, by which are conveniently conducted to the river those miserable victims whom it is their interest to remove. Seen in 1793, the conciergerie liberally disgorged its prisoners, within the hour arrested and condemned to die upon the scaffold. At this epoch the old prison of St. Louis was literally the Hold of Death. Under the arches some gates were hung, and at night a red lantern was suspended there, fit emblem of this abode of misery and despair.

The evening preceding the day when Louis, Maurice, and Geneviève were breakfasting together, a dull rumbling shook the pavement of the quay, and rattled the windows of the prison, then ceased before the arched gate. The gendarmes knocked with the handles of their swords, the gates opened, and a voiture entered the court; when the hinges had turned and the rusty bolt ground round, a female descended. The gaping wicket opened immediately to receive her, and closed upon her. Three or four curious heads protruded to gaze upon the prisoner by the light of the flambeau, appeared in mezzo-tinto, then vanished in the darkness, while vulgar jokes and rude laughter passed between the men leaving, who could be heard, though not seen. The person thus brought remained at the wicket with the gendarmes; she saw it would be necessary to pass through a second, but forgot at the same time to raise the foot and lower the head, as there is a step to ascend and a beam which descends. The prisoner, although unfortunately habituated to prison architecture, notwithstanding her long sojourn there, omitted to stoop, and struck her forehead violently against the bar.

"Are you much hurt, citoyenne?" demanded one of the gendarmes.

"Nothing can hurt me now," she replied, tranquilly; and passed on without uttering a single complaint, although sanguinary traces of the injury remained upon her brow.

Shortly, the armchair of the porter became visible—a chair more venerated by the prisoners than the throne of the king by his courtiers; for the concierge of a prison is the dispenser of favor, and all mercy is important to a prisoner, as sometimes the smallest kindness may change the darkest gloom to a heaven of light. The concierge, Richard, installed in his armchair, felt a due perception of his own importance. He remained undisturbed even when the rumbling of the carriage announced a new arrival. He inhaled some snuff, regarded the prisoner, opened a large register, and looked for a pen in the little ink-horn of black wood, where the ink, incrusted on the sides, retained in the center a moldy humidity, as in the midst of the crater of Vesuvius there always remains a certain degree of heat.

"Citizen Concierge," said the chief of the escort, "write, and write quickly, for they are impatiently awaiting us at the Commune."

"I will not be long," said the concierge, at the same time emptying into the inkstand some drops of wine remaining at the bottom of his glass; "we are a good hand at this, thank God! Your name and surname, citoyenne?" said he, and, dipping his pen at the same time into this improvisatory ink, he commenced writing at the bottom of a page already nearly filled. The new arrival, while standing behind his chair, the Citoyenne Richard, a female of benevolent aspect, contemplated, with a mixture of astonishment and respect, this woman, so sad, so noble, and so proud.

"Marie Antoinette Jean Joseph de Lorraine," replied the prisoner, "Archduchess of Austria and Queen of France."

"Queen of France!" repeated the concierge, raising himself in astonishment by the arms of his chair.

"Queen of France," repeated the prisoner, in the same voice.

"Otherwise called the widow of Capet," said the chief of the escort.

"Under which of these names am I to designate her?" demanded the concierge.

"Whichever you please, only do it quickly," said the chief of the escort.

The concierge reseated himself, and with a trembling hand wrote down the name, surname, and titles given him by the prisoner, inscriptions of which the ink still appears visible this day upon the register of which the revolutionary rats of the conciergerie had nibbled the leaf but respected the parts most precious. Richard's wife still retained her position behind her husband's chair, and remained standing with her hands clasped together, commiserating the situation of the unfortunate being before her.

"Your age?" continued the concierge.

"Thirty-seven years and nine months," replied the queen.

Richard wrote this down, then the description, and finished with the regular notes and forms.

"There," said he, "that is completed."

"Where shall we conduct the prisoner?" said the chief of the escort.

Richard helped himself to a second pinch of snuff, and looked at his wife.

"Dame," said he, "we did not anticipate this, and have not long known it."

"You must find out," said the brigadier.

"There is the council chamber," said Richard's wife.

"Too large," murmured Richard.

"So much the better; you can the more easily place the guards."

"Go to the council chamber," said Richard. "But it is not habitable at this moment; it has no bed."

"True," replied his wife; "I had quite forgotten that."

"Bah!" said one of the gendarmes, "you can put a bed there to-morrow, and to-morrow will soon be here."

"Besides, the citoyenne could occupy our chamber for one night; could she not, my man?" said Richard's wife.

"And what are we to do?" said the concierge.

"Oh, we can do without a bed for one night; and, as the citizen gendarme observes, the night is nearly gone."

"Then," said Richard, "conduct the citoyenne to my chamber."

"And in the meanwhile you will prepare our receipt?"

"It shall be ready on your return."

Richard's wife took the candle from the table, and went first to lead the way. Marie Antoinette followed without uttering a word, calm and pale as usual. Two turnkeys, at a sign from Richard's wife, accompanied them.

The queen was shown her bed, on which the woman proceeded to place clean sheets. The turnkeys installed themselves outside; the door was closed, then double locked. And Marie Antoinette was left at last alone. How she passed that night no one ever knew. Probably in close communion with her God. On the next day the queen was conducted to the council chamber. This was a long, four-sided room, of which the wicket-door opened upon a corridor of the conciergerie, divided the whole length by a partition, which did not reach the height of the ceiling. One of these compartments was occupied by the men on guard. The other was the chamber of the queen. A window, thickly grated with small iron bars, lighted both these cells. A folding-screen, the substitute for a door, secluded the queen from the guards, and closed the aperture in the middle. The whole of this room was paved with brick. The walls, at one period or another, had been decorated with gilt picture-frames, where still hung some shreds of paper fleur-de-lis. A bed was placed opposite the window, and a single chair near the light. This was all the furniture the royal prison contained. On entering, the queen requested her books and works might be forwarded to her. They brought her the "Revolutions d'Angleterre," which she had commenced in the temple, the "Voyages de Jeune Anacharse," and her tapestry. The gendarmes established themselves in the adjoining compartment. History has preserved their names, as it has done that of many others more infamous, associated by destiny in these great events, and who saw reflected on them a fragment of that light cast by the thunderbolt which destroys the thrones of kings, perhaps even the kings themselves. They were called Duchesne and Gilbert. These two men were selected by the Commune, who knew them to be stanch patriots. They were to remain at their posts in their cell till the sentence of Marie Antoinette. They hoped by this measure to avoid the irregularities consequent upon a change of office several times during the day, and therefore laid the guards under a heavy responsibility. The queen first became acquainted with this new regulation from the conversation of the gendarmes, who, omitting to speak softly, their discourse reached her ears. She experienced at once joy and disquietude; for if, on the one hand, she felt that these men ought to be trustworthy, since they had been chosen from a multitude, on the other side, she reflected her friends might more easily corrupt two known men at their post, than a hundred unknown individuals selected by chance, passing near her occasionally, and then only for a single day. On the first night before she retired, one of the gendarmes, according to his usual custom, began to smoke. The noxious vapor glided imperceptibly round the screen, and through the aperture, enveloping the unfortunate queen, whose misfortunes had irritated instead of deadening her nerves. She soon felt herself seized with nausea and swimming in the head; but, true to her indomitable system of firmness, she uttered no complaint. During her melancholy vigil, while nothing disturbed the deep silence of the night, she fancied she heard plaintive cries outside. These cries were mournful and prolonged; there was about them something unearthly and piercing, like the howling of wind in the dark and deserted corridor, when the tempest borrows the human voice to animate the passions of the elements. She soon recognized the noises that had at first startled her, the doleful and persevering cry, as that of a dog running along the quay. She immediately remembered her poor little Jet, whom she never thought of when they removed her from the Temple, and now believed she could recognize his voice. Indeed, the poor little animal, who by his mistaken vigilance had ruined his mistress, had, unperceived, descended behind her, and followed the carriage as far as the grating of the conciergerie, where he continued till he narrowly escaped being cut in two by the double door of iron which closed behind her. But the faithful creature had soon returned, and, comprehending that his mistress was confined in this great stone building, he howled and whined, waiting, within ten feet of the sentinel, a caressive reply. The queen replied by a heart-broken sigh, which reached the ears of her guards ; but as this sigh was not repeated and no other sounds proceeded from the queen's chamber, they again composed themselves, and relapsed into their former state of drowsiness.

At break of day the queen rose and dressed herself, then took her seat near the window, the light from which, intercepted by the grating of iron bars, fell with a bluish tint upon her emaciated hands, in which she held a book. She was apparently reading, but her thoughts were far away. The gendarme Gilbert half opened the screen, and regarded her in silence. The queen heard the noise of the screen, but did not turn her head. She was so seated that the gendarme could see her head bathed in the morning light. Gilbert made a sign to his comrade to advance and look through the opening with him. Duchesne approached.

"Look," said Gilbert, in a low tone ; "how very pale she is ; it is frightful. Those red circles round her eyes denote her suffering. She has surely been weeping."

"You well know," said Duchesne, "Capet's widow never weeps. She is too proud for that."

"Then she must be ill," said Gilbert, and raising his voice, "Tell me, Citoyenne Capet," said he, " are you ill ? "

The queen slowly raised her eyes, and fixed an inquiring look upon the two men.

"Did you address me, messieurs ?" demanded she, in a voice full of sweetness, for she fancied she detected the accent of kindness in him who had spoken to her.

"Yes, citoyenne, we spoke to you," replied Gilbert ; "we feared you were ill."

"Why so ?"

"Because your eyes are so red."

"And at the same time you are so pale," added Duchesne.

"No, thank you, messieurs, I am not ill, only I suffered much last night."

"Ah! yes, your misfortunes."

"No, messieurs, my miseries are always the same; and my religion having taught me to carry them to the foot of the cross, I do not suffer more one day than another. No; I am ill because I could not rest last night."

"Ah! your new lodging, and different bed," said Duchesne.

"And then the lodging is not very comfortable," added Gilbert.

"Ah! it is not that, messieurs," said the queen, shaking her head. "Lofty or lowly, it is all the same to me."

"What is it, then?"

"I ask pardon for telling you; but I have suffered much inconvenience from the smell of tobacco, which monsieur is inhaling at this moment."

Indeed, Gilbert was smoking, for, like many others, it was his habitual occupation.

"*Mon Dieu!*" cried he, much grieved, from the kindness with which the queen had expressed herself. "Why did you not tell me so, citoyenne?"

"Because I thought I had no right to deprive you of any enjoyment."

"Well you shall be incommoded no more—by me, at least," said Gilbert, casting away his pipe, which broke upon the tiles, for I will smoke no more."

He turned round, his companion followed, and he closed the screen.

"Possibly they may cut off her head; that is an affair of the nation; but why should we cause her any suffering, this poor woman? We are soldiers, and not hangmen, like Simon."

"It rather savors of the aristocrat, comrade, what you did just now," said Duchesne, shaking his head.

"What do you term an aristocrat? Explain yourself."

"I call aristocrats all those who annoy the nation and succor its enemies."

"Then according to your theory, I annoy the nation because I discontinue smoking before the widow of Capet? Go along, then. As for me, I remember my oath to my country, and the order of my brigadier. As for my order, I know it by heart. Not to permit the prisoner to escape, not to allow any one to see her, to resist all correspondence she may endeavor to continue, and to die at my post. This is what I promised, and to this will I keep. *Vive la nation!*"

"That is what I tell you," said Duchesne. "It is not that I wish you to do so, but from my fear lest you should compromise yourself."

"Hush! here is some one."

The queen had not lost one word of this last conversation, although carried on in a low voice. Captivity had rendered her hearing doubly acute.

The noise which had attracted the attention of the two guards was the sound of several steps approaching the door. It opened, and two municipals entered, followed by the concierge and some of the turnkeys."

"Well," they inquired, "where is the prisoner?"

"Here she is," replied the two gendarmes.

"How is she lodged?"

"You can see."

And Gilbert touched the screen.

"What do you wish?" demanded the queen

"It is the visit of the Commune, Citoyenne Capet."

"This man is kind," thought the queen, "and if my friends——"

"Very good, very good," said the municipals, both entering the queen's chamber; "there is not much ceremony requisite here."

The queen did not even raise her head, and it might have been believed, from her impassibility, that she neither saw nor heard them, but fancied herself alone. The delegates of the Commune curiously observed everything around the chamber, sounded the wainscoting, the bed, shaking the grating of the window which looked upon the court of the Commune, and then, having recommended to the gendarmes the utmost vigilance, took their departure without having addressed a word to the queen, who, on her part, seemed not to have been aware of their presence

CHAPTER XXXV.

LA SALLE DES PAS-PERDUS.

Toward the decline of the day on which we have seen the municipals so carefully inspecting the queen's prison, a man attired in a gray blouse, his head covered with a mass of black hair, and on his head one of those hairy bonnets which then among the people was a distinguishing mark of the most exaggerated patriotism, walked into the large hall so philosophically termed "La Salle des Pas-Perdus," and seemed most attentively observing all the goers and comers forming the general population of this hall, a population considerably augmented at this period, when actions had acquired greater importance, and when the only pleading was to dispute their heads with the hangman and with Fouquier Tinville, their indefatigable purveyor.

The attitude assumed by this man whose portrait we are about to sketch was in very good taste. Society at this epoch was divided into two classes: the lambs and the wolves. The one naturally inspired the other with fear, since one half of society devoured the other. Our fierce promenader was rather short, and wielded in his dirty black hand one of those knotted cudgels then called "constitutions." It is true, the hand that flourished this horrible weapon might have appeared rather small to any one who might amuse himself by acting *vis-à-vis* to this strange visitor, who arrogated to himself the right to do so to others, but no one felt the least inclined to risk it, for this man's aspect was far too terrible. Indeed, it was supposed this man with the cudgel caused much disquietude to several groups of scribes engaged in the discussion of public affairs, which at this time daily progressed from bad to worse, or from better to better, according as they were considered in a conservative or revolutionary point of view. These valorous folks looked askance at his black beard, his green eyes surmounted by overhanging eyebrows of tufted hair, and trembled whenever the promenade of the mighty patriot (a promenade the whole length of the hall) brought them in near contact with each other. This terror was augmented when each time they saw him approaching, or even looked at him too attentively, the man with the cudgel struck with its full weight upon the pavement his powerful weapon, which almost tore up the stones upon which it fell with a sonorous and clashing sound. But it was not only these brave men among the scribes, designated generally as the "rats of Paris," who received this formidable impression; it was also the various individuals who entered La Salle des Pas-Perdus by the great door, or through some of its narrow vomitaries, who also quickened their pace on perceiving the man with the cudgel, who obstinately continued his journey from one end of the hall to the other, finding each moment some pretext for dashing his weapon on the pavement. If the writers had been less timorous and the promenaders more clear-sighted, they would have discovered that our patriot, capricious like all eccentric or extreme natures, appeared to evince a preference for certain flag-stones, those for instance situated a little distance from the wall on the right, near the center of the hall, emitting a clear and ringing sound. He even finished by concentrating his anger upon some particular stones in the center of the hall. At the same time, he so far forgot himself as to stop and measure with his eye something in the distance. True, it was a momentary absence only, and he immediately resumed his former expression, which a gleam of pleasure had for a moment obliterated. Almost at the same moment another patriot —for at this epoch every one wore his opinions on his forehead, or, rather, on his dress—almost at the same moment, say we, another patriot entered by the door of the gallery, and without appearing the least in the world to partake of the fear generated by the former occupant, began to cross the hall at a pace equal to his own, so that in the center of the promenade they encountered each other. The new arrival had, like the former, a hairy bonnet, a gray blouse, dirty hands, and in one of them a cudgel; indeed, in addition he carried a sword, which struck against the stones at every step; and, on the whole, he appeared a greater subject for terror than his predecessor. The first had an air of ferocity, the last seemed replete with sinister cunning.

Although these two men appeared to belong to the same cause, and partook of the same opinions, the assembly ventured to watch the result, not of their meeting, for they were not walking in the same line, but their approach toward each other. At the first turn they were disappointed, as the patriots contented themselves with exchanging looks; at the same time, the smaller of the two turned slightly pale, only from an involuntary movement of the lips it was evident it was not caused by fear but by nausea. However, at the second turn, as if the patriot had made a violent effort, his countenance, till now so overcast, cleared up suddenly, and something like a smile passed over his lips as he inclined slightly to the left, with the evident intention of stopping the second patriot on his course. Near the center they joined each other.

"Eh, *pardieu!* here is the Citizen Simon," said the first patriot.

"Himself. But what do you want with the Citizen Simon? and who are you, first?"

"It seems, then, that you do not know me?"

"I do not know you, and for an excellent reason—I never saw you."

"Not recognize me!—when I had the honor to carry the head of the Princess Lamballe!"

At these words, pronounced with savage fury, and bursting passionately from the mouth of the patriot, Simon started.

"You?" said he, "you?"

"Well, that is surprising! I thought that you would remember your friends better than that, faith! Ah, citizen, you have forgotten me!"

"That is all very well," said Simon; "but I do not recognize you."

"It is a great privilege to act as guardian to the young Capet; it brings you into notice. As for myself, I both know and esteem you."

"Ah! Thank you."

"It is not that. Are you taking a walk?"

"Yes; I am waiting for some one. And you?"

"I also."

"What is your name? I will make mention of you at the club."

"I am called Theodore."

"What else?"

"Nothing else; is not that quite sufficient?"

"Oh, perfectly. Who are you waiting for, Citizen Theodore?"

"A friend to whom I wish to make a pretty little denunciation."

"Indeed! Tell me, then."

"A whole covey of aristocrats."

"What are their names?"

"No, indeed; I only tell that to my friend."

"You are wrong; for here is mine advancing toward us, who, it seems to me, is sufficiently acquainted with business to settle at once all this affair."

"Fouquier Tinville!" cried the first patriot.

"No one less, *cher ami.*"

"That's all right."

"Yes. Good-day, Citizen Fouquier."

Fouquier Tinville, calm and pale, opening wide, according to habit, his large black eyes, shaded by his bushy eyebrows, at this moment entered by a door at the end of the hall, his register in his hand, and a bundle of papers under his arm.

"Good-day, Simon," said he; "anything new?"

"Several things. The first. a denunciation from

Citizen Theodore, who carried the head of the Princess Lamballe. I will introduce him to you."

Fouquier fixed his scrutinizing glance upon the patriot, who, notwithstanding his strong nerves, felt rather uneasy while undergoing this examination.

"Theodore!" said he; "and who is Theodore?"

"I," said the man in the blouse.

"You carried the head of the Princess Lamballe?" said the public accuser, with a great expression of doubt.

"I. Rue St. Antoine."

"But I know a person who boasts that he did so," said Fouquier.

"I know ten," replied the Citizen Theodore, courageously; "but, indeed, as they all make some demand, and I ask nothing, at least I ought to have the preference I hope."

This reply excited Simon's laughter, and dispersed the cloud on the accuser's brow.

"Right," said he; "and if you did not do it, you ought to have done so. But leave me now; Simon has some business to transact with me."

Theodore retired, rather wounded by the frankness of the public accuser.

"One moment," cried Simon. "Do not send him away so; let us first hear his denunciation."

"Ah!" said Fouquier Tinville, with an absent air, "a denunciation?"

"Yes; a covey," replied Simon.

"All in good time. Speak—what is the matter now?"

"Ah! not much; only the Chevalier de Maison Rouge and some of his friends."

Fouquier advanced a step, while Simon raised his arms toward heaven.

"Is this the truth?" they exclaimed, both together.

"The pure truth; will you take them?"

"Directly. Where are they?"

"I met the Chevalier de Maison Rouge in La Rue de la Grande Tissanderie."

"You are mistaken; he is not in Paris," replied Fouquier.

"I tell you I have seen him."

"Impossible; they have sent a hundred men in pursuit of him; he would not show himself in the streets of Paris."

"It was him," said the patriot. "Very brown, and a beard like a bear."

Fouquier shrugged his shoulders disdainfully.

"More folly," said he; "the Chevalier de Maison Rouge is short, pale, and has not a sign of a beard."

The patriot dropped his weapon with an air of consternation.

"Never mind, your good intention was all the same. Come, Simon, we must both make haste; they require the register, this is the time for the carts."

"Well, there is nothing new; the child is well."

The patriot turned his back that he might not appear indiscreet, but remained in a position which enabled him to listen.

"I will go," said he, "lest I should intrude."

"Adieu!" said Simon.

"Good day," said Fouquier.

"Tell your friend that you were deceived," added Simon.

"Well, I shall wait."

And Theodore removed to a short distance, and stood resting on his cudgel.

"So the child goes on well?" said Fouquier; "but the rest?"

"I mold him to my will."

"He will speak, then?"

"When I choose."

"I think he will be afraid in the trial of Antoinette."

"I think not; indeed, I am sure."

Theodore was leaning against a pillar, his eyes directed toward the door. But his eye was wandering, while his ears were erect and uncovered under the hairy bonnet he wore. Perhaps he saw nothing, but most assuredly he heard something.

"Reflect well," said Fouquier, "and do not make what is termed a blunder of this commission. You feel sure that Capet will speak?"

"He will say all that I require."

"Has he told you what we are going to ask him?"

"He has told me."

"It is important, Simon, that you should promise this; the child's evidence is fatal to the mother."

"I count upon that, *pardieu!* "

"There will have been nothing equal to it seen since the intimacy between Nero and Narcisse. Once more, reflect, Simon."

"One would fancy you took me for a brute, repeating constantly the same thing. Take this as an example: when I put leather in water it becomes supple, does it not?"

"But—I do not know," replied Fouquier.

"It becomes soft, then. Well, in my hands the little Capet becomes supple as the softest leather. I have my own method for that."

"It may be so," said Fouquier. "Have you anything else to say?"

"I forgot. There is a denunciation."

"Again? You will overwhelm me with business," said Fouquier.

"One must serve the country."

Simon presented a small paper, black as the leather he had just mentioned, but certainly less supple. Fouquier received it and read the contents.

"Again the Citizen Louis; you have a great hatred for this man."

"I am always at daggers drawn with him. He said, 'Adieu, madame,' to a woman who saluted him from a window yesterday evening. To-morrow I hope to give you a little information concerning another 'suspect'; that Maurice who was municipal at the Temple when that affair of the red carnation occurred."

"Precisely, precisely," said Fouquier, smiling at Simon.

He held out his hand, and then turned away with an eagerness that evinced little favor toward the shoemaker.

"What the devil do you want more ? Many have been guillotined for much less."

"Patience," replied Fouquier, quietly; "everything cannot be done at the same time ;" and he passed quickly through the wicket.

Simon looked round for the Citizen Theodore, to console himself with him. He was no longer to be seen. He had hardly gone beyond the western iron gate, when Theodore reappeared at the corner of a writer's hut. The occupant of the hut accompanied him.

"At what hour are the iron gates closed ?" said Theodore to this man.

"At five o'clock."

"And then what do they do here ?"

"Nothing ; the hall remains empty till to-morrow."

"No rounds, no visits ?"

"No, monsieur ; our barracks are locked."

The word "monsieur" made Theodore knit his brows and look around with defiance.

"Are the crowbar and pistols safe in the barracks ?" said he.

"Yes, under the carpet."

"Return home, then. Apropos, show me again the chamber of the tribunal that has not a grated window, and looks upon the court near La Place Dauphine."

"To the left, between the pillars under the lantern."

"Go now, and have the horse ready at the place assigned."

"A glorious chance ! a glorious chance ! Depend fully upon me."

"Now is your time. No one is looking. Open your barrack."

"It's done, monsieur; I will pray for you."

"It is not for me you ought to pray. Adieu."

And the Citizen Theodore, after an eloquent look,

glided so adroitly under the low roof of the barrack, that he disappeared like the shadow of the waiter who closed the door. The worthy scribe drew the key from the lock, took some papers under his arm, and went out of the vast saloon with the delightful thought that the stroke of five would disperse all these registers like an arrear guard of idle bees.

CHAPTER XXXVI.

THE CITIZEN THEODORE.

THIS immense saloon was enshrouded by the gray veil of night, of which the wretched echoes had learned to repeat the severe words of the advocates and the suppliant ones of the pleaders. From afar, in the distance, in the midst of the obscurity, upright and immovable, a white column seemed watching, in the center of the hall, like a phantom protector over the sacred place. The only noise heard in this darkness was the nibbling and galloping of innumerable rats, who rummaged the papers enclosed in the writer's huts, having first commenced by gnawing the wood. Sometimes the sound of a carriage penetrated as far as this sanctuary of Themis (an academician, so called), and the loose clashing of keys, which appeared to proceed from under the ground; but all this only reverberated in the distance, and nothing resembling a noise ever interrupted the silent darkness, which was not even broken upon by the apparition of a star. Most unquestionably, much terror was occasioned at this hour by the saloon of a palace, whose walls of the exterior were yet stained with the blood of the victims of September—whose staircases had witnessed the descent in one day of twenty-five human beings condemned to an ignominious death, and separated only by a few feet from the cells of the conciergerie peopled with bleached skeletons. Notwithstanding, in the middle of this frightful night—in the midst of this almost solemn silence, a low grinding was heard;

the door of a writer's hut turned upon its creaking hinges, and a shadow, darker than the shadow of night, glided cautiously out of the barrack. Then the fierce patriot we have heard addressed as "Monsieur," but who called himself Theodore, stepped lightly over the uneven stones. He held in his right hand a ponderous iron lever, and with his left felt in his belt to ascertain the safety of his double-barreled pistol.

"I reckoned twelve stones to this part of the cell, and here is the end of the first," murmured he; and, as he calculated, groping with the point of his foot, to discover the chinks which time had rendered daily more perceptible.

"Let me see," said he, stopping; "have I taken my measurement correctly? Shall I possess strength sufficient? And she—will she have the courage? Oh, yes; her courage is known to me. Oh, *mon Dieu! mon Dieu!* when I shall take her hand—when I can say, 'Madame, you are saved!'"

He suddenly paused, as if crushing this hope beneath his feet.

"Ah!" replied he, "fearful and foolish project. They say the others hid themselves under their bedclothes, or contented themselves by roaming about dressed as lackeys through the conciergerie; but they have not my motive for daring all—it is, that I not only desire to serve the queen, but the woman. Well, to work; we will sum up the whole. To raise the stone is nothing, to leave it open is the danger—they may perhaps come the rounds; but yet they never do so. They cannot suspect anything, for I have not any accomplices, and what is required with an ardor like mine to overcome the dark passage? In three minutes I am under her chamber; in five minutes I raise the stone which is on the hearth. She will hear me working, but has too much firmness to feel alarmed; on the contrary, she will understand that a friend is near, and laboring for her deliverance. She is guarded by two men, who will doubtless hasten to the spot. Well, after all," said the patriot, with a melancholy smile, looking first at the weapon concealed in his girdle, and then at the one he held poised in his hand, "a double shot from this pistol, or a couple of strokes from this iron bar. Poor creatures! they will die like others not more culpable than themselves."

And the Citizen Theodore resolutely pressed his lever between the chinks of the flag-stones. At this moment a vivid light gleamed like a ray of gold across the stones, and a noise, repeated by the echoes of the vault, caused the conspirator to turn, and then with a single bound to conceal himself in the stall. Soon voices, weakened by the distance, and softened by the emotion experienced by every one at night in a large and desolate building, reached the ears of Theodore. He stooped down, and through an aperture in the stall perceived first a man in military costume, whose large saber, dangling against the pavement, partly produced the sound which had attracted his attention; then a man in a pistachio-colored suit, holding a rule in his hand, and a roll of papers under his arm. Thirdly, a man in a large waistcoat of rateen and fur bonnet; and lastly, a fourth, with wooden shoes and a blouse. The iron gate, Des Merciers, ground upon its sonorous hinges, rattling the chain intended to keep it open during the day. The four men entered.

"A round," murmured Theodore. "God be praised! five minutes later and I should have been ruined."

He then, with the utmost attention, endeavored to recognize the individuals who composed the round—indeed, three of them were known to him. He who walked first, clad in the costume of a general, was Henriot; the man in the hairy bonnet was Richard, the concierge, and the man in the blouse was, in all probability, a turnkey. But the man in the pistachio-colored coat he had never seen —he was totally unknown to him. Who or what could this man be? and what brought, at ten o'clock at night, to the Salle des Pas-Perdus, the general of the Commune, the guardian of the conciergerie, a turnkey, and this man unknown? The Citizen Theodore remained kneeling, with one hand on his loaded pistol, while with the other he replaced his bonnet, which his precipitous movement had somewhat disarranged.

Up to this moment the nocturnal visitors had kept silence, or, if they had spoken, their words had not reached the ears of the conspirator; but, when about ten paces from his lurking-place, Henriot spoke, and his voice was distinctly heard by the Citizen Theodore.

"We are now," said he, "in the Salle des Pas-Perdus. It is for you now to guide us, Citizen Architect, and to endeavor to convince us that your revelation is no idle story; for, you see, the Revolution has done justice to all this folly, and we believe no more in these subterranean passages than in ghosts. What do you say, Citizen Richard?" added Henriot, turning toward the man in the fur bonnet and rateen vest.

"I have never said there was any subterranean passage under the conciergerie," said he. "There is Gracchus, who has been turnkey for ten years, and, consequently, is acquainted with the whole of the conciergerie; and he ignores the existence of the vault of which the Citizen Giraud has spoken. However, as the Citizen Giraud is the city architect, he ought to know better than any of us. It is his business."

Theodore shivered from head to foot on hearing these words.

"Fortunately," murmured he, "the saloon is large, and before they find what they search for, two days at least must expire."

But the architect opened his great roll of papers, put on his spectacles, and knelt down to examine more fully the plan by the trembling light of the lantern which Gracchus held in his hand.

"I fear," said Henriot, ironically, "that the Citizen Giraud has been dreaming."

"You will see, Citizen General, if I am a dreamer. Wait a little—wait."

"You see, we are waiting," said Henriot.

"Good!" said the architect; and he began to calculate. "Twelve and four make sixteen," said he, "and eight are twenty-four ; which, divided by six, makes four, and then half remains; that is it. I maintain my opinion ; and, if I am deceived, call me an ignoramus, that's all."

The architect pronounced these words with an assurance which terrified the Citizen Theodore.

Henriot regarded the plan with a species of respect, seeing he admired more than he comprehended it.

"Now, follow what I say."

"Where ?" said Henriot.

"Upon the chart which I have drawn. *Pardieu!* here we are. Three feet from the wall is a movable stone I have marked A ; do you see ?"

"Certainly, I see A," said Henriot. "Do you think I do not know how to read ?"

"Under this stone," continued the architect, "is a staircase ; do you see ? It is marked B."

"B!" said Henriot ; "I see B, but I do not see the staircase;" and the general smiled at his own facetiousness.

"When once the stone is raised, the foot once upon the last step, count fifty paces, look up, and you will find yourself exactly at the register where the subterraneous passage terminates, passing under the cell of the queen."

"Capet's widow, you mean, Citizen Giraud," said Henriot, knitting his brows.

"Yes, Capet's widow."

"Why did you say the queen ?"

"The old custom."

"You say, then, it may be found under the register ?" demanded Richard.

"Not only in the register, but also I will tell you in what part you will discover it ; under the stone."

"That is curious," said Gracchus, "for I have noticed that every time I dropped a log in that place the stone resounded. In short, if we find your statement correct, Citizen Architect, I shall pronounce geometry a fine thing."

"Then declare it, Citizen Henriot, for I am now going

to conduct you to the place indicated by the letter A."
The Citizen Theodore made his nails pierce his flesh.

"When I have seen it," said Henriot, "when I have seen it; I rather resemble St. Thomas."

"Ah! you said St. Thomas."

"Yes, as you said 'the queen,' from mere habit; but they cannot accuse me of conspiring with him."

"Nor I with the queen."

After this retort the architect delicately placed his rule, reckoned the distance, then stopped, having apparently finished his calculation, and struck upon a particular stone. This was the identical stone struck by the Citizen Theodore in his fit of frantic rage.

"It is here, Citizen General," said the architect.

"You fancy so, Citizen Giraud."

Our concealed patriot so far forgot himself as to strike his thigh with his clinched hand, with difficulty suppressing a deep groan.

"I am positive," said Giraud; "and your examination, combined with my report, will prove to the Convention I have not been deceived. Yes, Citizen General," continued the architect, with emphasis, " this stone opens upon a subterranean passage, terminating at the register, and passing below the cell of the Widow Capet. Let us raise the stone, descend with me, and I will convince you that two men, even one man, could effect a rescue in a single night, without any one suspecting it."

A murmur of terror and admiration, elicited by the architect's words, ran through the group, and faintly reached the Citizen Theodore, who seemed turned to stone.

"Look at the danger we run," continued Giraud. "Well, now, with a grating which I shall place in the middle of this underground passage, before it reaches the cell of the Widow Capet, I shall save the country."

"Ah, Citizen Henriot," said Giraud, "that is an idea bordering on the sublime."

"Perdition seize you, addle-pated fool!" grumbled the patriot, with redoubled fury.

"Now, raise the stone," said the architect to the Citizen Gracchus, who, in addition to a lantern, carried a crowbar.

He commenced his work, and in a second the stone was raised. The passage appeared open, with the staircase lost in its profundity, while the moist air escaped like a pestilent vapor.

"Another abortive attempt," murmured the Citizen Theodore. "Alas! Heaven does not will that she should escape, and her cause must be accursed!"

CHAPTER XXXVII.

THE CITIZEN GRACCHUS.

For an instant the three men remained petrified at the entrance to the vault, while the turnkey plunged his lantern into the opening without being able to penetrate its depth. The architect triumphantly exulted over his companions from the summit of his genius.

"Well?" said he, at length.

"*Ma foi!* yes," replied Henriot, "here, incontestably is the passage. It only remains to know where it leads to."

"Yes," repeated Richard; "it remains to know that."

"Well, then, descend yourself, Citizen Richard, and then you will see if I have told you the truth."

"I have something better to do than go in there," said the concierge. "We will return with you and the general to the conciergerie. There you can raise the hearthstone, and we shall see."

"Very well," said Henriot; "we will return."

"But we must be careful," said the architect; "this stone remaining unclosed may offer an idea to some one."

"Who the devil do you imagine ever comes here at this hour?" said Henriot.

"Besides," said Richard, "the hall is deserted, and to leave Gracchus here is sufficient. Remain here, Citizen Gracchus, and we will return to you from the other side of the subterranean passage."

"Let it be so, then," said Gracchus.

"Are you armed?" demanded Henriot.

"I have my sword and this crowbar, Citizen General."

"Keep strict watch; in ten minutes we will be with you."

And, having closed the iron gate, the three took their departure by the Gallery des Merciers, to find this particular entrance to the conciergerie.

The turnkey watched their receding footsteps, and followed them with his eyes as far as he could see and listen as long as he had anything to hear; then all relapsed into silence, and, supposing himself in perfect solitude, he placed his lantern on the ground, then sat down, his legs overhanging the depths of the vault, and began to dream. The turnkeys did dream sometimes, but did not often trouble themselves to find out what was the subject of their dreams. All at once, in the midst of this profound reverie, he felt a hand pressed upon his shoulder. He turned round, and attempted, on seeing a stranger, to give the alarm, but at the same instant a pistol gleamed before his eyes. The accents were arrested in his throat, his arms fell listlessly by his side, and his eyes assumed the most suppliant expression.

"Not a word," said the intruder, "or you are a dead man!"

"What do you want, monsieur?" said the turnkey.

Even in '93, there were moments when they had not sufficiently tutored themselves, and omitted to say "Citizen."

"I wish," said the Citizen Theodore, "to be allowed to enter down there."

"What for?"

"Never mind."

The turnkey regarded the person who proffered this request with the most profound astonishment; but in the meantime his interlocutor fancied he detected a ray of intelligence on the man's countenance. He lowered his pistol.

"Do you refuse to make your fortune?"

"I don't know. Hitherto no one has ever made me a proposition on the subject."

"Well, then, I will begin."

"You offer to make my fortune?"

"Yes."

"What do you mean by a fortune?"

"Fifty thousand golden livres, for instance."

"Money is scarce, and fifty thousand livres now are worth a million."

"Well, I offer you that sum."

"To go down there?"

"Yes; but on condition that you come with me, and afford me your assistance in my undertaking."

"But what are you going to do? In five minutes this passage will be filled with soldiers, who will arrest you."

The Citizen Theodore was forcibly struck by this argument.

"Cannot you prevent the soldiers from descending there?"

"I have no means of doing so; I know none, I search in vain."

Indeed, it was evident the turnkey taxed all the powers of his mental energies to discover some means of realizing the sum of fifty thousand livres.

"But," demanded the Citizen Theodore, "could we not enter to-morrow?"

"Yes; but to-morrow a grate of iron will be placed across the passage, occupying the whole width, and for the greater security it is arranged that this partition should be entirely solid, and without even a door."

"Then we must think of something else," said Theodore.

"Yes; we must find some other way," said the turnkey.

It may be seen from the manner in which Gracchus had been experimentalized with, that an alliance was already formed between himself and the Citizen Theodore.

"Look at me," said Theodore. "What do you do at the conciergerie?"

"I am a turnkey."

"What do you do?"

"I open the doors and shut them."

"Do you sleep there?"

"Yes, monsieur."

"Do you take your meals there?"

"Not always. I have my hours of recreation."

"And then?"

"I avail myself of them."

"What to do?"

"To pay my respects to the mistress of the Cabaret du Puits-de-Noe, who has promised to marry me when I am possessed of twelve hundred francs."

"Where is the Cabaret du Puits-de-Noe?"

"Near the Rue de la Vieille Draperie."

"Very well."

"Hush, monsieur!"

The patriot listened.

"Ah, ah!" said he.

"Do you hear?"

"Yes. Voices and footsteps."

"They are returning."

"You see, we should not have had time."

This momentarily became more evident.

"That is true; you are a brave youth, citizen, and are, through me, predestined——"

"To what?"

"To be rich one day."

"God grant it?"

"You, then, still believe in God?"

"Sometimes one thing, sometimes another. To-day, for example."

"Well?"

"I willingly believe."

"Believe, then," said the Citizen Theodore, putting ten louis into the man's hand.

"The devil!" said he, regarding the gold by the light of the lantern.

"Is it serious?"

"It could not be more so."

"What must I do?"

"Meet me to-morrow at the Puits-de-Noe. I will then tell you what I require of you. What is your name?"

"Gracchus."

"Well, Citizen Gracchus, get yourself dismissed from here to-morrow by the Concierge Richard."

"Dismissed! Give up my place?"

"Do you reckon on remaining a turnkey, with fifty thousand livres?"

"No; but being a turnkey and poor, I am certain of not being guillotined."

"Certain?"

"Or nearly so; while being free and rich——"

"You will hide your money, and make love to a tricoleuse, instead of to the mistress of Puits-de-Noe!"

"Well, then, it is settled."

"To-morrow, at the cabaret."

"At what hour?"

"At six in the evening."

"Flee quickly; there they are. I tell you to be quick, because, I presume, you descend and go through the arches."

"To-morrow," repeated Theodore, hastening away.

And not before it was time, for the voices and steps approached, and lights were already visible in the obscurity of the underground passage. Theodore gained the gate indicated by the owner of the hut, then opened the lock with his crowbar, reached the window, threw it open, dropped softly into the street and found himself upon the pavement of the Republic once again. Before quitting the Salle des Pas-Perdus he heard the Citizen Gracchus again question Richard, and also his reply.

"The citizen architect was quite right, the passage passes below the chamber of the Widow Capet, and it was dangerous."

"I believe it," said Gracchus; and in this instance he told the entire truth.

Henriot reappeared at the opening of the staircase.

"And the workmen, Citizen Architect?" demanded he of Giraud.

"Before daybreak they will be here, the supporters fixed, and the gate hung," replied a voice which seemed to proceed from the bowels of the earth.

"And you will have saved the country," said Henriot, half in jest, half in earnest.

"You little know the truth of what you say, Citizen General," murmured Gracchus.

CHAPTER XXXVIII.

THE ROYAL CHILD.

IN the meantime, as we have seen in the chapter preceding, the queen's trial was about to take place. It was already surmised that by the sacrifice of this illustrious head, the popular hatred, so long since displayed in murmurs, would at length be satisfied. The means were not wanting for the completion of this tragedy, and in the meantime, Fouquier Tinville, that fatal accuser, had resolved not to neglect the new mode of accusation which Simon had promised to place in his hands. The day after he and Simon had met in the Salle des Pas-Perdus, the noise of arms still continued to startle the prisoners who remained in the Temple. These prisoners were Mme. Elizabeth, Mme. Royale, and the child, who, after having been called "Your majesty" from his cradle, was now styled the "little Capet." General Henriot, with his tricolored plume, his splendid horse, and large sword, followed by several of the National Guard, dismounted, and entered the dungeon where the royal child languished. By the general's side walked a registrar of a very unprepossessing appearance, carrying a writing-desk, a large roll of paper, and waving in his hand a pen of immoderate length. Behind the scribe walked the public accuser.

We have seen, we know, and shall find that, at a still later period, this dry, jaundiced, cold man, with his bloodshot eyes, made tremble before him the ferocious Henriot, even when cased in his armor. Several National Guards and a lieutenant followed them. Simon, smiling hypocritically, and holding his bonnet in one hand, and his shoemaker's stirrup in the other, walked before to show them the way. They arrived at a very dirty chamber, spacious and cold, at the end of which, seated upon his bed, was the young Louis, in a state of immobility. When we have seen the poor child fleeing from the brutal anger of Simon, he still retained a species of vitality, resenting the unworthy treatment of the shoemaker of the Temple; he fled, he wept, he prayed; then he feared and suffered, but still he hoped. But now both fear and hope had vanished; without doubt the suffering still existed, but if it still remained, the infant martyr, whom they had made pay after so cruel a fashion for his parents' faults, buried it in the depths of his heart, and veiled it under an appearance of total insensibility, and did not even raise his head when the commissioners walked up to him. Without further ceremony they instantly installed themselves. The public accuser seated himself at the head of the bed, Simon at the foot, the registrar near the window, the National Guard and their lieutenant on the side, and rather in the shade. Those among them who regarded the little prisoner with the slightest interest, or even curiosity, remarked the child's pallor, his extraordinary *embonpoint*, resulting from his bloated appearance and the curvature of his legs, of which the joints began already to swell.

"The child is very ill," said the lieutenant, with an assurance that caused Fouquier to turn round, though already seated, and prepared to question his victim.

The little Capet raised his eyes to discover who had uttered these words, and recognized the same young man who had already once before saved him from Simon's cruelty in the court of the temple. A sweet and intelligent glance shot from his deep blue eye, and that was all.

"Ah, ah! is that you, Citizen Louis?" said Simon, thus calling the attention of Fouquier Tinville to the friend of Maurice.

"Myself, Citizen Simon," said Louis, with his usual

nonchalance. And as Louis, though always ready to face danger, was not a man uselessly to seek it, he availed himself of this circumstance to bow to Fouquier Tinville, which salutation was politely returned.

"You observed, I think, citizen," said the public accuser, "that the child was ill; are you a doctor?"

"I have studied medicine, at least, if I am not a medical man."

"Well, and what do you discover in him?"

"What symptoms do you mean?" said Louis.

"Yes."

"I find the cheeks and eyes puffed up, the hands thin and white, the knees swollen; and were I to feel his pulse, I should certainly count eighty or ninety pulsations in a minute."

The child appeared insensible to the enumeration of his sufferings.

"And to what does science attribute the condition of the prisoner?"

Louis rubbed the tip of his nose, murmuring:

> "Phyllis wants to make me speak,
> I am not the least inclined.

Ma foi, citizen," replied he, "I am not sufficiently acquainted with the little Capet's constitution to reply. However——"

Simon lent an attentive ear, and laughed in his sleeve to find his enemy so near committing himself.

"However," said Louis, "I think he does not have sufficient exercise."

"I believe the little scoundrel," said Simon, "does not choose to walk."

The child remained quite unmoved by this apostrophe of the shoemaker. Fouquier Tinville arose, advanced to Louis, and addressed some words to him in a low tone. No one heard the words, but it was evident they assumed the form of interrogatories.

"Oh, oh! do you believe that, citizen? It is a serious charge for a mother——"

"Under any circumstances, we shall find out. Simon pretends he has heard him say so, and has engaged to make him acknowledge it.

"This would be frightful," said Louis; "but indeed it is possible; the Austrian is not exempt from sin, and, right or wrong, does not concern me; they have made her out a Messalina, but, not content with that, they wish to make her an Agrippina. I must acknowledge it appears to me rather hard."

"That is what has been reported by Simon," said the impassible Fouquier.

"I do not doubt that Simon has said all this. There are some men who stick at nothing, even the most impossible accusations. But do you not find," said Louis, fixing his eyes steadily on Fouquier, "do you not find—you, an intelligent and upright man, possessed with a strong mind —that to inquire of a child concerning such circumstances as those which all the most natural and most sacred laws of nature command us to respect, is to insult the whole human nature in the person of a child?"

The accuser did not frown, but took a note from his pocket and showed it to Louis.

"The Convention enjoins me to inform," said he; "the rest does not concern me. I inform."

"It is just," said Louis; "and I declare that if this child acknowledges——"

And the young man shook his head, expressive of disgust.

"Besides," continued Fouquier, "it is not only upon the denunciation of Simon that we proceed; the accusation is public."

And Fouquier drew a second paper from his pocket. This was a number of a work entitled, "Le Père Duchesne," which, as it is well known, was written by Hebert. The accusation indeed appeared there in full.

"It is written and even printed," said Louis, "but till I hear a similar declaration proved from the lips of the child—mind, I mean voluntarily, freely, and without menaces, notwithstanding Simon and Hebert, I shall disbelieve it, much as you in reality do yourself."

Simon impatiently awaited the issue of this conversation.

The miserable creature was not aware of the power exercised upon an intelligent man, the looks which he receives from the crowd, expressive either of sympathy or subtle hatred. But Fouquier Tinville had felt the keen observance of Louis, and was anxious to be fully understood by him.

"The examination is now about to commence," said the public accuser. "Registrar, resume your pen."

This individual, who came to draw out the procès-verbal, was waiting, like Henriot, Simon, and all the rest, till the colloquy between Fouquier and Louis had ceased. The child alone appeared perfectly a stranger to the scene in which he was soon to become the principal actor, and had withdrawn the look which for an instant had gleamed with such bright intelligence.

"Silence," said Henriot, "the Citizen Fouquier is going to interrogate the child."

"Capet," said the public accuser, "do you know what has become of your mother?"

The little Louis turned from an ashy paleness to a brilliant red, but made no reply.

"Did you hear me, Capet?"

He still remained silent.

"Oh! he hears well enough," said Simon, "only he is like the ape, he will not reply for fear he should be taken for a man, and so made to work."

"Really, Capet," said Henriot, "it is the commission from the Convention that interrogates you. You must show obedience to its laws."

The child turned pale, but did not reply. Simon made a frantic gesture of rage. With natures so stupid and brutal as his, anger becomes madness, more especially when accompanied by symptoms of drunkenness.

"Will you reply, you wolf's cub?" showing him the strap.

"Be quiet, Simon," said Fouquier Tinville; "you have not the parole."

This word, which had taken its rise from the Revolutionary Tribunal, had escaped him.

"Do you hear, Simon?" said Louis. "This is the second time you have been told this in my presence; the first was when you accused Tison's daughter, whom you had the pleasure of bringing to the scaffold."

Simon was silent.

"Does your mother love you, Capet?" asked Fouquier.

Still the same silence.

"They say not," continued the accuser.

Something like a ghastly smile passed over the child's pale lips.

"But then, I say," roared Simon, "he has told me she loves him too much."

"Look here, Simon," said Louis, "you are angry that the little Capet chatters so much when you are together, and remains silent before company to-day."

"Oh! if we were together," said Simon.

"Yes, if you were alone; but, unfortunately, you are not alone. Oh! if you were, brave Simon, excellent patriot, how you would belabor the poor child, hey? But you are not alone, and dare not show your rage before honest men like us, who know that the ancients, whom we endeavor to take for our models, respected all who were weak. You dare not, for you are not valiant, my worthy man, when you have children of five feet six inches to combat with."

"Oh!" muttered Simon, grinding his teeth.

"Capet," said Fouquier, "have you confided any secrets to Simon?"

The child never turned round, but his face assumed an expression of irony impossible to describe.

"About your mother?" continued Fouquier.

A look of supreme contempt passed over his countenance.

"Reply, yes or no," cried Henriot.

"Say yes," roared Simon, holding his leather stirrup over the child's head.

The child shuddered, but made no movement to avoid the blow. Those present uttered a cry expressive of their disgust. Louis did more. Before the wretch could lower his arm he darted forward and seized him by the wrist.

"Will you let me go?" roared Simon, purple with rage.

"There is no harm," said Fouquier, " in a mother loving her child. Tell us in what way your mother loved you, Capet. It may be useful to her."

The young prisoner started at the idea of being useful to his mother.

"She loves me as a mother loves her son, monsieur," said he; "there are not two ways for mothers to love their sons, or sons to love their mothers."

"And I, little serpent, declare that you have told me your mother——"

"You have dreamed that," interrupted Louis, quietly; "you must often have the nightmare, Simon."

"Louis, Louis," growled Simon, grinding his teeth.

"Yes, again, Louis. There is no way of beating Louis, since he chastises the wicked; there is no way to denounce him for what he did in arresting your arm, as it was done before General Henriot and Fouquier Tinville, who approved it, and they are not lukewarm in the cause. There is, then, no way to bring him to the guillotine, as you did poor Héloise Tison. It is very grievous, very vexatious, very enraging; still it is so, my poor Simon."

"Too late! too late!" replied the shoemaker, with his mocking laugh.

"Yes, dear friends," said Louis; "I hope, with the help of the Supreme Being— Ah! you expected I was going to say with the help of God, but I hope, with the assistance of the Supreme Being and my sword, to disembowel you first; but more aside, Simon, you prevent me from seeing."

"Brigand!"

"Be silent; you prevent me from hearing."

And Louis silenced him with a threatening look Simon clinched his black hands and shook his fists, but, as Louis had told him, he was obliged to keep within bounds.

"Now he has begun to speak," said Henriot; "he will continue, no doubt. Go on, Fouquier."

"Will you reply now?" demanded Fouquier.

The child returned to his former silence.

"You see, citizen, you see," said Simon, "the obstinacy of this child is strange," troubled in spite of himself at this royal firmness.

"He is badly advised," said Louis.

"By whom?" demanded Henriot.

"By his patron."

"Do you accuse me?" cried Simon, "do you denounce me? Ah! that is curious——"

"Take it coolly," said Fouquier. Then, turning toward the child, who, as we have said, remained perfectly insensible. "My child," said he, "reply to the National Commission; do not aggravate your situation by refusing us any useful information. You have spoken to the Citizen Simon about your mother, how you caress her and love her, how she caresses and loves you?"

Louis threw a glance around the assembly, which gleamed with hatred when it rested on Simon, but he did not reply.

"Do you feel yourself unhappy?" demanded the accuser, "are you uncomfortably lodged, and badly fed, and unkindly treated? Would you wish more liberty, better food, another prison, another guardian? Would you like a horse to ride upon, and some companions of your own age?"

Louis still maintained the profound silence he had only once broken—to defend his mother. The commission was utterly confounded at so much firmness and intelligence evinced by a child.

"These kings," said Henriot, in a low voice, "what a race! They are like tigers, and all the young ones inherit their wickedness."

"How are we to write the procès-verbal?" asked the register much embarrassed.

"As there is no charge, Simon, there is nothing to write," said Louis; "that will settle your affairs exactly."

Simon again shook his fist at his implacable enemy.

Louis began to laugh.

"You will not laugh like that the day you will sneeze in the sack," said Simon, drunk with fury.

"I do not know whether I shall precede or follow you in the little ceremony you menace me with," said Louis; "but this I do know, that many will laugh when your turn comes. Gods!—I have spoken in the plural, gods! —you will not be ugly then, Simon; you will be hideous."

And Louis retired behind the commission, with a fresh burst of laughter. The commission, having nothing more to attend to, withdrew, when the poor child, released from his tormentors, threw himself upon his bed and began to sing a melancholy song which had been a great favorite of his deceased father.

CHAPTER XXXIX.

THE BOUQUET OF VIOLETS.

As it might be foreseen, the felicity of Geneveive and Maurice was not of long continuance. In the tempest which unchains the wind and hurls the thunderbolt, the nest of the dove is shaken in the tree where it had retired for shelter. Geneviève passed from one terror to another. She no longer feared for Maison Rouge, she now trembled for Maurice. She knew her husband sufficiently well to feel convinced, the moment of his disappearance, he was saved, but, sure of his safety, she thought now of her own. She dared not confine her griefs to the man, the least timid, at this epoch when no one was devoid of fear, but it was plainly evinced by her red eyes and pallid cheeks.

One day Maurice softly entered, so quietly, indeed, that Geneviève, buried in a profound reverie, did not notice his entrance. He stopped upon the threshold and saw Geneviève sitting immovable, her eyes fixed on vacancy, her hands lying listlessly on her knees, her head hanging pensively upon her bosom. He gazed at her for a moment, with an expression of sadness, for all that was passing in the young girl's heart was suddenly revealed, as if he had read even to her latest thought. He stepped up to her.

"You have ceased to care for France, Geneviève; confess it is so. You fly from the air you breathe, and not without the greatest reluctance will you even approach the window."

"Alas!" said Geneviève, I know I cannot conceal my thoughts from you, Maurice; you have divined rightly."

"It is, nevertheless, a fine country," said the young man; "life is here important, and well occupied now. This bustling activity of the tribune, the clubs, the conspiracies, etc., renders sweeter the hours spent by our own fireside. One loves it the more ardently, may be from the fear of not being able to love it on the morrow, for on the morrow one may have ceased to exist."

Geneviève shook her head.

"An ungrateful country to serve," said she.

"Why so?"

"Yes, you who have labored so much for the cause of liberty, are you not to-day more than half suspected?"

"But you, dear Geneviève," said Maurice, with a look of tenderness, "you a sworn enemy to this liberty, you who have done so much against it, you yet sleep peaceable and inviolate beneath the roof of a Republican, and there, you see, is my recompense."

"Yes," said Geneviève, "but that cannot last long, that which is wrong cannot endure."

"What do you mean?"

"I mean to say that I, that is to say, an aristocrat, that I who dream quietly of the defeat of your party, and the ruin of our plans; I who conspire, even in your house, the return of the ancient régime; I who, recognized, you would condemn to death and dishonor, pursuant to your opinions, at least; I, Maurice, will not remain here as the evil genius of your house, I will not drag you to the scaffold."

"And where would you go, Geneviève?"

"Where shall I go, Maurice? One day, when you are out, I shall go and denounce myself, without saying where I come from."

"Oh!" cried the young man, wounded to the heart's core, "already ungrateful."

"No," cried the young woman, throwing her arms round Maurice's neck, "it is love, and the most devoted love, I swear. I did not wish my brother should be taken and slaughtered as a rebel; I do not wish my lover to be arrested and guillotined as a traitor."

"And you will do this, Geneviève?"

"As truly as there is a God in heaven," replied the young woman; "besides, I not only experience fear, but remorse;" and she bowed her head as if it were a burden too heavy to be borne.

"Oh, Geneviève!" said Maurice.

"You will understand all that I say, all that I feel, Maurice, for you experience this remorse. You know I gave myself to you while I belonged to another, and you have taken me without my possessing the right to dispose of myself."

"Enough," said Maurice, "enough." He turned pale, and a melancholy expression suffused his clear countenance, and firm resolution burned in his clear eyes. "I will show you, Geneviève, how entirely I love you," said the young man, "I will prove to you that no sacrifice is beyond my love. You hate France. Well, let it be so. We will quit France."

Geneviève clasped her hands, and regarded her lover with enthusiastic admiration.

"You will not deceive me, Maurice?" murmured she.

"Have I ever deceived you?" said Maurice, "and is this the time? I am dishonoring myself for you."

Geneviève approached her lips to Maurice's, and remained hanging on the neck of her lover.

"Yes, you are right," said Geneviève; "it is I who

deceive myself. What I feel is not remorse, perhaps it is a degradation to my love; but you will comprehend, at least, I love you far too much to feel any other emotion than the all-engrossing one, the fear of losing you. Let us go far away, Maurice; let us go far away, where no one can reach us."

"Oh, thanks!" said Maurice, transported with joy.

"But how can we flee?" said Geneviève, trembling at the thought. "It is not so easy to escape nowadays from the poniard of the assassins of the 2d of September, or the hatchet of the hangman of the 21st of January."

"Geneviève," said Maurice, "God will protect us. Listen to me. A good action which I endeavored to perform, apropos to this 2d of September, which you have just named, is now about to receive its reward. I wished to save a poor priest who had studied with me. I went to Danton, and at his request the Commune of Public Safety signed a passport for the unfortunate man and his sister. This passport Danton forwarded to me, but the unhappy man, instead of seeking it at my house, as I had recommended him to do, was shut up by the Carmelites, and there he died."

"And the passport?" said Geneviève.

"I have it now. It is worth a million. It is worth more than that, Geneviève; it comprises both life and happiness."

"Oh, God be praised!" cried the young woman.

"Now, my property, as you are aware, consists of an estate, managed by an old servant of the family, a stanch patriot, and strictly loyal, in whom we may confide. He will send a remittance whenever I wish. On arriving at Boulogne we will go to his house."

"Where does he reside, then?"

"At Abbeville."

"When shall we go, Maurice?"

"Within an hour."

"No one need know of our departure."

"No one will know it. I will run to Louis; he has a cabriolet and no horse, while I have a horse and no carriage. We will set out immediately on my return. You remain here, Geneviève, and prepare everything for our departure. We want but little luggage; we can purchase all that we require in England. I shall give Scevola some commission that will remove him out of the way. Louis will explain our departure to him this evening. By that time we shall be far away."

"But if we should be stopped upon the road?"

"Have we not our passports? We shall go to Hubert's house; that is the steward's name. Hubert forms part of the municipality of Abbeville; from Abbeville to Boulogne he will accompany us as safeguard. At Boulogne we will purchase and freight a vessel. I could, besides, proceed to the committee and make them give me a mission to Abbeville. But no, not by fraud, Geneviève. Is it not better to risk our lives to save and secure our happiness?"

"Yes, yes, *mon ami;* and we shall succeed. But how you are perfumed this morning," said the young woman, concealing her face on Maurice's breast.

"True; I purchased a bunch of violets for you this morning, passing before the Palace d'Egalité; but, on my return, finding you so sad, I thought of nothing but inquiring the cause of your distress."

"Oh, give it to me; I will return it."

Geneviève inhaled the odor of the bouquet with intense delight, when suddenly her eyes suffused with tears.

"What is it?" said Maurice.

"Poor Héloïse!" murmured Geneviève.

"Ah, yes!" said Maurice, with a sigh; "but let us think of ourselves, and leave the dead, wherever they may be, to rest in the grave dug by their devotion. Adieu! I am going."

"Return quickly."

"In less than half an hour I shall be here again."

"But if Louis is not at home?"

"What does it matter? his servant knows me. And even in his absence I can take what I please, as he would do here in mine."

"Very well."

"Now, my Geneviève, prepare everything; but, as I have told you, confine yourself to necessaries. I do not wish our departure to appear like a removal."

The young man advanced a step toward the door.

"Maurice," said Geneviève.

He turned round, and saw the young woman extend her arms toward him.

"*Au revoir, au revoir,* dear love," said he; "in half an hour I shall be here."

Geneviève remained alone, occupied, as we have said, in preparations for their departure. She accomplished her task in feverish haste. As long as she remained in Paris, the part she was acting appeared to her doubly culpable. Once out of France, once among strangers, it seemed that her crime—a crime rather of fatality than her own, would weigh the less heavily on her conscience. She even hoped, isolated and in solitude, she might finish by forgetting the existence of any other man than Maurice. They would fly to England; everything was arranged. There they would hire a little cottage, standing alone, very retired, shut out from all eyes; they would change their names, and instead of two names would have one. Then they would have two servants, who would be perfectly ignorant of the past. Fortunately, both Geneviève and Maurice spoke English. Neither the one or the other left anything to regret in France. Thus Geneviève commenced making preparations for their voyage, or, rather, flight. She took singular pleasure in selecting from the rest those objects for which Maurice had evinced any predilection. The coat setting off his tall figure to advantage, the cravat and waistcoat suitable to his complexion, the books whose leaves he had most frequently drawn upon. She had already made her selection; already the waiting trunks were on the floor, while clothes, linen, and books were strewn on the chairs, the sofa, and the piano. Suddenly she heard the key turn in the lock.

"Why, Scevola has returned!" said she. "Surely Maurice could not have met him."

And she continued her occupation. The doors of the

saloon were open, and she heard Scevola moving in the ante-chamber. She held a roll of music in her hand, and was looking for some string to tie round it.

"Scevola!" cried she.

An approaching step sounded in an adjoining room.

"I am here," said a voice.

At the sound of his voice, Geneviève turned quickly round, and uttered a terrific cry.

"My husband!" cried she.

"Himself," said Dixmer, coolly.

Geneviève was upon a chair, searching for some string in the wardrobe. She felt her head turn round, and extending her arms, fell backward, wishing she could precipitate herself into an abyss beneath. Dixmer took her in his arms, and carried her to a sofa, where he seated himself also.

"What is the matter, my dear? What is it? My presence seems to have produced a most disagreeable effect upon you."

"I am dying," murmured Geneviève, turning from him, and pressing both hands over her eyes, that she might shut out the frightful apparition.

"What," said Dixmer, "did you believe me dead, my dear, and did you take me for a ghost?"

Geneviève looked round her with a bewildered air, when, perceiving the portrait of Maurice, she glided from the sofa and fell upon her knees, as if to implore the assistance of this powerless and insensible image, which still continued to smile. The miserable woman fully comprehended the menaces concealed by Dixmer under his affected calmness.

"Oh, my dear child," continued the master tanner, "it was well for me, perhaps, that you thought I was far from Paris; but I remained there. The day after I had quitted the house, I returned, and found in its stead a heap of ruins. I inquired after you. No one had seen you. I then commenced a search after you, and have had much trouble to find you. I vow I did not think you were here; however, I had my suspicions. So, as you see, I came. So here I am, and you see me. And how is dear Maurice? Indeed, I fear you have suffered much. You so stanch a Royalist, compelled to seek shelter under the roof of a Republican."

"My God! my God!" murmured Geneviève, "take pity upon me!"

"After all, my dear," continued Dixmer, "what serves to console me most is that you are so comfortably lodged here, and that you do not appear to have suffered much from the proscription. As for myself, since the burning of our house, and the ruin of our fortune, I have had my share of wandering adventures, sometimes living in a cave, another time a boat, and sometimes even in the common sewers with which the Seine abounds."

"Monsieur!" said Geneviève.

"You have there some beautiful fruit; as for me, I have often gone without any dessert, not having had any dinner." Geneviève, sobbing bitterly, supported her head between her hands. "Not," continued Dixmer, "that I was destitute of money. I have, thank God! generally carried with me thirty thousand francs in gold, which at this time is worth five hundred thousand francs; by means of which the 'collier,' the 'fisherman,' or the 'rag merchant' drew the louis from his pocket to purchase a morsel of cheese or a sausage. Eh, my God! yes, madame, I have successfully adopted these three costumes. To-day, the better to disguise myself, I am *en patriote, en exagère, en Marseillais.* I lisp and I swear; an outlaw cannot conceal himself as easily in Paris as a young and pretty woman, and I have not the happiness of knowing an ardent young Republican who would hide me from every eye."

"Monsieur! monsieur!" cried Geneviève, "have mercy upon me; you see that I am dying."

"Anxiety; I can understand that you have had much anxiety about me; but console yourself, you see me now. I have returned, and we will now part no more, madame."

"Oh, you will kill me!" cried Geneviève.

Dixmer regarded her with a frightful smile.

"Kill an innocent woman! Oh, madame, what makes you say so? It must be that grief for my absence has turned your brain."

"Monsieur!" said Geneviève, "monsieur, I beseech you to kill me at once, rather than torture me with these cruel railleries. No, I am not innocent; yes, I am criminal; yes, I merit death. Kill me, monsieur, kill me——"

"Then, you acknowledge that you merit death?"

"Yes, yes!"

"And to expiate this crime of which you accuse yourself, you will submit to death without complaint?"

"Strike, monsieur; I will not utter a cry, and, instead of cursing, I will bless the hand that strikes me."

"No, madame; I do not wish to strike you, though, in all probability, you will die. Only your death, instead of being, as you seem to fear, an ignominious one, shall be most glorious. Thank me, madame, while punishing, I will immortalize you."

"What, then, will you do, monsieur?"

"You will follow the end to which we were tending when interrupted on our route. In your own eyes and in mine you die guilty; in the eyes of the world you will die a martyr."

"Oh, my God! you will drive me mad by speaking thus. Where are you conducting me? where are you dragging me?"

"In all probability, to death."

"Leave me to offer up one prayer!"

"To whom?"

"It matters not to you. The moment you deprive me of life, my debt is canceled—my debt paid, I owe you nothing."

"True," said Dixmer, retiring into another room; "I will await you."

And he left her once more alone.

Geneviève sunk on her knees before the portrait, pressing her hands against her bursting heart.

"Maurice," said she, in a low tone, "pardon me; I could not expect to be happy, but I hoped to have made you so. Maurice, I am depriving you of a joy that constituted your life; pardon me for causing your death, my best beloved!"

Then, severing a ringlet from her mass of curls, she bound it round the bouquet of violets, and placed them beneath the portrait, which, insensible and speechless as it was, still appeared to assume an expression of grief at her departure. At least, so it appeared to the unfortunate Geneviève, as she gazed at it through her tears.

"Well, are you ready, madame?" demanded Dixmer.

"So soon!" murmured Geneviève.

"Oh, take your time, madame," replied Dixmer; "I am in no hurry. Besides, I dare say, Maurice will not be long, and I shall be delighted to thank him for all his kindness and hospitality toward you."

Geneviève trembled with terror at the idea of a meeting between her lover and husband. She raised herself by an effort, saying, calmly:

"It is finished, monsieur, and I am ready now."

Dixmer went out, first, and the trembling Geneviève followed him. With half-closed eyes, her head turned round to look her last, she ascended the carriage which was waiting at the door. It rolled away. As Geneviève had truly said—it was finished.

CHAPTER XL.

THE CABARET DU PUITS DE-NOE.

THIS man, attired in the blouse, whom we have seen traversing with long and rapid strides the Salle des Pas-Perdus, whom we have heard (during the expedition of the architect Giraud, General Henriot, and Richard) conversing with the turnkey left to guard the subterranean passage, this enraged patriot, who had introduced himself to Simon as having carried the head of the Princess de Lamballe, found himself, on the next evening, about seven o'clock, at the Cabaret du Puits-de-Noe, situated,

as we have said, at the corner of La Rue de la Vieille
Draperie. He was seated at the end of a dirty room,
redolent of tobacco and candles, pretending to devour a
plate of fish swimming in black butter. The room where
he supped was nearly deserted; two or three *habitués* of
the house alone remained after the rest who enjoyed the
privilege of a daily visit to this establishment. The tables
were, for the most part, empty; but we ought to remark,
in honor to the Cabaret du Puits-de-Noe, that the stained
tablecloths denoted the departure of a satisfactory number of satisfied guests. The three last successively disappeared, and at about a quarter to eight the patriot found
himself alone. Then, with true aristocratic disgust, he
pushed away the greasy plate, which an instant before he
had appeared to think so delicious, and drew from his
pocket a tablet of Spanish chocolate, which he ate slowly,
and with a very different expression to that we have endeavored to portray on his countenance. From time to
time, while eating his chocolate and black bread, he cast
toward a glass door, shaded by a red and blue-checked
curtain, anxious and impatient glances. Sometimes he
interrupted his frugal repast to listen; in short, evinced
an absence of mind sufficient to induce the mistress of the
mansion (seated at her counter, and near the door on
which the patriot so eagerly fixed his eyes) to conclude,
that she might without vanity consider herself as the object of his preoccupation. At length the door-bell
sounded in a way that made him start; he drew the plate
again before him, and, without attracting the woman's
observation, threw half the contents to a famished-look-
ing dog, and the remainder to a cat, who, spitefully seizing
the dog's dainties, received in return some strokes from
his paws. The door opened, and a man entered, dressed
almost the same as the patriot, with the exception of the
hairy cap, which he had replaced with the bonnet-rouge.
An enormous bunch of keys hung from his girdle, from
which also depended a sword.

"My soup! my chop!" cried the man, entering the public room without removing his bonnet, or even saluting the

mistress of the house by an inclination of his head, but, with a sigh of fatigue, seated himself at a table adjoining that where our patriot was discussing his black bread and chocolate. The mistress of the cabaret, in consequence of the deference she entertained for the newcomer, rose herself to order the requisite viands. The two men turned—one to look into the street, the other toward the end of the room —not a word was exchanged between them till the mistress of the cabaret had totally disappeared. When the door had closed behind her, and the light from a single candle, suspended from the end of an iron wire so as to divide the light equally between the two guests, when at length the man in the bear-skin bonnet—thanks to the light placed before him—saw that the room was deserted:

"*Bon soir,*" said he to his companion, without turning round.

"*Bon soir,*" said the newcomer.

"Well," said the patriot, with the same affected indifference, "where are we now?"

"Well, it is done."

"What is done?"

"As we agreed, I have had some conversation with Father Richard about the situation. I complained of swimming in the head, dimness of eyesight—in short, of general ill-health, and a continual pain altogether."

"What then?"

"Father Richard called his wife, and she rubbed my temples with vinegar, and that revived me. Then, as we had arranged between us, I said that want of air produced the swimming in the head, that I made blood too fast, and that the duty at the conciergerie, which contains at the present moment four hundred prisoners, was killing me."

"What did they say to that?"

"Richard's wife pitied me, and he took me to the door."

"It was not enough to take you to the door."

"But wait. Then his wife, who is a good soul, reproached him with having no heart, seeing that I was the father of a family."

"What did he say to that?"

"He said that she was right; but that the very first condition annexed to the situation of turnkey was to remain within the prison to which he was attached; that the Republic did not jest, but would, without ceremony, cut the throats of those who grew dizzy in the exercise of their duty."

"*Diable!*" said the patriot.

"And he was not far from wrong either; for since the Austrian has been there, it is a perfect hell of surveillance. Confound her!" The patriot here gave his plate to the dog to lick, who was directly bitten by the cat.

"Go on," said he, without turning round.

"At last, monsieur, I began to groan, and to say that I felt very ill; asked concerning the infirmary, and said I was certain my children would die of hunger if this pain was not removed."

"And Father Richard?"

"The Father Richard replied that turnkeys had no business with children."

"But you had his wife on your side, I suppose?"

"Fortunately. She made a great to-do with her husband, reproached him with possessing a bad and hard heart, and Richard finished by saying to me:

"'Well, Citizen Gracchus, speak to some one of your friends who will give you some security for his attendance, present him to me, and I promise to accept him as your substitute.' Upon which I left him, saying:

"'Very good, Father Richard, I will directly seek one.'"

"And you have found one, my brave fellow."

At this moment the mistress of the establishment entered, bringing the Citizen Gracchus his soup and chop. This did not suit either the patriot or Gracchus, who had still some communication to make.

"Citoyenne," said the turnkey, "I have received a slight remuneration from Father Richard to-day, which will permit me to treat myself to some better fare. So bring me some pork, a drinking-horn, and a bottle of

Burgundy wine; send your servant to fetch the one from the pork butcher's, and bring me the other yourself fresh from the cellar."

The hostess immediately left to execute his orders.

"Well," said the patriot, "you are an intelligent lad."

"So far intelligent that I do not hide from myself what, notwithstanding all your fine promises, will be the end of us both. Do you suspect what it may be?"

"Yes, perfectly."

"We stake both our necks."

"Do not be uneasy about mine."

"It is not yours, monsieur, I must confess, that causes me the greatest uneasiness."

"It is your own?"

"Yes."

"But what if I estimate it at double its worth?"

"Ah, monsieur, there is nothing more precious than one's neck!"

"Not yours."

"Why not mine?"

"At this moment, at least."

"What do you mean by that?"

"I mean to say your neck is not worth an old coin, seeing that if I, for example, were an agent of the Committee of Public Safety, you would be guillotined to-morrow."

The turnkey suddenly turned round so brusquely that the dog barked at him. He was pale as death.

"Neither turn round nor turn pale," said the patriot, "but, on the contrary, finish your soup quietly. I am not an agent, friend. Let me once enter the conciergerie, install me in your situation, give me the keys and to-morrow I will count out to you fifty thousand livres in gold."

"Is this true, at least?"

"Well, you have excellent security. My head."

The turnkey considered for some seconds.

"Come," said the patriot, who could not see him in the glass, "do not indulge in meditations of evil. If you denounce me, as you will only have done your duty, you will not receive a sou from the Republic ; if you serve me, and, on the contrary, are deficient in this same duty, as it is unjust in this world to do anything for nothing, I will give you fifty thousand livres."

"I understand perfectly," said the turnkey. "I have all the inclination to do what you require, but I fear the results——"

"The results! And what have you to fear? I will not denounce you ; on the contrary."

"No doubt."

"The day after I am duly installed, take a turn through the conciergerie, and I will count you twenty-five rouleaux each containing two thousand francs. These you can easily dispose of in your two pockets. With the money I will give you a card to leave France. You go, and wherever you are you will be not only rich, but independent."

"Well, it is settled, monsieur ; let what will happen. I am a poor devil who never meddled in politics. France has always got on very well without me, and will not perish through any fault of mine ; if you do a wicked action, so much the worse for you."

"At all events," said the patriot, "I think I shall never do worse than they are doing at this moment."

"Monsieur, permit me to decline passing an opinion upon the politics of the National Convention."

"You are a pattern of philosophy and carelessness. When, however, will you present me to Father Richard?"

"This evening, if you please."

"Yes, certainly ; but who am I?"

"My cousin Murdoch."

"Murdoch let it be, then ; the name pleases me. What trade?"

"A breeches-maker."

"Either breeches-maker or tanner. I have that at my fingers' ends."

"Are you a tanner?"

"I could be one."

"True."

"At what time will you present me?"

"In half an hour if you like."

"At nine o'clock, then."

"When shall I have the money?"

"To-morrow."

"You must be enormously rich."

"I am in easy circumstances."

"A *ci-devant*—is it not so?"

"What does it matter?"

"To possess money and give it away to run the risk of being guillotined; surely the *ci-devants* must be great blockheads."

"What would you have? The *sans-culottes* have too much sense to leave any for others."

"Hush! here is my wine."

"This evening, in front of the conciergerie."

"Yes."

The patriot paid his bill and went out. At the door was heard the stentorian voice:

"Come, citoyenne, quick! the ribs of pork and the drinking-horn, my cousin Gracchus is dying of hunger."

"Murdoch is a good fellow," said the turnkey, tasting the wine poured out for him by the *cabaretière*, and regarding her tenderly.

CHAPTER XLI.

THE REGISTRAR OF THE MINISTER OF WAR.

The patriot left but he had not gone far. Through the curtained window he kept watch over the turnkey to discover if he entered into conversation with any of the agents of the Republican police, one of the best that ever existed, since one half of the society closely watched the other, less from the great glory of government than for the still greater security of their heads. But nothing occurred to excite the patriot's fears. At a few minutes before nine the turnkey rose, pinched the chin of the hostess, and went out. The patriot rejoined him at the quay of the conciergerie, and they entered the prison together. On the same evening the affair was concluded, and Father Richard accepted Murdoch as a substitute for Gracchus. Two hours before this arrangement took place, another scene had been enacted in a different part of the prison, which, although apparently of no interest, was possessed of vital importance to the principal personages of this history. The registrar of the conciergerie, fatigued with his day's labor, was folding up his papers, and preparing to leave, when a man, conducted by the Citoyenne Richard, presented himself in his office.

"Citizen Registrar," said she, "here is your fellow-registrar of the minister of war, who comes on the part of the citizen minister to hasten some military matters."

"Ah, citizen," said the registrar, "you are too late; I have just put away all my papers."

"Dear brother, pardon me," said the newcomer; "but we are really so overwhelmed with business that even running does not make up for lost moments, and our lost moments only are those occupied by others in eating and sleeping."

"That alters the case, my dear fellow; so make haste, for, as you observe, it is near supper-time, and I am very hungry. Have you your documents?"

"Here they are," said the registrar of the minister of war, exhibiting a portfolio of papers, which his brother, busy as he was, scrutinized with the strictest attention.

"Oh, they are all right," said Richard's wife, "and my husband has already thoroughly inspected them."

"Never mind, never mind," said the registrar, continuing his examination. The registrar remained like a man patiently awaiting the accomplishment of all due formalities. "Perfectly correct," said the registrar of the conciergerie, "and you can now commence as soon as you please. Have you many entries to make?"

"A hundred. That will occupy you for several days.

Therefore, dear brother, I wish to form a small establishment near you; that is to say, if you will permit me."

"How am I to understand you?" said the registrar of the conciergerie.

"I will explain it to you fully if you will join us at supper this evening. You say you are hungry?"

"I do not deny it."

"Well, you shall see my wife, who is a good housekeeper, and you know me, and will acknowledge me for a good companion."

"*Ma foi!* yes; you strike me as such, and my dear brother; yet, notwithstanding——"

"Oh! come without ceremony, and partake of some oysters that I will purchase as I pass La Place du Châtelet, a poulet of our own roasting, and a few dishes which Madame Durant excels in."

"You tempt me, my brother," said the registrar of the conciergerie, astonished at the bill of fare, to which he was totally unaccustomed as a registrar paid by the Revolutionary Tribunal at the rate of ten livres, in assignats, equal to two francs at the utmost.

"Then you will accept my invitation?"

"Yes, willingly."

"In that case, to work to-morrow; till this evening we part."

"Now we must part."

"You will come early?"

"In an instant, only I must first inform the gendarmes who guard the Austrian."

"Why must you tell them?"

"So that when they know that I am absent, and that there is no one at the wicket, they may become suspicious of every noise."

"Ah! that is a very wise precaution, faith!"

"You understand now?"

"Perfectly."

"Go then."

The registrar of the conciergerie proceeded hastily to the wicket, which was opened by one of the gendarmes.

"Who is there?"

"I, the registrar, you know. I am going out. *Bon soir*, Citizen Gracchus."

"*Bon soir*, Citizen Registrar;" and the wicket was shut.

The registrar of the minister of war had paid the greatest attention to this scene, and while the door of the queen's prison remained opened, his looks rapidly penetrated to the first compartment, where, seeing the other gendarme, Duchesne, seated at table, he felt perfectly assured the queen had only two guards, and when the registrar of the conciergerie turned round, his face had resumed its expression of perfect stolid indifference. As they went out of the conciergerie two men entered. They were the Citizen Gracchus and his cousin Murdoch. The cousin Murdoch and the registrar of the minister of war, each by a simultaneous movement arising from the same feeling, appeared to shrink, the one at the sight of the hairy bonnet, the other from the broad-brimmed hat pulled down over the eyes.

"Who are these men?" asked the registrar of the minister of war.

"I only know one of them—it is a turnkey, named Gracchus."

"Ah!" said the other, with affected indifference, "do the turnkeys then go out of the conciergerie?"

"They have their day."

The investigation did not proceed any further, and the new friends took the road to the Pont au Change. At the corner of the Place du Châtelet, the registrar of the minister of war, according to agreement, purchased some oysters, and continued his way by the Quay de Grève. The dwelling of this individual was simple. The Citizen Durand inhabited three rooms on La Place de Grève, in a house without any porter. Each tenant had a key of the door in the passage, and it was agreed that if any one had omitted to take his key, he should intimate the same by one, two, or three raps with the knocker, according to the story he inhabited, and any one who was waiting, and heard the signal, then descended and opened the door; but the Citizen Durand, having provided himself with his key, had not any occasion to knock. They ascended two flights of stairs, when the Citizen Durand drew another key from his pocket, and they both entered. The registrar of the palace found his friend's wife much to his taste. She was a charming woman ; indeed, an expression of profound melancholy diffused over her countenance, stamped it with an expression of deep interest. It has always been allowed that sadness is seductive in women, especially pretty women. It attracts all men, without exception, even turnkeys ; and turnkeys are but men, after all ; and what man possessed with natural feeling would not wish to console a pretty woman in affliction, and as the Citizen Dorut remarks, "To change the pale tint, of the white rose to a roseate hue!" The two registrars did full justice to their excellent supper ; it was only Mme. Durand who ate nothing. In the meantime, conversation proceeded. The registrar inquired of his brother registrar (with a curiosity the more remarkable in these days, when such frightful dramas were daily enacted) concerning the customs of Paris, the days of judgment, and the means of surveillance. The registrar of the palace, delighted at being listened to with so much deference, replied with the greatest complaisance, spoke of the manners of jailers, of Fouquier Tinville, and lastly of the Citoyen Sanson, the principal actor in the tragedy daily performed upon the Place de la Revolution. Then, in his turn, addressing his colleague and host, he made various inquiries concerning his vocation and ministry.

"Oh!" said Durand, "I am not so well informed as yourself, being a person of much less importance, seeing that I am rather secretary to the registrar than the incumbent of the place. I do the work of the registrar-in-chief —an obscure employment for me, at least, but highly profitable to them ; but that is the way with all these revolutionary commissioners. Heaven and earth may perhaps change one day, but these things never."

"Well, I will assist you, citizen," said the registrar of

the palace, charmed with the excellence of his host's wine, and, above all, with the *beaux yeux* of Mme. Durand.

"Thanks," said he to whom this offer had been made; "anything to vary the habits and locality is some distraction to a poor employé. I wish to hasten my work at the conciergerie, rather than to procrastinate it, and therefore thought if I might every day bring Madame Durand with me to the office, who is very dull here——"

"I do not see any inconvenience in that," said the registrar of the palace, delighted with the prospect of the charming recreation afforded him by his colleague.

"She can dictate the papers," said the Citizen Durand, "and occasionally, when our work is finished, if you have not found this evening unpleasant, you can return and spend an hour or two with us."

"Yes; but not too often," replied the registrar of the palace, foppishly; "for I declare I shall be scolded if my visits are less frequent than usual at a small house in La Rue du Petit Muse."

"Well, here is some one who will settle all these affairs. Is it not so, *chère amie?*"

Mme. Durand, pale and melancholy, as usual, raised her eyes toward her husband, and replied:

"What you wish shall be done."

Eleven o'clock struck, announcing it was time to retire. The registrar of the palace rose, and took leave of his two friends, expressing the great pleasure he felt in making their acquaintance. The Citizen Durand conducted his friend to the landing, then reentered the apartment.

"Go, Geneviève, go to bed," said he.

The young woman made no reply, but rose directly, took her lamp, and withdrew to the bedroom on the right. Durand, or, rather, Dixmer, watched her departure, remained stationary for a moment with an expression of deep grief depicted upon his countenance, then passed into his own chamber on the opposite side.

CHAPTER XLII.

THE TWO BILLETS.

FROM this time the registrar of the minister of war worked every evening most indefatigably in his colleague's office, while Mme. Durand dictated from the registers previously prepared, which Durand copied with avidity. Durand strictly examined everything, while appearing to notice nothing. He had remarked that every evening at nine o'clock, a basket of provisions, carried by either Richard or his wife, was placed at the door. The instant the registrar said to the gendarme, "I am going, citizen," one of the guards, either Gilbert or Duchesne, came out, took the basket, and carried it to Marie Antoinette. During three consecutive evenings, when Durand had remained rather late at his post, the basket also was left untouched; since it was only when opening the door to say adieu to the registrar that the gendarme took in the basket containing the provisions, which, a quarter of an hour afterward, was returned empty to the same place by one of the two guards. On the evening of the fourth day, it was the beginning of October, when, after the ordinary sitting, the registrar of the palace had withdrawn, and Durand, or, rather, Dixmer, remained alone with his wife, he laid down his pen, looked around and listened, as if his very life was at stake; he then rose hastily, and running toward the door of the wicket, raised the cloth which covered the contents of the basket, and in the new bread destined for the prisoner concealed a small silver purse. Pale and trembling with emotion, he quickly regained his seat, and sank down overpowered, placing one hand on his forehead, the other on his heart. Geneviève regarded him in silence; indeed, since the day her husband had taken her from Maurice, she had never spoken till he addressed her first. But this time she first broke silence.

"Is it to be this evening?" she inquired.

"No; to-morrow," replied Dixmer.

He then rose, and having again looked and listened, closed the registers, and, approaching the wicket, knocked at the door.

"What?" said Gilbert.

"Citizen," said he, "I am now going."

"Well," said the gendarme, from the end of the cell, "good-night."

"Good-night, Citizen Gilbert."

Durand heard the grinding of the bolt, and knew that the gendarme was opening the door. He went out.

In the passage leading to the apartment of Father Richard by the court he rushed against a turnkey dressed in a bear-skin bonnet and dangling a heavy bunch of keys. Dixmer was much alarmed. Perhaps this man, brutal as the generality of his species, was about to interrogate him, to watch him, and perhaps finally to recognize him. He drew his hat over his eyes, while Geneviève concealed herself, as she best could, in the folds of her cloak. But he was mistaken.

"Pardon!" said the turnkey only, although he was the man who had been nearly overthrown.

Dixmer trembled at the sound of that sweet, soft voice.

But the turnkey was doubtless pressed for time; he glided into the passage, opened Richard's door and disappeared. Dixmer continued his road, leading Geneviève.

"It is strange," said he, when outside, and the gate had closed behind them, and the freshening breeze had cooled his fevered brow.

"Oh, yes; 'tis very strange!" murmured Geneviève.

In former times they would have communicated to each other the cause of their astonishment, but Dixmer now confined his thoughts to his own breast, and combated them as an hallucination; while Geneviève contented herself, on turning the angle of the Pont au Change, by casting a last look at the dark and gloomy palace, where something like the phantom of a lost friend awoke in her memory many sweet and bitter remembrances. Thus they both reached La Grève without having exchanged a single word. During this time the gendarme Gilbert had brought in the basket of provisions intended for the queen. It contained some fruit, a cold chicken, a bottle of white wine, a carafe of water, and half a loaf. Having first raised the napkin, and ascertained that everything was arranged as usual, he opened the screen.

"Citoyenne," said he, "here is your supper."

Marie Antoinette divided the bread, but as her fingers pressed it, they came in contact with the silver. In an instant she comprehended the bread contained something unusual. When she looked around her, the guard had disappeared. The queen remained a moment immovable, calculating his retiring footsteps. When she felt certain he was seated by his comrade, and not till then, she drew the purse from its place of concealment. It contained a billet, which she opened, and read as follows:

"MADAME,—Be ready to-morrow at the hour when you receive this billet, as to-morrow at this hour a female will be introduced into your majesty's prison. This female will exchange dresses with you, and you will then quit the conciergerie on the arm of one of your most devoted servants. Do not be alarmed at any noise that passes in the first compartment; let neither cries nor groans deter you, only attire yourself quickly in the dress and mantle of the female who comes to take your majesty's place."

"This is devotion!" murmured the queen. "Thank God, I am not, as it is said, an object of execration to all."

She then reread the billet, when the second part attracted her attention: "Let neither cries nor groans deter you."

"Oh! that means they will sacrifice my two guards. Poor men! who have evinced so much kindness and pity toward me! Oh! never—never!"

She tore off part of the letter, and, having no pen or ink, pricked on the paper the following words:

"I neither can nor will accept the sacrifice of any one's life in exchange for my own.   M. A."

She then replaced the paper in the purse, which she concealed in the other half of the broken bread. This operation was just completed when ten o'clock struck, and the queen, holding the piece of bread in her hand, sadly counted the strokes which vibrated slowly and distantly, when she heard at one of the windows opening upon the court termed "La Cour des Femmes," a grating sound, like that produced by a diamond dividing the glass. This noise was followed by a clash upon the window, and was several times repeated, intended to conceal the cough of a man. Then, at the corner of the glass, a small roll of paper appeared, which glided slowly, and fell on the inside of the wall. The queen then heard the sound of keys jingling and clashing against each other, and receding footsteps on the pavement. She was aware that the window was perforated at this corner, and that through this aperture the departing individual had conveyed a paper, which doubtless contained a billet. It was now lying on the ground. The queen covered her eyes, listening if either of her guards were approaching, but heard them conversing in a low tone as usual, as if with the intention of not annoying her with their voices. Then she moved softly, holding her breath, and secured the paper, which contained some minute and hard substance concealed in a case, which, falling on the bricks, sounded like metal. It was the most exquisite file that could be imagined—more of the jewel than the tool—one of those inventions in steel with which the most feeble and uninitiated hand could, in a quarter of an hour, divide a bar of iron.

"Madame," said the paper, "to-morrow, at half-past nine, a man will be conversing with the gendarmes who guard you, through the window of the Cour des Femmes. During this time your majesty will saw the bar of your window, going from the left to the right. Cut slanting; a quarter of an hour will suffice for your majesty; and then be prepared to escape through the window. This advice reaches you from one of your most devoted and faithful subjects, one who has consecrated his life to your majesty's service, and would be happy also to sacrifice it for you."

"Oh!" murmured the queen, "it must be a snare. But no; this writing appears familiar to me—it is the same as at the Temple. It is—it must be the Chevalier de Maison Rouge! God is perhaps willing that I should escape."

And the queen fell on her knees, and took refuge in prayer, the only balm and consolation undenied to the unfortunate prisoner.

CHAPTER XLIII.

THE PREPARATIONS OF DIXMER.

The morrow, prefaced by a sleepless night, at length arrived. The day broke at last, presenting a terrible appearance, when it might, without exaggeration, be said the sky was the color of blood; indeed, each day at this epoch, and in this year, however beautiful the sun, had a livid hue. The queen at length slept, but it was a sleep without repose. With her eyes closed, she saw nothing but blood; with her understanding deadened, she heard nothing but smothered cries of despair. She had dropped asleep with the file in her hand. One part of the day was devoted by her to prayer, and the guards seeing her often thus engaged, did not feel any alarm at what they considered an increase of religious feeling. From time to time, however, she examined the file transmitted to her by one of her intended deliverers, and compared the fragility of the instrument with the strength of the bar. Fortunately, these bars were only secured in the wall on one side—that is to say, at the lower part. The upper part was set in a cross-bar; the lower part divided, there was only to pull the bar, and it, of course, would yield. But it was not these physical difficulties which arrested the queen. She perfectly comprehended the thing was practicable, and it was this very possibility which caused hope, like a brilliant meteor, to flash before her eyes. She felt that, to reach her, her friends must necessarily sacrifice her guards; and could she at any price consent to the death of the only individuals who, for a length of time, had evinced any interest in her, or pity for her? Then, opposed to this argument, were the iron bars she was to saw asunder, and the bodies of these two men on the other side, who must fall in preventing her friends from coming to her deliverance. This comprised life, liberty, and perhaps vengeance—three things, above all, so sweet, that she asked pardon of God for so earnestly desiring them. She believed, as to the rest, that not the slightest suspicion agitated the minds of her guards, that they had not any idea of a snare (if such a thing existed) into which it was intended the prisoner should fall. These simple men would have betrayed themselves to eyes so much exercised as those of this woman habituated to detect evil from having so severely suffered from it. The queen entirely abandoned the idea that these combined overtures were contrived as a trap; but as the fear of being betrayed into this snare disappeared, the still greater apprehension increased of some bloody scene being enacted before her very eyes.

"Strange destiny! sublime sight!" murmured she; "two conspiracies united to save a poor queen, or, rather, a poor female prisoner, who has had no means of inducing or encouraging these conspiracies, which are about to take place at the same monent. Who knows? Perhaps there may be one only. Perhaps it may be a double mine, leading to one and the same point. If I will it, I might then be saved. But a poor woman sacrificed in my stead! two men killed before this woman could reach me. God might perhaps forgive me. Impossible! impossible!"

Then passed and repassed in her mind visions of the great devotion of servitors for their masters, and the ancient tradition of the right exercised by masters over the lives of their retainers—a phantasy almost effaced by the royal doom and death.

"Anne of Austria might have accepted this," said she. "Anne of Austria would have yielded every consideration to the safety of the royal person. Anne of Austria is of the same blood, and was almost in the same situation as myself. What madness to be following the royal career of Anne of Austria in France! Was I not brought hither? Two kings said it is important that two royal children, who have never seen or loved each other, who perhaps never may love each other, should be married at the same altar, to die upon the scaffold. And then, will not my death accelerate that of my poor child, who in the eyes of my friends is still King of France? And when my son, like his father, is dead, will not their shades both smile on me in pity, seeing that to spare some drops of plebeian blood I have stained with my blood the remains of the throne of St. Louis?"

In this anguish of thought, this fever of doubt, every pulsation redoubled, and in a tempest of terror and fear, the unhappy queen continued till the arrival of night. She had several times closely scrutinized her guards, but they exhibited an air of the greatest calm. Never had she been more forcibly struck by the invariable kindness and attention of these two uneducated men. When the darkness of night reigned in the cell, when the steps of the round, the noise of resounding arms, and the barking of dogs, awoke the echoes of the gloomy vaults; when all the horrors of the prison revealed themselves, gloomy and hopeless, Marie Antoinette, subdued by the natural weakness of a woman, succumbed to terror.

"Oh, I will fly! I will fly!" said she. "Yes, yes; I will fly! When he comes, when he speaks, I will saw the bar. I will await what God and my deliverers ordain me. I owe it to my children; they shall not murder them. And if they are sacrificed, and I am free—oh, then, at least, I——"

She did not conclude; her eyes closed, and her deep emotion checked all utterance. This was a frightful vision to the unfortunate queen, inclosed with gratings and iron bars. But, as usual, it soon disappeared, and in its stead another presented itself to her view. She saw herself in the midst of a dark, stern, inflexible army; she orders the fire to consume, the swords to be drawn, and vengeance to be taken on a nation she will no longer claim as her own.

During this time Gilbert and Duchesne were tranquilly preparing their evening repast. At this time, also, Dixmer and Geneviève entered the conciergerie, and installed themselves in the office, as usual. At the end of an hour the registrar of the palace, having completed his business, according to custom took his departure, leaving them alone to themselves. Directly the door had closed on his colleague, Dixmer rushed toward the empty basket placed at the door in exchange for that of the evening. Then, seizing the bread, he found the purse, and turned pale while reading the letter of the queen. Geneviève observed him tear it into a thousand pieces, and throw them into the mouth of the burning stove.

"It is well," said he; "all is arranged." Then, turning toward Geneviève: "Come here, madame," said he; "I must speak with you."

Geneviève, motionless and cold as marble, gave a gesture of assent, and approached him.

"The time has arrived, madame; listen to me."

"Yes, monsieur."

"You prefer a death beneficial to your cause—a death that will insure you blessings from one part and pity from the whole of the nation—is it not so?—to an ignominious and revengeful end of life."

"Yes, monsieur."

"I might have killed you on the spot when I recognized you at the house of your lover; but a man who, like myself, consecrates his life to a holy and honorable cause, ought to be able to fling aside and forget his own private griefs, by rendering them subservient to this cause. This I have done, or, rather, I intend to do. I am, as you see, denied the pleasure of doing myself justice, and have also spared your lover." Something resembling a bitter but fugitive smile flitted over the lips of Geneviève. "But as for your lover, you who know me should well be aware, I only bide my time."

"Monsieur," said Geneviève, "I await my fate. Then, wherefore all this prelude?"

"Are you ready?"

"Yes, I am ready. Kill me, if you choose; you have good cause to do so."

Dixmer looked at Geneviève, and started, in spite of himself. She at this moment appeared sublimely beautiful; a glory the most brilliant of all shone around her— the glory that emanated from love.

"To continue," said Dixmer, "I have informed the queen; she expects you, notwithstanding she will, in all probability, raise numerous objections. You must overrule them all."

"Give me your orders, monsieur, and I will execute them."

"At the moment," continued Dixmer, "I knock at the door, Gilbert opens it, and with this poniard"—here Dixmer threw open his coat, and, half drawing from its scabbard a double-edged poniard, "with this I shall kill." Geneviève shuddered. Dixmer made a motion with his hand to command her attention. "The instant I strike him, dart into the second chamber—that of the queen. There is, as you are aware, no door, only a screen. You will exchange clothes with her, while I despatch the other man. Then I shall take the queen's arm, and pass through the wicket with her."

"Very well," said Geneviève, coldly.

"You understand me?" said Dixmer. "You have been seen each evening in your black taffeta mantle, which conceals your face. Place your mantle upon her majesty, and dress her precisely as you have been accustomed to dress yourself."

"All shall be done as you desire, monsieur."

"It remains now for me to pardon, and to thank you, madame."

Geneviève shook her head with a scornful smile.

"I neither want your pardon nor your thanks, monsieur," said she, extending her hand. "What I have done, or, rather, am about to do, effaces my crime. I have only been guilty of weakness; and again, this weakness (recall your own conduct), monsieur, you all but forced me to commit. I withdrew myself from him; you drove me into his arms; so you are at the same time instigator, judge, and avenger. It remains for me to pardon you my death, and I do pardon you. It is I who should thank you for death, since life has become insupportable to me, separated from the only man I love; since that hour especially when you severed by your savage vengeance every tie that bound me to him."

Dixmer drove his nails into his flesh. He strove to reply, but his voice failed him. He moved toward the wicket.

"Time passes," said he, at last. "Madame, every moment is of consequence. Are you ready?"

"I have told you, monsieur," replied Geneviève, with the calmness and courage of a martyr, "I attend you."

Dixmer collected his papers, saw the gates were fast closed, so that no one could enter the wicket, and then wished to reiterate his instructions.

"It is unnecessary, monsieur," said Geneviève. "I know perfectly well all I have to do."

"Then adieu;" and Dixmer extended his hand, as if at this supreme moment all recrimination was effaced before the grandeur of the situation and the sublimity of the sacrifice, Geneviève, shuddering, touched with the tips of her fingers the proffered hand of her husband.

"Place yourself near me, madame, and the moment I have struck Gilbert, pass on."

"I am ready."

Then Dixmer pressed with his right hand his large poniard; with his left he knocked at the gate.

CHAPTER XLIV.

THE PREPARATIONS OF THE CHEVALIER.

DURING the scene described in the preceding chapter as passing at the door of the wicket leading into the prison of the queen, or, rather, into the first compartment occupied by the two gendarmes, other preparations were also taking place on the opposite side—that is to say, in the Cour des Femmes. Suddenly a man appeared, like a statue of stone which had detached itself from the wall. He was followed by two dogs, and was humming the " Ça ira," a song much in fashion at this period. He held in his hand a large bunch of keys, which, in passing, he had rattled against the bars which barricaded the window of the queen. The royal prisoner at first started; but recognizing the signal, immediately opened her window softly, to commence her work, with a hand more experienced than would have been believed, for more than once (in the blacksmith's shop, where her royal husband amused himself by passing part of the day) she had often with her delicate fingers handled instruments similar to that upon which at this moment depended her every chance of safety and deliverance. Directly the man with the keys heard the queen's window open, he knocked at that of the gendarmes.

" Ah, ah ! " said Gilbert, looking through the window, " here is the Citizen Murdoch."

" Himself," said the turnkey. " Well, but it appears you keep strict watch."

" Much as usual, Citizen Key-bearer. It seems to me you do not often find us at fault."

" Ah ! " said Murdoch, " and vigilance is more than ever necessary to-night."

" Bah ! " said Duchesne, who had now approached.

" Truly."

" Why, then ? "

" Open the window, and I will tell you all about it."

Gilbert opened it, and shook hands with Murdoch, who had already made friends with the two gendarmes.

"What is it, Citizen Murdoch?" repeated Gilbert.

"The sitting of the Convention has been rather warm to-day. Have you read it?"

"No. What passed, then?"

"It was first stated the Citizen Hebert had made a discovery."

"What?"

"It is that the conspirators believed to be dead are found to be living. There are three living."

"Oh, yes," said Gilbert; "Delessert and Thierry; I have heard speak of that. They are in England, the scoundrels!"

"And the Chevalier de Maison Rouge," said the key-bearer, raising his voice so that the queen might hear.

"What, is he in England, too?"

"Not at all," said Murdoch; "he is in France," still speaking in the same loud key.

"He has returned, then?"

"He has never quitted it."

"Well, he has good courage," said Duchesne.

"Indeed he has."

"Well, are they going to arrest him?"

"Certainly; but that is much easier said than done."

At this moment the queen's file grated so forcibly upon the iron bar that the key-bearer feared it might be heard, notwithstanding all his efforts at concealment. He hastily trod upon the paw of the nearest dog, who uttered a prolonged howl of pain.

"Oh, poor beast!" said Gilbert.

"Bah!" said the key-bearer, "he had not put on his sabots. Be quiet, Girondin; will you be quiet?"

"Is your dog named Girondin, Citizen Murdoch?"

"Yes; that is the name I have given him."

"And you say this?" said Duchesne, who, imprisoned himself, took a lively interest in all that related to prisoners. "You say this?"

"Truly, I say this, that in the Citizen Hebert you see

a good patriot. I say that the Citizen Hebert has made a proposition to return the Austrian to the Temple. Dam! Because they pretend she has only been withdrawn from the Temple to remove her from the immediate inspection of the Commune of Paris."

"Yes; and from the attempts of this cursed Maison Rouge," said Gilbert, "it seems that the subterranean passage did exist."

"That was the reply the Citizen Saintez made; but Hebert said the instant that was defeated there was no more danger; that at the Temple fewer precautions were requisite for the security of Marie Antoinette than here; and finally, that the Temple was differently inclosed to the conciergerie, and another thing altogether."

"*Ma foi!*" said Gilbert, "I wish they would remove her to the Temple."

"I understand you are tired of the confinement?"

"No; but it makes me melancholy."

Maison Rouge coughed loudly, as the noise of the file biting through the iron bar was distinctly heard.

"What have they decided on?" said Duchesne, when the key-bearer's cough had subsided.

"It is settled that she remains here; but her trial will take place immediately."

"Poor woman!" said Gilbert.

Duchesne, whose sense of hearing was no doubt more acute than that of his colleague, or his attention less engrossed by the recital of Murdoch, stooped down to listen on the left side of the compartment.

The key-bearer saw the movement.

"So, you see, Citizen Duchesne, the attempts of the conspirators will become the more desperate, from the fact of their having less time before them for their execution. They are going to double the guards of the prisons, so look out, Citizen Gendarme, since the matter in question is nothing less than the irruption of an armed force into the conciergerie. They will murder all, sacrifice every impediment, till they effect an entrance to the queen —to the widow of Capet, I tell you."

"Ah, bah! How can they get in?"

"Disguised as patriots, they will appear to recommence the 2d of September. Poor wretches! and when once the gates are open. *Bon soir.*"

There was an instant's silence, produced by the astonishment of the guards, while the key-bearer heard with emotions of joy and terror the continued grating of the file. Nine o'clock struck. At the same moment there was a knock at the wicket, but the gendarmes, preoccupied, did not reply.

"Well, we shall see, we shall see," said Gilbert.

"And, if necessary, will die at our posts like stanch Republicans," said Duchesne.

"She ought soon to have finished," said the key-bearer to himself, wiping the drops of perspiration from his face.

"And you, on your side," said Gilbert, "keep on the lookout, I presume? They would spare you no more than us were such an event to take place."

"I should think so," said the key-bearer. "I pass the night in going the round, thus I am always on the alert; the rest of you, at least those who are relieved, can sleep every other night."

At this moment a second summons at the wicket was heard. Murdoch started; any event, however trifling, might mar the execution of his project.

"What is it, then?" demanded he, in spite of himself.

"Nothing, nothing," said Gilbert; "it is only the registrar of the minister of war. He is going now, and came to inform me of it."

"Oh, very well," said Murdoch.

The registrar still continued to knock.

"*Bon, bon!*" cried Gilbert, without leaving the window. "*Bon soir.* Adieu."

"I think he is speaking," said Duchesne, turning toward the door.

The voice of the registrar was then heard.

"Come here, Citizen Gendarme," said he, "I wish to speak to you."

This voice, which appeared overpowered by emotion,

and deprived of its natural accent, startled the key-bearer, who fancied he recognized it.

"What do you want, Citizen Durand?" said Gilbert.

"I wish to speak a word with you."

"Well, you can tell me to-morrow."

"No, this evening; it must be this evening," replied the same voice.

"Oh!" murmured the key-bearer, "what is about to happen now? It is Dixmer's voice."

Sinister and vibrating, this voice seemed to borrow something funereal from the far-off echoes of the gloomy corridor. Duchesne turned round.

"Well," said Gilbert, "if he wishes it, I must go," and he directed his steps toward the door.

The key-bearer availed himself of this moment when the attention of the two gendarmes was thus occupied by this unforeseen circumstance. He ran toward the window of the queen.

"Is it done?" said he.

"I have more than half finished," said the queen.

"Oh, *mon Dieu, mon Dieu!*" murmured he, "make haste, make haste!"

"Well, Citizen Murdoch," said Duchesne, "what has become of you?"

"Here I am," said the key-bearer, returning quickly to the window of the first compartment.

At that very same moment, even as he turned to resume his former station, a frightful cry resounded through the prison, then an imprecation, and a noise of a sword being drawn from the scabbard.

"Villain! brigand!" cried Gilbert, and the sound of a struggle was heard in the corridor,

The door then opened, displaying to the eyes of the turnkey two shadows struggling in the wicket, and thus affording a free passage to a female, who, pushing aside Duchesne, rushed into the queen's chamber. Duchesne, without noticing the woman, ran to his comrade's assistance. The turnkey sprung toward the other window, and beheld the female on her knees before the queen, praying and supplicating her majesty to exchange dresses with her. He lowered his burning eyes, endeavoring to gain a clearer view of this woman, whom he feared he had already recognized. All at once he uttered a dreadful cry.

"Geneviève! Geneviève!" murmured he.

The queen had dropped the file from her hand, and seemed transfixed with despair. Here, alas! was another attempt rendered abortive.

The turnkey seized the bar with both hands, shook it with all his strength, but the file had not accomplished its work; the bar of iron would not yield to his efforts. During this time Dixmer had, wrestling, struggling with Gilbert, reached the prison, and there attempted to force his entrance with him; but Duchesne, leaning against the door, prevented him. But he was unable to close it, for Dixmer, in despair, had placed his arm between the gate and the wall. In his hand he still retained the **poniard,** which in the contest, blunted by the buckle of the belt, had glided over the turnkey's breast tearing open his coat and lacerating his flesh. The two men encouraged each other to reunite their efforts, at the same time calling loudly for assistance. Dixmer felt his arm must break; he placed his shoulder against the door, shook it violently, and succeeded in withdrawing his bruised arm. The door closed with a great noise. Duchesne drew the bolts, while Gilbert turned the key; a rapid step was heard in the corridor, then all was over. The two gendarmes searched everywhere around them. They detected the sound of the assumed turnkey wrenching the bar; then Gilbert rushed into the queen's chamber, where he found Geneviève entreating her majesty, on her knees, to exchange clothes with her. Duchesne seized his gun and ran to the window; he discovered a man hanging to the bar, which he shook with rage, frantically endeavoring in vain to break it.

He pointed his gun; the young man saw it leveled at him.

"Oh, yes, yes!" said he, "kill me, kill me!" and, sublime in his despair, he bared his breast to the storm.

"Chevalier," said the queen, "chevalier, I entreat you to live."

At the sound of the queen's voice the chevalier sank upon his knees. The gun was discharged, but this movement saved him; the ball passed over his head. Geneviève, imagining her friend was dead, fell upon the ground without sense or motion. When the smoke was dissipated, no one remained in the Cour des Femmes. Ten minutes afterward, thirty soldiers, led by two commissaries, searched the whole of the conciergerie, even its most inaccessible retreats. They discovered no one; the registrar had passed, calm and smiling, before Father Richard's armchair. As to the turnkey, he had gone out crying:

"Alarm! alarm!"

The sentinel opposed his egress with his bayonet, but the two dogs seized him by the throat. It was only Geneviève who was arrested, interrogated, and imprisoned.

CHAPTER XLV.

THE INQUIRY.

We can no longer leave in forgetfulness one of the principal personages of this history, he who, during the accomplishment of the various incidents of the preceding chapter, had suffered most of all, and whose anxieties merit the liveliest sympathy on the part of our readers. The sun shone gloriously in La Rue de la Monnaie, and the gossips were discoursing merrily at their doors (as if for the last ten months a mist of blood had not hung over the city, tinging all nature with its sanguinary hue), when Maurice returned home, bringing, as he had promised, the cabriolet with him. He gave the bridle of the horse to a shoe-black on the pavement of St. Eustache, and hastily ran up-stairs, his heart filled with joy.

Love is a vivifying sentiment. It animates hearts long deadened to every other sensation—it peoples the desert—it resuscitates before the eyes the shade of the beloved object—it causes the voice which sings in the soul of the lover to display before him the entire creation illumined by the brilliant rays of hope and happiness, at the same time it is egotistical, blinding him who loves to all but the existence of the beloved object.

Maurice neither saw these women nor listened to their commentaries, he alone saw Geneviève preparing for a departure which was at last to bring them durable happiness; he only heard Geneviève singing carelessly her customary song, and this little song burred so sweetly in his ear that he might have sworn he was listening to the varied modulations of her voice, mingled with the less harmonious sound of closing locks. Upon the landing, Maurice stopped; the door was half open; it was generally kept closed, and this circumstance surprised Maurice. He looked all round, thinking Geneviève was in the corridor. She was not there. He entered, looked in the ante-chamber, the dining-room, the saloon. He visited the bedchamber, but anteroom, saloon, and bedchamber were all empty. He loudly called. No one replied. The official, as he knew, had gone out. Maurice imagined that, during his absence, Geneviève had perhaps required some cord to fasten her trunk, or *provision de voyage* to store in the carriage, and had gone out to purchase it. He thought it imprudent, but although every moment his anxiety increased, he in reality feared nothing.

Maurice waited for some time, walking up and down the room with long impatient strides, and occasionally leaning out of the window, which, half opened, admitted puffs of air charged heavily with rain. But soon he fancied he heard a step upon the staircase; he listened, it was not that of Geneviéve; he ran to the landing, looked over the palisade, and recognized the official, who leisurely mounted the stairs after the manner of domestics.

"Scevola!" cried he.

The official raised his head.

"Ah! is it you, citizen?"

"Yes. Where is the citoyenne?"

"The citoyenne?" demanded Scevola, with much surprise, as he continued mounting the stairs.

"Have you seen her below?"

"No."

"Go down, then, and ask the porter, and inquire of all the neighbors."

Scevola descended.

"Quicker! quicker!" said his master. "Do you not see I am burning with impatience?"

After waiting five or six minutes, and Scevola not having made his appearance, Maurice reentered the apartment and again leaned out of the window. He saw Scevola enter several shops and leave them without having gained any fresh intelligence. He called him. The official raised his head, and saw his master impatiently looking from the window. Maurice signed to him to come up.

"It is impossible she can have gone out," said Maurice to himself; and again he called: "Geneviève! Geneviève!"

All was silent as death; even the solitary chamber appeared no longer to have an echo. Scevola reappeared.

"Well?" demanded Maurice.

"The porter is the only person who has seen her."

"The porter has seen her! How was that?"

"He saw her go out."

"She is gone out, then?"

"It seems so."

"Alone! It is impossible Geneviève would go out alone!"

"She was not alone, citizen; she had a man with her."

"How! a man with her?"

"That is what the porter says, at least."

"Go and seek him. I must find out who this man is."

Scevola made a step toward the door; then, turning: "Wait," said he, appearing to reflect.

"What is it?" said Maurice. "Speak, or you will be the death of me."

"Perhaps it was the man who ran after me?"

"What for?"

"To ask me for the key."

"What key?"

"The key of your apartments."

"You gave the key of the apartments to a stranger?" cried Maurice, seizing with both hands the official by the collar.

"It was not to a stranger, monsieur, it was to one of your friends."

"Ah! yes, to one of my friends. It is Louis, no doubt, it is so. She has gone out with Louis;" and smiling a ghastly smile, Maurice wiped away the drops of agony which had gathered on his brow.

"No, monsieur; no, it was not he. I know Monsieur Louis very well."

"Who was it, then?"

"You know the man who came here one day?"

"What day?"

"The day when you were so sad, and he took you away with him, and you returned so happy."

Scevola had remarked all these things. Maurice regarded him with a bewildered air; a cold shudder ran through all his veins. Then, after a long silence:

"Dixmer!" cried he.

"*Ma foi!* yes. I think it was him, citizen."

Maurice tottered, and fell back upon the chair.

"Oh, my God!" murmured he. When he reopened his eyes they encountered the violets, forgotten, or, rather, left there by Geneviève. He rushed toward them, seized and kissed them, remarking where she had placed them: "Doubtless," said he, "these violets—it is her last adieu."

When Maurice turned round he perceived for the first time the trunk was half full, the rest of the linen remained on the ground, or in the half-opened wardrobe. The cord which lay upon the ground had no doubt fallen from Geneviéve's hand at the apparition of Dixmer. It was all explained now. The scene rose vivid and terrible before his eyes, between these four walls that had lately witnessed so much happiness. Till now Maurice had remained crushed and heart-broken. Now the reaction was fearful. His rage was bordering on frenzy. He rose, closed the window, took from the top of his secretaire a pair of pistols, ready loaded for their intended journey, looked to the priming, and finding all right, placed them in his pocket. He also furnished himself with two rouleaux of louis, which, notwithstanding his patriotism, he had thought it politic to conceal at the bottom of a drawer, and taking his saber in his hand :

"Scevola," said he, "you are attached to me, I think; you have served my father and myself for fifteen years."

"Yes, citizen," replied the official, terrified at the pallor and nervous trembling he had never before remarked in his master, who had always been justly considered one of the most courageous and vigorous of men, "yes ; what are your orders for me ? "

"Listen. If this lady who lived here——" He stopped ; his voice trembled so much in pronouncing these words, he was unable to proceed. "If she should return," continued he, after a moment's pause, " receive her, close the door after her, take this gun, and station yourself upon the staircase, and, for your head, for your life, for your soul, do not permit a single person to enter here. If any one should force the door, defend it. Strike ! kill ! kill, and fear nothing, Scevola, for I will answer for all."

The young man's impetuous harangue, his vehement confidence, electrified Scevola.

"I will not only kill, but will even suffer death for the Citoyenne Geneviève," said he.

"Thanks. Now, attend. This apartment is odious to me, and since I cannot find her I will no longer remain here ; if she has been able to effect her escape, if she has returned, place before the window the Japan vase, with the pearls, which she loves so much. That is, during the day. At night put a lantern. Every time I pass the end of the street I shall know, and if I see neither vase nor lantern I shall still continue my researches."

"Be prudent, monsieur ! Oh, pray be prudent !" continued Scevola.

His master made no reply, but, rushing from the chamber, flew down the staircase as if possessed of wings, and ran toward Louis' house. It would be difficult to paint the astonishment and rage of our worthy poet when he heard the news, much as he wished to recommence the touching elegies addressed by Orestes to Pylades.

"And you do not know where she is?" he repeated, incessantly.

"Lost! disappeared!" shrieked Maurice, in a tone of despair; "he has killed her, Louis—he has killed her!"

"No, my dear friend; no, Maurice; he has not killed her; it is not after so many days of reflection that he would be likely to kill a woman like Geneviève. If he had thought of doing so, he would have done it on the spot, and have left her corpse there in token of his just vengeance. No, no; he has taken her away, only too happy at having regained his lost treasure."

"You do not know, Louis—you do not know; this man had something fatal in his look."

"You are mistaken," said Louis; "he always struck me as a brave man. He has taken her as the sacrifice. He will stop with her, and they will die together. Where, then, is the danger?"

These words redoubled Maurice's fury.

"I will find her! I will find her, or perish in the attempt!" cried he.

"Oh! as to that, we are certain to find her," said Louis; "only calm yourself. They fail in success who do not reflect; and when agitated as you are, we reflect badly and unwisely."

"Adieu, Louis, adieu!"

"Where are you going, then?"

"I am going."

"You will leave me, then? Why is that?"

"Because this concerns me only. I alone should risk my life to save Geneviève's."

"Do you wish to die?"

"I will face all. I will find out the president of the Committee of Surveillance. I will speak to Hebert, to Danton, to Robespierre. I will avow all, that she may be restored to me."

"Very well," said Louis; and, without adding another word, he rose, adjusted his belt, put on his military cap, and, as Maurice had done, provided himself with a pair of pistols, ready loaded, which he put in his pocket.

"Let us go," said he, simply.

"But you will compromise yourself," said Maurice.

"Well, what next?"

"Where shall we seek her first?" said Maurice.

"We will first search in the old quarter; you know. Vieille Rue St. Jacques; then we will watch for Maison Rouge, as where he will be, doubtless Dixmer will be also; then we will draw near the houses in La Vieille Corderie. You know they talk of transferring Marie Antoinette to the Temple; believe me, men like them will not, till the last moment, abandon the hope of serving her."

"Yes," repeated Maurice, "you are right. Maison Rouge, do you think he is in Paris?"

"Dixmer is there."

"It is true, it is true; of course they will be together," said Maurice, to whom these vague ideas seemed partially to restore reason.

The two friends went out to commence their search immediately, but all in vain. Paris is large, and well adapted for concealment. Never was a pit known to conceal more obscurely the secret confided to its keeping by crime or misery. A hundred times Maurice and Louis passed over La Place de Grève; a hundred times glanced at the house that contained Geneviève, watching without ceasing for Dixmer, as the priests watch the victim destined for a sacrifice. Geneviève, on her side, seeing herself destined to perish, like all generous souls, accepted the sacrifice, and only wished to die quietly and unnoticed; besides, she dreaded less for Dixmer than the cause of the queen—the publicity that Maurice would not fail to give to his vengeance. She kept, then, a silence as profound as if death had already sealed her lips.

In the meantime, without saying anything to Louis, Maurice had applied to the members of the terrible Committee of Public Safety; and Louis, without speaking to

Maurice, had, on his part, determined on a similar proceeding. Thus, on the same day, a red cross was affixed by Fouquier Tinville to both their names, and the word "suspects" united them in a sanguinary embrace.

CHAPTER XLVI.

THE SENTENCE.

On the 23d day of the month of the second year of the French Republic, one and indivisible, corresponding to the 14th of October, 1793, old style, as it was then called, a curious crowd had, since the morning, invaded the galleries of the hall where the revolutionary sittings were held. The passages of the palace, the avenues of the conciergerie, were lined with greedy and impatient spectators, who made over one to another their reports and passions, as the waves transmit their froth and foam. Notwithstanding the curiosity which agitated each spectator—an agitation caused by this curiosity—every wave of this troubled sea, enclosed between two barriers—the exterior one which propelled them, and the interior which repelled them—this flux and reflux of human beings were thus kept almost stationary in the places they had at first taken. Thus, those more conveniently situated, comprehending it was necessary they should obtain forgiveness for their good fortune, kept this object in view by transmitting to these their neighbors less comfortably and commodiously placed than themselves, and who, in their turn, recounted to others the first words they heard and all they saw.

Near the door of the tribunal a group of men was collected, rudely disputing for ten lines of space in width and height—for ten lines in breadth sufficed to see between two shoulders the corner of the hall and the form of the judges—for ten lines in height was sufficient to overlook the entire hall and the figure of the accused. Unfortunately, this entrance to the passage of the hall, this narrow defile, was almost entirely filled by a man with broad shoulders, and his arms akimbo, who most effectually excluded the wavering crowd, ready to drop into the hall if this rampart of flesh were to give way.

This immovable man was young and handsome, and at every push bestowed on him by the crowd, he shook his head of hair, thick as a lion's mane, under which gleamed a dark and resolute expression, then, when either by a look or a movement he had repelled the crowd and resisted their violent attacks, he fell back into his attentive immobility. A hundred times this compact mass had, notwithstanding, striven hard to overthrow him—as from his great height, to see anything behind him was utterly impossible; but, as we have said, firm as a rock, he stood his ground. In the meantime, at the other extremity of this human sea, in the midst of the crushing crowd, another man was forcing a passage, with a perseverance almost amounting to ferocity. Nothing impeded his indefatigable exertions; neither the cries of those he left behind, the fearful imprecations of those he almost stifled in passing, nor the wails of the women—for there were many females in this crowd.

To blows he responded with blows; to imprecations, by a look before which the most courageous quailed; to complaints, by a carelessness bordering on disdain. At last he arrived behind the powerful young man, who, so to speak, closed the entrance to the hall in the midst of the general expectation—for all were anxious to see how the contest between two such rude antagonists would terminate—he essayed his peculiar method, which consisted in planting his elbows between two spectators, and thus breaking through. He was, notwithstanding, a short young man, whose wan face and emaciated appearance betokened latent illness.

His elbows had scarcely touched the young man before him, when he, indignant at the aggression, turned sharply round, at the same moment raising his clinched fist, which threatened, in falling, to crush the slender form of the intruder.

The two antagonists now found themselves face to face, when a cry of recognition escaped from each.

"Ah, Monsieur Maurice," said the delicate young man, with an accent of inexpressible anguish, "permit me to pass; only let me see her, I entreat you; then kill me afterward."

Maurice—for it was he—felt himself affected by admiration and compassion, excited by this ceaseless devotion, this adventurous daring.

"You here!" murmured he. "How imprudent!"

"Yes; but I am exhausted. Oh, *mon Dieu!* she speaks. Let me see her—let me listen to her."

Maurice drew aside, and the young man passed before him, and being at the head of the crowd, there was nothing now to intercept the view of him who had undergone so many blows, so much buffeting to attain his end. All this scene, and the murmurs it occasioned, aroused the curiosity of the judges. The accused also turned round, and immediately perceived and recognized the chevalier. A shudder ran through the queen's frame, seated in the iron arm-chair. The interrogation, conducted by the President Harmand, interpreted by Fouquier Tinville, discussed by Cheveau Legarde, the defender for the queen, lasted as long as the strength of the judges and the accused permitted. During all this time, Maurice remained motionless in his place, while several times already the concourse was renewed both in the hall and the corridors. The chevalier leaned against a pillar. He was no less pale than the marble that supported him. The day was succeeded by a dark night; some lighted candles on the tables of the jurors, and some smoky lamps on the walls of the hall, threw a red and sinister expression on the noble face of that woman who had formed the bright and beautiful ornament of the splendid fêtes at Versailles. She was alone there, replying in brief and dignified language to the questions of the president, and occasionally addressed some words to her counsel in a low voice. Her white and polished forehead retained all its original pride. She was neither humbled nor cast down. She was attired in a black dress, which she had worn ever since her husband's death. The judges retired from the hall. The sitting had terminated.

"Have I evinced too much hauteur, monsieur?" said she, addressing herself to Cheveau Legarde.

"Ah, madame," replied he, "you are always right when you act like yourself."

"How proud she is!" cried a woman among the audience, as if a voice from the people had replied to the question of the unfortunate queen to her advocate.

The queen turned and looked at her.

"Yes," repeated the woman, "you are proud, Antoinette; and I tell you pride has been the ruin of you."

The queen blushed. The chevalier turned toward the female who had uttered these words, and replied, softly:

"She was queen."

Maurice seized him by the wrist, saying, in a low tone:

"Take care; do not forget yourself."

"Oh, Monsieur Maurice," replied the chevalier, "you are a man yourself, and you know you are speaking to a man. Tell me, oh, tell me, do you think they will condemn her?"

"I do not think," said Maurice; "I am sure of it."

"What, a woman?" said the chevalier, with a deep groan.

"No, a queen," said Maurice; "you have yourself said so."

The chevalier, in his turn, seized Maurice by the wrist, and with a force of which he appeared to be incapable, compelled him to bend his ear. It was half-past three in the morning. Many vacuums were visible among the spectators, and a few lights burning here and there served only to render darkness visible. In one of the most obscure parts of the hall were the chevalier and Maurice, listening to what the former was telling him.

"Why are you here? what brings you here?" demanded the chevalier; "you, monsieur, who have not a tiger's heart?"

"Alas!" said Maurice, "to discover what has become of an unfortunate woman."

"Yes, yes," said Maison Rouge; "she whom her husband forced into the queen's cell, the female it surprised me so to see."

"Geneviève?"

"Yes, Geneviève."

"Then, Geneviève is a prisoner, sacrificed by her husband, killed by Dixmer. Oh! I comprehend all, I understand all now. Chevalier, tell me all that has occurred, tell me where she is, tell me where I can find her. Chevalier, this woman constitutes my life; do you hear me?"

"I witnessed all. I was there when she was arrested. I was there also to effect the escape of the queen, but our different projects not having been communicated to each other, injured instead of assisting our mutual cause."

"Why did you not save her, at least—your sister, Geneviève?"

"How could I, when an iron bar divided us? Oh! if you had only been there, if you had united your efforts with mine, the bar must have yielded, and both might have been saved."

"Geneviève!" Geneviève!" murmured Maurice.

Then, regarding Maison Rouge with an indefinable expression of hatred and rage:

"And Dixmer, where is he?" demanded he.

"I know not; he saved himself, as I did also."

"Oh!" said Maurice, grinding his teeth, "if ever I meet him——"

"Yes, I understand. But there is nothing yet to despair about concerning Geneviève," said Maison Rouge; "her case is not yet desperate; but the queen. Oh, stop, Maurice, you are a sensitive man, an influential man. You have friends. Oh! I pray to you as I would pray to my God. Maurice, help me to save the queen. Maurice, Geneviève supplicates you through me."

"Pronounce not that name, monsieur. Who knows

but that, like Dixmer, you may have sacrificed this unhappy woman?"

"Monsieur," replied the chevalier, haughtily, "when I attach myself to a cause, I know better than to sacrifice any one but myself."

Maurice was about to reply, when the door of the chamber of debate opened.

"Silence, monsieur, silence," said the chevalier, "the judges are returning."

And Maurice felt the hand tremble which Maison Rouge had placed upon his arm.

"Ah!" murmured the chevalier, "my heart fails me now."

"Have courage and constrain yourself, or you are lost," said Maurice.

The tribunal reentered, and the news of its return spread rapidly through the corridors and galleries. The crowd again congregated in the hall, and even the dim lights appeared to burn brighter at this solemn and decisive moment. The queen rose, and stood erect, haughty, and immovable; her eyes fixed, her lips closed. The decree was then read which doomed the queen to death. She heard her sentence without even turning pale or uttering a sigh; her countenance evinced not the slightest emotion. Then, turning toward the chevalier, she regarded him with a long and eloquent look, as if to indicate her gratitude to this man whom she had ever seen a living statue of devotion, and supported on the arm of the officer of the gendarmes who commanded the forces, with a calm and dignified demeanor, she quitted the court.

Maurice drew a deep sigh.

"Thank God!" said he, "nothing in this declaration can compromise Geneviève; there is yet hope."

"Thank God!" murmured the chevalier on his side. "It is all finished, and the struggle at length terminated. I have not strength to go further."

"Courage, monsieur," said Maurice, in a low voice.

"I will take courage, monsieur," replied the chevalier; and, having shaken hands, they disappeared by different outlets. The queen was reconducted to the conciergerie; the large clock struck four as she entered. At the end of Pont Neuf, Maurice was stopped by Louis.

"Halt!" said he; "you do not pass here!"

"Why?"

"First, where are you going?"

"I am going home. I can return there now, since I know what has become of her."

"So much the better; but you must not enter there."

"For what reason?"

"The reason is, that two hours ago the gendarmes went there to arrest you."

"Ah!" cried Maurice. "Well, there is the greater reason."

"Are you mad? And Geneviève?"

"You are right. But where are we to go?"

"To my house. *Pardieu!*"

"But I shall ruin you."

"The more reason," said Louis, dragging Maurice away with him.

CHAPTER XLVII.

THE PRIEST AND THE EXECUTIONER.

ON leaving the court, the queen had been conducted back to the conciergerie. On reaching her chamber she had taken a pair of scissors and cut off her long and beautiful curls, rendered still more so from the absence of powder, which had been totally abolished two years since; these she enclosed in a packet, and on the paper was inscribed, "For my son and daughter." She then seated herself, or rather, sunk into a chair, and, worn out with fatigue, the trial having lasted eighteen hours, she fell asleep. At seven o'clock the noise of the opening screen roused her from her troubled sleep, and turning round, she beheld a man perfectly unknown to her.

"What do you want?" demanded she.

THE CHEVALIER DE MAISON ROUGE.

He approached and saluted her as respectfully as if she had not been the queen.

"I am called Sanson," said he.

The name was sufficient. The queen slightly shuddered.

"You are here in good time, monsieur; could you not have made it rather later."

"No, madame," replied Sanson; "I received orders to come."

As he uttered these words, he advanced still nearer to the queen. At this moment everything about this man was expressive and terrible.

"I understand," said the prisoner, "you wish to cut off my hair."

"It is necessary, madame," replied the executioner.

"I know it, monsieur; and I wished to spare you the trouble. My hair is on the table."

Sanson followed the direction of the queen's hand.

"Only," said she, "I wish these curls sent to my children to-night."

"Madame," said Sanson, "this does not concern me."

"However, I thought—notwithstanding——"

"Oh! I get nothing," replied the executioner; "the clothes, the jewels, unless formally made over to me, all go to La Salpetrière, and are allotted to the poor of the hospital. The Committee of Public Safety arrange these things."

"But, monsieur," persisted Marie Antoinette, "may I at least, depend upon this packet being forwarded to my children?"

Sanson remained silent.

"I will endeavor to do so," said Gilbert.

The prisoner cast upon him a look of deep gratitude.

"I came," said Sanson, "to cut off your hair; but since you have done so, I can, if you wish it, leave you for a short period alone."

"I entreat you to do so, monsieur. I wish to collect my scattered thoughts, and offer up a prayer."

Sanson bowed, and retired, when the queen once more

found herself in solitude. While the condemned threw herself upon her knees before a low chair which served her as a *prie-dieu*, a scene no less terrible was passing in the parsonage of the small church of St. Laudry, in the city. The curé was dressing, the old housekeeper had prepared the humble morning meal, when a loud summons at the gate was heard. Even in our day, an unexpected visit is in general the precursor of some event, either a baptism, a marriage, *in extremis*, or a confession; but at this epoch the visit of a stranger would announce some matter of far graver import. Indeed, at this period the priest was no longer the mandatory of God, but rendered his account to man. However, the Abbé Giraud was of the number of those who had least cause for fear, as he had taken an oath to the constitution—in him conscience and probity had spoken louder than *amour propre* or religious spirit. No doubt the Abbé Giraud admitted the possibility of a proficiency in the government, and much regretted the abuses committed under the name of the Divine will, and had, while retaining his God, accepted the fraternity of the Republican régime.

"Go and see, Dame Jacinthe," said he, "who disturbs us at this early hour, and if the business is of no very pressing nature, say that this morning I have been sent for to the conciergerie, and must go there directly."

Dame Jacinthe, otherwise called Madeline, had accepted this flowery appellation in lieu of her own, as the Curé Giraud had taken the title of citizen instead of that of abbé. At the suggestion of her master, Jacinthe hastened down the steps to the little garden leading to the entrance gate. She drew back the bolts, when a thin, pale young man, much agitated, but with a frank and sweet expression, presented himself before her.

"Monsieur l'Abbé Giraud?" said he.

Jacinthe, not slow to remark the disordered dress, the neglected beard, and the nervous tremor of the newcomer, augured unfavorably of him.

"Citizen," said she, "there is here neither monsieur nor abbé."

"Pardon me, madame," replied the young man, "I meant to say the Curé of St. Laudry."

Jacinthe, notwithstanding her patriotism, was struck by the word "madame," with which they only have addressed an empress. She, however, replied:

"You cannot see him now; he is repeating his breviary."

"In that case I will wait," replied the young man.

"But," said Jacinthe, in whom this obstinate persistence revived the first unfavorable impression, "you will wait in vain, for he is summoned to the conciergerie, and must go there immediately."

The young man turned frightfully pale, or, rather, from pale, to livid.

"It is, then, true," murmured he; then, raising his voice. "This, madame, is the subject which brings me to the Abbé Giraud."

And in spite of the old woman, he had, while speaking, effected an entrance; then coolly but firmly drawing the bolts, and notwithstanding the expostulations and even menaces of Dame Jacinthe, he not only entered the house, but also the chamber of the curé, who, on perceiving him, uttered an exclamation of surprise.

"Forgive me, Monsieur le Curé," immediately said the young man, "I wish to speak to you on a very serious subject; permit us to be alone."

The aged priest had experienced deep sorrow, and knew what it was to endure. He discerned deep and devouring passion in the confusion of the young man, and intense emotion in his fevered tones.

"Leave us, Dame Jacinthe," said he.

The visitor impatiently followed with his eyes the receding steps of the housekeeper, who, from being accustomed to the confidence of her master, hesitated to comply, then, when at length the door was closed:

"Monsieur le Curé," said the unknown, "you will first wish to know who I am. I will tell you. I am a proscribed man, doomed to death, who only at this moment lives from the power of audacity; I am the Chevalier de Maison Rouge."

The abbé started in horror from his armchair.

"Fear nothing," said the chevalier; "no one has seen me enter here, and those who even might see me would never know me. I have altered much these last two months."

"But what do you wish, citizen?" asked the curé.

"You are going this morning to the conciergerie, is it not so?"

"Yes the concierge has sent for me."

"Do you know why?"

"To an invalid, or some dying person, perhaps even to one condemned."

"You are right; it is to one condemned."

The old priest regarded the chevalier with astonishment.

"But do you know who this person is?" demanded Maison Rouge.

"No; I do not know."

"This person is the queen."

The abbé uttered an exclamation of grief.

"The queen? Oh, my God!"

"Yes, monsieur, the queen. I made inquiry as to the priest who would attend her, and I learned it was you. I, therefore, came directly to seek an interview."

"But what do you require of me?" asked the curé, alarmed at the wild accents of the chevalier.

"I wish—I wish nothing, monsieur. I implore. I entreat, I supplicate you."

"For what, then?"

"To allow me to enter with you into the presence of her majesty."

"You are mad!" said the curé; "you would not only ruin me, but would sacrifice yourself."

"Fear nothing."

"The poor woman is condemned, and that is the end of her."

"I know it, and it is not to make any attempt to save her that I wish to see her, it is— But listen to me, my father; you are not listening."

"I do not listen to you, since what you ask is impossible; I do not listen to you, since you act like a man bereft of his senses," said the aged man. "I do not listen to you, because you terrify me."

"My father, reassure yourself," said the young man, endeavoring to calm himself; "believe me, my father, I am in my senses. The queen, I know, is lost; but if I could only for an instant prostrate myself at her feet, it would save my life. If I do not see her, I will kill myself, and as you will have caused my despair, you will at the same moment destroy both body and soul."

"My son! my son!" replied the priest, "you ask me to sacrifice my life for you. Old as I am, my existence is still necessary to the unfortunate; old as I am, to precipitate my own death is to commit an act of suicide."

"Do not refuse me, my father," replied the chevalier; "you must have a curate, an acholothist; take me, let me go with you."

The priest tried to maintain his firmness, which was gradually giving way.

"No, no," said he; "this would be a defalcation from duty; I have sworn to the constitution, and I am bound heart, soul, and conscience. The unhappy woman condemned to death is a guilty queen; I would accept death if by so doing I could benefit a fellow-creature, but I will not depart from the path of duty."

"But," cried the chevalier, "when I have told you, and again repeat, even swear to you, I do not want to save the queen; here by the Evangelist, by the crucifix, I swear I do not go to the conciergerie to prevent her death!"

"What is your motive, then?" said the old man, affected by his undisguised accents of despair.

"Hearken," said the chevalier, whose soul seemed to speak from his lips; "she was my benefactress, she is attached to me, to see me for the last time will afford her happiness, and will, I am certain, prove a consolation to her."

"And this is all that you desire?" demanded the curé, yielding to these irresistible accents.

"Absolutely all."

"And you have woven no plot to attempt to rescue the condemned?"

"None. I am a Christian, my father, and if there rests in my heart a shadow of deceit, if, as I hope to live, I deal falsely in this, may God visit me with eternal damnation!"

"No, no," said the curé; "I can promise nothing," as the innumerable dangers attendant on an act so imprudent returned to his mind.

"Now listen to me, my father," said the chevalier, in a voice hoarse with emotion; "I have spoken like a submissive child, I have not uttered one bitter word or uncharitable sentiment, no menace has escaped my lips; yet now my head whirls, fever burns in my veins, now despair rushes into my heart; now I am armed; behold! here is my dagger."

And the young man drew from his bosom a polished blade which threw a livid reflection on his trembling hand. The curé drew back quickly.

"Fear nothing," said the chevalier, with a mournful smile; "others knowing you to be so strict an observer of your word, would have terrified you into an oath. But no; I have supplicated, and I still continue to supplicate, with hands clasped, my forehead in the dust, that I may see her for a single moment. Look! here is your guarantee."

And he drew from his pocket a billet, which he presented to Giraud, who opened it, and read as follows:

"I, René, Chevalier de Maison Rouge, declare by God and my honor, that I have by threats of death compelled the worthy curé of St. Laudry to carry me to the conciergerie, nowithstanding his refusal and great repugnance to do so. In proof of which I have signed:

"MAISON ROUGE."

"It is well," said the priest; "but swear to me once again that you will be guilty of no imprudence; it is not sufficient that my life is saved, I am answerable also for yours."

"Think not of that," said the chevalier. "Then you consent?"

"I must, since you so absolutely insist. You can wait outside, and when she comes to the wicket, you will see her."

The chevalier seized the hand of the old priest, and kissed it with all the ardor and respect he would the crucifix.

"Oh!" murmured the chevalier, "she shall die at least like a queen, and the hand of the executioner shall never touch her."

CHAPTER XLVIII.

THE CART.

IMMEDIATELY after having obtained this permission from the curé of St. Laudry, Maison Rouge withdrew into a cabinet, the door of which, being half opened, he had recognized as the priest's dressing-room. There his long beard and mustachios speedily disappeared under the stroke of the razor; and then only he was fully aware of his frightful pallor and altered appearance. It was terrible to behold. He reentered perfectly calm, and seemed to have forgotten that notwithstanding the absence of his beard and mustachios, he might probably be known at the conciergerie. He followed the abbé, whom, during his momentary absence, two officials were seeking, and with the cool audacity which casts aside suspicion, entered the iron gate at this time opening into the court of the palace. He was, like the Abbé Giraud, dressed in black, sacerdotal habits at that period being abolished. In the register they found about fifty persons assembled; some employed about the prison, some deputies, some commissaries, all waiting in the expectation of seeing the queen pass; there might be some mandatories, and many idlers. His heart bounded so violently on finding himself opposite the wicket, that he heard not even the parley that ensued between the abbé, the gendarmes, and the concierge.

Only a man with a pair of scissors in his hand and a piece of stuff newly cut, pushed against Maison Rouge upon the threshold. He turned round and recognized the executioner.

"What do you want, citizen?" demanded Sanson.

The chevalier endeavored to repress the shudder which, in spite of himself, ran through his veins.

"You see, Citizen Sanson," replied the chevalier, "that I accompany the curé of St. Laudry."

"Oh, very well," said the executioner, drawing himself on one side, and issuing orders to his assistant.

During this time Maison Rouge had passed into the interior of the register, and from there into the compartment inhabited by the two gendarmes. These men were overcome by contending emotions. Proud and haughty as she had been to others, how sweet and condescending she had ever been to them! They seemed more like her servants than her guards. In his present position the chevalier could not obtain a view of the queen—the screen was closed! It had opened to give entrance to the curé, but directly closed behind him. When the chevalier entered, the conversation had already commenced.

"Monsieur," said the queen, in a clear and firm voice, "since you have sworn yourself to the Republic, to those who have condemned me to death, I have no confidence in you. We do not worship the same God."

"Madame," said Giraud, struck by this profession of faith so unworthy of her, "a Christian about to die should dismiss all hatred from her heart, and ought not to repulse her God, under whatever form He may be presented to her."

Maison Rouge advanced a step to open the screen, hoping that when she saw him, and knew what brought him, she would change her opinion in regard to the curé; but the gendarmes detected the movement.

"But," said Maison Rouge, "I am acholothist to the curé."

"Then, since she refuses the curé," said Duchesne, "she does not require you."

"But still, perhaps she may accept me," said he, raising his voice ; "it is impossible she would refuse me."

But Marie Antoinette was too much engrossed by the sentiment which agitated her either to hear or recognize the chevalier's voice.

"Go, monsieur," continued she; "leave me," addressing Giraud, "since at this time we in France live under the régime of liberty, I claim the right of dying according to my own fashion."

Giraud offered some resistance.

"Leave me, monsieur," said she. "I desire you to leave me."

Giraud endeavored to speak.

"I will not hear you," said she; "leave me!" with the gesture of Marie Therese.

Giraud went out.

Maison Rouge essayed to gain a glimpse of her through the opening in the screen, but the prisoner had turned her back. The executioner's assistant crossed before the curé ; he came in holding a cord in his hand. The two gendarmes pushed the chevalier toward the door ; before, amazed, despairing, and utterly bewildered, he had been able to utter a cry, or make the slightest movement to effect his purpose, he found himself, with the curé, in the corridor of the turnkey. This corridor brought them again into the register, where the news of the queen's refusal had already circulated, where the Austrian pride of Marie Antoinette was to some the pretext of the coarsest invectives, and to others the subject of secret admiration.

"Go," said Richard, to the abbé, "return home, since she repulses you, and let her die as she likes."

"She is in the right," said Richard's wife, "and I would act the same."

"Then you would do wrong, citoyenne," said the curé.

'Be silent," said the concierge, opening his eyes very wide ; "what does this concern you ? Go, abbé, go !"

"No," said Giraud, "no. I will, notwithstanding all, accompany her; one word, only one word, if she will listen, might bring her back to duty ; besides, I am sent by the order of the Commune, and I must discharge my office."

"Send back your sexton, then," brutally observed the adjutant-major, commandant of the armed forces.

He had been formerly an actor of French comedy, named Grammont. The eyes of the chevalier flashed lightning, as he thrust his hand into his breast, where Giraud knew he had concealed a poniard. He arrested him with a suppliant look.

"Spare my life," said he, in a low voice; "you see all your hopes are lost; do not ruin hers. I will mention you on the route; I swear to you I will tell her you risked your life that you might see her once more on earth."

These words calmed the effervescence of the young man, and the ordinary reaction taking place, he sunk into a state of quiescence. This man of heroic mind, of marvelous power, had arrived at the termination of both strength and will, and glided, irresolute, or, rather, exhausted and vanquished, into a state of torpor that might have been imagined to be the precursor of death.

"Yes, I believe," said he, "it should be thus; the cross for Jesus, the scaffold for her, gods and kings drink deep of the chalice presented to them by men."

This thought produced resignation, and now, totally prostrated, he allowed himself to be pushed without offering any resistance, except an occasional involuntary groan, to the outer gate, passive as Ophelia when, devoted to death, she found herself borne away by the remorseless waves.

At the foot of the gate, and at the doors of the conciergerie, a crowd was assembled, which, unless once seen, it was impossible to describe. Impatience rules every passion, and each passion speaks its own language, and these combined formed an immense and prolonged uproar, as if the whole noise and the entire population of Paris were on this occasion concentrated in the quarter of the Palais de Justice. In front of this crowd the whole army was encamped, with guns intended to guard the procession, and also to secure the enjoyment to those who came to witness the last act of the tragedy.

It would have been vain to attempt to pierce this profound rampart, increasing gradually, since the condemnation of the queen was now known not only at Paris, but by the patriots of the faubourgs. Maison Rouge, expelled from the conciergerie, naturally found himself in the first rank among the soldiers, who instantly demanded who he was. He replied, "He was the curate of the Abbé Giraud, but having bound himself by the same oath, he, like the curé, had been dismissed and refused by the queen;" on which the soldiers, in their turn, pushed him into the first row of spectators, where he was again compelled to repeat what he had previously told them.

Then the cry arose: "He has just left!" "He has seen her!" "What did she say?" "What did she do?" "Is she as haughty as usual?" "Is she cast down?" "Does she weep?" The chevalier replied to all these questions in a feeble but sweet and affable tone, as if this voice was the last manifestation of life suspended on his lips. His answer was couched in the language of truth and simplicity. It contained an elogium on the firmness of Marie Antoinette, and that which he recounted with the sublimity and faith of an evangelist, cast sorrow and remorse over many hearts.

When he spoke of the little dauphin, and of Mme. Royale, of this queen without a throne, of this wife without a husband, this mother bereft of her children, this woman alone and abandoned, without a friend, surrounded by executioners, more than one face here and there assumed a sad expression, and more than one tear of regret was clandestinely wiped from eyes previously animated by hatred. The palace clock struck eleven. All murmuring at this moment ceased. One hundred thousand human beings counted these strokes, echoed by the pulsations of their own hearts. When the last vibration had ceased and died away in the distance, a loud noise was heard within the gates, and, at the same time, a cart advancing from the side of the Quai aux Fleurs broke through the crowd, then the guards, and drew up at the bottom of the steps. The queen soon appeared on the top of the staircase; she made a motion of astonishment and horror; her respiration was laborious and slow; her hair was cut short, the greater portion had turned gray during her captivity, and this shade of silver rendered still more delicate the mother-of-pearl pallor which at this moment lent an almost angelic beauty to this daughter of the Cæsars. She was attired in a white robe, her hands were fastened at her back. When she appeared with the Abbé Giraud on her right, who, notwithstanding all opposition, would still accompany her, and the executioner on her left, both dressed in black, there ran throughout the crowd a murmur that God alone, who reads all hearts, could comprehend and sum up the truth. A man passed between the executioner and Marie Antoinette; it was Grammont. He conducted her to the fatal car. The queen recoiled.

"Mount!" said Grammont.

This word was distinctly heard by all. Emotion held every breath suspended on the lips of the spectators. A blush suffused the face of the queen, mounting even to the roots of her hair, but immediately receded, leaving her face a ghastly paleness, and blanching her half-open lips.

"Why a cart for me," she said, "when the king had a carriage to convey him to the scaffold?"

The Abbé Giraud advanced, and addressed a few words to her in a low tone; doubtless he condemned this last cry of royal pride. The queen remained silent, but tottered so much that Sanson held out his arms to support her; but she recovered her self-possession before he could touch her. She then descended the staircase, while the assistants placed a foot-board behind the cart. The queen went first, the abbé followed her. When the cart was in motion it caused a great movement in the assemblage: and the soldiers, at the same time, ignorant of its cause, united their efforts to push back the crowd, and, consequently, a large space was cleared between the people and the vehicle of death, when suddenly a mournful howling was heard. The queen started, and instantly rose, looking around her. She then saw her little dog, which had been lost for two months, who, unable to follow her into the conciergerie, regardless of kicks, blows, and thrusts, rushed toward the cart; but almost directly poor Jet, thin even to emaciation, starving and bruised, disappeared under the horses' feet. The queen followed him with her eyes; she could not speak, for her voice was drowned in the noise; she could not raise her hands, for they were tied; and had she been able to do either, who would have listened to her. Having closed her eyes for an instant, she soon revived. He was in the arms of a pale young man, who, standing on a cannon, was conspicuous above the crowd, and prompted by an inexplicable impulse, pointed toward heaven. Marie Antoinette looked upward and smiled sweetly.

The chevalier uttered a groan, as if this smile had broken his heart; and as the fatal cart turned toward the Pont au Change, he fell back among the crowd, and disappeared.

CHAPTER XLIX.

THE SCAFFOLD.

Upon La Place de la Revolution, leaning against a lamppost, two men were waiting. Of those who followed with the crowd, some were carried to La Place du Palais, others to La Place de la Revolution, while the rest spread, impatient and tumultuous, over the whole road separating the two places. When the queen reached the instrument of punishment, which, defaced by the sun and storm, worn by the hand of the executioner, and, most horrible, blunted by too frequent contact with its victims, it reared its head with a sinister pride over the subjacent mass, like a queen ruling her people. The two men, arm in arm, and speaking by fits and starts, with pale lips and contracted brows, were Louis and Maurice. Lost in the crowd, but not in a way calculated to excite suspicion, they continued in a low tone their conversation, which was perhaps not the least interesting one circulating among the various groups, which, like an electric chain, agitated this living sea from the Pont au Change to the Place de la Revolution.

"See," said Maurice, as the hideous monster reared her red arms; "might it not be said that she calls us, and smiles from her wicket, in anticipation of a frightful mouthful."

"I," said Louis, "must confess I do not belong to the school of poetry which sees everything *couleur de rouge*. I see it *en rose*, and even at the foot of this dreadful machine, I will sing and hope still. '*Dum spiro, spero.*'"

"You hope, when they murder women?"

"Maurice," said Louis, "child of the Revolution, do not deny your mother. Ah! Maurice, remain a stanch and loyal patriot. She who is condemned to die is unlike all other women; she is the evil genius of France."

"Oh! it is not her that I regret; it is not for her I weep!" cried Maurice.

"Yes, I understand, it is Geneviève."

"Ah!" said Maurice, "there is one thought that drives me mad. It is that Geneviève is in the hands of those purveyors to the guillotine, Hebert and Fouquier Tinville; in the hands of the men who sent here the poor Héloise, and are now sending the proud Marie Antoinette."

"Well," said Louis, "it is this thought that inspires me with hope. When the anger of the people has feasted two tyrants it will be for some time satiated at least, like the boa-constrictor, who requires three months to digest what he has devoured. Then it will swallow no more; and, as it is said by the prophets of the faubourg, 'the lesser morsels will have no cause for fear.'"

"Louis! Louis!" said Maurice, "I am more positive than you, and I say it in a whisper, but am ready to repeat it aloud; Louis, I hate the new queen, who seems destined to succeed the Austrian whom she destroys. It is a sad queen whose purple is daily dyed in blood, and to whom Sanson is prime minister."

"Bah! we shall escape."

"I do not believe it," said Maurice, shaking his head; "to avoid being arrested at your house, we have no resource but to live in the street."

"Bah! we can quit Paris; there is nothing to prevent us. We need not complain then. My uncle will await us at St. Omer; money, passport, nothing will be wanting. There exists not the gendarme who shall arrest us; what do you think? We remain in Paris because we choose to do so."

"No, that is not correct, excellent friend, devoted and faithful as you are. We remain because I wish to continue here."

"And you wish to remain to discover Geneviève. Well, nothing is more simple, just, or natural. You think she is in prison; nothing more probable. You wish to keep watch over her, and on that account we cannot quit Paris."

Maurice drew a deep sigh; it was evident his thoughts were wandering.

"Do you remember the death of Louis XVI.?" said he.

"I can see him yet, pale with pride and emotion. I was then one of the chiefs in this crowd, where I conceal myself to-day. I was greater at the foot of the scaffold than the king upon it had ever been. What changes, Louis! and when one thinks that nine short months have sufficed to work this change."

"Nine months of love, Maurice! Love lost Troy."

Maurice sighed; his wandering thoughts now took another direction.

"Poor Maison Rouge!" said he, "it is a sad thing for him."

"*Hélas!*" said Louis, "shall I tell you what appears to me the most melancholy thing about the revolution?"

"Yes," said Maurice.

"It is that one often has for friends those we should prefer as enemies, and for enemies those we would wish——"

"It gives me much pain to think of one thing," interrupted Maurice.

"What?"

"It is that he did not invent some project to save the queen. He must be mad!"

"A man with the strength of ten thousand."

"I tell you he was mad. I know that to save Geneviève——"

Louis frowned.

"I again tell you, Maurice," said he, "you are wild. No; even were it possible for you to save Geneviève, you would only become a bad citizen. But enough of this. Maurice, let us listen. Look how the heads undulate; see, there is Sanson's valet raising himself from under the basket, and looking in the distance. The Austrian arrives.

In short, as if to accompany this movement which Louis had remarked, a shuddering, prolonged and unceasing, pervaded the crowd. It was one of those hurricanes which commence with a whistle and terminate with a bellow. Maurice raised himself by the help of the lamppost, and looked toward La Rue St. Honoré.

"Yes; said he, shuddering, "there it is."

And another machine now made its appearance, almost as revolting as the guillotine. It was the fatal cart. On the right and left glittered the arms of the escort, while in front marched Grammont, replying with flashes of his saber to the shouts and cries of some fanatics. But even as the cart advanced, these cries subsided under the haughty courage of the condemned. Never had a countenance commanded more respect, never had Marie Antoinette looked more the queen. Her proud courage inspired her assistants with terror. Indifferent to the exhortations of the Abbé Giraud, who still accompanied her, her face moved neither to the right nor left; her deep thought was as immutable as her look; even the jolting motion of the cart upon the uneven pavement did not by its violence disturb the rigidity of her features; she might have been taken for a royal statue riding in the cart, had it not been for her brilliant eyes, and her hair, which had escaped from her cap, being waved about by the wind. A silence equal to that of the desert fell suddenly upon those three hundred thousand spectators of this scene, witnessed by the heavens for the first time by the light of the sun. On the right, where Maurice and Louis were standing, the wheels of the cart were heard, and the breathing of the horse. The cart stopped at the scaffold. The queen, who, doubtless, was not conscious at the moment, awoke, and understood it all; she threw a haughty glance upon the crowd, and again encountered the restless eyes of the pale young man she had previously seen standing on the cannon. He was now mounted on a stone, and repeated the respectful salutation he had before offered her as she left the conciergerie. He then disappeared. Many persons seeing him, it was soon reported, from his being dressed in black, that a priest was in attendance on Marie Antoinette, to give her absolution ere she ascended the scaffold. As to the rest, no one disturbed the chevalier. There is in the highest moments a supreme respect for certain things. The queen cautiously descended the steps from the cart, supported by Sanson, who to the last moment, in accomplishing the task to which he himself appeared to be condemned, treated her with the most marked respect.

As the queen walked toward the steps of the scaffold some of the horses reared, and several of the foot-guards and soldiers appeared to oscillate and lose their equilibrium; then a shadow was seen to glide under the scaffold, but tranquillity was almost instantaneously reestablished, since no one was willing to quit his place at this solemn moment—no one was willing to lose the minutest detail in the dreadful tragedy about to be accomplished. All eyes were directed toward the condemned. The queen was already on the platform of the scaffold. The priest still continued to address her; an assistant softly placed himself behind her, while another removed the handkerchief from her shoulders. Marie Antoinette felt the touch of the infamous hand upon her neck, and, making a brusque movement, trod upon Sanson's foot, who, without her having seen him, was engaged in fixing the fatal plank. Sanson drew back.

"Excuse me, monsieur," said the queen; "I did not do it intentionally."

These were the last words pronounced by the daughter of the Cæsars, the queen of France, the widow of Louis XVI.

As the clock of the Tuileries struck a quarter after twelve, the queen was launched into eternity. A terrible cry—a shout comprising at once joy, terror, sorrow, triumph, expiation—rose like a storm, smothering in its birth a feeble burst of lamentation which issued from beneath the scaffold. The gendarmes heard it, notwithstanding, feeble as it was, and advanced some steps in front. The crowd, now less compact, expanded like a river whose dike has been enlarged, threw down the fence, dispersed the guards, and rushed like the returning tide to beat the foot of the scaffold, which was already shaking. Each one wished for a nearer view of the royal remains of her whom they had considered the destruction of France. But the gendarmes had another object in view—they sought the shadow which had repassed their lines, and glided beneath the scaffold. Two of them returned leading between them by the collar a pale young man, whose hand contained a bloodstained handkerchief, which he pressed to his heart; he was followed by a little spaniel howling piteously.

"Death to the aristocrat! death to the *ci-devant!*" cried some men of the people; "he has dipped his handkerchief in the Austrian's blood—to death with him!"

"Great God!" said Maurice to Louis. "Do you recognize him? do you recognize him?"

"Death to the royalist!" repeated these madmen; "take away the handkerchief he wishes to preserve as a relic, wrest it from him, tear it from him."

A haughty smile flitted across the young man's lips, he tore open his shirt, bared his breast, and dropped the handkerchief.

"Gentlemen," said he, "this blood is not the queen's, but my own. Let me die in peace."

And a deep gushing wound appeared widely gaping

under the left breast. The crowd uttered one cry, and retired. The young man sank slowly upon his knees, and gazed upon the scaffold as a martyr looks upon the altar.

"Maison Rouge," whispered Louis to Maurice.

"Adieu!" murmured the young man, bowing his head with an angelic smile, "adieu! or, rather, *au revoir!*" and he expired in the midst of the stupefied guards.

"There is still the expedient, Louis," said Maurice, "before becoming an unworthy citizen."

The little spaniel turned toward the corpse, terrified and howling lamentably.

"Why, here is Jet!" said a man, holding a large club in his hand; "why, here is Jet! Come here, old fellow."

The dog advanced toward him, but was scarcely within arm's-length of the man who had called him, when the brutal wretch raised his club and dashed out his brains, at the same time bursting into a hoarse laugh.

"Cowardly wretch!" cried Maurice.

"Silence," said Louis, "or we are lost. It is Simon."

CHAPTER L.

THE VISIT TO THE DOMICILE.

Louis and Maurice returned to their mutual home, but the latter, in order not to compromise his friend too openly, usually absented himself during the day, and returned at night. In the midst of these events, being present always at the removal of the prisoners to the conciergerie, he watched daily for the sight of Geneviève, not having been yet able to discover her place of imprisonment. Louis, since his visit to Fouquier Tinville, had succeeded in convincing him that on the first ostensible act he was lost, and would then have sacrificed himself without having benefited Geneviève, and Maurice, who would willingly have thrown himself into prison in the hope of being united to his mistress, became prudent from the fear of being separated from her forever. He went every morning to the Carmelites at Port Libre, the Madelonnettes at St. Lazare, from

La Force to the Luxembourg; he stationed himself before these prisons to watch the carts as they came out to convey the accused to the Revolutionary Tribunal. Then, when he had scanned the victims, he proceeded to the other prisons to prosecute this hopeless search, as he soon became aware that the activity of ten men would prove inadequate to keep watch over the thirty-three prisons which Paris could boast of at this period. He, therefore, contented himself by going daily to the tribunal, there to await the coming of Geneviève. He was already beginning to despair. Indeed, what resources remained to a person condemned, after their arrest? Sometimes the tribunal, whose sittings commenced at ten o'clock, had condemned twenty or thirty people by four o'clock; those first condemned had six hours to live, but the last, sentenced at a quarter to four, fell at half-past beneath the ax. To resign Geneviève to submit to a similar fate would be ceasing to fight then against destiny. Oh! if he had known beforehand of the imprisonment of Geneviève, how Maurice would have tracked the blind human justice of this epoch! how easily and promptly he had torn Geneviève from prison! Never were escapes more easy, and it may be said never were they so rare. All the nobles once placed in prison, installed themselves as in a château, and died at leisure. To fly was to withdraw from the consequences of a duel; the women even blushed at liberty acquired at this price.

But Maurice would not have shown himself so scrupulous. To kill the dogs, to alter the door-keys, what more simple? Geneviève was not one of those splendid names calculated to attract general attention. She would not dishonor herself by flying, and besides, when could she be disgraced? Oh! as he bitterly called to mind the gardens of Port Libre, so easy to scale, the chambers of Madelonnettes, so easy of access to the street, the low walls of the Luxembourg, and the dark corridors of the Carmelites, where a resolute man could so easily penetrate by opening a window!

But was Geneviève in one of these prisons? Then, devoured by doubt and worn out with anxiety, he loaded Dixmer with imprecations; he threatened, and nourished his hatred against this man, whose cowardly vengeance concealed itself under an apparent devotion to the royal cause.

"I will find him out thus," thought Maurice : "if he wishes to save the unhappy woman, he will show himself; if he wishes to ruin her, he will insult her. I will find him out, the scoundrel, and it will be an evil day for him!"

On the morning of the day when the events occurred which we are about to relate, Maurice went out early to take his usual station at the Revolutionary Tribunal, leaving Louis asleep.

He was suddenly awakened by a loud noise at the door, the voices of women, and the butt-ends of guns. He threw around him the startled glance of a surprised man, who wished to convince himself that nothing that could compromise him was in view. Four sectionaries, two gendarmes, and a commissary entered at the same moment. This visit was sufficiently significant, and Louis hastened to dress himself.

"Do you come to arrest me?" said he.

"Yes, Citizen Louis."

"What for?"

"Because you are suspected."

"Ah! all right."

The commissary muttered some words in a low tone about arrest by procès-verbal.

"Where is your friend?" said he immediately.

"What friend?"

"The Citizen Maurice Lindey."

"At home, probably."

"No; he lodges here."

"He! go along! Search, and if you find——"

"Here is the denunciation," said the commissary; "it is plain enough," offering Louis a paper with vile writing and enigmatical orthography.

It stated that every morning the Citizen Lindey was seen going out of the Citizen Louis' house, suspected, and ordered for arrest. The denunciation was signed "Simon."

"Why, the cobbler will lose his practise, if he follows two trades at the same time—a spy and boot-mender. He is a Cæsar, this Monsieur Simon," and he burst into a fit of laughter.

"The Citizen Maurice, where is the Citizen Maurice?" said the commissary. "We summon you to deliever him up."

"When I tell you he is not here?"

The commissary passed into the chamber adjoining, then ascended to the loft where Louis' official slept, and at last opened a lower apartment, but found no traces of Maurice. But upon the dining-room table a recently written letter attracted the attention of the commissary. It was from Maurice, who had deposited it there on leaving in the morning (as they slept together) without awakening his friend.

"I go to the tribunal," said Maurice; "take breakfast without me. I shall not return till night."

"Citizens," said Louis, "however anxious I may feel to obey your commands, I cannot follow you *en chemise*. Allow my official to assist me."

"Aristocrat," said a voice, "do you require assistance to put on your breeches?"

"Ah, *mon Dieu!* yes," said Louis; "I resemble the Citizen Dagobert—mind, I did not say king."

"Well, dress," said the commissary; "but make haste."

The official came down to help his master to dress. However, it was not exactly that Louis required a *valet de chambre*, it was that nothing might escape the notice of the official, and that, consequently, he might detail everything to Maurice.

"Now, messieurs—pardon, citizens. Now, citizens, I am ready, and will follow you; but permit me, I beg, to carry with me the last volume of 'Lettres à Émile,' by Monsieur Demonstier, which has just appeared, and I have not read. It will enliven the hours of my captivity."

"Your captivity," said Simon, sharply, now become municipal in his turn, and entering, followed by four sectionaries, "that will not last long. You figure in the procès of the woman who wanted to assist the Austrian to escape. They try her to-day, and to-morrow your turn will come."

"Cobbler," said Louis, "you cut your soles too quickly."

"Yes; but what a nice stroke from the leather-cutting knife!" replied Simon; "you will see, you will see, my fine grenadier."

Louis shrugged his shoulders.

"Well," said he, "let us go; I am waiting for you."

As each one turned round to descend the staircase, Louis bestowed on the municipal Simon so vigorous a kick with his foot that he sent him rolling and howling down the entire flight of stairs. The sectionaries could not restrain their laughter. Louis put his hands in his pockets.

"In the exercise of my functions," said Simon, livid with rage.

"*Pardieu!*" said Louis, "are we not all here in the exercise of our functions?"

He got into the carriage, and was conducted by the commissary to the Palais de Justice.

CHAPTER LI.

LOUIS.

IF for the second time the reader is willing to follow us to the Revolutionary Tribunal, we shall find Maurice in the same place where we have already seen him, only now infinitely more pale and agitated. At the moment our scene again opens upon the lugubrious theater, whither we are led by a tissue of events rather than by our own inclinations, the jury were deliberating, a cause had just been tried; two of the accused had already, by one of those insolent precautions by which they ridiculed the judges, attired themselves for the scaffold, and were conversing with their counsel, whose words somewhat resembled those of a physician who despairs of the life of his patient. The people of the tribune were this day in a ferocious mood, calculated to excite the severity of the jury placed under the immediate surveillance of the tricoteuses and inhabitants of the suburbs. The juries under these circumstances became more excited and energetic, resembling an actor who redoubles his efforts beneath the eyes of a censorious public. Since ten in the morning five condemnations had already taken place under the decisions of these harsh and insatiable juries. The two individuals who now found themselves on the bench of the accused awaited the decisive moment, when "yes" or "no" would return them to life or doom them to death. The people of the nation, rendered savage by the daily occurrence of these spectacles, now become their favorite pastime, prepared themselves by exclamations and anticipations for the awful moment.

"There! there! look at the tall one," said a tricoteuse, who, not having a bonnet, wore a tricolored cockade, large as a hand, on her breast—"there! is he not pale? they say he is almost dead now."

The condemned regarded the woman with a contemptuous smile.

"What do you say?" said her neighbor; "why, he is smiling."

"Yes, the wrong side of his mouth."

One of the men looked at his watch.

"What is the time?" inquired his companion.

"A quarter to one. This has lasted three quarters of an hour."

"The same as at Dagobert, that unfortunate town, where you arrive at noon, and are hung in an hour."

"And the short one! the short one!" cried another person, "will he not be ugly when he sneezes in the sack?"

"Bah! it is done so quickly you will barely have time to perceive it."

"Then we will demand the head from Sanson; one has a right to see it."

"Look! what a beautiful blue coat he has on, the tyrant! It is rather a pleasant thing that the poor can shorten the rich and well dressed people."

Indeed, as the executioner had told the queen, the poor inherited the spoils of each victim; they were carried immediately to the Salpetrière, after the execution, and distributed among the indigent; and there even the clothes of the unfortunate queen had been conveyed.

Maurice heard this whirlwind of words without paying any attention; every moment was occupied by one engrossing thought, to the exclusion of all else. For several days his heart beat only at certain moments, and by fits and starts, as from time to time hope or fear appeared to suspend all vital action, and these perpetual oscillations to bruise the most tender sensibilities of his soul.

The jury returned to their places, and, as had been fully anticipated, the president pronounced the condemnation of the two accused, who were directly removed, walking with a firm and erect step; for at this epoch every one learned how to die boldly.

The solemn and sinister voice of the usher was again heard.

"Citizen, the public accuser against the Citoyenne Geneviève Dixmer."

A shudder ran through Maurice's frame, and a cold sweat bedewed his brow. The little door by which the accused entered suddenly opened, and Geneviève appeared. She was dressed in white; her ringlets were tastefully arranged, instead of being cut short, hanging in long masses of clustering curls. Doubtless, at the last Geneviève wished to create a favorable impression on those who would see her.

Maurice beheld Geneviève, and felt that all the strength he had collected was inadequate to this occasion, notwithstanding he had awaited this blow, since for twelve days he had not omitted a single sitting, and three times already had the name of Geneviève proceeded from the mouth of the public accuser and reached his ear; but there are certain griefs and miseries so profound that it is quite impossible to sound the depths of the abyss.

All those who witnessed the appearance of this young female, so lovely, so pale and innocent, uttered a simultaneous cry, some of fury—for at this period there existed a class of people who detested everything bordering on superiority of beauty, riches, and even of birth—others of admiration, and some of pity. Geneviève, doubtless, among all these cries had recognized one cry, amid all these voices had distinguished one voice, for she turned in the direction of Maurice, while the president, looking up from time to time, turned over the law papers of the accused.

At the first glance she discovered Maurice, concealed as his features were under the broad brim of a large hat which he wore; and, turning round with a sweet smile, and a gesture still more engaging, she pressed her rosy but trembling hands upon her lips, and depositing her whole soul with her breath, she gave wings to a last kiss which only one in that vast crowd had the right to appropriate to himself. A murmur of interest ran through the hall. Geneviève recalled, turned toward her judges, but stopping suddenly in the midst of this movement, her eyes dilated, and fixed with an undefinable expression of horror toward one point of the hall. Maurice in vain raised himself on his toes; he saw nothing, or, rather, something of more consequence claimed his attention upon this scene—that is to say, the tribunal.

Fouquier Tinville had commenced reading the act of accusation. This act stated that Geneviève Dixmer was the wife of an obstinate conspirator, suspected of having assisted the ex-Chevalier de Maison Rouge in all his successive attempts to rescue the queen. She had, besides, been surprised at the feet of the queen, entreating her to exchange garments with her, and offering to die in her stead. This absurd fanaticism, continued the act, merited, no doubt, the admiration of the contre-revolutionists; but in our day every French citizen owes his life to the nation; it is, therefore, double treason to sacrifice it to the enemies of France.

Geneviève, when interrogated as to having been recognized on her knees before the queen, as stated by the two gendarmes, Gilbert and Duchesne, and entreating her to exchange vestments, simply replied:

"Yes."

"Then," said the president, "inform us of your plan, and what hope you entertained of its success."

Geneviève smiled.

"A woman might conceive hopes," said she, "but a woman could not form a plan like this of which I am the victim."

"How came you here, then?"

"Not of my own account. I was driven to it."

"Who compelled you?" demanded the public accuser.

"Those who menaced me with death if I did not obey;" and again the agitated look of the young woman was centered on that part of the hall invisible to Maurice.

"But to escape from this death which menaced you, did you not face death which must result from your condemnation?"

"When I consented, the knife was at my throat, while the guillotine was only in perspective. I succumbed under present violence."

"Why did you not call for assistance? All good citizens would have defended you."

"Alas! monsieur," said Geneviève, in a voice at once so sad and sweet that it caused Maurice's heart to beat tumultuously, "I had no one near me."

Commiseration succeeded to interest, as interest had succeeded to curiosity. Many heads were lowered, some to conceal their tears, many to allow them to flow freely. Just then Maurice perceived on his left an immovable head and an inflexible countenance. It was Dixmer, standing dark, gloomy, and implacable, never for a moment losing sight of Geneviève or of the tribunal.

The blood rushed to the young man's temples, rage mounted from his heart to his forehead, filling his whole being with an intense desire for vengeance. He flung at

Dixmer a look so replete with burning hatred, so condensed and powerful, that he, as if attracted by the electric fluid, turned his head toward his enemy. Their glances encountered like two flashes.

"Tell us the names of your instigators," said the president.

"There was only one, monsieur."

"Who?"

"My husband."

"Do you know where he is?"

"Yes."

"Inform us of his retreat?"

"He has been brutal, but I will not be a coward. It is not for me to tell you his retreat, but for you to find him." Maurice looked at Dixmer. He never moved. One idea flitted through the young man's brain. It was to denounce him himself; but he quickly suppressed the thought. "No," said he, "it is not thus that he should die."

"Then you refuse to assist us in our search?" said the president.

"I think, monsieur, I could not do so without rendering myself as contemptible in the eyes of others as he is in mine."

"Are there any witnesses?" demanded the president.

"There is one," replied the usher.

"Call the witness."

"Maximilien Jean Louis!" shouted the usher.

"Louis!" cried Maurice, "oh, *mon Dieu!* what has happened, then?"

This scene took place the same day that Louis had been arrested, and Maurice was in utter ignorance of all that had occurred.

"Louis!" murmured Geneviève, looking round with anxious solicitude.

"Why does not the witness answer to the call?" demanded the president.

"Citizen President," said Fouquier Tinville, "upon a recent denunciation the witness was arrested at his own house; he will be here directly." Maurice started. "There is another still more important witness, but we have not yet been able to find him."

Dixmer turned toward Maurice, smiling. Perhaps the same idea flitted through the mind of the husband which had before entered that of the lover. Geneviève, pale and horror-stricken, uttered a low groan.

At this moment Louis entered, followed by two gendarmes. After him, and by the same door, Simon appeared, who came to take his seat in the judgment hall, according to custom in that locality.

"Your name and surname?" inquired the president.

"Maximilien Jean Louis."

"Your trade?"

"An independent gentleman."

"You will not remain so long," muttered Simon, shaking his fist.

"Are you related to the prisoner at the bar?"

"No; but I have the honor of being one of her friends."

"Did you know there was a conspiracy to carry off the queen?"

"How could I know it?"

"She might have confided in you."

"In me! a member of the Section of the Thermopyles?"

"Notwithstanding, you have sometimes been seen with her."

"That might have been seen often."

"Did you recognize her as an aristocrat?"

"I knew her as the wife of a master tanner."

"But her husband did not in reality follow the business which he pretended to."

"Of that I am ignorant; her husband was not one of my friends."

"Tell me what you know of this husband."

"Oh, very willingly. He is a villain, who——"

"Monsieur Louis," said Geneviève, "have mercy."

Louis continued, unmoved:

"He is a villain who has sacrificed this poor woman before you, not even to his political opinions, but to private hatred. Pooh! I look upon him as lower and more degraded even than Simon."

Dixmer became livid with rage. Simon wished to speak, but a gesture from the president imposed silence.

"You appear to know the whole history, Citizen Louis," said Fouquier; "continue your account."

"Pardon me, Citizen Fouquier," said Louis, rising; "I know nothing more."

He bowed, and reseated himself.

"Citizen Louis," said Fouquier, "it is your bounden duty to enlighten this tribunal."

"It will not be much enlightened by all I have to say. As to this poor woman, I again repeat she has only acted under compulsion. Look at her; does she look like a conspirator? What she has done she was compelled to do. That is all."

"You think so?"

"I know so."

"In the name of the law," said Fouquier, "I require that the witness Louis shall be placed before this tribunal as an accomplice of this woman."

Maurice groaned, while Geneviève buried her face in her hands. Simon screamed out in a transport of joy.

"Citizen Accuser, you are the savior of your country!"

As to Louis, he leaped over the balustrade without making any reply, and seating himself near to Geneviève, took her hand, and respectfully kissed it, saying, "*Bon jour*, madame," with a coolness which electrified the assembly; "how do you find yourself?" Then he took his seat on the bench of the accused.

CHAPTER LII.

SEQUEL TO THE PRECEDING.

ALL this scene had passed before Maurice like a fantastic vision. Leaning upon the handle of his sword, which he had never quitted, he saw his friends precipitated one after another into that gulf which never yields back its victims; and this dangerous fancy so affected him that he asked himself why he, the companion of these unfortunates, should still cling to the brink of the precipice, and not surrender himself to the infatuation which was dragging him with them. In leaping the balustrade, Louis saw the dark figure and sneering features of Dixmer. When, as we have said, he had placed himself near her, Geneviéve whispered in his ear.

"Ah, *mon Dieu!*" said she, "do you know that Maurice is here?"

"Where? Do not look round directly; one look might prove his ruin. Calm yourself."

"Behind us, near the door. What a trial for him, if we are all condemned!"

Louis regarded the young woman with tender sympathy.

"We shall be," said he. "I conjure you not to doubt it. The deception would be too cruel if you were to permit yourself to hope."

"Oh, *mon Dieu!*" said Geneviève, "pity our poor friend, who will remain alone in the world."

Louis then turned round toward Maurice, and Geneviève also could not refrain from glancing at him. His eyes were fixed upon them both, and one hand was placed upon his heart.

"There is one way to save you," said Louis.

"Are you sure?" said Geneviève, her eyes sparkling with joy.

"Oh, of that one I am sure," replied Louis.

"Oh, if you can save me, how I will bless you!"

"But this way," replied the young man.

Geneviève read his hesitation in his eye.

"You have also seen him?" said she.

"Yes, I saw him. Will you be saved? Let him, in his turn, take his seat in the iron armchair, and you shall be safe."

Dixmer, doubtless from Louis' look and the expression of his countenance, divined what he uttered. He at first turned pale, but soon recovered his satanic look and sinister smile.

"Impossible!" said Geneviève; "the most I can do is to hate him."

"Say that he knows your generous nature, and defies you."

"No doubt; for he is sure of him, of me, of us all."

"Geneviève, Geneviève! I am less perfect than yourself. Let me entreat you. Let him perish."

"No, Louis, I conjure you. Nothing in common with this man, not even death. It seems to me I should be unfaithful to Maurice were I to die with Dixmer."

"But you will not die."

"To live by his death."

"Ah!" said Louis, "Maurice has reason to love you; you are an angel, and heaven is the angels' home. Poor, dear Maurice!"

In the meantime, Simon, who could not overhear the conversation between the accused, devoured their looks instead of their words.

"Citizen Gendarme," said he, "prevent those conspirators from continuing their plots against the Republic, even in the Revolutionary Tribunal."

"You know, Citizen Simon," replied the gendarme, "they will conspire here no more, and if they do so now it will not be for long. These citizens are only conversing together, and since the law does not forbid them to do so in the cart, why should it be forbidden at the tribunal?"

This gendarme was Gilbert, who, having recognized the prisoner taken in the queen's chamber, avowed with his ordinary honesty the interest which he could not help

"I decidedly think I shall kill you, Maurice," said Dixmer, "you tremble so much."

The Chevalier de Maison-Rouge
—p. 393

according to her courage and devotion. The president having consulted the benchers, by the request of Fouquier Tinville, commenced his questions.

"Accused Louis," demanded he, "of what nature was your acquaintance with the Citoyenne Dixmer?"

"Of what nature, Citizen President? Friendship's pure flame bound us to each other. She loved me as a sister, I loved her as a brother."

"Citizen Louis," said Fouquier Tinville, "your poetry is out of season here, and the rhyme is bad."

"Why so?"

"You have a syllable too long."

"Cut it off! cut it off, Citizen Accuser; that is your trade, you know."

The imperturbable countenance of Fouquier Tinville assumed a pallid hue at this horrible pleasantry.

"And in what light," demanded the president, "did the Citizen Dixmer view this *liaison* of a man, a pretended Republican, with his wife?"

"As to that I can tell you nothing, declaring to never having been intimate with the Citizen Dixmer, and never having felt any desire to be so."

"But," said Fouquier Tinville, "you did not tell us that your friend, Maurice Lindey, formed the link of this pure friendship between yourself and the accused."

"If I did not say so," replied Louis, "it was because it seemed to me wrong so to speak, and I find that you even might take example from me."

"The citizen jury," said Fouquier Tinville, "will appreciate this singular alliance between an aristocrat and two Republicans, and at the very moment even when this aristocrat is convicted of the blackest plot that could be concocted against the nation."

"How should I know anything concerning this plot you speak of?" demanded Louis, disgusted by the brutality of the argument.

"You were acquainted with this woman, you were her friend, you term yourself her brother, you speak of her as your sister, and you knew all her proceedings. Is it then probable, as you have yourself remarked," continued the president, "that she would have committed this act imputed to her alone?"

"She did not commit it alone," replied Louis, repeating the technical words used by the president; "since, as she has told you, and I have told you, and again repeat it, her husband compelled her."

"Then, how is it you are not acquainted with her husband," said Fouquier Tinville, "since the husband was united with the wife?"

It remained only for Louis to recount the first disappearance of Dixmer, to mention the *amours* Geneviève and his friend, and, in short, to relate the manner in which Dixmer had carried off and concealed his wife in some impenetrable retreat. It needed only this to exculpate himself from all connivance, and to elucidate the whole mystery. But for this he must betray the secrets of his two friends; to do this would be to shame Geneviève before five hundred people. Louis shook his head, as if saying no to himself.

"Well," demanded the president, "what do you reply to the public accuser?"

"That his logic is crushing," said Louis; "and I am now convinced of one thing which I never even suspected before."

"What is that?"

"That I am, it appears, one of the most frightful conspirators that has ever been seen."

"This declaration elicted a roar of laughter; even the jury could not refrain, so ludicrous was the young man's pronunciation of these words. Fouquier felt the ridicule; and since, with his usual indefatigable perseverance he had managed to possess himself of all the secrets of the accused, as well known to him as to themselves, he could not help feeling toward Louis a sentiment of pity mingled with admiration.

"Citizen Louis," said he, "speak and defend yourself. The tribunal will lend a willing ear. We are acquainted with your previous conduct, and it has always been that of a stanch Republican."

Simon essayed to speak; but the president made him a signal to remain silent.

"Speak, Citizen Louis," said he; "we are all attention."

But Louis only shook his head.

"This silence is confession," said the president.

"Not so," said Louis. "Silence is silence, that is all."

"Once more," said Fouquier Tinville, "will you speak?"

Louis turned toward the audience to encounter the eyes of Maurice, and to learn from them what course he would wish him to pursue; but Maurice made no sign to speak to him, and Louis maintained his former silence. This was self-condemnation. All that followed was quickly executed. Fouquier resumed his accusation, the president continued the debates, the jury retired, and unanimously returned a verdict of guilty against Louis and Geneviève. The president condemned them both to suffer the penalty of death. Two o'clock sounded from the large clock of the palace. The president had just time sufficient to pronounce the condemnation as the clock struck. Maurice heard the double sound, and confounded one with another. When the vibration had ceased, his strength was utterly exhausted. The gendarmes led away Geneviève and Louis. who had offered her his arm. Both saluted Maurice, but in different ways. Louis smiled; but Geneviève, pale and trembling, wafted him a last kiss upon her fingers, bathed in tears. She had till the last moment nourished the hope of life, and now wept, not for the loss of life, but love, which must perish with her. Maurice, half mad, had not replied to his frends' farewell. He rose, pale and bewildered, from the bench on which he had fallen. His friends had disappeared. He felt only one sentiment alive within him. It was the hatred which corroded his heart. He threw a last look around him and recognized Dixmer, who was leaving with the rest of the spectators, and at that moment stooped to pass under the arched door of the passage. With the eagerness of a prohibited cause, Maurice sprung from bench to bench, and reached the door. Dixmer had already passed through, and descended into the darkened corridor. Maurice followed behind him. At the moment Dixmer planted his foot on the pavement of the grand hall, Maurice placed his hand upon his shoulder.

CHAPTER LIII.

THE DUEL.

AT this epoch it was always a serious thing to feel a touch upon the shoulder. Dixmer turned, and recognized Maurice.

"Ah, *bon jour*, Citizen Republican," said Dixmer, without evincing any other emotion than an almost imperceptible start, which he immediately repressed.

"*Bon jour*, Citizen Coward," replied Maurice. "You were waiting for me, were you not?"

"That is to say," replied Dixmer, "that, on the contrary, I had ceased to expect you."

"Why was that?"

"Because I had expected you sooner."

"I still arrive too soon for you, assassin!" added Maurice, with a voice, or, rather, a murmured growl, since it resemble the grumbling of a storm, gathered in his heart, as his looks were like the lightning's flashes.

"You fling fire from your eyes, citizen," replied Dixmer. "We shall be recognized and followed."

"Yes, and you fear to be arrested, do you not? You dread lest you might be conducted to the scaffold, where you send others. Let them arrest us; so much the better; for it seems to me that not to do so now is a culpable omission on the part of national justice."

"Like omitting your name in the list of people of honor. Is it not so—since yours has disappeared?"

"Well, we shall speak about all that, I hope; but in the meantime, you are revenged—miserably revenged—upon a woman. Why, since you have waited for me elsewhere, did you not do so at my house, when you stole away Geneviève?"

"You were the first thief, I believe."

"Neither by your spirit or your words have I ever estimated you, monsieur. I judge you better by your actions—witness the day when you wanted to murder me. That day your true nature displayed itself—that day your genuine nature spoke."

"And I have more than once regretted I did not listen to it," said Dixmer, coolly.

"Well," said Maurice, touching his sword, "I offer you your revenge."

"To-morrow, if you like, but not to-day."

"And why to-morrow?"

"Or this evening."

"Why not directly?"

"Because I am engaged till five o'clock."

"Another hideous project!" said Maurice; "another ambush!"

"Really, Monsieur Maurice, you are rather ungrateful," replied Dixmer. "In truth, you are. Here, for six months I have allowed you to make love to my wife—for six months have permitted your meetings, and have not noticed your smiles. Never man, you must confess, has evinced so little of the tiger in his composition as myself."

"That is to say, you thought I might be useful, and you could mold me to your purpose."

"Without doubt," returned Dixmer, calmly, who ruled his own passion to increase that of Maurice. "Without doubt; while, that you might betray your Republic, rob me of the affections of my wife, that you might dishonor yourselves—you by your treason, she by her adulterous love, I remained the sage and hero. I waited, and I triumphed."

"Horrible!" said Maurice.

"Is it not? Yes, you appreciate your own conduct fully, monsieur. It is horrible! it is infamous!"

"You deceive yourself, monsieur; the conduct I term horrible and infamous is that of the man, to whom the honor of a woman being confided, had sworn to guard this honor pure and unsullied, and who, instead of keeping his word and oath, employed her beauty as a shameful bait where love had already insnared her feeble heart. It was your sacred duty, beyond all others, to protect this woman, and, instead of protecting her, you have sold her."

"That is what I had to do, monsieur," replied Dixmer. "I am going to tell you I had to save my friend who united with me in this sacred cause. Even as I have sacrificed my property to this cause, so have I sacrificed my honor. As for me, I am completely forgotten, completely struck out; I have considered myself the last. Now my friend is no more; he died by the poniard. My queen is no more; she died an ignominious death on the scaffold. Now, now, I can think of my revenge!"

"Say of your assassination."

"One does not kill an adulteress at a blow; she is punished for her crime."

"This sin you imposed upon her, therefore it was rendered lawful."

"You think so," said Dixmer, with a devilish smile. "Judge from her remorse if she believes she has acted lawfully."

"Those who punish strike at once. You, you do not punish, for while striking you fly, and while casting her head to the guillotine you conceal yourself."

"Me? I fly? I hide myself? When did you see that, poor idiot that you are?" demanded Dixmer. "Is it concealing myself to assist at her condemnation? Is it flying when I go into the Salle des Morts to fling her my last adieu?"

"You are going to see her again? to fling her a last adieu?" cried Maurice.

"Decidedly you are not expert at revenge, citizen," replied Dixmer, shrugging, his shoulders. "Thus in my situation, you would abandon these events to their strength alone, these circumstances to their natural course; thus, for example, the adulterous woman having merited death, the moment she has received the punishment of death I am quits with her, or, rather, she is quits with me. No, Citizen Maurice, I know better than that. I have discovered a way to return this woman the evil she has done me. She loves you and will die far from you ; she detests me, and I will be near her again. There !" said he, drawing a pocket-book from his pocket, " do you see this ? It contains a card signed by the registrar of the palace. With this card I can gain near access to the condemned. I will penetrate to Geneviève ; I will call her ' adulteress ;' I shall see her curls fall under the hand of the vile executioner, and as they are severed she shall still hear my voice repeating ' adulteress !' I will even accompany her to the fatal cart, and, as she plants her foot upon the scaffold, the long, last sound that greets her ear shall be the word, ' adulteress !'"

"Take care ; she has not strength to support so much cowardice ; she will denounce you."

"No," cried Dixmer ; " she hates me too much for that. If she had wished to denounce me she would have done so when her friend urged her so softly. If she did not denounce me to save her life, she will not do so that I may die with her, for she well knows, in that case, I should retard her execution for a day ; she well knows that if she denounces me, I shall go with her not only to the lowest step of the palais, but even to the scaffold ; she well knows that, instead of leaving her at the foot of the ladder, I will ascend into the cart with her, and that, seated by her side the whole length of the road, I will constantly repeat the one dreadful word, ' adulteress ;' that even on the scaffold I will continue to do so till the moment she sinks into eternity and the accusation falls with her."

Dixmer was frightful in this state of anger and hatred. He seized Maurice by the hand and shook it with a force unknown to the young man, upon whom this had acted with a contrary effect ; as Dixmer became excited Maurice grew calm.

"Listen," said the young man, " in your vengeance you have omitted one thing."

"What ?"

"That you will be able to tell her, on leaving the tribunal, ' I have seen your lover, and have killed him.'"

"On the contrary, I prefer telling her that you live, and will suffer for the remainder of your days, from the spectacle of her death."

"You shall kill me, notwithstanding," said Maurice, "or," added he, turning round, and finding himself nearly master of his position, "I will kill you."

And pale with emotion, and excited by fury, finding his strength redoubled, from the restraint he had imposed upon his feelings, while listening to the unfolding of Dixmer's horrible project, he seized him by the throat, and drew him backward toward a staircase, which led toward the high bank of the river. At the contact with his hand, Dixmer, in his turn, felt hatred rush over him like a boundless wave.

"You need not compel me by force; I will follow."

"Come, then. Are you armed?"

"I will follow you."

"No, go first; but I give you notice, at the least sign or gesture, I will cleave your skull in twain with my sword."

"You know I am a stranger to fear," said Dixmer, with a smile rendered frightful from his pallor.

"Fear of my sword," said Maurice, "no; but fear of losing your revenge, Now, however, we are face to face —dismiss that fear."

They had, indeed, arrived at the water's brink; and had any one seen and followed them, they could not have arrived in time to prevent the duel from taking place; besides, an equal desire for vengeance now animated both. While speaking, they had descended the little staircase, and gained the nearly deserted quay; for as the condemnations continued, seeing it was two o'clock at least, the crowd still filled the judgment hall, the corridors, and the courts. They appeared equally to thirst for each other's blood.

They plunged themselves under one of those arches leading from the cells of the conciergerie to the river, at this time drained, but then foul and saturated with water, serving more than once as a means of conveyance for the corpses, which floated far away from the dungeons, leaving no trace behind. Maurice placed himself between Dixmer and the water.

"I decidedly think I shall kill you, Maurice," said Dixmer, "you tremble so much."

"And I, Dixmer," said Maurice, taking his sword in hand, and carefully inclosing him, so as to cut off all retreat, "I, on the contrary, believe that I shall kill you; and, having killed you, shall remove from your pocket-book the card signed by the registrar of the palace. Ah! you have buttoned up your coat beautifully; but my sword shall open it, were it even formed of brass, like the cuirasses of old."

"And this paper," roared Dixmer, "you will take it, will you?"

"Yes," said Maurice, "I will make use of this card. I, with this talisman, will secure an entrance to Geneviève. I will sit next her in the cart, I will murmur in her ear, while life remains, 'I love thee;' and when the last stroke has fallen, I will murmur still, 'I have loved thee.'"

Dixmer made a movement with his left hand to take the card from his right, and together with the pocket-book to cast them into the river, when, rapid as a thunder-bolt, sharp as a hatchet, Maurice's sword fell upon his hand, nearly severing it from the wrist. The wounded man uttered a cry, and shaking his mutilated limb, flung himself furiously on his antagonist. There, in the obscurity of this gloomy vault, the deadly combat commenced. The two men were inclosed in a space so narrow that the sword strokes, swerving from the line of the body, glided upon the humid pavement, and were with difficulty prevented from striking the sides of the arch, more especially as these impediments redoubled the attacks and impatience of the combatants. Dixmer, who, as he felt his life-blood flow, was aware that his strength diminished, also charged Maurice so furiously that he was compelled to step backward; in so doing he lost his footing, and his enemy's sword entered his breast. But by a movement rapid as thought, kneeling as he was, he raised the blade with his left arm, and turned the point toward

Dixmer, who, maddened with rage, darted forward, and, impelled by the inclining ground, fell on the sword, the point of which entered his body. Thus impaled, and uttering a fearful imprecation, the two bodies rolled to the outside of the arch. One only rose. It was Maurice— Maurice, covered with blood, but that blood the blood of his enemy. He drew his sword toward him, and as he slowly raised it the blade appeared to him even to thirst for the remnant of life which still agitated with a nervous shuddering the limbs of Dixmer. Then, when assured that he was dead, he stooped toward the corpse, opened the dead man's coat, withdrew the card, and hurried away directly. But on looking at himself, he felt assured that in his present state he should not proceed far without being arrested. He was literally covered with blood. He approached the water's edge, and bending toward the river, washed his hands and coat, and then rapidly ascended the staircase, casting a last look toward the arch, whence a red smoking stream issued, advancing slowly toward the river. On arriving near the palace, he opened the pocket-book, and there found a card signed by the registrar.

"Thanks, just God!" murmured he; and he rapidly mounted the steps leading to La Salle des Morts. It struck three.

CHAPTER LIV.

LA SALLE DES MORTS.

It must be remembered that the registrar of the palace had opened his jailer's book to Dixmer, and had also entered into an arrangement with him which the presence of madame rendered peculiarly agreeable. This man, it may be imagined, was terribly alarmed when the news of Dixmer's plot was communicated to him. He would doubtless be considered as nothing less than an accomplice of Dixmer, his false colleague, and therefore condemned to die with the wretched Geneviève. Fouquier Tinville had summoned him to appear before him. It may easily be understood that this poor man would have some trouble to prove himself innocent in the eyes of the public accuser; he had, however, succeeded in so doing, thanks to Geneviève, whose declaration had clearly established his utter ignorance of the plot of her husband. He had succeeded, thanks to Dixmer's flight, and, above all, from the interest excited in Fouquier Tinville, who wished to preserve his administration free from all stain.

"Citizen," said he, flinging himself upon his knees before Fouquier, "pardon me, for I have been deceived."

"Citizen," replied the public accuser, "a man who in these days permits himself to be deceived deserves to be guillotined."

"I may have been a blockhead, citizen," replied the registrar, who was longing to call Fouquier Tinville monseigneur.

"Blockhead or not," replied the rigid accuser, "no one should allow his love for the Republic to sleep. The spies of the Capitol were only geese, yet they were sufficiently awake to save Rome."

The registrar looked upon this argument as totally unanswerable; he groaned, and remained waiting.

"I pardon you," said Fouquier Tinville. "I will go so far as to defend you, since I do not wish one of my employés to be even suspected; but you will bear in mind that at the least word that reaches my ears, the least revival of this affair, you will leave instantly."

It is scarcely necessary to say with what anxiety this man sought the newspapers, always ready to tell what they know, and sometimes more than they can certify, even if they caused the heads of ten men to fall on the scaffold. He sought Dixmer everywhere, to recommend him to keep his own counsel; but he had very naturally changed his apartments, and was nowhere to be found. Geneviève had been placed on the bench of the accused, but had already, without any reservation, declared that neither herself nor husband had any accomplices, and he thanked the poor woman with his eyes as she passed before him to surrender herself to the tribunal. While she was passing, and he was returning to the office to fetch some law papers for Fouquier Tinville, he all at once saw Dixmer's apparition approaching him with a calm and quiet step. This vision petrified him.

"Oh!" said he, as if he had seen a specter.

"Do you not know me?" said the newcomer.

"Do I know you? You are the Citizen Durand, or, rather, the Citizen Dixmer."

"Just so."

"But are you dead, citizen?"

"Not yet, as you see."

"I wish to tell you they will arrest you."

"Who wants to arrest me? No one knows me."

"But I know you, and it only needs one word from me to send you to the guillotine."

"And two words from me only will send you there with me."

"It is too bad of you to say that."

"No; it is logic."

"How do you make that out? Make haste, speak quickly, for the less time we are together, the less danger we incur from each other."

"My wife is about to be condemned, is it not so?"

"I greatly fear for her, poor woman!"

"Well, I wish to see her once more, to bid her adieu."

"Where?"

"In La Salle des Morts."

"Would you dare to enter there?"

"Why not?"

"Oh!" said the registrar, like a man whose thoughts made him shudder.

"There must be some way," continued Dixmer.

"To enter La Salle des Morts? Without doubt there is."

"How?"

"To procure a card."

"And where are these cards procured?"

The registrar turned frightfully pale, and murmured:

"Where are they procured, you ask?"

"I inquire where are they to be procured," replied Dixmer; "the question is plain enough, I think."

"They are procured—here."

"Ah! true; and who usually signs them?"

"The registrar."

"But you are the registrar?"

"Doubtless, I am."

"Then, as it has so happened," said Dixmer, seating himself, "you can sign a card for me."

The registrar made one bound.

"Do you ask for my head, citizen?" said he.

"No; I ask you for a card, that is all."

"I am going to arrest you, unhappy man," said he, summoning all his energy.

"Do," said Dixmer, "and the next moment I will denounce you as an accomplice, and instead of leaving me to enter the famous salon alone, you shall accompany me."

The registrar turned ghastly pale.

"Villain!" said he.

"There is no villainy in that," said Dixmer; "I wish to speak to my wife, and all I require of you is a card to enable me to do so."

"Is it, then, so imperative that you should speak to her?"

"It seems so, since I risk my head by coming here."

This seemed very plausible to the registrar, and Dixmer immediately perceived that this staggered him.

"Rest assured," said he, "no one shall know anything. The devil! why, surely sometimes a similar case to mine must present itself to your notice."

"Very rarely; it is by no means a common occurrence."

"Well, then, let us arrange it in another way."

"If it is possible. I should ask nothing better."

"Nothing is more possible. Enter by the door of the condemned; there a card is not required; then, when you have spoken to your wife, call me, and I will let you out."

"That will not answer," said Dixmer; "unfortunately, there is a story current in the city."

"What story?"

"The history of a poor hunchback, who mistook the door, thinking to enter the archives, but instead of so doing, found himself in the salon of which we are now speaking. Only since he had entered by the door of the condemned, in lieu of the large door, as he had no card to prove his identity, once there, he was not permitted to go out. They strenuously maintained that since he entered the door with the other condemned, he was condemned likewise. In vain he protested, swore, appealed; no one believed him, no one came to his assistance, no one helped him to get out. So that, notwithstanding his protestations, his imprecations, and supplications, the executioner first cut off his hair, and then finished by cutting his throat. Is this anecdote true, Citizen Registrar? You ought to know better than any one else."

"Alas! yes, it is too true," said the registrar, trembling.

"You must see, then, that with such antecedents, I should be a fool to enter this cut-throat place without a card."

"But I shall be there, I tell you."

"If when you were called you should be otherwise engaged? If you should forget?" Dixmer laid particular stress on these last words, "if you should forget."

"But, then, I promise you."

"No; besides, it would compromise you. They would see me speaking to you; and, in short, it does not suit me; I prefer having a card."

"Impossible!"

"Then, *cher ami*, I will speak, and we will both take a journey together to La Place de la Revolution."

The registrar, frantic with terror, and half dead with fear, signed the pass for a citizen. Dixmer rose and went out precipitately, to take his station in the judgment hall, where we have already recognized his presence. The rest is known to us. At the same moment the registrar, to avoid all accusation of connivance, seated himself near Fouquier Tinville, leaving the management of the office to his head clerk. At ten minutes before three, Maurice, furnished with a card, crossing a hedge of turnkeys and gendarmes, arrived without interruption at the fatal door. When we say fatal, we exaggerate, for there were two doors, the principal one by which those possessing cards entered and returned, and the door of the condemned, by which no one departed except to the scaffold. The place that Maurice entered was divided into two compartments. One of these was set apart for those employed in registering the names of the arrivals, the other, furnished only with wooden benches, was appropriated for the reception of those who were arrested and those who were condemned, which at this period amounted to pretty much the same thing. The hall was very dark, lighted only from a glass window of the partition which divided it from the registrar's office. A female dressed in white, in a half-fainting attitude, lay in a corner, supported against the wall. A man was standing in front of her, from time to time shaking his head. His arms were crossed upon his breast, and he hesitated to speak to her, as if fearful of restoring her to the consciousness she appeared to have lost. Around these two individuals several condemned persons were scattered promiscuously, some giving vent to their feelings in sobs and groans, others joining in patriotic songs, while the remainder walked rapidly up and down, as if to chase away the thoughts which devoured them. This was indeed the antechamber of death, and the furniture rendered it worthy of the name. Here were seen half-open coffins filled with straw, seeming as if to invite the living to their beds of repose, the provisional receptacles for the ashes of the dead. A large wardrobe was erected in the wall opposite the window.

A prisoner, prompted by curiosity, opened it, but recoiled with horror. It contained the bloodstained garments of those executed on the preceding evening; long tresses of hair hanging here and there, the executioner's perquisites, who sold them to the relatives when not enjoined by the authorities to burn these precious relics. Maurice, trembling with emotion, at length opened the door, when the whole tableau at once presented itself to his view. He advanced three steps into the hall, and fell at Geneviève's feet. The unfortunate woman uttered a cry which Maurice stifled on her lips. Louis, weeping, pressed his friend in his arms; these were the first tears he had shed. Strange it was that all these unhappy individuals assembled to die together scarcely looked even at the touching tableau presented to their view by their unfortunate fellow-creatures, but every one suffered too much himself to take part in the miseries of others. The three friends remained for a moment united in a deep silence, happy, almost joyous. Louis first disengaged himself from the wretched group.

"Are you, then, condemned also?" said he to Maurice.

"Yes," replied he.

"Oh, happiness!" murmured Geneviève.

But the joy of those who have only one hour to live cannot last even as long as their life. Maurice, having contemplated Geneviève with looks of ardent and profound affection, turned toward Louis.

"Now," said he, taking Geneviève's hands within his own, "let us talk together."

"Yes," said Louis, "let us converse while the time remains to us. It is only a right to do so. What do you wish to say to me, Maurice?"

"You have been arrested through me, condemned for her; as for Geneviève and I, let us pay our debt; it is not fair, at the same time, that you should be made to pay also."

"I do not understand you."

"Louis, you are free."

"I, free? you are mad!" said Louis.

"No, I am not mad; I repeat that you are free; see, here is the pass. They will inquire who you are; you are employed at the register of the Carmelites, and are going to speak to the registrar of the palace; you have, from motives of curiosity, requested a pass from him to see the condemned; you have seen them, and are now leaving, perfectly satisfied with your visit."

"This is a joke, is it not?"

"No, indeed, my friend; here is the card, take advantage of it. You are not a lover, like myself; you do not wish to die that you may be enabled to pass a few more minutes in the society of the well-beloved of your heart, and not to lose a second of eternity with her."

"But, Maurice," replied Louis, "if one might be able to get out from here—a circumstance I swear to you I could not have believed possible—why do you not save madame first? as to yourself, we will consider afterward about that."

"Impossible!" said Maurice, with a frightful oppression at his heart; "this card is for a citoyen, not for a citoyenne; besides, Geneviève would not depart and leave me here to live herself, while knowing that I remained to die."

"If she would not, then why should I? Do you imagine I possess less courage than a woman?"

"No, dear friend; I know and acknowledge your bravery, but nothing can excuse your obstinacy in this case. Then, profit by this moment, and allow us the supreme felicity of knowing and feeling that you are free and happy."

"Happy!" said Louis. "You are facetious, surely— happy without you, eh? What the devil am I to do in this world without you? In Paris, without my usual avocations, without seeing you again; to weary you no more with my *bouts-rimés;* ah, *pardieu*, no!"

"Louis, my friend——"

"Exactly; it is because I am your friend that I persist in my opinion, with the prospect of recovering you both; were I a prisoner, as I now am, I would tear down the walls, but to save myself, and go out from here alone into the streets, my head bowed down with a feeling resembling remorse, and a continued cry in my ears, ' Maurice— Geneviève!' To pass into certain quarters, and before certain houses, where I have seen your persons, but shall now only recognize your shadows; to arrive at last to execrate this dear Paris that I love so well; ah, *ma foi*, no! And I find there was good reason to proscribe these kings; might not this be the motive of King Dagobert?"

"And what relation has King Dagobert with what concerns us?"

"What? Did not this frightful tyrant say of the grand Eloi, 'He is not such good company that one cannot quit him.' Ah, well! I am a Republican. I say one never ought to quit good company, even the guillotine; I feel very comfortable here, and I will remain."

"Poor fellow! poor fellow!" said Maurice.

Geneviève said nothing, but looked at them with eyes suffused with tears.

"You regret your life, then?" said Louis.

"Yes, on her account."

"And I have nothing to regret in mine, not even on account of the Goddess Reason, who, I had forgotten to tell you, has latterly behaved most shamefully to me; who will not take the trouble even to console herself, like the other Arthemises of old. I shall go to my death perfectly cool and rather facetious. I will amuse all the beggarly wretches who follow the cart. I will repeat a pretty quatrain to Monsieur Sanson, and wish the company good-night—that is to say—wait, then——" Louis interrupted himself. "Ah! if so," said he, "I will go out. I well know I love no one, but I forgot that I hated some one. The time, Maurice, the time!"

"Half-past three."

"I have time, *mon Dieu*! there is time."

"Certainly," cried Maurice; "there are nine more accused persons still to be tried, this will not terminate before five o'clock; we have, therefore, nearly two hours' respite."

"That is all that I require; lend me your card, and also twenty sous."

"Ah, *mon Dieu*! what are you going to do?" murmured Geneviève.

Maurice pressed his hand; it was important to him that Louis should go out.

"I have my own plan," said Louis.

Maurice drew his purse from his pocket, and placed it in his friend's hand.

"Now, the card, for the love of God—I ought to say, for the love of the Supreme Being."

Maurice gave him the pass. Louis kissed Geneviève's hand, and availing himself of the moment when a fresh batch of the condemned were ushered in he leaped the benches, and presented himself before the principal entrance.

"Eh!" said the gendarme, "here is one, it appears to me, trying to escape."

Louis drew himself up, and presented his card.

"Hold, Citizen Gendarme," said he, "and learn to know people better."

The gendarme recognized the signature of the registrar, but, belonging to a class of functionaries rather wanting in confidence and as at this moment the registrar himself came down from the tribunal with a nervous shudder, which had not left him since he had so imprudently hazarded his signature:

"Citizen Registrar," said he, "here is a pass bearing your signature, with which this person wishes to leave La Salle des Morts; is it all right?"

The registrar turned pale with fright, and, feeling convinced that if he turned his eyes in that direction it would only be to encounter the terrible figure of Dixmer, hastily seizing the card, quickly replied:

"Yes, yes, it is my signature."

"Then," cried Louis, "if it is your signature, return it to me."

"No," said the registrar, tearing it into a thousand pieces, "these cards can only be once available."

Louis remained for a moment irresolute.

"So much the worse," said he; "but, above all things, it is necessary I should kill him;" and he passed through the office.

Maurice had followed Louis with an emotion easy to comprehend. When he had disappeared, Maurice returned, saying, with an exultation nearly amounting to joy:

"He is saved, Geneviève; the card is destroyed, therefore he cannot return. Besides, even if he were able to do so, the sitting of the tribunal will have terminated at five o'clock. He will return, but we shall have ceased to live."

Geneviève shuddered, and breathed a deep sigh.

"Oh, press me in your arms!" said she, "and let us separate no more. Why is not possible, oh my God! for one blow to annihilate us both, that together we might breathe our last sigh?"

Then, retiring into the deep shade of the gloomy hall, Geneviève placed herself near Maurice, who closely twined his arms around her. Thus they remained, rendered by the strength of their love insensible to the surrounding scene, almost to the approach of even death itself. Half an hour passed thus.

CHAPTER LV.

WHY LOUIS WENT OUT.

SUDDENLY a loud noise was heard; the gendarmes opened the lower door; behind them appeared Sanson and his assistants, the latter carrying rolls of cord.

"Oh, *mon ami, mon ami!*" said Geneviève, "the fatal moment has arrived, and I feel that my senses are leaving me."

"There you are wrong," said the cheering voice of Louis.

"Here you are wrong, *en vériét*,
Since death is now *la liberté*."

"Louis!" cried Maurice, in despair.

"Well, that is good, now, is it not? I have adopted your opinion since yesterday evening, and could not be so contemptible——"

"Ah! that is the question. You are returned, unhappy man, you are returned!"

"I considered that was our agreement. But listen, as what I have to say to you will also interest madame."

"*Mon Dieu! Mon Dieu!*"

"Allow me to speak, or I shall not have time to tell you all. I wished to go out that I might purchase a knife in La Rue de la Baullerie."

"What did you want with a knife?"

"I wished to despatch this nice Monsieur Dixmer."

Geneviève shuddered.

"Ah!" said Maurice, "I comprehend."

"I purchased it. Listen attentively to what I tell you, and you will understand your friend has a soul for logic; indeed, I begin to think I should have been a mathematician instead of a poet. Unfortunately, it is now too late. This is the way I reasoned: Monsieur Dixmer has compromised his wife; Monsieur Dixmer came to be present at her trial, and Monsieur Dixmer will not deprive himself of the pleasure of seeing her pass in the fatal cart; and, above all, he will accompany us. I will then look for him in the foremost of the spectators. I will glide near him, and say, '*Bon jour*, Monsieur Dixmer;' and then I will drive my knife into his ribs, or his heart."

"Louis!" cried Geneviève.

"Rest assured, dear friend, Providence has arranged all. Picture to yourself the spectators, instead of remaining stationary in front of the palace, according to their usual custom, making a demiturn to the right, and assembling on the borders of the quay.

"Oh!" said I to myself, it is doubtless a dog drowned. Why should not Dixmer be there? Even a dog drowning will serve to pass away the time. I approached the parapet, and beheld all along the high bank a troop of people, who, throwing their arms aloft in the air, and uttering loud exclamations, stooped down to gaze into the water beneath. I joined them and also looked down—there was something—guess what it was——"

"Dixmer!" said Maurice, in a gloomy tone.

"Yes. How could you guess that? Yes, it was

Dixmer, severely wounded. The unfortunate wretch killed himself in expiation, no doubt."

"Ah!" said Maurice, with a sad smile, "do you think so?"

Geneviève let her head drop between her two hands. She was too feeble to support these successive emotions.

"Yes, I thought so, from his blood-stained sword being found near him—at least sometimes—he had not met any one——"

Maurice, without reply, availing himself of the moment when Geneviève, overpowered by emotion, did not observe, opened his coat and displayed to Louis his waistcoat and shirt stained with blood.

"Ah! this alters the case," said Louis, as he held out his hand to Maurice. "Now," said he, whispering in his ear, "they have not searched me, seeing that I entered in Sanson's suite. I have the weapon still if the guillotine is too revolting to your feelings."

Maurice seized his arm with a joyful expression.

"No," said he, "she would suffer too much."

And he returned the knife to Louis.

"You are right," said he, "long live Monsieur Guillotine! Why, what is it, after all? a filip on the neck, as I observed to Danton. And what is that, after all?" And he flung his knife in the midst of a group of the condemned, one of whom immediately seized and buried it in his breast. He was dead in an instant. At the same moment Geneviève awoke and uttered a piercing cry. She felt the pressure of the executioner's hand upon her shoulder.

CHAPTER LVI.

"LONG LIVE SIMON!"

At the sound of this cry, Maurice understood that the struggle was about to commence. The influence of love may be able to exalt the love to heroism—it may, against natural instinct, impel a human being to desire death, but it had not, in his instance, extinguished the fear of pain. It was evident that Geneviève resigned herself the more patiently to death since Maurice was to die with her; but resignation did not exclude suffering, and to quit this world is not only to fall into the abyss termed fathomless and unknown, but also to suffer in the descent. Maurice, at a glance, embraced the entire scene and thought of what would follow. In the center of the hall lay the suicide, from whose breast the gendarme had just torn the weapon of destruction, fearing, probably, it might be useful to some others. Around him were several individuals, mute with despair, and scarcely heeding him, inscribing in their pocket-books some indistinct words, or pressing one another's hands; some repeating, without any intermission, a cherished name, as if imbecile, or bathing with tears a portrait, a ring, or tress of hair; some hurling imprecations against tyranny, a word banished and cursed by each one in turn, and sometimes even by the tyrants themselves. In the midst of these unfortunates, Sanson, grown old, less from his fifty years than his miserable and dispiriting occupation; Sanson, of a mild disposition, and as much their consoler as his terrible vocation permitted him to be, to this one offered advice, to that one some sad consolation or encouragement, finding some Christian responses to their accents of despair as well as to bravado,

"Citoyenne," said he to Geneviève, "I must remove the handkerchief, and raise or cut off your hair, if you please."

Geneviève began to tremble

"Come, *m'amie*," said Louis, softly, "take courage."

"May I remove madame's hair?" demanded Maurice.

"Oh, yes!" cried Geneviève; "I entreat you to permit him to do so, Monsieur Sanson."

"Do so, then," said the old man, turning away his head.

Maurice gently removed the handkerchief from her neck, and Geneviève, stooping, fell on her knees before the young man, presenting her charming head, appearing more beautiful in her grief than she had ever been in her days of sunshine and happiness.

When Maurice had completed his funereal operation, his hands were so tremulous and his countenance betrayed so much grief, that Geneviève exclaimed:

"Ah! I am courageous, Maurice."

Sanson turned round.

"Is it not so, monsieur?" said she; "am I not courageous?"

"Certainly, citoyenne," replied the executioner, in a mild voice, "for yours is true courage."

In the meantime, the first assistant had run over the list forwarded by Fouquier Tinville.

"Fourteen," said he.

Sanson counted the condemned.

"Fifteen, including the dead," said he; "why, how is this?"

Maurice and Geneviève counted after him, both struck by the same thought.

"You say there are only fourteen condemned, and that there are fifteen," said she.

"Yes; the Citizen Fouquier Tinville must have been mistaken."

"Ah! you spoke falsely, then," said Geneviève, turning to Maurice; "you were not condemned."

"And why wait for to-morrow, when you die to-day?" said Maurice.

"*Ami*," said she, smiling, "you reassure me; I now am convinced it is easy to die."

"Louis," said Maurice, "now for the last time—no one

here can recognize you—say that you came to bid me adieu—say that you have been shut in by mistake ; call the gendarme who saw you go out. I will be the true condemned who ought to die. But you, my friend, we supplicate to live to guard our memory ; there is yet time, Louis ; we entreat you."

Geneviève joined her hands in an attitude of prayer. Louis took both her hands and kissed them.

" I have said no, and I mean no," said Louis, in a firm voice ; " say no more on the subject, or I shall think I am a constraint upon you."

" Fourteen," repeated Sanson, " and here are fifteen ; " then, elevating his voice, " Is there any one here who can protest against this ? " said he ; " is there any one here who can prove he is here by mistake ? "

Perhaps some lips half opened at this question, but closed again without uttering a single word, since those who might have lied were ashamed to do so, and those who would not have lied were determined not to speak.

A silence of several minutes ensued, during which the assistants continued their mournful office.

" Citizens, we are ready," was then pronounced in the dull and solemn tones of old Sanson.

He was answered only by sobs and groans.

" Well," said Louis, " let it be so.

" To die for our country
Is of all fates the best !

Yes, to die for our country ; but decidedly I begin to think we do not die for her, but for the pleasure of those who witness our deaths. *Ma foi !* Maurice, I have adopted your opinion. I am disgusted with the Republic."

" The call ! " said a commissary, at the door.

Several gendarmes entered the hall, closing up the issues, thus placing themselves between life and the condemned, as if to prevent them from returning to it. The summons was repeated. Maurice, who had seen the condemned who had destroyed himself, when his name was called answered in his stead, and then found the number was correct. The corpse was removed from the hall, but if his identity had been established, and he had been recognized as one condemned he would have been guillotined with the rest, although already dead. The survivors were pushed toward the outlet, in order that as each passed before the wicket their hands might be tied behind their backs. For the space of ten minutes not a word was exchanged between these unfortunates, the executioners alone seemed endowed with life or motion.

Maurice, Geneviève, and Louis, not being any longer able to retain their hold of one another, successively presented themselves, that they might not be separated. When the condemned were removed from the conciergerie into the conrt, the scene became truly appalling. Several fainted at the sight of the carts, and the turnkeys were compelled to assist them to mount the steps of these vehicles of death. Behind the still closed doors was heard the confused murmur of the crowd, and it might be imagined from the sound that the concourse was immense. Geneviève courageously ascended the car; Maurice at her side sustained her; he sprung in rapidly after her. Louis did not hurry himself, but carefully selected his seat at the left of Maurice. The doors opened, and foremost in the crowd stood Simon. The two friends immediately recognized him; indeed, the recognition was mutual. He was standing upon a stone near which the carts must pass, for there were three of them. The cart containing our three friends moved first.

"Eh, *bon jour*, brave grenadier," said Simon to Louis; "you are going to try the effect of my leather-cutting machine, I suppose?"

"Yes," said Louis, "and I will be careful not to notch it, that it may be ready when your turn comes."

The two remaining carts now followed the direction of the first. And now commenced a terrific tempest of cries, shouts, groans, and maledictions, surrounding and following the condemned.

"Courage, Geneviève, take courage," murmured Maurice.

THE CHEVALIER DE MAISON ROUGE. 411

"Oh!" replied the young woman, "I do not regret life, since I die with you. I regret only that my hands are tied, and I cannot embrace you before I die."

"Louis," said Maurice, "feel in my waistcoat pocket, there you will find a knife."

"*Mon Dieu*!" said Louis, "a pen-knife; I should be ashamed to die, garroted like a calf."

Maurice placed his pocket on a level with his friend's hands; Louis found the knife, which between them they succeeded in opening. Maurice then placed it between his teeth, and severed the cord which bound Louis' hands, who, the moment they were free, performed the same office for Maurice.

"Make haste," said the young man; "Geneviève is fainting."

In fact to accomplish this operation, Maurice had for a moment turned from Geneviève, when, as if all her strength had been derived from him, her eyes closed, and her head sank upon her breast.

"Geneviève, open your eyes, *mon amie*," said Maurice; we have only a few minutes more to see each other in this world."

The cords wound me," murmured the young woman.

"Maurice unbound them. She immediately reopened her eyes, and rose, radiant with almost celestial beauty. She threw one fair arm around Maurice's neck, with the other hand seized that of Louis, and thus, all three standing in the cart, with two more victims lying at their feet, wrapped in the stupor of anticipated death, they gazed toward heaven with a look of ardent gratitude for having been permitted to support and console each other, while those who had outraged and insulted them previously were now perfectly silent. The scaffold was in sight. Maurice and Louis beheld it. Geneviève did not; she saw naught beside her lover. The cart stopped.

"I love thee," said Maurice to Geneviève; "I love thee."

"The woman first, the woman first!" shouted a thousand voices.

"Thanks, good people," said Maurice; "who, then, can call you cruel?"

He took Geneviève within his arms, pressed his lips fondly upon hers, and delivered her to Sanson.

"Courage!" cried Louis, "courage!"

"I have it," said Geneviève, "I have it."

"I love thee," murmured Maurice; "I love thee."

They were no longer victims about to be slaughtered, but friends making a festival of death.

"Adieu!" cried Geneviève to Louis.

"*Au revoir*," replied he.

And Geneviève disappeared under the fatal swinging-gate.

"To thee, Louis! To thee, Maurice!"

"Hark! she calls you."

At this moment Geneviève uttered the last cry.

"Come," said she.

A furious uproar ascended from the crowd. The fair and graceful head had fallen. Maurice rushed forward.

"It is exactly correct," said Louis; "let us follow logic. Are you listening, Maurice?"

"Yes."

"She loved you, and they have murdered her first; you are not condemned, and therefore die the second; and I, who have done nothing, being the greater criminal of the three, die the last.

> "And thus you see 'tis all explained
> Through studying logic.

"*Ma foi!* Citizen Sanson, I promised you a quatrain, but you must be content with a distich."

"I did love thee!" murmured Maurice, lying on the fatal plank, and smiling at the head of his beloved, "I did lo——" The knife cut short the last word.

"Now for my turn," said Louis, bounding on the scaffold, "and be quick, or I shall lose my head. Citizen Sanson, I have committed bankruptcy for two verses, instead of which I offer you a pun."

Sanson placed him in his turn.

"Let us see," said Louis, "it is the fashion to cry long live something, when dying. Once it was *'Vive la roi!'* but now there is no king; then once the cry was, *'Vive la liberté!'* but there is no more liberty. *Ma foi!* Long live Sanson, who unites us all three!"

And the head of the generous and noble-hearted young man fell near those of Maurice and Geneviéve.

THE END.